# JARED MOVED CLOSER.

So close that she could feel the warmth of him, smell the seductive, musky, male scent of him. With a heady feeling of dizziness, Kitty leaned into him, and his hands grasped her shoulders. She looked up into his sensual dark eyes.

"I don't remember when I last had such an enjoyable time." Jared's husky voice and eyes sent a message that made Kitty shiver.

"It must have been the company," she said breathlessly.

"It was definitely the company." He lowered his head and kissed her forehead. "Good night, Kathleen."

Then there was only emptiness in the spot that his warmth had once filled. Funny how she once had thought him cold.

## *Other* AVON ROMANCES

The Bride Sale *by Candice Hern*
Heart of Night *by Taylor Chase*
His Unexpected Wife *by Maureen McKade*
The Lily and the Sword *by Sara Bennett*
My Lady's Temptation *by Denise Hampton*
Pride and Prudence *by Malia Martin*
A Seductive Offer *by Kathryn Smith*

*Coming Soon*

A Rebellious Bride *by Brenda Hiatt*
Tempt Me With Kisses *by Margaret Moore*

*And Don't Miss These*
**ROMANTIC TREASURES**
*from Avon Books*

Claiming the Highlander *by Kinley MacGregor*
Too Wicked to Marry *by Susan Sizemore*
A Touch So Wicked *by Connie Mason*

THE
MACKENZIES
JARED

# ANA LEIGH

AVON BOOKS
An Imprint of HarperCollinsPublishers

This is a work of fiction. Names, characters, places, and incidents are products of the author's imagination or are used fictitiously and are not to be construed as real. Any resemblance to actual events, locales, organizations, or persons, living or dead, is entirely coincidental.

AVON BOOKS
*An Imprint of* Harper Collins*Publishers*
10 East 53rd Street
New York, New York 10022-5299


ISBN: 0-380-82007-2
**www.avonromance.com**



First Avon Books paperback printing: March 2002



Printed in the U.S.A.

10 9 8 7 6 5 4 3

In loving memory, to my brother Mike

*"Home is the sailor, home from the sea . . ."*

# Prologue

*Texas, 1893*

"*Ashes to ashes, dust to dust.*"

Kathleen MacKenzie Drummond observed hollowly as her brother, uncles, and cousins lowered her husband's casket into the deep hole. The light sound of dirt splattering on the wooden coffin echoed like deafening drumbeats, and she sucked in a deep, shuddering breath that ended in a sob. Her mother clasped Kathleen's hand, and the strong arm of her father closed around her shoulders. She shut her eyes and leaned against the solid strength of him.

The quiet ceremony ended and Pastor Frank approached. She welcomed the warmth of his hand when he held her icy ones between his own as he offered a few final words of comfort.

"Honey, Luke," he said, in a good-bye to her parents.

"Thank you for everything, Reverend Frank," her mother said. Her father exchanged a few words with him, shook hands, and then the pastor departed.

"Let's go back to the house, Kitten," her father said.

"You all go back, Daddy. I'll be along shortly."

He kissed her on the forehead, then he and her mother followed the others up the hill to the house.

For a long moment, Kitty gazed down at the grave. As youths she and Ted had always been loyal friends, despite the childhood disease that weakened his heart. Eventually their friendship had grown into love, and three years ago, when they believed Ted had overcome the condition, they had married. Yesterday the attack had come swiftly; no warning signs, no chance to say good-bye—no chance to tell him just one more time how much she loved him. Ted was gone. Never again would she know the touch, the laughter, of the gentle and devoted man she had married.

Tears slid down her cheeks as she struggled to accept that reality.

"I love you so much, my darling. Please forgive me, because I'll never forgive myself."

# Chapter 1

*1895*

Kitty goaded her mount, crested the butte, and reined the mare to a halt. Her gaze swept the rolling countryside below and fixed on a distant group of men gathered around a fire. She smiled fondly when she saw her father and uncles ride up and join the group. Within minutes they were working side by side with the younger men.

The rites of spring, she thought reflectively: the rounding up and branding of the calves. When had she known a spring without it? Sighing deeply, Kitty dismounted and sat down. As far as the eye could see lay the Triple M Ranch. She had traversed its range from the time her father had put her on a pony when she was six years old.

Her somber gaze scanned the sage-covered valley abounding with clumps of white birch and copses of ponderosa pine. For twenty-two years she had climbed the buttes and mesas that capped it, had explored the plateaus and canyons of its plains, and had swum in the streams and creeks that snaked through its gorges and ravines. She had picked the bluebonnets of its springs and endured the rugged chills of its winters.

The Triple M had been and always would be the center of her universe—but the time had come to leave it.

Sadly, she rose and mounted her mare, then began her descent.

Saying good-bye to her family the next morning almost broke Kitty's resolve to leave. She could see the confusion in their eyes and hear the heartache in their voices as they stood on the platform of the train depot.

Tears pooled in her mother's eyes. "How long do you think you'll be gone, sweetheart?"

"I have no idea, Mom. As long as it takes, I guess."

"That's the kind of answer I'd expect from your father," her mother said, smiling through the tears she fought to restrain.

"I honestly don't know myself, Mom. I'll stay in Dallas with the Carringtons for a while, and decide there what I'll do next."

"I still don't think it's right or proper for a gal to go off on her own," her father declared, trying to disguise his concern under a mien of gruffness.

"Daddy, since when did you give a hoot or a holler to what's proper?" But in truth, she knew that her father was one of the most respected men in the territory. Before he'd finally settled down as a rancher, the name of Luke MacKenzie had conjured up an image of a dedicated lawman to both those who loved and those who feared him.

"Furthermore, Daddy, it didn't bother you and Mom when Josh left the Triple M."

"He came back, didn't he?"

"And someday I will, too."

"What makes you think your brother's leaving didn't bother us?" her mother asked. "At least we understood why he did it, though."

"Then try to understand why I must go, too."

"It's not the same, Kitty." Her father's voice deepened with reproach. "It's plumb natural for a young man to test his wings, but it's just plain wrong for a gal to—"

"Daddy, it's been two years since Ted died, and I've tried to get on with my life. But I can't do that as long as I remain here, where everything reminds me of Ted. I've got to find out for myself if I have the same strength and fortitude as the rest of you—and you all look after me as if I'm a fragile doll that will break if I stumble and fall."

*Was that why you stayed, Ted, to protect me like the rest of them do?*

"Daddy, Mom and Aunt Garnet did it when they were younger, and Aunt Adee ran away from home. Even Em and Rose were on their own when Josh and Zach met them."

"You planning on becoming a Harvey Girl, like they were?"

"Maybe. I don't know, Daddy. I just know I have to stop leaning on you and Mom. Had I been more independent, I would have encouraged Ted to leave and start a business elsewhere. Instead, I wanted to remain here, where I felt safe and secure. If I'd thought more about Ted's contentment instead of my own—"

"Kitty, Ted had a weak heart," her mother said gently.

"I know that, but—"

"Then surely you aren't holding yourself responsible for his death."

"Maybe Ted would have been happier elsewhere, Mom."

That struck a nerve with her father. "What in hell was wrong with the Triple M?"

She was pouring salt into an already gaping wound. How could she make him understand? Her father loved the ranch as much as his brothers did—as much as she did, Josh did, and her cousins did. It was inconceivable to him why others wouldn't.

"Oh, Daddy, Ted always felt inadequate compared to the men in my family. I sensed this and should have left, but I was too absorbed in my own needs to consider his."

"So you think you can make it up to him by leaving now? It won't bring him back, gal."

"Don't be angry with me, Daddy. Please try to understand?"

Her mother hugged her. "He does, sweetheart. We both do. We're just worried because it seems like you're running away from the problem, instead of staying here and facing it like—"

"—a MacKenzie, Mom?"

"Whether you recognize it or not, my darling

Kitty, you're as much of a MacKenzie as your brother and cousins—but I guess you'll have to discover that for yourself."

The sudden hiss from a burst of steam and the grating intrusion as metal ground against metal brought an end to the conversation.

"All aboard," the porter called.

"I'll write you from Dallas."

"Be sure and give Beth and Jake our love."

"I will, Mom." They hugged and kissed, and for a lingering moment their gazes held. Throughout her life, the two had exchanged this same look between them: a look that said more about love and support than any spoken words ever could.

Then Kitty turned to her father, and closed her eyes when his strong arms drew her into his embrace. That wall of strength had always been there for her in any crisis she'd faced. She fought the temptation to seek it again.

"I love you, Daddy." She kissed him, and finally climbed on the train.

She didn't look back.

The wound he'd sustained in India ached like hell, and Jared had stepped off the train to stretch his leg. His attention was drawn to a young woman and an older couple on the platform. From their expressions, it was obvious a farewell was being enacted. Both women were dabbing at their eyes.

Drat women, anyway! Why did they always have to weep, shed tears that could haunt a man forever? A man could be leaving with the prospect of a most exciting event, and there would still be tears. Like his mother's tears that long-ago day when he'd left for West Point. He'd been excited about entering the military academy; she had wept. It was the last time he'd seen her alive, because she had died six months later. Her tears were his final memory of her.

The porter called out again for them to board, and he watched the young woman turn to depart. Despite her female propensity for tears, he felt admiration for her grit. Despite her sadness, her step didn't falter; she carried herself with steadfast resolution.

When she disappeared behind a cloud of steam and evaporating morning mist, for an inexplicable moment he visualized her in bright sunlight, laughing as she romped through a meadow of wildflowers. Then the vapor diminished enough for him to see her disappear onto the train. Why in the world had his thoughts strayed to such absurdities? Obviously he still had a touch of fever. He gave his aching leg a final shake, then climbed on the train.

Returning to his seat, he discovered that the woman from the platform now occupied it.

"Madam, I'm afraid you're sitting in my seat." She appeared oblivious to his remark and continued to stare out the window. Jared cleared his throat. "Madam, you are sitting in my seat." This time his declaration was considerably more forceful.

Jared was pleased to see he finally got through to her. She turned her head and looked up at him with a sad expression in her dark blue eyes. "I beg your pardon?"

"You are occupying my seat, madam, and I would appreciate your moving."

"Oh, I'm sorry. I didn't realize this seat was occupied." She glanced at the opposite Pullman seat facing them. "I wonder if you'd object to taking that seat, sir. It's the only available one, and I have a tendency to become ill when I ride backward."

"Regrettable, madam. However, if you find that seat undesirable, I'll be glad to ask the porter to find you an accommodation in an adjoining car. In the meantime, *I* have a tendency to become irritated with delays—they tax my good nature."

"Whatever *good* nature you may possess, sir, is certainly not in evidence at the moment." Clearly irritated, she stood and gathered up the gloves and purse she had placed beside her on the seat.

Suddenly the train lurched forward. His wounded leg buckled, causing him to plop down on the seat just as she started to move toward the opposite one. Thrown off balance, she fell backward, sprawling in his lap.

Jared grabbed her reflexively and found himself staring down into her startled eyes. They actually were the color of sapphires and were tipped with long, dark lashes. Indeed, they were extraordinary, and for a brief moment he was mesmerized.

"If you please!" she demanded.

It took several seconds for Jared to realize he still held her in a firm grasp, and she was struggling to stand up. He released her, and she shifted to the opposite seat.

Jared bent over and picked up her glove, which had fallen to the floor. Her fascinating eyes flashed in annoyance when he handed it to her.

"Thank you," she snapped, and proceeded to adjust the bonnet that had slipped down on her forehead. Drawing out a hat pin, which appeared to be only slightly more lethal than the bonnet's ridiculously long feather, she struggled to repin the hat on top of her dark curls.

"My advice, madam, is that you remove that outrageous weapon before its feather blinds someone."

"Your advice, sir, is neither sought nor appreciated." She finally abandoned the effort and laid the hat beside her.

When a scathing glare failed to wipe the smirk off his face, Kitty turned her head and stared out the window.

Fuming, she watched the countryside whiz past. What a dreadful man! Undoubtedly the rudest one she'd ever known. Was he an example of what she'd continue to encounter outside the protective boundaries of her home? But the husbands of her father's three cousins, whose roots had never been nurtured on the Triple M, were unfailingly polite. What it boiled down to was that this stranger was simply nasty and cantankerous. She stole a glance at him, and saw that his eyes were closed.

He was wearing a military uniform, which wasn't a rare sight where she'd been raised, at some point most men in Texas joined either the cavalry or the Texas Rangers. But he probably wasn't a Texan, anyway.

He was tall, well built, with dark hair and brown eyes. But he wasn't what she considered a handsome man, perhaps due to the scar that ran from his left cheek to his eyebrow. It kind of tugged at the corner of the brow, giving the impression of an arched brow. It was a recent wound, still vivid and red, and she wondered how he had sustained it.

She decided the wound had nothing to do with why she found this man unattractive, though: it was his overbearing, domineering, arrogant personality. He was downright, rattlesnake mean.

He opened his eyes, and Kitty quickly turned her head and resumed staring out the window.

As soon as the train reached Dallas, she rose hastily and left. After claiming her luggage she climbed into a cab, and saw her traveling companion walking toward an elegant carriage. Limping, actually.

Kitty felt a flash of guilt. Perhaps she had been too critical. Between that unappealing scar and his limp, he might have good cause to be so disagreeable.

"No more snap judgments," she declared, then broke into a grin. She and this stranger *had* snapped at each other, like two turtles claiming the same sunny spot on the sand, or in this case, the same seat on a train.

Smiling over the foolishness of it, she leaned back to enjoy the sights of Dallas.

The stately mansions, with their trimmed lawns and ornamental yards, were a beauteous sight as the carriage moved up Rose Avenue. These opulent mansions were the homes of Dallas's elite.

Kitty had visited Dallas for the first time when she was just a child. Michael Jacob Carrington, affectionately known as Jake to family and close friends, was a wealthy entrepreneur whom her father's cousin, Elizabeth MacKenzie, had married. Kitty had never forgotten her first sight of the crystal chandeliers and marble floors, the mahogany balustrades on the elegant stairway, and the high ceilings of the luxurious Carrington mansion.

As soon as the cabbie turned into the long driveway, a groom appeared to assist her out of the carriage. The front door opened and Beth and Jake stepped out to greet her. Within minutes, Kitty was seated in their comfortable drawing room having tea and filling them in on the latest MacKenzie news.

"Has Cole returned from Alaska yet?" Jake asked.

"No, he hasn't, but he wrote Uncle Cleve that he's convinced he's going to strike gold soon."

Jake chuckled. "Knowing Cole, he probably will, too."

"What about Jeb?" Beth asked. "Have Cleve and Adee heard from him?"

"Not since he left to join Cole. Aunt Adee's worried sick about him; she's afraid he might have changed his mind and joined the army."

"Oh, dear," Beth said. "Jeb's so young."

"He's twenty."

Beth shook her head. "Poor Adee. I must write to her."

"Jonathan Fraser's son, who's in the army, was wounded in India, you know," Jake said.

Beth nodded. "Yes, I heard. I don't know what I'd do if our Mike ever gets the notion to go off and join the army."

"Honey, I don't think we have to worry," Jake said. "It would take an invasion of the United States to get our son off the ranch." He grinned at Kitty. "When we finished the roundup on La Paloma, our kids and their Kincaid cousins all went up to Colorado to spend the summer on the Roundhouse. Angie and Giff will have their hands full."

"My sister and her husband love it," Beth said. "And the Roundhouse is so large, the children really get a taste of ranching. I miss them already, though." Then she stood up. "But enough of this talk. Let's get you situated upstairs, Kitty. You've arrived in time to join a dinner party we're having tonight."

"I don't want to impose, Beth. I'll just remain in my room."

"Nonsense! I won't hear of it." Beth tucked her arm through Kitty's as they climbed the wide stairway. "I'm so glad you came, honey. This place is like a mausoleum when the children aren't here. If it weren't for a stockholders' meeting Jake would never have come back from La Paloma, either; he's worse than the children when it comes to that ranch."

Kitty nodded. "I know what you mean. I used to think it must have something to do with being a MacKenzie. What is the fascination men find with sitting on a horse chasing a cow?"

"I'd say it had more to do with being Texan, except my sister and brother-in-law are just as bad. It's harder than pulling teeth to get Angie and Giff off their ranch."

*You were so different, Ted. Weren't you?* Kitty thought somberly.

Once in one of the bedroom suites, Beth sat down and chatted as Kitty unpacked.

"Beth, you went to school in the East; did you like it?"

"Do you mean school or the East?"

"The East. I haven't quite made up my mind where to go. Do you think I'd like New York?"

"It's a very interesting city, but I wouldn't want to live there. I was always homesick for the Roundhouse. But when I married Jake and had to leave Colorado, I couldn't bear to think of Texas as home at first, either." Beth hesitated. "Kitty, may I ask you a very personal question? Why *are* you leaving the Triple M? I always had the impression you loved it."

"I do. And I miss it already."

"Then why did you leave?"

"I had to get away. My life isn't going anywhere, Beth. I feel I need a drastic change."

"It's more than that, isn't it, dear?"

Beth was a kind and caring person, and Kitty knew the question was asked out of concern for her. "I've been so unhappy since Ted died, Beth."

"Kitty, I'm not one to advise you, because I can't bear to even think of an existence without Jake. But you're young, dear—there's so much life ahead of you yet. I don't think there's anything wrong in trying a change. The trouble is, your deepest problems accompany you wherever you go—there's no escape from them. If you're still grieving over Ted, you're not going to stop somewhere else. Grieving needs its own time—not a place."

"That's practically what my mother said. I just feel the Triple M holds too many painful reminders of him."

*Reminders of my own dark feelings, which overshadow any happy memories. One day I'll return to the Triple M and be able to fill my heart again with only sweet recollections of our love.*

Sighing, Kitty sank to the edge of the bed. "It's more than just grieving, Beth. I feel guilty, too."

Beth came over and sat down beside her on the edge of the bed. "Guilty about what?"

"I don't think that Ted was happy on the Triple M."

"Why wouldn't he be? Your family loved him, didn't they?"

"Oh, yes! They've known Ted since we were children."

"Did he love them?" Beth asked.

"I believe so."

"Then what makes you think he was unhappy there?"

"You know how formidable my family is, Beth. Ted was just the opposite. He was intimidated by them. I knew this, so I should have suggested we leave the Triple M and go elsewhere."

"Or *he* should have, if he was unhappy."

Kitty was surprised by the acerbity in Beth's reply. "Beth, you're married to a a strong-willed, successful man who could probably accomplish anything he put his mind to. Ted wasn't like that."

"I understand, Kitty—but if he was unhappy at the Triple M, it was his responsibility to say so, not yours to try and read his mind."

"I believe he was putting my happiness ahead of his own."

"And doing more harm than good to his marriage. Which one of you suggested you remain on the Triple M after you were married?"

Kitty thought about her wedding day and the events that followed. "Ted did."

"Didn't that come as a surprise to you?"

"Well . . . yes, at the time, but it pleased me not to have to leave the ranch."

"And it solved a big problem for Ted, too: he didn't have to take the initiative of providing for you."

"Beth, that's unfair. Ted carried as heavy a workload on the ranch as any of the men. Keeping the warehouse stocked was an important responsibility and a lot of work."

"Well, looking objectively at it, Ted really had no cause to be intimidated by your family, any more than you now have cause to feel guilt over the decision he made. So why punish yourself by leaving the ranch?"

"I left for my own peace of mind, Beth. I think I'm independent enough to make it on my own, but if I don't prove it to myself, I'll have to live the rest of my life with the guilt that he was right."

"You're going to do just fine, dear. And you're welcome to remain with us as long as you wish. There's plenty of room."

"You're very kind, Beth, but I think I might try going out East. It should be a drastic enough adjustment that I won't have time to wallow in self-pity."

Beth stood up to depart. "I think you're being very courageous, Kitty. And you've got a lot of grit to do what you're doing. That's why I'm convinced you'll work it out, dear. Now, why don't you rest for now? Dinner's at eight."

Despite feeling too pent-up to sleep, Kitty lay down to rest. The past nights of restlessness caught up with her, and she woke to a tapping on the door. Startled, she sat up when a maid entered.

"My apologies, ma'am, I'm Nellie, the upstairs maid. I've brought you fresh linens, and I'll just be puttin' them in the bathroom and be on me way."

"Thank you, Nellie."

Within seconds, the young woman returned. "Will you be needin' anything else, ma'am?"

Still stupefied that she'd even fallen asleep, Kitty glanced at the clock and was shocked to see it was almost seven o'clock. She had slept away the whole afternoon.

"Nothing, Nellie. Thank you."

As soon as the maid left, Kitty drew a bath and luxuriated in the warmth and sweet fragrance of lavender bath salts. After dressing and grooming her hair, she descended the stairway just as the clock in the foyer chimed the hour.

Beth introduced her to the dozen guests, and at dinner Kitty found herself seated next to a pleasant, gray-haired gentleman named Jonathan Fraser. He was a delightful dinner companion, and she soon learned that he was a business associate of Jake's. Fraser dwelt little on that fact, though, choosing instead to talk about his twin granddaughters, whom he obviously adored. By the time dinner was over, Kitty and he were on a first-name basis.

Following dinner, Jonathan Fraser remained at her side, and before Kitty realized it, she had told him she was widowed and of her intention to start a new life in the East.

"I admire your intrepidness, my dear, but how do you intend to support yourself?" he asked kindly.

Bemused, she looked at him. "Actually, I'm not sure. I'm very proficient at ranching, but I doubt there's much use for such skills in the East. I have no secretarial capabilities, but I did assist my husband in operating the general store on the ranch. Perhaps I can find a position clerking in a store."

"Do you have children, Kathleen?" When she shook her head, Jonathan asked, "Have you had any experience with young children?"

Laughing, Kitty rolled her eyes. "Now, *that's* a whole different thing. Between my cousins and the hired hands on the Triple M, there were always young children of all ages around. The Triple M is a community in itself, and children have always been an important part of it. My cousins and I all grew up together."

"Well then," Jonathan said, "have you thought of becoming a nanny or tutor as a possibility?"

Although Jonathan's suggestion didn't offer the opportunity of having her own household, which Kitty had been accustomed to the past five years, she had to admit it was a credible idea.

"The reason I mention it, Kathleen, is I'm in need of a nanny for my granddaughters at the moment. The one we had left rather abruptly today."

"I really don't think I'm qualified to accept such a position, Jonathan."

"You'd be doing me an immense favor, my dear. If you'd prefer, it could just be temporary until I can advertise and interview a permanent one. Do consider it, Kathleen."

Kitty was still hesitant. True, it would enable her not to have to impose on Beth and Jake's hospitality, as well as give her time to decide about her future. Perhaps she could even post letters applying for positions—something she should have considered doing before leaving the Triple M.

Before she could reply, Beth walked over and slipped her arm through Kitty's. "Jonathan, how is Jared doing?"

"Quite well, Elizabeth. He's home now, and the doctor said it's just a matter of recuperation."

"That's wonderful to hear. I'm sure Jennifer and Rebecca are happy to have their daddy home."

"Yes, indeed. He's been away so often, I'm afraid my granddaughters have had little opportunity to get to know their father. At least his recuperation will give them all a chance to get reacquainted." He offered a sheepish grin, which made him appear puckish. "Elizabeth, I've a confession to make. I've been trying to persuade this lovely young lady to become the girls' nanny. At least temporarily until I can hire one."

"That's a wonderful idea, Jonathan. And the girls are delightful, Kitty. You'd love them."

"I'm sure I would. I'm just not certain I could do a proper job of it."

Jonathan grasped her hand. "Kathleen, my dear, I'm confident you could do a proper job of any endeavor you undertook."

His sincere confidence was the very encouragement she needed to expel some of her self-doubts.

Her purpose in leaving her home was to prove her independence, wasn't it? This could be the beginning of doing just that.

"Very well, Jonathan. I'll give it a try . . . on a temporary basis only."

Later, Kitty lay in bed wondering about the wisdom of her hasty decision. As much as she loved children, she'd never had to care for them on a day-in, day-out basis. Well, her new life was all about confidence, wasn't it?

Smiling, she closed her eyes. *Besides, anyone can handle two little girls.*

# Chapter 2

Bright and early the next morning, Kitty arose and took a walk in the Carringtons' lovely flower garden, which abounded with sweet-smelling spring flowers and blooming shrubs.

On the Triple M it was impossible to sustain a successful flower garden. Lord knew, she and her mother had tried often enough.

She sat down on a bench and breathed in the delightful fragrance of apple blossoms, magnolias, and lilacs. The garden was refreshing and peaceful, and her confidence that she was doing the right thing grew with every breath. This day would be the beginning of a new journey.

After an enjoyable breakfast with Beth and Jake, Kitty dressed for her appointment with Jonathan Fraser, optimistically packed her belongings, and with luggage in hand, sallied forth on her new adventure.

Even though the Fraser mansion was just a short

distance from the Carrington house, a carriage waited outside to transport her. Used to a hardy ranch life, Kitty would have preferred to walk. Despite the many diversions the city had to offer, the life of a lady living in one of these mansions, with butlers and maids to do her biding, seemed too idle an existence for her liking. She surmised the novelty would wear off easily.

Set back from the street, the gracious white Fraser mansion, with its pillared portico, was as stately as the oak trees that lined the driveway.

A liveried butler answered the door. He was tall and slim, with a receding hairline and an impassive expression.

"Good morning, Mrs. Drummond. Mr. Fraser is expecting you in the study."

He took her luggage and then led her to a large and well-appointed study. Jonathan Fraser's lively face broke into a wide smile as he jumped to his feet.

"Good morning, Kathleen. A beautiful morning, isn't it? I hope your presence indicates that you haven't changed your mind."

"No, Jonathan, I haven't," Kitty assured him. "I'm looking forward to it, as long as we understand it's only temporary."

He chuckled in delight. "And I won't hold you to that arrangement if you decide at a future date you'd like to make it a permanent position."

"That's very unlikely. I've made up my mind that I'm going to New York. I've heard so much about the city."

"Let's hope we can convince you otherwise,"

Jonathan said. He tugged on a bellpull and the butler appeared instantly.

"Charles, will you ask the twins to join us?"

"I shall *ask*, sir," Charles said, and departed.

Kitty found the man's response most unusual, but Jonathan appeared undisturbed by it, so she shrugged aside her curiosity.

"How old are your granddaughters, Jonathan?"

"Eight years old. They're adorable girls, Kathleen. Truly adorable."

"I'm sure they are," Kitty replied, suspecting there was more than a little bias in the grandfather's opinion.

"The poor darlings lost their mother when they were four."

"Oh, how tragic." Overcome with sympathy for the young girls, she asked, "Was it accidental or had their mother been ill?"

"One could say it was an illness. Their mother abandoned them. Ran off to Europe with the scion of some Italian duke, and she's made no effort to contact my son or inquire about her children's welfare in the past four years."

Kitty was shocked. Having yearned for children herself, she found it inconceivable that a woman who was fortunate enough to have children could then desert them.

"What of the children's father? Didn't he attempt to stop her?"

"Of course he tried through legal channels, but was unsuccessful."

"Legal channels! I would have thought he'd pursue it in person." Any man in her family would have done so.

"My son is a career military officer, Kathleen. He has spent most of the past four years in foreign service, most of that in India."

It sounded to Kitty as though the children lacked a father as much as they did a mother. "At least your granddaughters are fortunate to have such a caring grandfather."

"My granddaughters' welfare is the most important mission in my life, Kathleen." His somber look changed instantly when the two young girls in question appeared in the doorway.

Jonathan hadn't exaggerated: the eight-year-old girls *were* adorable. And they were identical right down to the length of their long, dark hair. Bright blue eyes in oval-shaped faces glowed with love as they greeted their grandfather

"You wanted to see us, Poppie?" they asked in unison.

"Yes, come in, darlings."

They ran over and each kissed one of his cheeks, then they stood at the sides of his chair and looked at Kitty with blatant curiosity.

"Girls, I'd like you to meet Mrs. Drummond. She will be your nanny until I can hire a permanent one." Two sets of bright blue eyes studied her intently as he continued. "Kathleen, my granddaughters: Becky on my right, and Jenny on my left."

Dipping in curtsies, they said together, "How do you do, Mrs. Drummond."

"How do you do," Kitty said, her motherly juices

flowing as rapidly as a brook after a spring thaw. "I know I'm going to enjoy our relationship."

The girls looked at each other and smiled. "Thank you," they said.

"Darlings, why don't you show Mrs. Drummond to her room?"

Kitty stood up, and he walked her to the door. "Take your time and get settled in, Kathleen. I'll see you at lunch. Hopefully, the twins' father will be joining us."

The girls waited for her at the foot of the wide staircase that dominated the marbled foyer.

"I'm sure it's nice to have your father home again," Kitty said as they climbed the stairs to the floor above.

"Yes, it is," the girls said in accord.

"I'm afraid that for a while I'm going to have a hard time telling you girls apart. You'll have to be patient with me."

"We will."

"Do you girls always speak in unison?" Kitty asked.

"Not always," they responded together.

The upstairs of the mansion was as impressive as the lower floor, and Kitty was dumbfounded when the twins took her to a large suite complete with a sitting room, a bedroom, and private bathroom.

"This is my room?" she exclaimed, looking around, astounded. She'd never imagined an employee's quarters would be so lavish. "It's very elegant. And where are your rooms?"

"We share a room," one of them said.

"Are you Becky or Jenny?" Kitty asked.

"I'm Becky," She pointed to her sister. "She's Jenny. I'm older than she is."

"Is that so? By how much?"

"Ten minutes."

Kitty winked at Jenny. "It's nice to have an older sister, isn't it, dear? I always wished I had one." Her humor failed miserably, and they looked at her blankly. "I'd like to see your room now, girls."

They proceeded down the hallway to a different wing of the house.

"Our rooms are quite a distance apart, aren't they?" Kitty said. "That seems rather unusual, as well as impractical."

"If you prefer, I'm sure Poppie will give you a different room, Mrs. Drummond," one girl said.

"It doesn't matter. I won't be here that long, anyway."

"No, you won't," the girls replied in harmony, and exchanged one of their private looks.

The twins also had a suite, though the sitting room was more of a playroom. Kitty saw the girls couldn't possibly want for any toy; there were two of everything.

"How do you tell which toy belongs to whom?" she asked.

"What's hers is mine," one said.

"And what's mine is hers," the other finished. "Except for Bonnie and Bibbie." They glanced at two dolls placed side by side in miniature rocking chairs. Since the dolls looked identical and were dressed identically, Kitty thought they'd be as impossible to tell apart as any of the other toys.

She perused the reading books on a table, and went through some of the teaching material on the two children's desks in the corner.

In a series of short lessons, Kitty was impressed that both girls were skillful in reading and arithmetic, and could print and write in cursive. Unfortunately, there was no telling their handwriting apart.

The job was going to be more challenging than she'd anticipated. Kitty finally left their room and returned to her suite, but saw no sign of her luggage. Thinking a maid had already unpacked it, she opened the top drawer of the chest.

The contents were not hers. The same was true of the next drawer.

"Who are you, and what the devil are you doing here?"

Startled, Kitty slammed the drawer shut and whirled around. She gasped in shock at the sight of the man who stood in the bathroom doorway, naked except for a towel wrapped around his waist and hips.

"You!" Appalled, Kitty stared at the disagreeable stranger from the train. She couldn't help but notice that he had a beautifully proportioned body that looked even more powerful naked than it had restrained by a uniform. Drops of moisture from a recent bath glistened on broad shoulders that sloped into sinewy biceps. A patch of dark hair tapered in a seductive trail down the muscular brawn of his chest to a lean, flat stomach.

On the Triple M she'd often been surrounded by shirtless men with powerful physiques, yet now she could only stare awestruck at him.

"Good Lord, you're the twit from the train! Are you following me, madam?"

Bristling with indignation, Kitty found her voice. "Indeed not, sir! And will you kindly clothe yourself?"

If he found the situation awkward, it did not show. Moving with a measured pace to the bed, he picked up a robe. "Then who are you?" He pulled on the robe and belted it around his waist.

"I'm Mrs. Kathleen Drummond. I've been engaged as a nanny."

"I see. And just why are you in my room, riffling through my drawers?"

"I was told this was my room."

"You seem to have a proclivity, madam, for attempting to commandeer whatever strikes your fancy: first my seat on the train, now my quarters."

His cold disdain infuriated her. "That's not true," she cried out, sputtering with anger.

"And who do you claim told you this is your room?"

"The—" She choked back the words she was about to blurt out. She'd been tricked. So the twins were not as angelic as they led her to believe. Well, she had endured pranks from her cousins—especially Zach and Cole—enough times not to allow herself to be outsmarted by eight-year-olds. In good time, she'd settle this issue between them and her.

Right now, she needed to deal with this unbearable and practically naked man.

Swallowing back the lump of anger in her throat, Kitty said, "I assume you're Jared Fraser, Jonathan's son."

"You assumed correctly, Mrs. Drummond. And I find your familiarity in referring to your employer by his first name a bit informal, inasmuch as none of the other domestics do so and they've been with us for years. I prefer you wouldn't, either, in the presence of my daughters."

"I understand, Mr. Fraser."

"It's Captain Fraser. I'm in the army."

"In my defense, Captain Fraser, I would like to point out that your father and I met socially and were on a first-name basis before he even offered me this position."

"I understand perfectly . . . Mrs. Drummond." His tone was insinuating and insulting—and succeeded in refueling her anger.

"I don't think you do, Captain Fraser." She brushed past him and left the room.

Angrily, she strode down the hallway, the sound of muffled giggling and scattering footsteps preceding her. She would deal with the twins later; at the moment she had to control her temper and find out which was her room.

By the time she entered their room, the two girls were sitting at a table dressing their dolls in matching outfits. They glanced up innocently when she entered.

"That was very amusing, girls, but no more tricks."

"What have you little minxes done now?"

The question had come from the man lounging in the doorway.

"Uncle Seth!" The girls jumped to their feet and ran over to him.

He was a younger and handsomer version of Jared Fraser, but with a slighter frame and build. Having just viewed that frame and build wrapped only in a towel, she could easily make that assessment.

As the man hunched down and hugged them, he grinned up at her. "I'm Seth Fraser, the prodigal son. You must be the new nanny."

"Yes, I am. How do you do, Mr. Fraser; I'm Kathleen Drummond." She liked him instantly, and he was a refreshing contrast to his overbearing brother.

His smile was devastatingly charming. "I must say, Miss Drummond, you're much more attractive than the last nanny. Right, girls?"

"Right, Uncle Seth," came the harmonic reply.

"Thank you, Mr. Fraser. And it's *Mrs.* Drummond."

"Some men have all the luck. Father didn't tell me you had a husband."

"My husband died two years ago."

His sheepish smile was as appealing as it was contrite. "My apologies, Mrs. Drummond. I tend to put my foot in my mouth. I *am* sincerely sorry."

"Thank you, Mr. Fraser."

"Seth, please. Mr. Fraser is my father."

"As usual, Seth, you're wrong. Father is *Jonathan* to Mrs. Drummond," Jared said, entering the room.

Seth cocked a brow, and then chuckled. "Good for you, Mrs. Drummond. Ole Dad needs a bit of diversion."

Blushing profusely, Kitty declared, "Gentlemen, I must insist you refrain from such insinuation. It's unwarranted."

"Whatever you say, Mrs. Drummond. Nonetheless, you have my blessing." Seth bowed slightly and departed.

This was such a ludicrous situation, it was hard to believe it was actually happening. At any moment Kitty expected to wake up in her bed on the Triple M.

Sighing deeply, she turned around and was brought back to the grim reality that, indeed, she wasn't dreaming. Jared Fraser stood frowning at his daughters.

Both stood with downcast eyes, and the smiles that had lit their faces at the sight of their uncle had been replaced with distress.

"I apologize, Father," one said.

"I am not the one you should apologize to, Rebecca."

"I'm Jennifer, Father," the young girl said.

So he couldn't identify them any more than she could! The inflated Jared Fraser wasn't as infallible as he believed himself to be. Yet she couldn't help feeling sympathy for the young girls.

"I apologize, Mrs. Drummond," Jenny said softly.

"Rebecca," Jared pressed, his command hanging unspoken.

For the span of a drawn breath, Becky paused, and then said obediently, "I apologize, Mrs. Drummond."

Good God, she could fight her own battles. The girls had committed a childish prank, not a murder.

"No harm was done, girls. We'll just forget it even happened."

"I beg your pardon, Mrs. Drummond, but I'll be

the judge of what I deem is proper behavior for my daughters."

"Of course, Captain Fraser," Kitty replied, at the obvious reminder of her position in the household.

"I suggest, young ladies, you now direct Mrs. Drummond to the proper room." He departed as quickly as he'd arrived.

*Thank you for your apology, you despot.* If anyone should apologize it should be him for his outrageous insinuations.

"You told him," Becky hissed in anger.

So, now they were angry with her. However, an unexpected good had come from the incident: she had noticed that Rebecca tended to turn in the right corner of her mouth just before speaking. It was a faint mannerism, but recognizable to a discerning eye. Especially the discerning eye of Kathleen MacKenzie Drummond.

If she'd thought the episode with a semi-nude Jared was awkward, it couldn't compare to the afternoon meal. Passions were certainly naked, and tempers bare.

The tension between Jared and Seth was as heavy as the fragrance of the freshly cut roses in the center of the table—but far less sweet.

The two men barely spoke, and when they did it was more mocking innuendo than casual conversation. The situation was exacerbated by the twins' open adoration of their uncle. Seth joked with and teased them constantly, to the point where they ignored their father entirely.

Jonathan did his utmost to interject more amicable conversation, but his efforts failed miserably, and by the time luncheon was over Jared had retreated into a scowling silence.

Kitty said little, responding politely to Seth's and Jonathan's questions. Either there was very little love between Jared and his brother, or Jared was as much of an outsider to his family as she was. More likely, it was both. After all, he had just returned home the previous day.

Whatever the reason, by the end of the meal she began to believe that Jared Fraser's wife might have had good cause for leaving him.

Despite the unpleasant lunch, the afternoon was too sunny and bright to ignore; so after a grammar lesson Kitty took the twins for a walk. They appeared to enjoy the outing so much, she wondered how often they'd had this kind of opportunity. Their course followed the bank of a creek, and the girls laughed with pleasure as they hopped from stone to stone, back and forth from one bank to the opposite.

Upon returning to the house, Charles informed her that Captain Fraser wanted to see her in his suite.

Seated behind the desk, he looked dark and threatening. His mood clearly hadn't improved since lunch.

"I understand you were out walking with my daughters, Mrs. Drummond."

"That is correct, sir."

"In the future, I expect you to inform me before doing so."

"My apologies, Captain Fraser. I certainly didn't

intend to exceed my authority. I didn't realize I needed permission to take the girls for a walk."

He leaned back in his chair and regarded her with probing eyes. "Your authority is not the issue, madam. I am merely requesting that I am made aware of whenever my daughters are away. I trust my wishes will not constitute an additional burden on you, Mrs. Drummond."

"Not in the least, Captain Fraser. Am I excused now?" She didn't try to hide the sarcasm.

It did not go unobserved. "Mrs. Drummond, I don't understand your manner or what possible objection you could have to a father's concern over his daughters' whereabouts. It's a normal request, is it not?"

"This concern is newly discovered, Captain Fraser, since you've barely seen them in the past four years. I haven't witnessed your saying a kind word to them since I've been here, and your daughters appear terrified of you. Nevertheless, I shall make a point of informing you whenever I take the girls on an outing." Assuming the conversation was over, she turned to depart.

"There is another issue I wish to discuss," he said. "As you have pointed out—without delicacy, I might add—I am having a problem telling one of my daughters from the other. Therefore, I want them to cease dressing identically until I can do so."

"It's common for twins to dress alike, Captain Fraser."

"Perhaps so, but for the time being I want them to dress differently."

"By that do you mean one as a boy, the other a girl?" she asked, deliberately getting a rise from him.

"That's ludicrous, Mrs. Drummond."

"Some might be inclined to believe that a situation where a father cannot tell his daughters apart is more ludicrous."

"You are very impertinent, madam."

"Perhaps so, but I've observed your father and brother appear to have no problem identifying your daughters."

"And what about you, madam: do you have a problem doing so?"

"None in the least."

She was darned if she'd tell him how to identify them. He could figure it out for himself, just as she'd done. She had tested her theory on the walk they'd just taken, and it had worked. The only doubt occurred was when neither of them was speaking.

"And I shall inform you now that I intend to take the girls on an outing tomorrow."

"What kind of an outing, madam?"

"Shopping. I'll tell Charles we won't be here for lunch."

"Mrs. Drummond, we have a maid who shops for my daughters, and a cook to prepare their luncheon."

"If you understood the minutest iota about the opposite sex, Captain, you'd know there are two things in particular that a female enjoys doing: shopping and going out to lunch."

She actually saw a faint smile at the corners of his

mouth. "Interesting. I shall keep that in mind. Good day, Mrs. Drummond."

"Good day, indeed!" she muttered as she strode down the hallway. She doubted there'd be a *good day* until she was as far away from Captain Jared Fraser as she could get.

# Chapter 3

While the children rested in the late afternoon, Kitty walked out and sat in the garden, which was as peaceful and lovely as the Carringtons'. The layout and blooming shrubbery reminded her of pictures she'd seen of English gardens. There was even a small water fountain in its center. She sat down on a stone bench and thought about her meeting with Jared Fraser. Seeing how much the girls spoke and thought alike, she knew his orders would be devastating to them, and decided that tomorrow would be time enough to inform the twins of their father's wishes.

By the time she returned to her room and freshened up, Charles announced dinner.

The meal wasn't much better than the tension-filled luncheon. Jared didn't say more than a half dozen words throughout, and those were directed to his father. Seth was more subdued, but Jonathan was his usual pleasant self, and the twins devoted their attention to him.

After dinner, the family moved into the living room. Kitty sat down on the sofa next to Jonathan, and Jared took a chair and buried his head behind a newspaper. The twins pulled Seth over to the piano and sat on the piano bench with him. As he played, the three of them sang "The Old Gray Mare" at the tops of their voices. Kitty and Jonathan found it delightful, but Jared cringed and lowered the paper every time they hit a sour note.

"Come on over here and join us, Kathleen," Seth called when they finished.

He started a spirited rendition of "Little Brown Jug" and Kitty joined in. They followed it up with "Yellow Rose of Texas," which even drew Jonathan in for a verse. Then Seth said to her, "This one's for you, Kathleen."

The twins went over to the sofa and cuddled up next to Jonathan as Seth began to play and sing the haunting ballad "I'll Take You Home Again, Kathleen."

The song was one of her family's favorites. As Kitty listened to Seth's pleasant baritone, she recalled the many times she'd stood around a piano this very way at home as they sang.

Misty-eyed, Kitty glanced at Jared and saw he had lowered his paper enough to peer over the top, his gaze fixed on her. Blushing, she turned away.

Seth left shortly after, and Kitty took the twins upstairs and put them to bed. She was surprised Jared didn't appear to say good night to them. Returning to her own room, she undressed and went to bed, and lay thinking about her first day in the Fraser household. Jared Fraser truly was an unpleasant man, but since he appeared to spend most of his time alone in his suite, she did not foresee it as a problem. With a little cunning on her part, it would be easy to avoid him for the short time she'd be there.

Having made that resolve, Kitty shifted to her side to turn off the lamp. As she did so, she suddenly felt something touch her bare foot. Her breath froze in her throat, and she lay motionless, her heart pounding in her chest. Then she felt another brush against her foot. Was it a spider? A snake? She wanted to leap from the bed, but knew better than to move. Once a snake had crawled into her bed on the ranch, and her father's warning to remain still until he disposed of it had prevented her from being bitten. But this was the city. Surely there wouldn't be poisonous snakes crawling around in houses.

What if it was a scorpion—or a tarantula? She'd dealt with them countless times on the ranch, and their stings could be very painful and often caused serious infections.

She remained motionless and felt the perspiration forming on her brow. Dare she cry for help? Would she even be heard? The room closest to hers was the twins'. The rest of the rooms were in the other wing. It was up to her to get out of the predicament alone, or try not to move until morning, when someone came looking for her.

Suddenly she heard a sound that penetrated the cloak of fear that encompassed her. Galvanized into action, she jumped out of bed and threw back the counterpane and sheet.

With a loud croak, a frog hopped across the foot of the bed and down onto the floor.

So the twins were up to more shenanigans. She didn't know what she had done to deserve this kind of mischievous behavior. Despite those angel faces, the two girls were as nasty as their father. Well, she would put an end to it at once.

Kitty put on her robe and slippers, and then spent several minutes chasing down the frog. She poured a little water into the bottom of a glass, and put the frog into it. Then she strode down the hall to the twins' room, turned on the lamp, and shook them awake.

Rubbing their eyes, Becky and Jenny sat up in their beds.

"What's wrong, Mrs. Drummond?"

Recognizing the speaker as Becky, Kitty declared, "The time has come for the three of us to have an understanding. I will *not* tolerate any more of your misbehavior."

"I'm sleepy," Jenny whined. "I want to go back to sleep."

"Neither of you is going back to sleep until we settle this," Kitty said. "I want an explanation for this unacceptable behavior toward me."

"We don't need any nanny," Becky declared with a belligerent glare at Kitty.

"We can take care of ourselves," Jenny added.

"Your actions prove you do *not* have the maturity to take care of yourselves. Did you girls think you could actually drive me away with a frog! I was raised on a ranch. There are no paved roads and fancy mansions on a ranch. Spiders, frogs, and snakes are part of daily life. Furthermore, young ladies, you need to realize that your actions can have serious ramifications. A frog cannot survive for any great length of time out of water—especially when it's smothered in bedsheets."

Horrified, Jenny's eyes welled with tears. "You mean the frog's dead?"

"You killed it!" Becky cried out accusingly.

"No, Miss Rebecca Fraser, I didn't kill it—but your reckless, irresponsible conduct certainly could have. What if I hadn't retired until much later? The poor frog would have suffocated. Tomorrow, our first lesson will be a study of amphibians. Now get out of bed, and put on your robes and slippers."

"We don't want to get up," they said in unison.

"I don't care whether you do or not. Get out of those beds right now."

The girls crawled out of bed as ordered and put on their matching robes and slippers.

Jenny began sobbing. "We're going to tell Poppie how mean you are."

"And he'll make you leave," Becky warned, joining her sister in tears.

"Nothing would please me more," Kitty said. "But until then, I'm a MacKenzie, and MacKenzies honor their word."

"What's a MacKenzie?" Becky managed to ask between sobs.

Kitty put her hands on her hips. "You two rascals are about to find out. Where did you get the frog?"

"At the creek this afternoon."

"Very well. Follow me."

Kitty marched down the hallway to her room and

picked up the glass containing the frog, then, trailed by the girls, she descended the stairway.

The commotion had raised enough noise to attract Jared's attention. He came out of the library and waited at the foot of the stairs.

"What the devil's going on?"

"I would appreciate your remaining out of this, Captain Fraser. This issue is between me and the girls."

"Who happen to be my daughters."

Kitty was through trying to reason with either the father or daughters in this family. She gave him a hostile glare. "I must insist you return to the library and let me handle this."

"Am I to assume you are rendering some form of discipline, madam?"

"Your assumption is correct, sir." The sobbing behind her intensified.

"May I ask what they did to warrant this discipline?"

"That, too, is an issue between me and your daughters, Captain Fraser. Now please step aside."

Belting his robe, Jonathan Fraser came hurrying down the stairs. "What's wrong?" he asked, puffing from the exertion.

"Poppie!" the girls wailed out together. They rushed to him and he hugged them to his sides.

"What happened?"

"Unless you're prepared to suffer the wrath of Mrs. Drummond, Father, I advise you not to ask."

Confused, Jonathan looked at Kitty. "What happened, Kathleen?"

"As I explained to your son, Jonathan, it's nothing I can't handle. Come, girls," she ordered.

"We don't want to," they cried out. "Must we go, Poppie?"

"Do as you're told," Jared interjected, before his father could say anything.

Smoothing down his disheveled hair, Charles appeared from nowhere, accompanied by Mildred the cook, who was his wife. Kitty strode purposefully to the door, and the startled butler opened it automatically.

She stepped outside and nearly right into the arms of Seth Fraser, who reached out and steadied her to keep them from colliding. "I beg your pardon, Kathleen." The stench of whiskey was strong on his breath.

Kitty merely nodded and continued on her way, followed not only by the two whimpering twins, but by Jared, Jonathan, Charles, Mildred, and Seth.

The open front door provided enough light in the darkness for them to see as she led them to the garden. Once there, Kitty halted and handed the glass to Becky.

"I believe the fountain will do until you can return the frog to the creek tomorrow."

"But it's dark in the garden," Jenny whined.

"My sister is afraid of the dark," Becky added.

"Ah, but the righteous have no cause to fear darkness. Get going, girls."

"Come now, Mrs. Drummond," Jared said. "You've made your point. You heard the child; she's afraid of the dark."

"Will someone tell me what's going on here?" Seth asked.

"It appears Mrs. Drummond has cause to discipline the twins," Jonathan replied. "Am I correct, Kathleen?"

"Yes, you are," she said.

"Bravo, Kathleen!" Seth exclaimed. "It's about time someone did. As much as I adore these little minxes, they can be troublesome at times."

"Father, do we have to go?" The plaintive wail had come from Becky.

"I think you'd better listen to Mrs. Drummond," Jared said.

"You're just as mean as she is," Jenny lashed out.

The girls looked hopefully at their grandfather. "Poppie?" they pleaded. Sorrowfully, Jonathan shook his head.

"Don't be scared, Jenny," Becky said. "I'll take care of you." With the glass in one hand, and holding her sister's hand in the other, Becky led Jenny into the darkness.

Their sobs carried to the ears of those who waited anxiously. Everyone, that is, except Kitty. In her opinion, it was time those two little girls paid a price for their misdeeds. The fright and punishment the twins were enduring could not compare to those horrifying minutes she lay in bed, fearing a deadly snakebite. And the Lord only knew what mischief they'd done to previous nannies.

After a short time the twins returned, and Becky handed Kitty the empty glass.

"Thank you. You may go back to bed now."

To Kitty's surprise, Jared picked up one of them

in each arm and carried them back into the house. It was the first time she had witnessed a protective move on his part toward his daughters.

Once inside, the girls ran upstairs and the others went their separate ways. Before entering the library, Jared paused and looked back at her.

"Good night, Mrs. Drummond." His smile was more irritating than that damn croaking frog had been.

Long after the household had settled down for the night, Becky and Jenny lay whispering.

"She won't be as easy to get rid of as the others were," Jenny fretted. Yawning, she could barely keep her eyes open.

"We'll think of something," Becky replied confidently, right before she slipped into slumber.

Jared stood in the bedroom doorway and gazed at his sleeping daughters. They looked like angels, but they scared the hell out of him. Trouble was, he did the same to them. He was a stranger to them. He couldn't even tell one from the other.

Jared smiled tenderly. *That's not fair, girls. There's two of you and only one of me.*

If only he could catch one of them alone, then he might have a chance to get to know her better—but they were never apart. Even now, they preferred to share the same bed rather than be parted even in sleep.

They needed a mother badly. Damn Diane! How could she have abandoned their children so easily? Her actions should have remained an issue between the two of them; why had she made the children the victims of her adulterous behavior? He would have been willing to keep up a façade of marriage for the twins' sake, but she had run off for her own carnal satisfaction.

What did he know about little girls? He had no idea how to talk to them, what to say. He stared wistfully at the bed, his heart swelling with pride and love.

If only he knew how to tell them how much.

Yes, here he was: Captain Jared Fraser, United States Army. A veteran military campaigner who had been awarded a Victoria Cross by the British and the Legion of Honor by the French for heroism—*and he was afraid of two little girls!*

"Two very mischievous little girls," he murmured softly.

He turned away and went back to his room.

The next morning, with shaving brush in hand, Jared leaned over the sink for a closer inspection in the mirror. There were dark circles under his eyes, and although the scar on his cheek was not as vivid, it still appeared unsightly to him. No wonder his daughters avoided looking at him, shunned him as if he had the plague. Perhaps he should consider growing a beard and longer sideburns.

"Like hell I will," he declared, lathering his cheeks. He'd always preferred a clean-shaven look and he'd be damned if he'd let a scar drive him to hiding behind some overgrown stubble. He picked up his razor.

He hadn't slept well, either. Last night's incident

in the garden had disturbed him greatly. He had practiced self-restraint his whole life, and he'd observed since returning home that his daughters made no attempt to do so. His father didn't try to put any restrictions on the girls, but that didn't excuse their behavior. Still, last night the twins had been so frightened that it still preyed on his mind. He wiped the remaining soap off his face and tossed aside the towel.

But why try to blame his father for a responsibility he himself had neglected?

He pulled on his shirt. Lord knew, he was a poor excuse for a husband. His military career had kept them apart for most of their marriage, since Diane had refused to join him and abide the inconveniences and loneliness of an army wife. He glanced again into the mirror, this time with self-recrimination.

"And you were too damn self-serving to resign your commission in the army."

In truth, they'd been too young. Neither he nor Diane was mature enough for the compromises of marriage. He'd been overwhelmed by his graduation from West Point and then receiving his army commission; she had been swept up into the glamor of the uniform, military balls, and an archway of crossed swords at their wedding. The glow had faded swiftly when he'd been sent to a dusty army post in Kansas—and she'd become pregnant. She'd returned to Texas and never rejoined him.

He'd learned the hard way that love and marriage were only for the naïve. He'd never fall into that mirage again.

Women were a skirted army dedicated to making

his life miserable, or reminders of his failures. Diane, his daughters, even the haunting memory of his mother. Now he had to contend with this infuriating Kathleen Drummond and her incredible eyes. There was still the issue of last night to be settled. What the devil had the twins done? And more importantly, for the sake of fairness: did the crime warrant the punishment?

Incredible eyes or not, how dare she imply his concern for his daughters was newly discovered. She knew nothing about his feelings, yet she presumed to judge him. And why should she question his wishes to know his daughters' whereabouts? Wasn't that his right as their father?

He'd bloody well be happier when he could return to duty. At least in the army he dealt with men. Men had common sense. Men obeyed an order without attaching deep, emotional implications to it.

And as he descended the stairway, he thought it was a damn shame that a man had to prepare for battle in order to sit down for breakfast with his family.

# Chapter 4

Kitty awoke with a start and looked around at the unfamiliar room. It took several seconds for her to remember where she was and her purpose for being there.

Recalling the frog incident, she knew the twins would dislike her more than ever, now. But as much as she'd prefer their friendship, the twins were in serious need of firm guidance. And she would apply just that if they continued their pranks.

Rising, Kitty quickly dressed and went into the twins' room to wake them. Her cheerful morning greeting was met with scowls.

"Get out of here and leave us alone," Becky said.

"We want to go back to sleep," Jenny added, pulling the cover over her head.

"Get up now, girls. I thought that after breakfast we would have a brief lesson, and then what would you think of going shopping and having lunch in town?"

Jenny's head popped up from under the covers and they sat up.

"Do you mean it?" Both girls were staring at her with a combination of hope and distrust.

"Of course I do, if that's what you'd like."

"Aren't you angry with us for what we did last night?" Jenny asked.

"Certainly not. You were properly punished, so we can now put the incident behind us. Now get up, girls, and wash your faces and brush your teeth while I select dresses for you to wear."

The girls scrambled out of bed and rushed into their bathroom. Kitty went to the closet and saw two of every dress hanging side by side. She put a pink gown on Becky's bed and a white one on Jenny's. When the girls came out of the bathroom, they stared at them, befuddled.

"If you don't care for my selections you can pick out different ones, just as long as they don't match."

"We dress alike, Mrs. Drummond," Becky declared.

"Well, girls, I'm afraid there will be some changes made. From now on you will dress differently."

"No, we won't," they announced.

"Yes, you will," Kitty declared, just as decisively.

Becky was on the verge of tears. "You're just being mean because of what we did last night."

"No, I told you that incident is behind us. This will help to tell you apart." She saw no reason to tell them she was only carrying out their father's orders; she didn't want to remind them that their own father couldn't tell them apart.

Jenny's eyes were filled with tears. "But we've always dressed alike."

Kitty's heart went out to the heartbroken child. "It won't be as bad as you think, honey," she said kindly.

After Kitty pulled the white dress over Jenny's head, she did the same to Becky with the pink one. Then she took each by the hand and led them over to a long oval mirror in the corner.

"See for yourself, girls. Nothing's changed. You're the same person you always were. Now, get me your brushes and I'll do your hair."

They were too devastated to put up an argument as Kitty brushed out their long dark curls and tied them back with a white ribbon in Jenny's hair and a pink one in Becky's.

The twins were fully clothed and ready when Charles tapped on the door to tell them breakfast was awaiting their arrival.

Jared and Jonathan were seated at the dining table, but there was no sign of Seth. While Jonathan greeted them with his usual cheerfulness, Jared's "Good morning" came from behind the newspaper he was reading.

"And what is this?" Jonathan exclaimed. "What a surprise not to see you girls dressed the same."

"It's Mrs. Drummond's fault, Poppie," Becky quickly informed him.

"So she can tell us apart," Jenny said, resentment heavy in her voice. Both girls gave her aggrieved looks.

Jared glanced over the top of the newspaper.

"Mrs. Drummond is only carrying out my orders."

"We're twins. We're supposed to look alike," Becky said.

"Yeah, it's her problem, not ours," Jenny added.

Jared folded the newspaper and put it aside. "Mrs. Drummond is—"

"—capable of speaking for herself," Kitty interrupted. "And Mrs. Drummond is averse to being discussed as if she weren't present." She looked pointedly at Jared.

Fortunately the meal was served, ending the conversation. Jared said nothing, but Kitty observed that he took long looks at his daughters throughout the meal.

After lessons in reading and geography, Kitty left the girls to go to her room and dress for their outing. They were waiting in the carriage when she went downstairs. By the time they reached the shopping area, it was clear to see the girls were up to their tricks: Becky was now wearing the white dress and Jenny the pink one. And, naturally, they hadn't missed switching the ribbons in their hair. If the little devils thought they could fool her that easily, they were in for a big surprise.

When they reached the children's boutique, the girls tried on one dress after another, giggling and laughing at this new experience. But when she informed them they couldn't have identical ones, the situation became disastrous: the girls became desolate and refused to buy any of them.

To lift their spirits again, Kitty took them to a trinket store and suggested they pick out a special gift for each other with their own money.

"We've never done that before," Becky said.

"That should make it more fun," Kitty told them. "Remember, no peeking. The gift must be a big surprise to each other, Becky."

"I'm not Becky; I'm Jenny."

"I'm Becky," Jenny said. "Don't you remember, Mrs. Drummond, Jenny's wearing the white dress?"

"Jenny *was* wearing the white dress, but you're wearing the pink one now, aren't you, Jenny?"

They looked at each other in surprise.

"Girls, you haven't fooled me for a minute. I've been able to tell you apart since yesterday."

"Then why can't we dress alike?" they asked together.

"Because you're two different girls, and should distinguish yourselves so that people think of you as individuals."

"Why?" they asked in unison.

"And that's another thing, girls. We have twins in our family and they don't talk at the same time."

"We can't help it," they said.

Without thinking, she replied, "Didn't your mother teach you any manners? It's rude to speak when someone else is speaking—even if it is your twin."

"Our mother went away a long time ago," Becky said.

"She didn't teach us anything before she left," Jenny murmured sorrowfully.

"She didn't even say good-bye to us," Becky added.

Kitty wished that she could kick herself—or that

someone would do it for her. She felt horrible, seeing their sad little faces.

"Just try very hard, girls." She vowed that before she left the Fraser house, she'd try to get the girls to talk about their feelings. Until now she'd heard nothing but sass or deceptive remarks from them. Now she realized the young girls carried a lot of hurt inside them. But this was not the time; she wanted to raise their spirits, not lower them.

She told them to go their separate ways in the store, and not to tell what gift they selected for each other. They'd open them when they got home.

Trying to keep one eye on Becky and the other on Jenny, Kitty waited by the hosiery counter until each of the girls rejoined her, wearing broad smiles and carrying small, specially wrapped packages that they guarded tenaciously. It was probably the first time the twins had ever kept a secret from each other. Then, rather than take a carriage, they walked to the hotel and entered the dining room for lunch.

The twins were exceptionally well behaved in public, and Kitty couldn't help but be pleased. Looking angelic, they sat with their hands folded in their laps. If Kitty didn't know better, she'd be inclined to smile at them in passing just as other patrons in the restaurant were doing.

"I can't believe I've found the three loveliest ladies in Dallas," a male voice declared. With a theatrical sweep of his arm, Seth Fraser doffed his hat and bowed.

The twins broke into giggles immediately.

"Oh, Uncle Seth," Becky said.

"You're so funny." Jenny laughed as he tweaked her nose.

"And just what are you ladies up to, besides charming every man in the room?" His warm smile rested on Kitty.

"We're about to order lunch," she replied. "Would you care to join us?"

"I would, indeed," Seth said. He pulled out a chair and sat down. "I can't believe my brother didn't join you."

"I think lunch with the ladies holds no appeal to him."

"I think you're right, Kathleen. His tastes run more along the lines of eating in an army mess hall."

"What's a mess hall, Uncle Seth?" Becky asked.

"It's a big room filled with tables and chairs where soldiers are fed."

Glancing around, Jenny said, "This is a big room with tables and chairs. Is this a mess hall, Uncle Seth?"

"No, honey. In the army the food isn't as good or the company as charming," he said, looking deliberately at Kathleen.

When Kitty blushed profusely, Becky looked at Jenny and rolled her eyes. Throughout the rest of the meal, Seth kept up an entertaining conversation, delighting the children as much as he did her. But she felt uncomfortable with his outrageous flirting.

Jared Fraser stood outside and gazed longingly through the window at the four people seated at one of the tables. He imagined the sound of their laughter as they chatted with one another. His daughters appeared to hang on to every word his brother said, and Kathleen Drummond's face glowed whenever Seth looked at her.

Seth had that power over people; they gravitated to him as if he were the Pied Piper. While *he* had just the opposite effect on people.

For several minutes he stared at the quartet, watching the changing expressions on Kathleen's face. He'd overheard her tell Charles where they were having lunch, and had intended to join them. As if sensing his stare, she turned her head toward the window. Jared quickly stepped away and continued down the street.

As soon as they arrived home, the girls ran up to their room to exchange gifts. Kitty watched with pleasure as Jenny opened her package from Becky and pulled out a chain with a tiny locket.

"I love it!" Jenny exclaimed.

"I thought you could put a picture of us in it," Becky said.

"I will. Now open the one I gave you."

Smiling at her sister, Becky opened the package and squealed with pleasure at the sight of a thin gold band with a charm dangling from it.

"May I see the charm?" Kitty held it up to the light. "Why, it's a soldier."

"Just like our father," Jenny said.

Kitty would never have guessed that Jenny would choose that particular charm. It only confirmed her belief that these children's emotions ran much deeper than she'd suspected.

Once again, neither Jared nor Seth appeared at dinner. And later, when Kitty said good night to the children, she couldn't help smiling sadly as they kissed their respective gifts and tucked them under their pillows. Strange, how these two little girls, who had every toy or trinket available, could find such pleasure in the simple, inexpensive gifts they'd given each other.

Returning to her room, Kitty tried unsuccessfully to fall asleep. Recalling the extensive collection of books she'd seen in the library, she decided to select one to read.

Inside the library, Kitty looked around in awe. The walls were lined solidly with shelves of books. She loved to read, and began to peruse the shelves for a title that would catch her fancy.

After selecting a book to her liking, she saw one on a higher shelf that the twins might enjoy. Kitty stood on tiptoe but her fingertips only touched it. She struggled to work it out, but to no avail.

"Let me help you."

Startled by the voice at her ear, Kitty dropped the book in her hand and turned around. Jared Fraser was behind her, so close she could feel the heat of his body, breathe the bay fragrance of his shaving lotion. So close she could see the faint circles under his eyes and the bemused look that glimmered in those disturbing eyes.

A hot flush swept through her, her breath caught in her throat, and her pulse pounded in her ears. To her further distress, her trembling legs threatened to buckle beneath her. She stepped back, but met an immovable wall of shelves. She held her breath as he moved closer and plucked the book off the shelf, then stepped back and bent down to pick up the one she had dropped. He handed both of them to her.

"Thank you." To her dismay, her voice cracked.

"Do you enjoy reading, Mrs. Drummond?"

He walked over to the fireplace, and she realized he must have been sitting in one of the stuffed chairs there when she entered.

"I'm sorry to have disturbed you," Kitty said, and started to leave.

"I doubt you realize just how much you disturb me, Mrs. Drummond—but you didn't answer. I asked you if you enjoyed reading."

She turned to face him. "As a matter of fact I do." Her chin shot up defiantly.

"I find that a very admirable quality."

The condescension in his tone aggravated her. "It's not necessary to patronize me, Captain Fraser."

"That was not my intent, Mrs. Drummond."

If she allowed anger to control her, he'd always hold the upper hand. So instead, she nodded. "Then I apologize for my misconception. Good night."

This time she got as far as the door before he asked, "Do you read for knowledge or relaxation, Mrs. Drummond?"

Kitty drew a deep breath and turned to face him again. "What does it matter, Captain Fraser?"

"Just curious."

"For enjoyment. On a ranch, where I was raised, there weren't too many relaxing diversions."

"So you read fiction, not fact."

"That's right. But I think one gains knowledge from any good book."

"Such as?"

"Lessons in life. Insight into the differences between people. What motivates them. In fiction, the author reveals a great deal about human nature through the characters."

"But a Jane Austen character is far different from a Robert Louis Stevenson character. Perhaps the authors are merely appealing to their readership."

"Do you mean the female reader as opposed to the male?"

"Exactly. The happy ending offered to women is often the direct opposite of one written for men. The reality is that life doesn't have happy endings—everyone dies in the end."

"So you're not just a cynic, Captain; you're agnostic, too."

"It's not a question of faith, madam. Death is inevitable. Love is simply a distraction along the way. I don't accept the concept that people fall in love and live happily ever after. You should know that as well as anyone; I'm told you're widowed."

"Yes, my husband died two years ago from a congenital heart condition."

"I'm sorry. Did you love him?"

Her eyes flashed in anger as she slammed the books down on the desk. "That's an insulting question, sir. Of course I loved him. I've loved him since we were children. But unlike you, Captain Fraser, my husband didn't have a disability."

"My wounds are not permanent, madam. I'm told they will heal in time."

"I'm not referring to your wounds, Captain. Unlike you, my husband had the capacity to love."

His mocking laugh grated on her nerves, and she clutched her hands into fists.

"So you're of the opinion I'm incapable of loving, is that it? Some might consider that a virtue, or even an instinct."

"What instinct could it possibly be?" she lashed out.

"Self-preservation, madam."

"Your humor escapes me, Captain."

"It was not meant as humor, Mrs. Drummond."

"Then more's the pity, sir. I find it tragic that you're unable to love."

"And what qualifies you as an expert on the lack of my emotions?"

"The rejection of your own children. They're terrified of you. Your recent return should be a joyous occasion for you and your daughters, but I haven't heard you exchange a kind word with them since I've been here. And why aren't you there to kiss them good night when I put them to bed?"

"Perhaps it's for their own good, Mrs. Drummond."

"What lesson could two little girls learn from their father's rejection of them?"

"That if love is the gift you claim it to be," he said softly, "then they must learn to offer it to someone deserving of it."

"Deserving, or in need of it? The important thing is the willingness to give—not just to receive."

"I once believed that, too. But love can be a deceiving distraction."

"That is a very negative outlook, sir. In my opinion, love is neither deceiving nor a distraction."

"Even when you know a man is undeserving of being loved, but you don't have the heart to resist him? Could you love such a man, Kathleen?"

For what seemed an endless moment, their gazes were locked. This man was an enigma. Just when she was sure she hadn't misjudged him, he'd do or say something that opened her mind to doubts. Was he at war with society—or just with himself?

"I would like to believe I could. Most people are deserving of someone's love." She turned to the door.

"Mrs. Drummond, don't forget these." He picked up the books and read the titles, then handed them to her. "Your reading selections are quite diversified, madam."

"I intend to read *Pinocchio* to the twins. I'm curious to hear their reaction to the story. It might help me to understand them better."

"Surely you aren't suggesting my children are liars, Mrs. Drummond?"

"Not at all, Captain Fraser. They merely have a tendency toward rascality."

The warm, pleasant sound of his chuckle surprised her. "And why *The Strange Case of Dr. Jekyll and Mr. Hyde*?"

"I'm hoping it might help me to understand you better."

She left him staring bemusedly after her.

Later, as she lay in bed going over the incident, she realized that he had called her Kathleen.

* * *

As soon as Kitty had said good night and left, Jenny murmured, "I had a good time today, didn't you, Becky?"

Becky slid her hand under her pillow so she could touch the charm bracelet Jenny had given her. "Yes."

"Maybe Mrs. Drummond is different from the other nannies we've had. None of them ever took us shopping and to lunch."

"She's still a nanny," Becky said. "And we don't need one. Besides, she won't let us dress alike."

"I forgot about that. So what should we do?"

"I've got a good idea." Becky lowered her voice to a whisper and told Jenny her plan.

They pretended to be asleep when Mrs. Drummond came in and checked on them, before going downstairs. Becky and Jenny waited until she returned, and continued to check until the light went off in her bedroom. After a safe passage of time the two girls climbed out of bed, sneaked down the hallway, and cautiously opened the door to her room.

Once back in their beds, Jenny asked, "What if this doesn't work?"

"We'll just have to think of something else," Becky said.

# Chapter 5

Kitty awoke after a satisfying night's sleep and rolled over to get up. She let out a screech of pain when her head was yanked back. Horrified, she saw that hunks of her hair were stuck to something on the pillow. Picking up the feather-filled cushion enabled her to raise her head and sit up.

She discovered it was gum, and began to work her hair free from the wads that held the ends in a tangled mass. Once released, she went over to a mirror and tried unsuccessfully to work it out of her hair.

There was no doubt in her mind how the gum had gotten on her pillow. "Those little demons!" Their previous antics hadn't been harmful, but this was destructive: her hair would have to be cut away.

After yesterday's excursion to town she had believed she'd made great strides toward getting the girls to accept her. Stretching out a long hank of her hair, the ends of which were thick with gum, she realized that had been a delusion.

Throwing down the comb, she dressed quickly, tied a scarf over her head, and went downstairs.

She encountered Charles in the foyer. "Good morning, Mrs. Drummond.

"Good morning." She marched past him and opened the front door.

"Where are you going?" he asked.

"For a walk." She strode down the driveway and continued down the road until she reached the Carrington house.

Beth and Jake were at breakfast when their butler led her to the dining room.

Beth immediately broke into a smile. "Kitty, what a surprise. You're just in time to join us for—" Seeing the scowl on Kitty's face, Beth couldn't finish her sentence. "What's wrong?"

Jake got up and pulled out a chair for her, and Kitty plopped down in it. "See for yourselves." She removed the head scarf.

"Good Lord!" Jake murmured.

Beth stared speechlessly, her eyes rounded in shock.

"My sentiments exactly," Kitty said, feeling the rise of rage again that the walk had helped to lessen.

Beth came over and examined her head. "What is this in your hair?"

"Gum, that's what. Chewing gum!"

"But how . . . who—"

"Those two little demons."

"I don't understand." Beth returned to her chair.

"Becky and Jenny. Those two little miscreants could put Belle Starr to shame!"

"You mean they *deliberately* did this to you?"

"That's right. From the moment I entered that house, those girls have been trying to drive me out of it."

"But why would they do that?"

"They claim they don't need a nanny. If they were this obnoxious with others, I don't know how Jonathan was ever able to keep one. No wonder the last one left so abruptly."

"Oh dear," Beth said. "Come to think of it, there have been an excessive number of nannies and tutors."

Kitty eyed her apprehensively. "How many?"

Beth looked sheepish. "I haven't kept count."

"At least a dozen," Jake said.

"It's hard to believe Rebecca and Jennifer would be so difficult." Beth shook her head. "They always appear so angelic."

"Exactly what has gone on for the last couple days?" Jake asked.

As they ate their meal, Kitty related the attempts the twins had made to drive her out of the house. By the time she finished, Jake was chuckling, and Beth was trying to look sympathetic but failing miserably.

Somehow their amusement cooled her anger, and they all burst into laughter.

"Well, I suppose it is funny now, but at the time it was very exasperating," Kitty said finally.

Jake grinned broadly. "I'm visualizing the confrontation in his bedroom with Jared dressed only in a towel."

"Hmmm," Beth murmured, tapping her chin with a finger, "I've only met him once, but from what I remember, I'd think that wouldn't be exactly an unpleasant experience."

"Don't even think it, Mrs. Carrington. I'd better be the only fellow dressed in a towel that you encounter," Jake said.

"I admit Captain Fraser is built very handsomely, but at the time that it happened, it was very embarrassing."

"Captain Fraser?" Jake remarked. "Kitty, after *that* encounter, I'd think you'd be on a first-name basis by now."

Kitty couldn't help blushing, and Beth scolded him.

"I'm only teasing you, Kitty." He stood up. "As much as I'm enjoying the company and conversation, I have to leave." He came over and gave Kitty a peck on the cheek. "Hair grows back, honey," he said in a parting word of comfort.

He reached out a hand and pulled Beth to her feet.

"I'm just walking him to the door, Kitty. I'll be right back," she said.

Jake slipped an arm around Beth's shoulders as they left the room. The sight brought a winsome smile to Kitty. Beth and Jake were so in love one could feel it the way she did with her father and mother. Sometimes a simple gesture or a stolen glance could say so much more about feelings than any spoken word.

She frowned, recalling her reaction last night to Jared Fraser's nearness—the sudden, heated surge of awareness of him. Did it come from surprise and shock, or was it a reaction to his masculinity? Her lips quivered at the thought of such betrayal. *No, it can't be. I won't let you go, Ted.*

Suddenly Beth reentered the room, accompanied by her sister. "Look who I found at the front door."

"Cynthia!" Kitty exclaimed.

Cynthia MacKenzie Kincaid was like a Roman candle blazing across the sky. Madcap and unpredictable, she'd visited the capitals of the world while engaged to an Italian count, and men from kings to archbishops were captivated by her provocative beauty and enthusiasm. Upon returning to America, she had fallen in love with David Kincaid, the engineer in charge of the railroad her family was building. He was the only person who had ever succeeded in gaining an upper hand with her—and she'd married him.

Now, a pert Parisian bonnet perched atop Cynthia's dark upswept curls, her sapphire eyes glowing with warmth, she hugged and kissed Kitty in greeting. Then she stepped back and grimaced.

"Oh dear, Beth was right. We're going to have to do something about your hair."

"Pretty bad, isn't it?" Kitty said sorrowfully.

"I'm afraid we're going to have to cut it off, but with your bone structure, honey, you'll still look as beautiful as ever," Cynthia assured her.

The crisis had passed. Kitty knew Thia could accomplish anything she put her mind to—and whatever that might be, it would turn out successfully.

"Should we try ice first?" Beth asked.

Thia inspected several hanks of Kitty's hair. "We can try, but have the clippers handy."

Beth headed for the kitchen. "You two go up to my bedroom while I get the ice."

"This is going to be fun," Cynthia said. Grabbing Kitty's hand she hurried up the stairs.

After seating Kitty at a vanity table with her back to the mirror, Beth and Thia applied ice to the gum. As suspected, though, it did little good. Cynthia put it aside and picked up the clippers.

"Don't worry, dear," Beth assured her. "Thia is wonderful at cutting hair."

Despite her confidence in Cynthia, Kitty's heart sank to her stomach when a long hank of her hair fell to the floor.

"How in the world did this happen?" Thia continued to clip away as Kitty told her the whole story of her experiences at the Fraser house.

"I like the part about Jared in a towel," Thia said, merriment dancing in her eyes. "Was he extended or not?"

"Cynthia MacKenzie Kincaid! You're totally shameless," Beth declared.

"I know." She winked at Kitty. "But was he?"

"I didn't look," Kitty said, with a gummy-haired toss of her head.

"I sure would have," Thia replied. Kitty started giggling so hard, her shoulders shook. "Hold still, there's a master hand at work here."

"Then stop making those outrageous remarks, Thia," Beth told her.

"Well, what do you think?" Cynthia finally said, stepping back to view the results of her handiwork.

Kitty turned around and looked in the mirror. She gulped in shock. Her long dark hair had been reduced to a cap of short curls and ringlets that hugged her head.

"It's darling!" Beth exclaimed. "Oh, Kitty, you look like an adorable pixie."

"I guess I'll have to get used to it. And speaking of pixies, I'd better get back to those imps. I'd hate to get discharged for neglecting my responsibilities, although I'm certain it would give Captain Jared Fraser a great deal of satisfaction to do so."

"Isn't that just like a man," Thia said. "Compromises a woman, then can't wait to get rid of her."

"He did not compromise me, Thia."

Kitty's disgruntled look produced a wink from Cynthia. "Not yet, anyway."

Beth shook her head in defeat. "Don't pay any attention to her, honey. What do you plan to do about the twins now?"

"I suppose locking them in cages at night wouldn't be acceptable. I'll just have to think of something, or learn how to sleep with my eyes open."

Once downstairs she hugged and kissed them good-bye. "Thank you so much. I don't know what I'd have done without you."

As Kitty walked down the driveway, Thia called out, "Be sure and keep us informed. Especially if there are any more towel incidents."

As soon as she reached the Fraser house Charles opened the door. Mouth agape, he stared at her as if she were a circus freak. Kitty walked past him without offering any explanation.

"I regret to inform you that breakfast has been served already, Mrs. Drummond. And Captain

Fraser wished to see you as soon as you returned. But if you'd like, I'll have Mildred prepare you a tray afterward."

"Thank you, Charles, but that won't be necessary; I've already eaten," she said with a smile.

She was about to knock on Jared's door when she heard the raised voices of Jared and Seth coming from within. It wasn't her intention to eavesdrop, but the shouting was so loud, it was impossible not to overhear the argument.

"You're doing nothing but squandering the inheritance Mother left you on gambling and women," Jared shouted.

"It's my money," Seth retorted, just as loudly. "I'm not accountable to you or Father."

"Bullshit! I'd like to know how many times Father and his money have bailed you out of trouble while I was gone."

"It's none of your damn business, big brother."

"It is now. This bond scheme you're involved in is enough to bring down the family name."

"Billy Franks is a fraternity brother of mine. I had no reason to doubt his honesty when he approached me with the venture."

"Anyone with an ounce of common sense would have done some investigating before agreeing to join this damn investment fraud."

"Dammit, Jared, I told you I didn't know it was a fraud!"

"You do now. And you'd better hope Father can buy you out of it, or you'll be behind bars for a long time. Although a stint in prison might teach you a good lesson about responsibility."

"You're the last one to question someone else's responsibility. Where in hell were you when your wife ran off to Europe with her lover? And Father's been the only *father* your daughters have known for the past four years."

Kitty turned away. She'd heard more than enough. Granted, her father and uncles quarreled on issues, but they'd never made the arguments as personal as Jared and Seth were doing.

She had thought Seth was only making a light remark when he'd referred to himself as the prodigal son. It appeared the two brothers were total contrasts in character and personality.

However, Kitty had her own agenda to accomplish. With a new strategy in mind, she continued down the hallway to the twins' room. No longer dressed identically, the girls were seated at their table playing checkers. Bonnie and Bibbie were set in their rocking chairs and no longer were dressed alike, either. Reminding herself that she was a MacKenzie, Kitty sallied into the room with all the verve of a Jeb Stuart cavalry charge.

"Good morning, Mrs. Drummond," Becky said sweetly.

"Good morning, Mrs. Drummond," Jenny echoed just as sugary.

"What happened to your hair, Mrs. Drummond?" Becky asked with wide-eyed innocence.

"What do you think happened, Becky?" Kitty asked. "I had to have it cut off, of course, because of the gum you girls put in my bed."

Apparently they hadn't expected the prank would have such a drastic end. Shock registered on their faces, and Jenny, on the verge of tears, murmured, "We didn't think you'd have to cut off your hair, Mrs. Drummond."

Never raising her voice or showing any sign of irritation, Kitty said, "I want you to know that I consider you two the nastiest-behaved girls I have ever met." She flicked a piece of lint off her dress with her fingertip and said in a cheerful tone, "I suspect you both will grow up to be very ugly, because ugliness rises to the surface—just like cream in milk, you know."

Unmoved by the tears that had begun to streak their cheeks, Kitty continued in the same unruffled voice. "But no matter how nasty you act, I am not leaving here until I planned to do so. I was raised not to be a quitter, and was taught to love those who love me, and forgive those who do me wrong. So I forgive you, and I'll forgive anything else you try to do to me. I don't like you, but out of respect to my parents, I *will* forgive you."

Kitty walked to the doorway and paused to look back. Tears streaming down their cheeks, the girls sat with bowed heads in their little chairs, with their little dolls set beside them in even littler rocking chairs.

It was a pathetic sight.

"I must speak to your father now, so you girls continue with your checker game until I return."

As she strode down the hallway, her previous doubts lifted like a weight from her shoulders. She was in command of the situation now. She had won! Outnumbered, out flanked, she had met the enemy and defeated them. She might have lost the skirmishes, but she had won the war. She had triumphed over two eight-year-olds!

Kitty burst out laughing at the ridiculousness of it.

She paused and listened at the door. Either the argument was over or the brothers had killed each other. Tapping lightly, she entered in response to Jared's "Come in."

"You wanted to see me, Captain Fraser."

Seated behind his desk, he glanced up at her. "Good Lord, woman, what have you done to your hair?"

"I had it cut, sir."

"That's obvious. But why in the world did you do it?"

"I had my reasons, sir. May I ask why you summoned me?"

"It has been brought to my attention that you left the house this morning without notifying me or my father when you intended to return."

"I was under the impression I was to inform you of the twins' absences. I didn't realize I was included, too."

"We were unaware of your departure, madam, and the children were left unsupervised."

"Then you're fortunate they didn't burn down the house in my absence."

His arched brow inched higher. "Am I expected to guess what warranted such a comment, madam?"

"You'd know the answer to that, Captain, if you spent more time with your daughters instead of closeting yourself behind this door like some tortured hero in a gothic novel."

He burst into laughter. "Gothic novel, indeed! Tell me, madam, do you envision me as Bronte's Rochester, or Poe's Usher? God forbid if it's that wretched Ahab, stumbling around on a peg leg." Then he feigned remorse. "No, how remiss of me to forget. It's Jekyll and Hyde, isn't it, madam?"

The man must thrive on alienating people. She was determined not to let him rile her any more than his daughters. She was in control, wasn't she? So as much as she wanted to scratch the mocking look off his face, she smiled instead.

"Captain Fraser, I'd guess that you warrant a novel of your own." She opened the door. "In the future I'll be certain to inform Charles of my departure and time of return."

Kitty recognized a proper exit line when she heard one.

# Chapter 6

The twins were unusually quiet during their lessons and obeyed anything she told them to do without question, and Kitty began to think that she might have overdone her lecture earlier. Trouble was, they were such little actresses that she didn't know if they were acting from a sense of guilt or conjuring up further mischief. She'd like to believe they sincerely felt contrite, but the little minxes could be very deceiving when they chose to be.

After two hours, she told them to put their books away and get ready to take a walk to get some fresh air. She tapped on Jared's door to inform him of her intentions, and when there was no answer she returned to her room and slipped *Pinocchio* into the pocket of her gown. Before leaving, she checked her appearance in the mirror. It was still a shock to see her short hair, but as Jake had reminded her, hair eventually grew back.

Once downstairs, she peeked in the library, but it

was deserted. She found Charles and Mildred relaxing in the kitchen.

"Neither Mr. Jonathan nor Captain Fraser is home at this time," he told her. "Mr. Fraser is not expected back for several days and Captain Fraser had a lunch engagement."

That gave Kitty an inspiration. "I'm taking the girls for a walk. Mildred, do you think you could pack us a picnic lunch?"

"If you wish, Mrs. Drummond." Mildred set to the task at once and within five minutes had prepared a basket containing cheese sandwiches, fruit, slices of cake, and a red and white checkered tablecloth and napkins.

"I think this would be a good time to return the frog to the creek," Kitty told the girls once they were outside. They found the frog sunning itself on the edge of the fountain.

"Maybe we should just let him stay here in the garden," Becky said.

"But there's no other frogs here for him to play with," Jenny lamented. "And what if he's got a wife and babies at the creek who he misses . . . or who miss him?"

"Maybe the frog's a mommy and not a daddy," Becky ventured. "Mrs. Drummond, is this frog a boy or a girl?"

"I don't know, Becky." She was not about to explain the clinical reproduction of amphibians to the girls. "But I think every living thing seeks its own species."

This became a profound decision for the twins to make. Becky offered an analytical viewpoint. "Well, if it is a mommy frog and we took it away from its babies, that would be very sad."

Jenny approached it more pensively. "Maybe the frog was glad to leave its babies."

Her lower lip trembled, and Kitty knew the child had been thinking about her own mother. In a minute both girls would be in tears, and she'd probably be joining them. The conversation had made her aware of how much she was missing her own mom and dad.

"Let's just get the frog back to the creek where it belongs."

A short time later, she heaved a sigh of good riddance when they watched the frog hop across the water toward another frog sitting on a rock.

After choosing a grassy hillock near the creek to have their picnic, with the help of the twins Kitty spread out the tablecloth and they sat down and ate their lunch. As soon as they finished, she drew the book out of her pocket and the girls stretched out on their stomachs, propped their heads up on bended elbows, and listened with rapt attention as she read them *Pinocchio*, the story of the wooden puppet whose nose grew every time he told a lie.

For a long moment after she finished the story, the girls remained silent. Finally, Jenny said, "Pinocchio's story is like us growing uglier every time we do something bad, isn't it, Mrs. Drummond?"

"But in the end, he stopped lying and turned into a real boy," Becky argued.

"So if we stop doing nasty things, we won't grow uglier. Will we, Mrs. Drummond?" Jenny questioned.

She had reached them with the book. She now knew for certain she had not been hasty to claim a false victory. Smiling tenderly, she said, "That's right, honey; you'll grow up to be as beautiful as you are now."

Removing his hat, Jared slumped down on the ground and leaned back against a tree trunk. His leg ached like the devil. It had been foolish to believe he could walk the two miles between the Lorimer house and his own. Even taking the shortcut along the creek didn't help much.

He unbuttoned his suit coat and untied his cravat. This day had been a disaster from the moment he got out of bed: he'd cut himself shaving, Kathleen Drummond had confronted him acting like the cat that swallowed the canary—and what that was about, he was yet to learn—then he'd accepted the foolish lunch invitation, and now this confound attempt to walk home. What was he trying to prove? And to whom?

But accepting Stephanie's invitation was the most foolish thing he'd done to date. Curiosity, he supposed; it had been ten years since he and Stephanie were lovers. But he wasn't ready to socialize—especially with a former girlfriend who had married and was now widowed, looking for a new husband.

And Stephanie was like a tigress on a hunt. Had she always been so superficial? When he was eighteen he never noticed anything except her blond hair, blue eyes, and luscious curves. Her shallowness mattered not, because she willingly and generously bestowed her sexual favors on him. And with the appetite of an eighteen-year-old, he'd feasted on them voraciously. When she suddenly married Brian Lorimer, he'd been devastated. Looking back on it later, he'd come to realize he'd neither loved her, nor she him. His acceptance to the academy and meeting Diane Fleming had shoved any thought of Stephanie to the back of his mind. But when he saw her today, the memory had resurfaced. Could the sex between them be as great as it once had been? The "grieving widow" had offered it today with every movement and eye contact, and her poor husband wasn't even cold in the grave.

He was a man with normal needs and he'd be a fool to turn it down, but he'd be a bigger fool to accept it. The offer had too many strings attached—and he sure as hell didn't want to get involved in any permanent attachments.

Jared shrugged. What was he thinking? There wasn't any such thing as a permanent attachment. Hadn't he argued that very point with that persnickety Kathleen Drummond?

Now, *she* was a grieving widow. Her husband had been dead for two years and it was obvious she still mourned him. As much as he argued to the contrary, he admired her for it. Even though her husband would never return to her, she still carried her love for him in her heart. Dead or not, for a moment Jared envied the man. What quality did this Drummond possess to inspire such love and loyalty from her?

*As I told you last night, Kathleen Drummond, no one lives happily ever after.*

The sound of voices snapped him out of his reflections. He rose to depart, then sat back when

Kathleen Drummond and his daughters appeared in his view. They were unaware of him, so he chose to remain unobserved as they unpacked a picnic basket.

When was the last time he'd picnicked? It would have to have been with Stephanie. They'd always thought of ways to go off to some secluded area together.

He watched with interest as Kathleen and the girls chatted together, then his daughters' rapt attention when she read to them. What kept him from reaching out to them as he yearned to do—as he should be doing? Was it guilt—or fear of rejection?

He shifted his attention to Kathleen. With that elfin haircut, she didn't look much older than the twins. She was so unlike the Dianes and Stephanies he'd encountered that she was a puzzlement to him. And as infuriating as she could be, he enjoyed her company. She clearly considered herself on the same level as any man, and faced them without stooping to pandering or the wily methods so typical of women he'd known.

Surely this woman couldn't intimidate him. So why was he lurking in the shadows like a craven, instead of making his presence known? He brought a hand to his cheek. It was better to avoid others than subject them to the sight of him. The scar on his face was unsightly, and made people uncomfortable in his presence.

Resolved, he rose to return to the house, and as he did, Kathleen turned her head and saw him.

Drat the luck! Just another thing going wrong on this miserable day. He had no choice but to join them now.

As he approached, Kathleen put a finger to her lips to motion him to be quiet. He halted and saw that the twins had fallen asleep. She got up carefully and came over to him.

"Charles told me you and Jonathan were not expected for lunch, so I thought the girls would enjoy a picnic."

"You chose a lovely spot."

"I'm sorry if it's caused you an inconvenience, Captain Fraser."

"None whatsoever, Mrs. Drummond."

"Is there some reason you're seeking us, Captain?"

"Actually, madam, I didn't come seeking you. I was taking a shortcut back from a friend's house."

"Well, that's a relief. I know how easily you get upset and—"

He stiffened. "Mrs. Drummond, I do *not* get upset easily. I'm a military officer, trained to keep calm under any circumstances!"

"If you were any calmer, Captain, your shouting would wake up the children."

Her effort not to laugh had the same effect on him, and they broke into laughter.

She sat down and Jared joined her. "Did the girls enjoy *Pinocchio*?"

"I think so. It appeared to give them food for thought."

"So you now feel you understand them better."

"I think I understand them perfectly."

"Right now, I'd settle for being able to tell them apart."

"You need to spend more time with them, Captain. How long do you expect to remain home?"

"Until I've fully recovered from my wounds, I imagine."

"And then where do you go?"

"Wherever I'm sent."

"Jonathan mentioned you were wounded in India. I didn't realize we had troops there."

"We don't. I was a military attaché at the American embassy. India is a country of many sects and societies. Several of them are not sympathetic to the Western world—particularly England and America. One of those groups attacked the embassy." He arched a brow and rubbed his leg. "Ergo, I came back with several mementos."

"I'm certain your wounds will heal, Captain Fraser. My Uncle Flint had a similar wound on his cheek; through the years it's faded and shrunk to a thin line that I don't even notice anymore."

"It's not my face wound that concerns me, Mrs. Drummond. It's my leg."

"I'm sorry. Do you have much pain?"

"That, too, will pass. However, I fear the wound might cause enough of a limp to require me to resign my commission."

"I can understand why that might keep you from further military action, Captain Fraser, but surely you wouldn't have to leave the army."

"I can only hope you are right, Mrs. Drummond."

He stood up and offered her a hand. When she

slipped her hand into his, he felt his pulse escalate. His startled glance searched hers, and she appeared equally stunned.

"Thank you," she said when he pulled her to her feet. For an awkward moment their gazes remained fixed, then he released her hand and nodded.

"Enjoy your picnic, Mrs. Drummond."

Kitty watched him walk away. His limp was more perceptible today. She raised the hand he had held and stared at it as if expecting to see some mark, some evidence for the sudden surge of excitement his touch had generated. Why would she feel such a sensation? Jared Fraser was tyrannical and self-absorbed. Yet, underneath all his bombastic histrionics she had seen a glimmer of fear today, and had actually felt sympathy for him. He was a complex man. What other fears did he harbor beneath that intolerant, aloof exterior?

Kitty raised her head and watched him tread perseveringly along the bank of the creek. Jared Fraser was indeed a complex man, and he battled an internal pain as severe as the external one he struggled with so stoically.

Returning to the twins, Kitty sat down and watched Jared until he disappeared from sight. Against her will, she was being drawn deeper into the perplexities of this family, and she couldn't allow herself to become emotionally involved.

Staring pensively into the water, she sat quietly, with only the trill of birds and the babble of the creek lapping at the stones to break the silence as she waited for the twins to wake.

* * *

After the walk back, Jared could barely make it up the stairs. He sat down at his desk and riffled hurriedly through the mail Charles had put there. Pulling out an envelope marked *Office of the President of the United States,* he held the envelope in his hand for a long moment. From the time he'd awakened that morning, he'd had a feeling of foreboding. He'd even accepted Stephanie's offer of lunch just to get out of the house and try to shake it.

His hands felt clammy as he reached for the letter opener.

The letter thanked him for his courageous action in India, and regretted the wounds he'd sustained in the course of that action. It then went on to say that due to the recommendation of Colonel Hayes, the army's Chief of Surgeons, Jared was being ushered out of military service. The letter thanked him for his distinguished and dedicated service to his country, and then offered him a position in the diplomatic service.

The final paragraph requested him to attend an award ceremony in July, at which time he would receive the nation's highest honor, the Congressional Medal of Honor. The letter was signed by Grover Cleveland, President of the United States.

Jared poured himself a drink and slumped back in his chair, his worst fear now confirmed; he'd seen it in the expression on Colonel Hayes's face the last time the doctor had examined him. The thought of it had plagued his waking and sleeping hours.

He raised the glass in the air. "The Corps!" Then he quaffed the drink and, tossing the glass aside, he cupped his head in his hands. How he loved the army: the regimen, camaraderie, traditions. He'd always envisioned spending his adult life serving in it, and cursed the foul luck that had gotten him transferred to that damn Indian embassy!

So the army was through with him; booting him out with a pat on the shoulder and a medal.

"Well, President Cleveland, you can keep your damn accolades and medal."

He limped across the room, picked up the glass he'd thrown aside, and poured himself another drink.

Several hours later, he felt worse: his leg pained him and his head ached. Whiskey wasn't working, so he searched through the medicine chest looking for something to dull the pain. He'd used up the last of the laudanum several days ago, which was just as well. He didn't want to become dependent on it.

At this point he'd settle for an analgesic tablet or even a damn bicarbonate of soda. He tried both his father's and Seth's suites, but had no luck in either one. "Doesn't anyone ever get sick in this damn house!" Mildred would be sure to have some type of medicine, so he went downstairs. Hearing the sound of a piano, he went to the door of the living room. Kathleen and the twins were sitting on the piano stool, and she was teaching them how to play "Chopsticks."

His gaze rested on his daughters' nanny. She had a lovely profile: a combination of delicacy in the line of her jaw and pride in the set of her head. In truth, she had much more physical appeal than just those extraordinary eyes. He had just never been able to get past her eyes.

She struck a chord and started to sing, "Ta-ra-ra-boom-der-ay: did you see my wife today."

The twins sang back, "No, I saw her yesterday. Ta-ra-ra-boom-der-ay."

Jared couldn't help smiling as the song continued for several more verses, substituting "dog" and "cat" for "wife." When he'd originally heard the song sung at the burlesque, the words had been considerably more risqué.

In answer to the twins' request for another song, she said, "I shall now play Chopin's Minute Waltz in eighty seconds."

"But, Mrs. Drummond, a minute has only sixty seconds," Becky reminded her.

"So if it takes you eighty seconds, why don't you call it Chopin's Eighty-Seconds Waltz?"

"Mr. Chopin just liked to show off," she said. "Tell you what, though—tomorrow I'll play it in seventy-five seconds."

When she finished the piece, Jared was surprised to admit she was quite good, although he wasn't convinced that by the next day she'd have it down to seventy-five seconds.

He left before being observed, and it wasn't until he returned to his room that he realized he hadn't gotten anything to ease his pain.

He plopped down in a chair and reached for the whiskey bottle.

Jonathan had not returned for the evening meal, and Jared didn't join them, either. But their absences were compensated for by Seth's presence. With his usual charm he kept the twins' attention, and teased—even as he flattered—Kitty about her new hairstyle. She didn't welcome his outrageous flattery, but it was such a part of his gregarious personality that she didn't intend to discourage this attention from him.

Later, while she was putting the children to bed, Becky asked, "Mrs. Drummond, what do you have planned for tomorrow?"

"I haven't thought about it, Becky. Is there anything special you girls would like to do?"

"I'd like to go back to that mess hall and have lunch again," Jenny piped up.

Becky laughed. "Uncle Seth said that wasn't a mess hall."

"Well, whatever it was, I'd like to do that again."

"Let me think about it. I'm sure something will come to mind." She kissed each of them on the cheek, and wished them a good night.

Once in her room, Kitty thought about the next day. Since she'd taken them shopping, to lunch, and on a picnic already, she preferred to do something different. There certainly were many more ways to entertain eight-year-old girls.

Now, if she were on a ranch, there'd be . . . Of course, a pony ride. She'd have to get permission from their father, but she couldn't see why he'd object.

She went down to his room and rapped on the door. When there was no reply, she did it again. "Captain Fraser."

Kitty knew he was in his room; there was a light shining from under the door, so he hadn't retired. She rapped again, this time harder, and called out louder, "Captain Fraser, this is Kathleen Drummond. May I speak to you for a moment?"

"Go away!" he shouted back. "Dammit, madam, I don't want to be disturbed."

Good heavens, what a grouch! Jared Fraser was the most temperamental, unreasonable man she'd ever met.

Returning to her room, Kitty fluffed up her pillows, then reached for *The Strange Case of Dr. Jekyll and Mr. Hyde.* Perhaps the novel would help her to understand the very paradoxical Jared Fraser.

# Chapter 7

When Kitty opened the twins' door the next morning, she froze.

Hanks of their hair lay in scattered piles on the play table. Even Bonnie and Bibbie had fallen victim to the scissors.

"Oh, dear God! What have you girls done now?" Kitty cried, and rushed over to them.

"It was our fault you had to cut your hair, Mrs. Drummond," Becky said.

"So we thought we deserved to have our hair cut off, too," Jenny added.

"Oh, girls," Kitty moaned, "what am I going to do with you?"

"Are you mad at us again, Mrs. Drummond?" Becky asked, hanging her head.

Her hair hanging in shaggy lengths, Jenny looked at her sorrowfully. "We did it because we're sorry. Bonnie and Bibbie are sorry, too."

Kitty's heart swelled with such emotion she

wanted to cry. "Oh, girls." She sank to her knees and pulled them into her arms. "Your hair will grow back, darlings, but Bonnie's and Bibbie's never will." She hugged them for a long moment as she fought back her tears.

Finally she stood up. "Well, I'm afraid your family is going to be very upset. Let's see if I can repair some of the damage before they see you."

Kitty picked up the scissors. "Becky, you first." She sat her on the table and cut her hair so that the ends were even. By the time Kitty finished, Becky's hair hung to just below her ears, with the front trimmed in straight bangs across her forehead.

She stepped back to check it. "Becky, honey, your hair looks just like Bonnie and Bibbie's used to look. You're next, Jenny."

Kitty started on Jenny's hair, trimming the straggly ends until her hair was an even bob. Before she could trim the bangs, Jared came into the room.

"What have you done, woman?" His voice thundered with rage as he stared, appalled, at his daughters.

Kitty stood up and faced him. Anger had narrowed his lips to thin lines, and he glowered with fury.

"How dare you shear my daughters as if they're sheep! This time you've gone too far, madam. Your choice of punishment is petty and vicious. My God, you're dealing with eight-year-old girls—not hardened felons."

"Captain Fraser, you don't understand; I'm only trying to—"

"Spare me your explanations, Mrs. Drummond. Your services are no longer required in this household. I expect you to pack and leave immediately. A check for your services will be waiting by the time you depart."

He walked away without offering to listen to one word of explanation from her.

Throughout the tirade the twins had been petrified with shock and fear. As soon as he departed, they burst into tears.

"Hush, girls," Kitty cooed, gathering them to her.

Becky swiped at the tears in her eyes. "It's our fault Father yelled at you."

Jenny hugged her tightly. "We don't want you to go, Mrs. Drummond."

Kitty's eyes glistened as she fought back her own tears. She'd known from the beginning that this was a temporary position, but she had never expected to leave like this. And now that the time had come to actually leave, she felt a heaviness in her chest—she'd grown to care for the twins and felt guilty leaving them to the mercy of their tyrannical, self-absorbed father.

The girls sobbed profusely when she kissed them good-bye and departed hastily in fear of breaking down in front of them.

Her anger at Jared Fraser's unjust accusation increased with every piece of clothing she tossed into her suitcase. He was unreasonable, self-absorbed, pretentious, and overbearing. To think that yesterday she'd actually felt sympathy for him! A totally misdirected, wasted, honest emotion on her part.

"You're not on the Triple M anymore," she declared, slamming the suitcase closed. "Welcome to the real world, Kathleen Drummond."

Looking remorseful, Charles waited at the front door. "My wife and I are sorry to hear you're leaving, Mrs. Drummond."

"Thank you, Charles. You and Mildred have been very kind. And when he returns, please express my regrets to Mr. Fraser that I didn't have the opportunity to say good-bye to him."

"I will, Mrs. Drummond. Captain Fraser said to give you this."

Kitty glanced at the check in Charles's hand. "Tell Captain Fraser he can take his check and . . . and . . . choke on it. Good-bye, Charles. Thank you for everything."

Fuming with righteous anger, she strode down the driveway and passed Seth returning in a buggy.

He reined up sharply. "Hey, Nanny Kitty, where are you going?"

"Captain Fraser has discharged me. I'm going back to my cousin's house."

Seth jumped out of the buggy and took her bag. "I'll drive you."

"That's not necessary. It's just a few houses away; I can walk."

"I'll not hear of it. This bag is heavy, Miss Kitty." He put it in the back of the buggy, and then seated her.

"How did you find out my nickname?"

"I saw Jake Carrington last night. He told me about the hair incident. Those girls are lethal to nannies, but I adore them."

"I actually do, too. I finally broke through to them, and we were just becoming friends."

"Then why are you leaving, Kitty?" He reined up in front of the Carrington porch. "I know Father would love for you to remain."

"I told you; your brother discharged me."

"You mean he fired you?"

"The twins felt so guilty about my hair that they cut off their own."

"Good Lord!" Seth shook his head. "Those poor girls sure need a mother."

"Seth, I know it's none of my business, but I'm curious to know what their mother was like. I can't imagine how a mother could desert her children."

"If you'd ever met Diane, you'd understand. Jared should never have married her."

"Are you blaming him?"

"They're both to blame. Maybe if he hadn't committed himself to the army, things might have turned out differently. It's hard to say.

"When they met, Jared was one of Dallas's most eligible bachelors and on the verge of graduating from the academy. Diane had just moved to Dallas to live with an aunt, since her parents had died shortly before in a train disaster. They were both pretty young, but old enough to know what they were doing. Jared made no secret of his love for the army. He'd dreamed of a military career from the time he was little. If he hadn't been accepted at West Point, he'd probably have joined the army. Diane knew this when she married him."

"And Diane? What were her childhood dreams?"

"To be Diane. I sincerely believe, Kitty, that she

never thought beyond the next day. That was her charm. She loved parties, attention, and luxuries. A beautiful, blithe young spirit whom people enjoyed being with."

"I have a cousin who fits part of that description, except Cynthia's utterly devoted to her husband and children. There isn't a force strong enough to separate them."

"Well, they say that opposites attract, and if ever there were two people who embodied that cliché, it was Jared and Diane. They had nothing in common, and Jared was away most of the time."

"Surely she could have gone with him."

"She tried, but life on an army post was a dull existence to her."

"What could be dull about India? It sounds fascinating."

"India came many years after Jared was commissioned. Dusty Western outposts came first. I was away at school when Diane came home to have the twins. Dad told me that after they were born, she . . . well, she started up with other men. And after four years, she left with one of them."

"That may explain why she left Jared, but it doesn't explain why she'd leave her children behind."

"The twins were part of the mistake of her marriage. She put it all behind her when she left and divorced Jared."

"And she's made no effort to see them since?"

He shook his head. "Not even a letter."

"What was Jared's reaction to the breakup of his marriage?"

"I don't know; he doesn't talk about it to anyone. Now, you tell me why my big brother saw to discharge the best nanny his daughters ever had."

"Your brother came into their room when I was trying to even out the girls' hair, and accused me of cutting it as punishment."

"Didn't you tell him what happened?"

"He never gave me a chance. He ordered me out of the house."

"Jared's a hothead, but if he knew the truth I'm sure he'd change his mind."

Remembering the argument she'd overheard between the two brothers, Kitty doubted Jared could be fair about anything. "It's just as well, Seth. I intended to leave anyway. I only agreed to be a nanny until your father could find a replacement."

"What do you intend to do now?"

"Go to New York."

He helped her out of the buggy. After putting her bag on the porch, he took her hand and kissed it. "I'll miss you, Kitty. For a few days you lit up the darkness."

She felt a tug at her heartstrings. If Jared's accusations were true, what would become of this charming and likable man? "Take care of yourself, Seth."

She watched sadly as he drove away.

Beth and Jake were eating breakfast when Kitty burst into the dining room. "I'm back for good."

"Welcome home," Beth exclaimed. "And you're just in time for breakfast. Sit down and join us."

"It didn't take long for Jonathan to find a nanny," Jake said, pulling out a chair for her.

"Actually, he hasn't found one yet. In fact, he's been out of town for the past couple days."

"I don't understand," Beth said. "I thought you intended to remain there until he could find a nanny for Rebecca and Jennifer."

Kitty scowled. "That *was* my intention—but I was fired."

"Oh, yes, I'm sure you were," Beth scoffed.

"It's true, Beth. Jared Fraser fired me."

As they ate breakfast Kitty told them what had transpired in the past couple days, except for the quarrel she'd overheard between Jared and Seth.

Jake took a pragmatic view. "Sounds like the whole thing could be resolved with a simple explanation."

"Frankly, I'm relieved. I was beginning to develop a deep affection for the twins, so it's just as well I left before I became too attached to them. And maybe this will force Jared to devote more time to his daughters."

"How's Jared feeling since he came back?"

"I don't think I'm the right person to ask, Jake. My experience with him has been very limited—and unpleasant. I think his leg wound pains him greatly. But he's . . ."

Beth leaned forward. "He's what, Kitty?"

"He seems to be a man of dark moods. I have the impression he's a very unhappy man."

"Maybe rightfully so," Jake said. "After all, his wife deserted him and the twins, and he was wounded pretty badly in India." He put aside his napkin and stood up. "I'll see you lovely ladies at dinner. Behave yourselves."

As Beth walked Jake to the door, Kitty put her mind toward her future. She would check the train schedules today and formulate her plans to head East.

From the window of his suite, Jared had watched Kathleen walk down the driveway. He supposed the proper thing to do would have been to order a carriage for her, but she was such a headstrong woman he doubted she'd have accepted that courtesy anyway.

Why did he have this cursed propensity for misjudging women? First Diane, now Kathleen Drummond. He had believed what she'd said in the library when she spoke about giving love even if you didn't receive it from others. And yesterday by the creek, there appeared to be a gentleness about her that had touched him.

But it was all an act. No woman who professed everlasting love could be as vindictive and cruel as she had been. He suspected that the girls' childish pranks had somehow contributed to her cutting her hair, but why hadn't she discussed it with him, instead of resorting to such harsh cruelty? The twins were young and mischievous, but certainly didn't deserve to be chastised like prisoners.

He'd watched with interest when Seth met her in the driveway, and driven away with her. No doubt even the formidable Mrs. Drummond had fallen under Seth's persuasive charm. He'd seen how she blushed during meals in response to Seth's flirtation. The Lord only knew how many liaisons they'd probably shared already.

He'd been a fool to think Kathleen Drummond was different from other women.

He was still at the window when Seth returned. The short time he was gone could only mean he'd driven her to the nearby Carrington house.

Within seconds, Seth rapped on Jared's door. "Jared."

Jared ignored him. He was in no mood to talk to his brother. Obviously Seth had an opinion to express regarding Kathleen Drummond's dismissal. Well, he could jolly well keep his opinions to himself.

After a couple more raps Seth went to his room, and then drove away again shortly after. Jared went down the hallway to the twins' suite.

Mildred had brought breakfast trays to their room, and the girls were sitting at their table eating. As soon as they saw him, they burst into tears again and ran into their bedroom.

Mildred gathered up the trays and brushed past him with a scathing glare. Good Lord! What had he ever done to her, and to his daughters, to cause them to flee shrieking from the room as if he were a monster?

Did all females suffer an incapacity for common sense, or was it some devious conspiracy to drive him mad?

He yearned to return to the solidity of army life. He would more willingly face a murdering band of Thugees in India than cope with a household of females.

Biting the bullet, he went into his daughters' bedroom.

* * *

Laughing, Kitty and Cynthia entered the Carrington house after an afternoon of shopping.

Kitty glanced at her image in the foyer mirror. At Cynthia's insistence, she had bought the frivolous apricot straw toque with a Paradise plume of shaded yellow in front, and yellow and white daisies at the back and sides, now perched at a cocky angle on top of her short curls.

"Beth, where are you?" Cynthia called.

"In the drawing room, Thia," Beth called back.

The two women walked down the hall. "Wait until you see the darling hat Kitty—" Cynthia cut off her words when the man Beth had been entertaining put down his cup and rose to his feet. "Captain Fraser. How nice to see you; it's been a long time."

"It's a pleasure to see you again, Mrs. Kincaid. You're looking as lovely as ever."

"Thank you, Captain. You know our cousin, Kathleen Drummond, of course."

His gaze settled on Kitty. "Yes, of course."

Kitty wished she could turn around and leave, but it would be rude to Beth and Cynthia to do so.

Beth put aside her teacup. "Captain Fraser has been waiting to speak to you, Kitty."

"I'm sorry to hear that, because I have a dismal headache and I'm going directly up to my room."

"Perhaps if you could spare just a few minutes, Mrs. Drummond. It's imperative I speak to you."

"Captain Fraser, I'm not interested in anything you have to say. Your message was very clear this morning."

"Kitty, give the poor man a chance to apologize," Thia said, pouring herself a cup of tea.

Beth stood up and took the cup from Cynthia. "Thia, why don't we give Kitty and the captain some privacy."

"That won't be necessary, Beth," Kitty said.

She walked to the window. Obviously Beth and Cynthia were sympathetic to Jared. And she supposed the least she could do was accept his apology.

"Stay where you are and finish your tea. Captain Fraser and I can go into the garden."

Without looking back to see if he was following, Kitty hurried outside. She sat down on a bench, folded her hands in her lap, and took a deep breath. No matter what he had to say, she wouldn't lose her temper.

"Well, Captain Fraser, I'm waiting."

At the sight of his flushed and pained face, she couldn't help but feel a little guilty for forcing him to hurry. It seemed that Jared Fraser brought out the worst in her.

Kitty shifted over on the bench. "Sit down, Captain. I'm sorry; I forgot about your leg wound."

He took off his hat and patted the dots of perspiration on his forehead with a clean white handkerchief. "It's quite warm today, isn't it?"

"Yes, but I doubt you came here to discuss the weather."

He cleared his throat. "This is quite difficult for me to say, Mrs. Drummond."

She didn't try to make it easier, but stared at him with pained tolerance.

"After you left this morning I had a long talk with my daughters."

"Well, that must have been a first for all three of you."

He bolted to his feet. "Drat it, woman, this is difficult enough to say without your added sarcasm."

"And exactly what is so difficult for you to say?"

"I regret how I jumped to the wrong conclusion this morning, and I wish to apologize for my accusation. Becky and Jenny told me the whole story, including all they've done to drive you out of the house. I only wish you had told me."

"I can fight my own battles, Captain Fraser."

His mouth angled into the faint trace of a grin. "Unfortunately, you've made me aware of that on several occasions."

"And you, of course, find that annoying."

"Decidedly, madam. I'm in the habit of giving orders—and having them obeyed."

"And I'm *not* in your army, Captain Fraser."

Once again, he was glowering and she was glaring.

"Dammit, Kathleen, will you at least admit you have a propensity for insolence?"

"When you admit to being intolerant."

After another long moment, he threw up his hands. This time there was no mistaking his grin.

"It would appear we're at an impasse." He sat down and faced her. "Please come back to us, Kathleen." His tone had gentled. "The girls won't stop crying until you do, and their wailing is driving everyone out of the house."

"It won't last; by tomorrow they'll have forgotten me."

"I don't think so. You've touched something in them. According to Charles and Mildred, the twins have never formed this kind of attachment toward any nanny."

"Then perhaps it's just as well we part now. They knew I only intended to remain a short time."

"Then come back and give them a chance to accept the coming change. Somehow you reach them better than anyone else."

"I don't know, Captain Fraser. I've made plans to leave Dallas tomorrow."

"Plans can be changed. I'll reimburse you for any costs you've incurred, and I'll increase your salary by five dollars a week."

"That's not necessary. Jonathan's offer is already a very generous one."

"Then why are you adamant about leaving? I apologized for my outburst."

"Yes, but I doubt your apology changes your resentment of me, Captain Fraser. I think we'd always be in conflict."

"Sometimes I speak without thinking, but I can't change what I am, madam. Nor can you. For the twins' sake, I'm sure we're adult enough to maintain a working relationship." He looked at her intently. "Kathleen, you once spoke of how easy it is to give love. Can you give forgiveness as easily?"

"I'd like to believe I could, Captain Fraser. I've never been one to carry grudges."

"Then prove it by staying."

Torn with indecision, she turned away. It was difficult to think when she was looking into those brown eyes that had ceased glowering and now looked like a wounded deer's.

If she went back, she would become more emotionally involved with the twins—and that wouldn't do her any more good than it would them. What they needed was more involvement with their father.

Maybe she had a solution for that, after all.

Kitty turned back to Jared, who was staring at the ground, looking bleak and crestfallen.

"I'll come back under one condition, Captain Fraser."

His head jerked up. "What is it?"

"You have to promise to spend more time with your daughters—at least an hour daily."

He nodded. "It appears I'll have plenty of time for that." He offered his arm. "But I must add one other thing, Mrs. Drummond."

Kitty groaned silently. *Here it comes. No matter what, he has to have the final word.* "What is that, Captain Fraser?"

"I agree with Cynthia. That *is* a very fetching bonnet."

# Chapter 8

As they drove back to the house, Jared mused that the events in the past two days had turned his life around. Very shortly he'd be out of the service and would have to decide what he intended to do with the rest of his life. And drinking himself into a stupor each night wasn't a good solution.

Kathleen Drummond was beginning to give him food for thought, though. He always scoffed at concepts like providence, kismet, or the many other ideas to explain what mankind believed controlled destiny. The Hindus in India referred to it as karma. Could it be karma that Kathleen Drummond had appeared at this crisis in his life?

He'd already realized that she was an unusual woman. He'd never had to apologize to a woman before, much less plead with one. And he had to admit that she had offered an intelligent argument for why she shouldn't return. His daughters' continued association with Kathleen would most likely increase their bond with her.

How had she won their affection so quickly? According to Mildred and Charles, the twins had never formed such affection for any of their previous nannies. Karma?

Despite her infuriating obstinacy, she had many interesting attributes. Besides being attractive and quick-witted, she regarded people with an alert, open gaze that revealed intelligence and self-confidence. Her sense of humor clearly exceeded his own—of course, if one were to believe Seth's opinion, he had no sense of humor at all.

And if the way she had won over his daughters was any indication, the woman had a solid grasp on understanding human nature—which made him wonder why she challenged *him* so frequently.

So could it be providence—good karma—that she came into his and his daughters' lives at this time? A time when they needed a Kathleen Drummond more than at any other time in their lives?

The twins were waiting at the front door when he drove up with Kathleen. The Lord only knew what their reaction would have been if she hadn't been with him. For several moments, he watched them hug and kiss as if the woman were their long-lost mother. Then he walked past the closely huddled figures and continued up the stairway to his room, alone.

Kitty felt a moment of sympathy for Jared as he walked away. He had an air of defeat that she had never sensed before. In their excitement, neither Becky nor Jenny had thanked their father by word or action for his effort to persuade her to come back. Jared Fraser was a proud man, and maybe it had been unfair of her to set terms, but she was convinced more than ever that the agreement they'd made had been the right one. If it was the last thing she did before leaving this household, she'd break down the barrier between Jared and the twins.

The girls followed her up to her room and sat on her bed as she unpacked her clothes.

"There, I'm finished," she said, closing the dresser drawer. "I'm wearing out these clothes with all this packing and unpacking. Let's get to your room now, and I'll finish cutting Jenny's bangs."

"I decided I don't want bangs," Jenny said. "I'm going to wear my hair parted in the middle."

"What! Your sister has bangs."

"I know, but we're two different girls and should . . . should . . ." Jenny frowned and glanced helplessly at Becky for assistance.

"Distinguish," Becky prompted.

Jenny nodded. ". . . distinguish ourselves so that people—"

"—think of us as individuals," they said together, with wide smiles stretching across their faces.

"My feelings—and words—exactly," Kitty said.

Then in complete contradiction to what they'd just said, Jenny asked, "Does that mean we can dress alike again?"

"I would think so, but let me find out if your father agrees."

With an assertive bob of her head, Becky declared, "You see, Jenny, I told you it was Father's fault, because he can't tell us apart."

"Mrs. Drummond doesn't have any trouble."

Kitty decided to change the subject before it intensified. Her purpose was to bring the girls and their father together, not separate them.

"Girls, I think we're all friends, so I want you to call me Kitty, the way my friends do." They giggled with delight. "Okay, ladies, what's so funny?"

"You don't look like a kitty cat," Becky said.

"My real name's Kathleen; Kitty's my nickname. Just as you're called Becky, Rebecca."

Jenny still looked confused. "But Poppie says it's rude to call older people by their first names unless they give you permission."

"I've given you permission. And Poppie also expects me to instruct you ladies, so let's get moving. I'm sure we have time to get in a reading lesson before dinner."

When she entered the twins' suite, the first thing that caught Kitty's eye was Bonnie and Bibbie. The bangs on Bonnie's forehead had been untouched, but Bibbie's hair was now parted down the middle.

At least there was no doubt now which doll belonged to whom.

From her previous work with them, Kitty had observed that the girls enjoyed books. She was especially impressed with their reading ability. After thirty minutes of reading from their textbooks, they begged her to read to them. Kitty selected *Treasure Island*. Once again the twins stretched out on the floor and gave her their rapt attention as she began the story.

She hadn't read more than a couple of pages when Jared came into the room. "Captain Fraser, perhaps you'd like to read to the girls."

Jared looked at her, appalled. Her returning stare was a wordless reminder to him of the agreement they'd made.

"Yes, of course," he said, accepting the book she handed him.

Becky and Jenny raised their heads and exchanged looks of astonishment. However, they settled back down when Jared began to read.

Kitty thought it would be a good time to leave the three of them together, but her curiosity to see how it would go got the better of her; she sat down and listened.

His voice was deep and sensual, and she was mesmerized by the rich timbre that made Stevenson's words come alive. Occasionally, he'd raise his eyes above the page and glance at her with an enigmatic look.

The hour passed like seconds and she was startled when he put the book aside. "I think that's enough for today. We should consider getting ready for dinner, Mrs. Drummond."

"Oh, yes, of course," Kitty said, jumping to her feet.

"Kitty, can Father call you by your nickname, too?" Jenny asked.

Jared arched his brow. "What's this, Mrs. Drummond?"

"Kitty gave us permission to call her by her nickname, just like her friends do."

"Is that right, Becky?" The young girl preened at his recognition of her. There was a glint of amusement in his eyes when he turned back to Kitty. "And may I call you Kitty, too?"

A tremor rippled her spine in response to the huskiness in his voice. "Yes. Yes, of course, Captain Fraser."

He looked at her with a long stare. "My friends call me Jared."

He walked out of the room.

Kitty didn't understand why she'd reacted so strangely to him. Since the twins were watching her she tried to appear nonchalant, but her body was trembling.

"I think we should all freshen up for dinner," she said, and hurried from the room.

Becky grinned at Jenny. "Are you thinking what I'm thinking?"

"Of course I am. Did you see the way he looked at her?"

"And told her to call him Jared," Becky added quickly.

Jenny's eyes brightened with anticipation. "I think Kitty would make a good mother."

Becky's cheeks dimpled in a smile. "I think so, too. Looks like we'll just have to do something about that."

Later that evening after Kitty tucked the twins in bed, she wandered out to the garden in the hope of catching a cool breeze. Moonlight glistened on the petals of the flowers, and the only sound stirring the air was the light drip of the water fountain.

She sat on a bench and began to fan herself. It had been an extraordinary day and a very satisfying one as well. Even dinner had not been as tension-filled as she had grown to expect. Without Jonathan or

Seth present the twins had devoted their attention to Jared, with the bulk of the conversation devoted to *Treasure Island*. It had been a lively discussion between him and the girls, she thought proudly, and had given the twins an opportunity to reveal to their father what bright and alert minds they possessed.

Jared had even teased them about their shortened hairstyles, and even though the attempt appeared awkward and alien to his nature, she had to give him credit for trying. It was a giant step from the reticent and reclusive behavior she had encountered on her arrival. And it was all due to her efforts, she thought with satisfaction. Then she grinned. "Careful, Kitty, or you'll break your arm patting yourself on the back."

"I'm sorry, what did you say?" Jared's voice cut through her thoughts.

"Oh!" She was taken aback by his sudden appearance. "I thought I was alone, and didn't realize I was talking out loud. It was something my father used to say when my brother and I got too pleased with ourselves." She chuckled lightly. "Actually, he referred to it as being too big for our britches."

"And are you pleased with yourself, Kathleen Drummond?"

"I am. I see a big change in the girls. And you must have noticed at dinner how much they enjoyed your company."

"I think you're reading too much into it."

"It's a beginning, isn't it? They weren't as frightened of you as they were before."

"One dinner doesn't make a lifetime, Kathleen."

"You're too cynical, Captain."

"Perhaps I have good cause to be."

"I believe it was Oscar Wilde who described a cynic as one who knows the price of everything and the value of nothing."

"And perhaps that is why your Mr. Wilde is considered a humorist. Life has too many complexities to reduce them to simple definitions."

She jumped to her feet to face him, fanning herself rapidly. "Oh, you're the most exasperating man I've ever met! Can't you ever see the bright side of any situation? Today was the beginning of changing the relationship between you and your daughters. Don't you see that's the value? Look at what happened today: you apologized to me—and frankly, I suspect that's foreign to your nature—and you took an hour out of your busy day doing whatever you do behind that closed door to read to your daughters. Then you all spent an enjoyable dinner together. You don't consider that value!"

He abruptly said, "They're booting me out of the army, Kathleen. I got the letter yesterday."

So that would explain his rudeness last night. Knowing what the army meant to him, she looked at him with her eyes luminous with sympathy. "Oh, Jared, I'm so sorry."

"It was inevitable. I just held out hope that maybe . . . Oh, hell, I was a fool to think differently. I've never believed in happy endings, anyway."

"Everything happens for a reason, Jared. My Aunt Maude used to say that the Lord never closes a door without opening a window."

"Don't give me any clichés, Kathleen," he snapped. "I loved the army. It was my life."

"I understand the despair you're feeling right now, but you have two daughters who have needs, too. Maybe now they'll have a father there to kiss them good night, or stand between them and the bogeyman. And believe me, Jared, there are a lot of bogeymen in a little girl's life when she's growing up."

"I think I've heard a similar sermon from you before."

"Apparently you weren't listening too closely."

"Apparently." His shoulders sagged and his head drooped. He looked so sad, she wanted to hug him. "Believe it or not, Kathleen, I don't want to argue."

"Then let's not. When will you be leaving the army?"

"I'm not *leaving*, Kathleen, they're kicking me out. And they have the gall to tell me to come back to Washington to accept a damn medal."

"What medal is it?"

"The Medal of Honor."

Her eyes rounded in surprise. "The Medal of Honor! Jared, that's wonderful. Why, that's the highest honor—"

"Yeah, yeah. I've heard it all before. I'm not going. I don't need any damn medal."

"Stop calling it a damn medal—you do an injustice to the other men who've earned it. And you're going to accept it. If you won't do it for yourself, do it for your daughters."

"They wouldn't even know what it's all about."

"Maybe now they're too young to appreciate the significance, but someday they will. When I was a child I couldn't have loved my father any more than I did at the time. And when people spoke of how much they respected Sheriff Luke MacKenzie, I didn't understand what they really meant until I got older. Then I felt so much pride and respect. Not self-pride, but pride in someone you love. And now, my pride and respect for him equals that love I always felt."

"Well, my daughters don't love me, much less respect me."

"Jared Fraser, you're going to hear this whether you want to or not. When I took the twins shopping, I gave them a chance to pick out a special gift to give each other. Guess what Jenny picked out for Becky?"

"Must I?"

"It was a charm bracelet. And guess what charm was on it?"

"I'm sure you're going to tell me."

"The charm, you cynic, was a soldier, so that Becky could remember her father."

Jared looked up, clearly startled.

"Amazing, isn't it? With all the charms to choose from, your daughter picked out one that would remind her sister of you. Don't you see? Jenny wants Becky and her to have a father to love, Jared."

"And what did Becky think of her sister's choice?"

"She fell asleep with it clutched in her hand. Don't you see, *Captain*? That door may have closed, but the window's wide open. And though you're leery of clichés, you do have to learn to crawl before you walk."

"Or in my case, limp," he said bitterly.

"Is that your concern, that your leg won't fully

heal? If so, there are worse wounds you might have sustained—so keep it only a physical limp and count your blessings, Captain. Don't mentally limp through life, as so many do."

As if struck by a lightning bolt, Kitty gasped aloud and sank back down on the bench. "Oh, my God. That's what my parents have been trying to tell *me*!"

Jared sat down beside her, concern etched on his face. "What is it, Kathleen? Are you ill?"

She looked at him blankly. "I just realized that's exactly what *I've* been doing. For the past two years, I've been limping through life using Ted's death as a crutch. And he'd be the last person to ever want me to do that."

Jared took a long look at her. "How old are you, Kathleen?"

"Twenty-two."

"And how did you acquire such wisdom in twenty-two young years?"

"I had good and patient teachers."

"Your parents?" She nodded. "Tell me about them, Kathleen."

She chuckled. "You don't know what you're asking; I could talk about them for hours. My father was a sheriff in California when he met my mother. He'd been widowed during the war, and my brother Josh was six years old when our father remarried. Dad had decided he needed a wife, so he'd sent East for a mail-order bride."

"Your mother was a mail-order bride? Interesting. Obviously it worked out well."

"Actually, my mother took the place of the intended mail-order bride Daddy had sent for. When he found out, he arrested her in the hope she'd become a nursemaid for my brother. Naturally they fell in love and married. My family returned to Texas and the Triple M, and that's where I was born."

"I've heard of the Triple M. I understand it's quite a huge spread."

"One of the largest in Texas," she said proudly.

"Any other brothers and sisters?"

"No, just Josh and I."

"Are you and your brother close?"

"We're *very* close. I worship him. And he looks after me like the typical big brother."

"It would appear, Kathleen, you worship all of your family."

"I'm not ashamed of it, Captain, if that's what you're implying. My uncles, aunts, and cousins all live on the Triple M, too. And there's room for more when the time comes."

"And so everyone lives happily ever after." A tone of cynicism had crept back into his voice.

"Right again, Captain Fraser. And I refuse to listen to any of your skepticism on that subject."

"Then why are you talking about heading East?"

She was not about to expose her soul to him. He was too cynical to understand why she harbored such guilt. "I figured I needed a change to help me get over Ted's loss. When I'm ready, I'll return to Texas."

As Kitty started to get up, she dropped her fan. She bent to pick it up just as Jared stooped to do the same. His hand closed over hers, and tingling pleasure swept through her from the warm pressure. Only inches separated them, and his brown eyes held hers hypnotically. Her whole being filled with waiting as his gaze shifted to her lips, and he slowly lowered his head. Kitty closed her eyes.

Suddenly he stood up, and pulled her to her feet. She opened her eyes and saw a pensive look in his eyes.

"Good night, Kathleen Drummond."

As she watched him disappear into the darkness, Kitty felt more confused than ever. Long after he left, Kitty remained in the garden. Jared Fraser was a challenging and provocative man.

# Chapter 9

When Kitty entered the house later, she was pleased to see that Jonathan had returned home. As soon as he saw her hair, he insisted she sit down and tell him the whole story. His astonishment at what the twins had done paled next to his amazement when she told him Jared had swallowed his pride and asked her to come back.

"It's clear that my family has grown extremely attached to you, Kitty. I daresay even Jared, who has withdrawn from everyone since his return."

"Have you had a chance to speak to him yet?"

"No. I was just about to go up when you came in."

"I'll warn you that he's very disheartened right now, Jonathan. He got a letter yesterday notifying him that the army is discharging him."

"Because of his wound?"

She nodded. "They did offer him a diplomatic position, but he's not interested."

"Oh, dear God! The army is his life." He stared

sorrowfully into space. "Whatever can I say to him?"

She clasped the hand of the heartbroken man. "Jonathan, perhaps it's too early to say, but some good may come from it."

"Kathleen, as long as I can remember, Jared's wanted to be a soldier."

"This will enable him to spend more time with his daughters. They need their father, Jonathan."

His kindly face softened in a smile. "You're right, Kathleen."

"And I know you'll be proud to hear the government is awarding Jared the Medal of Honor."

Jonathan was flabbergasted. "My son! A Medal of Honor! He's never spoken of his actions during that attack on the embassy."

"They must have been very heroic or Jared wouldn't be getting a medal. He said he isn't going to Washington to accept it, though."

"He must. It's such an honor."

"His spirits are very low right now. I'm sure he's just reacting to the disappointment of having to leave the army. Jared just needs time; they say time heals all wounds."

"I'm afraid this wound will not heal as quickly as his physical ones will."

"But it will heal, Jonathan. Jared is an intelligent man. I can't believe he'd let this disappointment destroy the rest of his life."

Jonathan regarded her with a speculative look. "My elder son has always been a very private person, Kathleen. I'm surprised he discussed such personal issues with you."

Kitty reflected on how Jared had suddenly blurted out the news to her as if he could no longer contain it within him.

"Sometimes even the most private people can't keep their pain locked up forever. Jared needed someone to talk to, and I happened to have been handy. My mother always said letting it out is the first step in the healing."

"Your mother's right, Kathleen, but it takes someone very special to get people to reach out—and you have that quality, my dear."

"I wish that were so, Jonathan. But one has to heal oneself before hoping to heal others."

"You've come to mean so much to us, Kathleen. Will you consider staying? From what you've told me the twins hold a deep affection for you, and now even Jared has reached out to you."

"Jonathan, don't read too much into Jared's actions; he was reacting to a severe shock. Nothing more."

Was that why he almost kissed her? And he *had* intended to kiss her; there was no doubt about that. Fortunately, he hadn't.

"I can't stay, Jonathan. For two years, I've lived with doubts about my capability of functioning outside the protection of the Triple M. I know now I can. I've discovered I'm independent enough to start a new life anywhere I choose. If I remain here, I'd just be falling back into the same pattern of depending on others. Please understand, Jonathan, that no matter how attached I am to your granddaughters, I need to be the head of my own household, not live under someone else's roof. And for the first time in two years, I see the possibility of finding love again and having children of my own. The twins have proven how necessary that is in my life."

"Of course you do. I understand, my dear. Forgive an old man's selfishness." He stood up. "I'll wait and speak to Jared in the morning. It's been an exhausting trip, but worth the effort. I'll spare you the details, except to say that Seth had gotten himself involved in a business transaction that might end in a criminal complaint. Fortunately, young Mr. William Franks has admitted Seth's innocence in the scheme, so it looks hopeful. However, it's not resolved yet, so unfortunately Seth and I will have to return to New York to finalize the situation."

"I'm sure you're relieved, Jonathan." Kitty was glad to hear that the possibility of a prison sentence no longer hung over Seth's head.

"You see, my dear, no matter how old they may be, your children's problems remain with you. I'll warn you now, my dear, that parenthood is a double-edged sword. From the moment your children are born, you're never whole again: wherever they are, part of you goes with them. And when they're hurting, you bear their heartache. When they bleed, you bleed."

"The other edge of the sword must be the reward of having children."

"That's right. It's how your heart swells with love when they call you Dad. The trust you sense when they slip their hand into yours when they're small, or your pride in them when they shake your hand when they're men." His eyes shone tenderly with the memories of past days. "You know, my dear, you convince yourself that you've cut them free when they became men. But in your heart, you never give up the image of that little boy who slipped his hand into yours." He looked at her as if embarrassed. "Forgive me, I've run on too long. Good night, Kathleen."

She kissed him on the cheek. "Good night, Jonathan."

The next day Jared did not make an appearance at any of the meals, and Jonathan told Kitty he'd been unsuccessful in convincing Jared to go to Washington.

The following day started off the same way, with Jared noticeably absent from the breakfast table.

In late morning, a woman appeared at the door in response to the advertisement Jonathan had placed in the newspaper for a nanny.

The woman had recently come to Dallas from Boston. She didn't hesitate to inform Jonathan that she was currently living with a maiden sister who was very difficult to get along with.

Harriet Whipple was in her late forties, but appeared older due to the stark black widow's weeds she wore, even though her husband had been dead for ten years. Her countenance was as dour as her dress, and she carried herself in a stiff, standoffish manner.

In order to get her opinion of the applicant, Jonathan asked Kitty to join them in the drawing room for tea. Harriet Whipple would not have been Kitty's choice for a compassionate nanny to handle the twins, but the woman presented two letters to

Jonathan attesting to her efficiency and conscientiousness.

"Sugar or lemon?" Kitty offered, handing her a teacup.

"Just sugar. I like my tea sweet," the woman said.

"Have you had much experience with eight-year-olds, Mrs. Whipple?" Kitty stared when the woman put three large spoonsful of sugar into her teacup.

"Extensive experience, Mrs. Drummond. Before his death, my husband and I were licensed to operate an orphanage."

"I see; that is very impressive. Are there any particular questions you'd like to know about the twins' likes and dislikes?"

"None that I can think of, madam. I prefer to make my own evaluations."

"Of course." Kitty finished her tea and rose to leave. "I must get back to the girls. It was a pleasure meeting you, Mrs. Whipple."

"Excuse me a moment," Jonathan said, and followed Kitty into the hallway. "What do you think of her, Kathleen?"

"She's very experienced, I would say. Certainly more than I am."

"Are you certain you won't remain, Kathleen?"

"Yes, Jonathan. I'm certain."

"Very well. I'll tell her she can start tomorrow."

"Don't you think it would be advisable to have Jared interview her before you hire her?"

"He said he trusts my judgment."

Jared's indifference upset Kitty. What kind of father felt it unnecessary to take a few minutes to interview his children's future nanny?

Dinner that evening was as glum as a wake, and she felt like the deceased. Jared had joined them, as well as Seth. On the verge of tears, the twins sat with downcast eyes despite Seth's valiant attempts to cheer them up.

Jared had fallen back into reticence and said nothing, but before returning to his room he did thank her for her service and wished her well. Trouble was, he appeared more angry than gracious.

That night when she retired, Kitty cried herself to sleep at the thought that this was her last night there.

The following morning's farewell to the twins was heartrending; Kitty didn't know if she'd ever see them again. Choking back her tears, she dropped to her knees to embrace the sobbing girls. Amid the tears and hugs, she glanced up and saw Jared observing them from the top of the stairway. For a long moment they looked at each other, then he nodded slightly and returned to his room.

As Seth drove her to the Carrington house, Kitty tried to convince herself she was doing the right thing.

She yearned to leave immediately and go to New York, but bowing to Beth's and Thia's advice, she wrote letters to New York employment agencies and remained in Dallas to await a response.

Her cousins went out of their way to keep her busy and entertained with lunches and shopping excursions. Beth even persuaded Kitty to accompany her to the hospital where Beth volunteered her services one day a week.

Although all this was enjoyable, Kitty was

haunted with curiosity about what was happening at the Fraser house. She missed the twins badly, and at night she'd toss and turn thinking about Jared's brooding eyes and the excitement of his nearness. She even missed their arguments, for in truth, it was the only time they openly exposed their passions to each other.

On the fifth day, after she'd spent another restless night, the Carrington butler informed Kitty she had guests.

When she entered the drawing room, a cry of joy burst past her lips at the sight of Becky and Jenny. The girls rushed into her arms, and after a torrent of hugs and kisses, they asked her if they could stay with her.

"Darlings, you can't do that. In the first place, this isn't my house; I'm a guest here."

"Couldn't you get a house of your own, Kitty?" Jenny asked.

"No, dear. I don't have the money, and besides, your family wouldn't permit that. What happened to upset you?"

"Mrs. Whipple hit us!"

"She *what*?"

"With a ruler," Jenny replied.

The girls held out their hands, which still showed the redness from the punishment.

Kitty was horrified to see the red welts. "Why did she do this?"

"She said it was to teach us to behave."

"And she said she'd take out all the piss and vinegar from us. What does that mean, Kitty?" Jenny asked.

Kitty was more shocked than ever. "Did you tell your grandfather about this?"

"Poppie and Uncle Seth are in New York."

"What about your father?"

"He's in his room. We haven't seen him since you left."

"You haven't seen your father in five days!" She couldn't believe it, and felt a rise of anger. "Come with me, girls, I'll take you home. I have a few words to say to your father. And I'm sure when he hears of Mrs. Whipple's punishment, he won't tolerate it."

As they neared the Fraser house, Mrs. Whipple came hurrying up to them. She grabbed each of the twins by the shoulder and began to shake them. "Don't you dare do this again. I've been looking high and low for you."

"Take your hands off these girls," Kitty demanded.

"I'll not tolerate any more of their disobedience."

"The girls just came a few houses away to see me. We were on our way back."

"If I'm to have any success controlling these girls, Mrs. Drummond, I'd be thankful if you wouldn't interfere."

"It's not my intention to interfere, Mrs. Whipple. But if you continue to physically abuse them, I certainly will."

"Physical punishment is not abuse. They got their just deserts for what they did."

"And just what did they do to warrant you raising welts on their hands with a ruler?"

"They spread molasses on my . . ."

Kitty waited expectantly. Finally she asked, "On what? Your bed? A dress? The floor? Whatever it was, I'm sure it would wash off."

The woman arched her brows in disdain. "The seat of my toilet."

"Oh, my. Did you—" She couldn't get the question out.

"Yes. I sat down on it."

"Oh, my," Kitty repeated.

"And the day before that, I found a goldfish swimming in my bathtub."

Kitty briefly lowered her head to hide her amusement from the enraged woman. Considering what *she* had endured, she thought the twins were growing mellow.

"Nothing they did was so severe that you had to resort to striking them, Mrs. Whipple. There are other forms of punishment you can apply."

"I'll be the judge of that, thank you. Neither Mr. Fraser nor I has any need for your advice." Snatching each girl by the hand, she strode off with the twins stumbling to keep up with her.

Jenny turned around and waved so plaintively, Kitty's heart wrenched. Interference or not, she was going to speak to Jared. She knew he would not tolerate anyone striking the children. Most likely it would mean she would have to return again until another nanny could be found.

Kitty had just finished telling Beth her intentions when Charles appeared at the door of the Carrington house.

"Charles, what's wrong? Did that unpleasant woman hurt the twins again?"

"No, they were fine when I left. That's not why I'm here." He looked so solemn, she dreaded to hear the reason. Stepping aside, she said, "Come in, Charles."

He entered hesitantly. "I hate to bother you, Mrs. Drummond—"

"Please, call me Kathleen. What is wrong?"

"My wife and I are concerned about Captain Fraser. He's been drinking heavily, and hasn't come out of his room in almost a week. I've taken him trays of food, but he barely touches them or reads his mail. His room is in disarray, but he doesn't permit anyone to clean it up. He orders me out."

"He was very despondent over having to leave the army. Can't Mr. Fraser do something?"

"He and Mr. Seth have been gone for several days. My wife and I thought that if perhaps you spoke to him—"

"I was just preparing to come speak to him about Mrs. Whipple's treatment of the twins. But as far as his personal habits are concerned, he won't listen to me, either."

"We believe he will. You've always had a good effect on him. We're concerned that he might harm himself."

"I don't think he'd do any more harm to himself than he's done already. I'll see what I can do, Charles, but don't hold out any hope. Captain Fraser has a very strong will of his own."

"God bless you, Kathleen. The captain's a fine man. He's just run into bad times right now. If you're ready, I have a carriage outside."

After a quick good-bye to Beth, Kitty left with

Charles. When they drove up to the Fraser house, Harriet Whipple was out on the front lawn pacing back and forth. Jenny was crying, and Becky was lying on the ground.

Upon seeing Kitty and Charles the nanny shouted, "Help me!"

"What happened?" Kitty ran over and knelt down at Becky's side. The child's eyes were closed and there was a bloody blotch on her forehead.

"She killed her," Jenny screamed. "She killed my sister."

Mrs. Whipple shook her head. "I merely shook her, and she fell to the ground. She must have hit her head on a rock."

"Should I go for a doctor?" Charles asked.

"No. Get a policeman and have her arrested," Jenny cried out.

Kitty put her ear to Becky's chest to check her breathing, then glanced up at Charles. "I don't think a doctor will be necessary."

Harriet Whipple blanched. "You mean the child is dead!"

"My sister! My poor sister!" Jenny cried.

Kitty stood up and shook her head. "No, she's fine."

Jenny pointed an accusing finger at the nanny. "Arrest her. Cart her off to the gallows!"

"Jennifer Fraser, stop that ridiculous shouting," Kitty ordered.

"Jennifer?" Harriet Whipple exclaimed. "That screaming brat told me she was Rebecca."

"I told you she was mean, Kitty," Jenny pursued.

"I bet she's hurt a lot of other kids—even killed them."

"If she did, I doubt their blood smelled like ketchup. Becky, open your eyes and get up," Kitty ordered.

Becky's eyes popped open.

"You mean she isn't hurt!" The woman's eyes looked ready to pop out of her head. "Oh, you nasty girls!" Before Kitty guessed her intent, the nanny yanked Jenny around and slapped the child across the face. "I hate you little monsters!" She stormed back to the house.

Kitty hugged Jenny and looked at the ugly red mark on the child's cheek. "Oh, honey, I'm so sorry. Let's go inside and put a cool cloth on your cheek. But this was a very naughty trick, girls. What if Mrs. Whipple had a weak heart? She could have had a heart attack."

"Mrs. Whipple doesn't have a heart, so how could she have an attack?" Becky asked.

"The point is, you can carry your pranks too far. One of these days someone will be seriously hurt. I want you both to go in and apologize to Mrs. Whipple."

Becky groaned. "Must we?"

"We only did it as a joke," Jenny said.

"It wasn't very funny when she slapped you, was it?"

"No."

"Then it wasn't a good joke for you or her, was it?"

Jenny hung her head. "I guess not."

Kitty dug a handkerchief out of her skirt pocket and dipped it in the fountain. Then she sponged the ketchup off Becky's forehead. "I know Mrs. Whipple has been very mean to you, but this prank could have ended disastrously. Now get in there and say you're sorry."

"But that's a lie; we aren't sorry," Becky said. "You wouldn't want us to tell a lie, would you?"

"Since when did either of you two little Pinocchios have an aversion to telling a lie? I'm coming in there with you just to make sure you apologize. Let's get moving, girls."

The twins hung their heads and walked to the door.

Chaos reigned when they entered.

Mildred and Mrs. Whipple were shouting at each other. The twins flung their arms around Kitty's waist.

Casting her eyes heavenward, Mildred cried, "Thank God you've come back."

Mrs. Whipple snorted. "And it's a good thing, too. I'm not remaining in this house another minute. These nasty girls need a good thrashing, and their father should be incarcerated." She picked up a black suitcase and stormed out the door.

"And good riddance to you!" Mildred slammed the door.

"What started all this, Mildred?" Kitty asked.

"The prune-faced old harpy accused the twins of substituting salt in her sugar bowl. Seems she took a deep drink of tea and . . ." Mildred rolled her eyes, then sucked in her lips to keep from laughing.

"Look at me, girls," Kitty demanded. They tried

to look innocent but failed. "How could you do such a thing?"

"She was a witch, Kitty, truly she was," Becky declared.

"At night she'd change into a bat and fly around our room," Jenny added. "I saw it with my own eyes."

"If that's true, the two of you are very fortunate she didn't turn you both into toads. Now go up to your room and read a book; I have to speak to your father."

"Okay, Kitty." They linked hands and ran up the stairs.

"Mildred, does Captain Fraser know what's happened?"

"The old biddy said she tried to tell him, but he wouldn't open the door. She claims he threw something at it and told her to get out."

"Hmph—he's done the same to me in the past. Well, not this time!"

Kitty mounted the stairs and rapped on the door. "Jared, it's Kathleen Drummond. May I come in?"

"Go away."

"Jared, I must talk to you. Open this door."

When she heard the key click in the lock, Kitty waited for the door to open. After several more seconds, she turned the doorknob.

Jared stood with his back to her, staring out of the window. The air was stale and smelled of whiskey.

"Good Lord, open a window and get some fresh air in here!"

"Is that what you came to say?" He turned around and she stared in disbelief. His hair was disheveled and his clothes looked as if he hadn't changed them for a week. His eyes were bloodshot and a week's growth of whiskers covered his cheeks.

"Jared, why are you doing this? You look like you're drinking yourself into oblivion. Are you trying to kill yourself?"

"Hardly, madam, although the thought does have merit."

"Look at you," she said, disgusted. "Captain Jared Fraser, an officer and a gentleman."

"Captain Jared Fraser, retired," he corrected. He clicked his heels together and saluted.

"What rubbish! It's not the end of the world."

"It's the end of my world," he lashed out.

"*Your* world! *Your* needs! *Your* desires! *Your* wishes! That's all that's come from your mouth from the time I've met you. Doesn't anything else matter to you? Despite what you think, Captain, the earth hasn't stopped spinning, the sky hasn't fallen, and the sun hasn't disappeared from the heavens just because you have to leave the army."

"I don't expect you to understand, madam, nor am I interested in listening to your optimistic blather."

"Maybe you *are* a coward. I'm beginning to believe you really think there's nothing worth living for except the army. Try taking a deep breath of the sweet fragrance of that garden outside, or give your daughters a hug and kiss good night. Those alone are reasons to appreciate life. But maybe they aren't good enough for Captain Jared Fraser, United States Army, because life isn't playing out to your scheme of things. It's no wonder your wife left you. No woman could tolerate a narcissistic bastard like you," Kitty hurled at him.

His face turned white with anger, his eyes glowed with fury, and his hands balled into fists. She was afraid he was mad enough to strike her. "You are a heartless shrew, madam. Get out of my sight."

"Perhaps I am heartless—because when I lost the man I loved, I felt numbness, utter despair, and even guilt. But the worst was the overwhelming feeling of hopelessness, knowing there was nothing I could do to bring him back. Yet *never* did it enter my mind that there was nothing worth living for any longer. If you had the *heart* to love someone or something other than the army and yourself, you might understand the finality of losing some*one* you love, compared to merely losing some*thing* you love."

"I hate to disappoint you, but I am hardly about to fall on my sword, madam. I am simply taking some time to adjust to my new life. So get out of here and let me pursue that goal without further interference."

"Like it or not, Jared Fraser you're going to have to rejoin the world and tough it out. You may be a self-pitying egotist, but unless I miss my guess, you're not a coward." She started to leave, then halted. "And by the way, that abusive Mrs. Whipple has left, so fortify yourself, Captain: I'm back."

# Chapter 10

"Are you coming back for good?" Becky asked as soon as Kitty joined them.

"Girls, sit down and listen to me. You *have* to stop driving nannies away. Whether you want to accept it or not, you must have a nanny until you're old enough to take care of yourselves."

"But Kitty, why can't you be our nanny until then?" Jenny asked.

"Because I have my own life, too. Someday I might want to remarry and have children of my own. That's impossible if I remain here."

Becky's face brightened. "You could marry Father! That way *we'd* be your children."

"And you'd be our mother," Jenny added eagerly.

"Get that ridiculous idea out of your heads immediately. I'd never marry a man I didn't love, and your father and I don't even like each other, much less love."

"Couldn't you try to love him, Kitty?" Jenny

pleaded. "You didn't love us, but now you do, don't you?"

Becky's head bobbed in agreement. "And we love you, even if Father doesn't."

"It's much more complicated between men and women, darlings. You're too young to understand. And that's also why you have a problem about a nanny. Rather than trust what's best for you, or think about other people's feelings, you girls only consider what *you* want—just like your father does. That's a very selfish attitude, girls."

"But we weren't going to do that anymore," Jenny said, "because we didn't want to grow up to be ugly or have our noses grow like Pinocchio's did. We promised you we'd be good, remember?"

"And we would have been if that Mrs. Whipple wasn't such a mean lady, Kitty."

"But I don't believe all of the previous nannies were mean; and you drove *them* away. If you really love me like you say, you'll keep that promise to me and behave." She stood up and smiled down at them. "Now, let's go and get my clothes."

Jared was at the window when Kitty left with the twins. He was glad he'd taken her advice and opened the window; the fresh air felt good.

*Advice!* He scoffed. More like an order. Kathleen Drummond snapped out an order like a general barking a command at a shavetail lieutenant.

The woman might have a winning way with children, but she knew nothing about men. Only a shrew would accuse a man of drinking himself into a grave simply because he wanted to be alone to think out his future. Why couldn't she take into consideration that he'd just been fired from the only job he'd ever loved—the only life he'd ever known? He merely needed time to adjust to the thought of a new one. Wasn't that what she herself was trying to do? What was good for the goose was good for the gander, wasn't it? Drat the woman! She talked in clichés, and now she had him thinking in them.

So what if he sought the answer in solitude and an occasional drink? Hadn't she sought hers by riding those solitary hills of that ranch she spoke of with such love and pride?

My God—why hadn't he recognized the similarity before? They both had to give up the one thing that had been a sanctuary to each of them: he the army, she her beloved Triple M.

He glanced out of the window again. The three of them had clasped hands and were swinging their arms as they walked down the driveway. He had to give credit where credit was due: there was no denying the woman loved his daughters just as much as they loved her.

And there was no denying that he was physically attracted to her. He'd come so near to kissing her. Lord knew she was desirable enough, and he was only human.

But she *was* infuriating! And argumentative. Trouble was, her arguments often made sense—except when it came to issues concerning him. For example, her eternal carping about neglecting his daughters. Did she really believe he didn't love them? Didn't yearn for them to smile and laugh with him the way they did with her, or Seth and his father? If only he'd been able to be with them when they were infants. He had no memories of their first steps, their first words; and they had no memories of a father being there for them with a shoulder to cry on, or arms to hold them when they were frightened. Now that time had passed, and could never be brought back.

The few times he'd been home on leave, it had been a struggle to get reacquainted, and the older they got, the harder the struggle—and the more they withdrew from him.

When Diane left them, he should have requested duty here in the United States, or taken the girls with him to India. But he'd mistakenly thought they'd be happier and safer here.

How was he to reach them? He was as afraid of them as they were of him. Every night since his return, when the rest of the household was asleep, he'd look in on them, and his heart would ache just looking at their precious faces and thinking of what he had missed these past eight years. And the price they'd paid for his selfishness.

*Dammit, Kathleen, must your condemnation creep into every one of my waking thoughts?* She'd driven him to talking to her in his mind now!

Damn this inability to express his love to those he cared about. But had there ever been a time when he'd felt loved by those he loved? His mother had always doted on Seth and ignored him. His father had tried to be fair, but Seth's affectionate nature had always overshadowed his own reticent one. Even he and Seth, who had the capacity to love everyone, were never buddies. The same was true of the men he served with in the army: though friends, there were none he'd confide in.

Yet he'd foolishly rushed into a marriage expecting Diane to love him, when he didn't know how to give love himself.

And now he was faced with the hardest battle he ever had to wage: to win the love of his daughters. Could he face rejection again?

His gaze swung back to the driveway just as the three figures disappeared from view. Kitty had come back. It was karma. Good karma.

*Help me, Kathleen Drummond. I beg of you, help me.*

Charles met them in the foyer when Kitty and the twins returned. "Kathleen, may I speak to you for a moment?"

"Of course. Girls, go upstairs and wait for me in your room."

"Why do we always have to go to our room when you have to talk?" Becky asked. Kitty's reply was a deep frown. "Very well. Come on, Jenny, it's another thing we're too young to understand."

As soon as the girls disappeared, Kitty turned to Charles. "What is it, Charles?"

"I want to thank you, Kathleen. You've been a godsend to this house. My wife and I don't know what we'd do without you."

"The twins have become important to me, too, Charles."

"Not only the twins. You've helped Captain Fraser as well."

Kitty shook her head. "I don't think so, Charles.

I'm afraid the captain wasn't too impressed with what I had to say."

"Whatever you said appeared to have worked. After you left, he came downstairs and said he wanted his room cleaned up immediately, and to expect him for dinner. Then he bathed and changed."

"That *is* a surprise. Captain Fraser is a very confusing person, Charles. I don't think I'll ever understand him."

"I suspect you're being too modest, Kathleen. It's my observation that you understand him very well."

"Thank you, but I doubt the captain would agree. I do think, though, that I understand him well enough to know he wouldn't do anything he hadn't intended to do anyway."

Kitty started up the stairway, but Charles detained her. "One more thing, Kathleen. Mildred asks if there's anything special you prefer for dinner."

"Did Captain Fraser request anything in particular?"

"No, ma'am."

"I personally enjoy anything Mildred makes, but my suggestion would be to prepare Captain Fraser's favorite meal."

He grinned in understanding. "I'll pass that on to her."

Kitty had finished unpacking when she realized the twins hadn't come near her room. Since that was very unusual, she went to check on them. When she reached their room, she drew up in surprise: Jared sat in a chair reading to them.

Not only had he bathed, he now was cleanly shaven and his hair brushed back neatly. He looked incredibly handsome in a maroon smoking jacket and gray trousers.

"If I may interrupt, Captain Fraser, it's almost time for dinner. I'd like the twins to freshen up before we go downstairs."

Becky groaned. "Must we, Kitty? The story's getting real good now."

Jared surprised Kitty by saying, "The story will still be here when dinner is over. Mildred has prepared a meal, so the least we can do is show her we appreciate the trouble she's gone to on our behalf."

"But, Father," Jenny said, "you hardly ever go down for—"

"Come on, Jenny. Let's wash our hands," Becky said quickly. She grabbed her sister's hand and they disappeared behind the closed door of the bathroom.

"It appears being born ten minutes earlier than your twin makes you a little smarter," Jared said, amused.

"I'm surprised you noticed, Captain. Becky is definitely the leader of the two."

"Isn't that what life is all about, Kathleen: those who lead, and those who follow?"

"And which are you, Captain?"

He grinned. "That might depend upon whether you're around," he said as he departed.

Jared's good mood carried throughout the meal, even though he remained fairly quiet. The twins were animated and talkative, unaware of how their father studied their every move. But it didn't go unobserved by Kitty. He looked like the cat that swallowed the canary, and she wondered what he was up to.

Later, as soon as her duties were over for the night, Kitty sought the peace and quiet of the garden.

The smell of rain was in the air, and as she sat enjoying the serenity of the moment, she couldn't help reflecting on the course that day had taken. Life in the city was anything but dull.

"I thought I'd find you here."

Kitty wasn't surprised when Jared joined her.

"It appears we're in for a storm," he said.

"If not, we can always create one of our own."

"You have an engaging sense of humor, Kathleen. An irresistible combination when added with your beauty."

"This day must have been more taxing than I thought. Did I imagine a compliment, Captain?"

"That was my intention."

"Then you deserve one in return. Whatever your motive, thank you for the effort you're making with the twins. And I apologize if I sounded unkind today."

"No more than usual, Kathleen. We tend to do that with each other, no matter what we're discussing."

"I guess we do."

"Then it will take a greater effort on both our parts to curb it."

"Are you suggesting a truce, Captain?"

"For the children's sake, of course."

"I'm certainly willing if you are," she said.

Kitty hated to be skeptical, but he was wearing the "cat and canary" expression again. But if the twins benefited from it, she would be the last one to object.

"Shall we shake on it?"

He offered his hand and its warmth encompassed hers. Her fingers tingled from the contact and a jolt of tantalizing sensation flashed through her body. His gaze held hers in a mesmerizing suspension of time, a silence that each breath seemed to intensify. She had to do something—say something—to end it.

"Have you reconsidered going to Washington?" she asked, withdrawing her hand from his. The sudden contrast was like plunging her hand from the heat of a fire into icy water.

"Kathleen, the seam of this alteration of me has its limits. Let's not stretch it too far. You are the one who reminded me that one must learn to crawl before attempting to walk."

"Well, have you made a decision about your future?"

"Actually, I have. I've decided to write a book."

"Really! How interesting. What type of book?"

She expected nothing less from him than his depiction of the Spartan defense at Thermopyle or a complete rediagramming of the French and Russian armies at the Battle of Borodino.

"After considerable consideration, I have decided to write a novel with the protagonist an army officer."

"That's a relief," Kitty said.

"That I chose fiction?"

"No, that it's not an autobiography."

He threw back his head in laughter. A husky, delightful sound that was as warm as it was joyous.

"I don't believe it! You actually laughed aloud."

"God forbid if it becomes habit forming," he said in mock horror.

She laughed up into his eyes. "I doubt that, Captain. I doubt that very much."

The rumble of thunder and bright flashes of lightning nearby indicated the storm was approaching rapidly. Sighing, Kitty inhaled a deep breath of the perfumed air, and they hurried into the house just as large raindrops began to splatter the earth.

The crash of thunder seemed to shake the house, and Kitty jolted up to a sitting position. Through the curtained window she could see jagged bolts streaking the sky, each flash accompanied by the boom of thunder.

Suddenly her door flew open and two small figures raced to the bed. Kitty lifted the covers in invitation, and clutching Bonnie and Bibbie respectively, Becky and Jenny crawled in on either side of her. She could feel their little bodies quivering with fright as they huddled against her. Kitty slipped an arm around each of them and drew them closer.

"Aren't you afraid of lightning, Kitty?" Becky asked.

"Not as much as I once was. I think the noise scares me more than anything else."

"You mean you weren't even scared when you were little?" Jenny exclaimed.

"Oh, I used to be very scared then. I'll never forget the night I was frightened the most. I was six or seven at the time. Whenever there'd been a bad thunderstorm, I'd climb in bed with my mom and dad, but that night they weren't home. They'd gone into town and hadn't returned yet, so there was just my brother and me. Josh was about fourteen at the time. The thunder was booming and the lightning was crashing all around me. I thought the world was coming to an end."

"What did you do?" Jenny asked, snuggling even closer.

"I was so scared, I got out of bed and got into my parents' bed. I buried my face in my mom's pillow and could smell the fragrance of her perfume, and I touched the bed where my dad slept, and it was like I could feel his strength and warmth.

"Then Josh came to the door and asked me if I was scared. I didn't want him to think I was a sissy, so I told him that I wasn't. I remember he smiled and said, 'You'll be okay, Kitten.' Suddenly I wasn't scared anymore."

"Why? Did the storm stop?" Becky asked.

"No, honey. The storm didn't stop, but I felt safe, surrounded by people who love me."

"But you said your parents weren't there," Jenny said.

"They weren't physically; but lying in their bed I could feel them with me, and I knew they loved me and were worried about me just like Josh was. And the knowledge of that love made me feel safe. I'll tell you a big secret, if you promise not to tell anyone."

The two girls nodded. "We promise."

"Even though I'm no longer that little girl, whenever I'm really scared about anything, I think about my mom and dad, and I'm not scared anymore."

"We don't have a mom and dad," Jenny said. "We only have a father."

"Uh-uh," Becky objected, "we have a mother, too. Everyone has to have a father and mother."

"Why?" Jenny asked.

" 'Cause that's the rule," Becky replied. "Even if they don't love you."

"That's why I wish we had a mommy and daddy," Jenny said in her sad little voice. "Mommies and daddies love their children. Then we'd know we're loved and we wouldn't be so scared of lightning."

Kitty wanted to weep for the two little girls so desperately in need of feeling loved. She'd taken her parents' love for granted while she was growing up. How tragic that Jared Fraser couldn't recognize the twins' need for his love.

"Jenny, of course your father loves you."

"No, he doesn't," Jenny said. "Pretty soon he'll go away again, the same as our mother did."

Kitty actually welcomed the next crash of lightning, because it succeeded in changing the subject.

Becky buried her head from the frightening burst. "Kitty, what causes lightning?"

"It's got something to do with atmospheric electricity between clouds and the earth."

Jenny peeked out from under the cover she had pulled over her head. "What do you mean, 'at most fear it'?"

It took Kitty a few seconds to interpret the question. "The word is 'atmospheric,' Jenny. It's just a fancy word for the air that surrounds the earth."

"And what's electricity?" Becky inquired. "I heard Poppie tell Uncle Seth he's going to have electricity put in the house. Does that mean the house will be full of lightning, too?" Her eyes were huge.

"No, darling. Electricity's a current in nature. It has something called negative and positive electrons and protons."

"What does that mean?"

"I haven't the slightest idea," Kitty replied. That brought delighted giggles from the girls, and ended with them all breaking into laughter.

"I read that a man named Thomas Edison has figured out how to duplicate this current, to give us light," Kitty said. "That's what your grandfather was referring to. Tell you what, tomorrow we'll get a book and study all about it." She kissed each of them on the forehead. "Now go to sleep, girls. The storm will soon pass."

"Bibbie and I are too scared to sleep," Jenny murmured, on the verge of drifting into slumber.

"Bonnie and me are, too," Becky mumbled, barely able to keep her eyes open.

"And me, too," Kitty said, and closed her eyes.

The storm had wakened Jared and he sat up in bed. Concerned that the last clap of thunder might have scared the twins, he got up to check on them again. As he put on his robe, he remembered how frightened he'd been of lightning when he was their age. Not that he wasn't still skittish of it. A man would have to be witless not to respect nature on a rampage.

He hurried down the long hallway to the twins' room, only to discover they weren't in bed.

"Becky, Jenny," he called out softly. He stepped into the room, suspecting they were hiding from the storm. When there was no response, he lit a lamp and checked the bathroom and closet. He even looked under their bed. Wherever they were hiding was a mystery to him, but they had to be frightened to have left their room.

Jared continued down the hallway and was surprised to see the door to Kathleen's room ajar. She normally closed it at night.

A sudden lightning flash revealed an image he knew would remain in his memory forever: Kathleen lay asleep, and cuddled on each side of her were his sleeping daughters, their heads resting on her breast and her arms cradling them protectively to her sides.

It was the canvas an artist's soul dreamed of painting.

For a long moment he gazed at the awesome beauty of it, then he returned to his room.

His own bed had never felt so empty.

# Chapter 11

The fury of the electrical storm had begun to pass over when, as if in a final hurrah, a lightning bolt struck the birch tree near the house, cleaving it down the center. Part of the burning trunk toppled, gouging a big hole in the roof.

Sparks from the tree trunk landed on a pile of old magazines, and the dusty, yellowed pages immediately ignited. Within seconds the flames stretched out to the dried and brittle wood of a nearby chair, then leaped to a stack of old books. Slithering across the attic floor, the flames crept into the nooks and crannies, voraciously consuming anything in its path. Gray smoke began to billow through the hole in the roof and ooze through cracks and under the door to the floor below.

Jared felt the thud of the tree smash the roof and bolted to his feet. The twins' cries of fright sounded from the other wing at the same time he smelled the smoke. He opened his bedroom door to find that the hallway was billowed in gray smoke.

"Captain Fraser! Captain Fraser!" Charles shouted from below.

"Charles, the house is on fire. Get to the firehouse and take Mildred with you. I'll get the others out of the house."

"Jared," Kitty called.

"I'm coming," he yelled back.

As yet, the fire appeared not to have spread to the second floor, but the smoke in the hallway was becoming denser by the second, making breathing more difficult. It was essential to get Kitty and the girls out of the house before they inhaled too much.

Kitty had begun leading the girls by the hand down the hallway. He swooped up one of the twins in an arm, then grabbed Kitty's hand.

"Let's get out of here."

The smoke closed in around them and it became difficult to see. "Grab the back of my belt, Kitty, and don't let go," he ordered, releasing her hand. As soon as he felt her grab his belt, he groped along the wall until he reached the top of the stairway, relieved to be able to see the floor below.

Suddenly, Jenny exclaimed, "Bibbie! I forgot Bibbie!" She broke free from Kitty's grasp and ran back.

"Jenny, no!" Kitty cried, and tried to run after her, but Jared pulled her back and thrust Becky into her arms.

"Get her out of here!" He took off after Jenny.

"Jenny," he shouted, then began coughing from the smoke he sucked into his lungs. His eyes were stinging and watering. The smoke was so thick there was no visibility and he moved along the wall for direction. These same fumes were draining the life's breath out of his little daughter. What if she'd collapsed already, and he'd passed her by?

"Jenny, can you hear me?" he shouted in desperation.

Reaching the twins' room, he called, "Jenny, are you in here? Answer me."

"Daddy!"

The weak call had come from farther down the hall, and he realized she must have gone to Kitty's room.

The heat had intensified and he could glimpse fiery sparks in the smoke. Sickened, he realized the ceiling could crash down on their heads at any moment.

Jared reached the door opening to Kitty's room, but he couldn't see a thing. He followed the sound of Jenny's whimpering and found her in a heap on the floor. Scooping her into his arms, he hugged her to him as he looked around in desperation. He knew he'd never make it back to the stairway without becoming overcome with smoke. His only hope was the window.

An eddy of black smoke was sucked out through the opening as soon as he raised the window. Jared stuck out his head, gasping to bring some fresh air into his burning lungs. Lifting Jenny to the sill, he held her head out the window and his frantic gaze scanned the surroundings in search of an escape. There was a tree outside the window, but not close enough to leap to, even without holding a child in his arms.

Below on the ground, he saw Kitty and Becky just

as a carriage raced up the driveway. Jake and Beth Carrington, accompanied by Cynthia and Dave Kincaid, climbed out. Seeing Kitty, they hurried to her side.

"We were on our way home from the opera and saw the fire. Is everyone okay?" Beth asked.

"Jared and Jenny are inside!"

"Oh, dear God," Beth murmured.

Cynthia pulled off her cape and put it around Becky's shoulders. "Honey, why don't you let me put you in our carriage so you can get out of this rain?"

Becky shook her head. "I'm not going without my sister."

In an attempt to change the child's mind, Cynthia said, "But look, honey, your doll is getting wet, too."

"Bonnie understands. She wouldn't want to go, either, without Jenny and Bibbie."

As soon as Jared saw the new arrivals, he felt a glimmer of hope. He shouted to them for help and they all came running over to the window.

"We're trapped up here and this is the only way out," he shouted down to them.

"Is there a ladder in the carriage house?" Dave asked.

"None that I know of."

"I'm going to check anyway." Dave raced off.

"This ceiling's going to collapse any minute, Jake. If I drop Jenny down, do you think you could catch her?"

"You're damn right we'll catch her," Jake shouted. "We'll get you both out of there."

Dave returned, shaking his head. "No ladder, not even a damn rope."

"Jared wants to drop his daughter out the window."

"Yeah, that's the fastest," Dave agreed. "We'll need that cape you're wearing, Beth."

Kitty and the two couples spread the cape out to its fullest extent. "Keep it taut, and for God's sake, hold on to it when she hits," Dave said.

With time running out, Jared looked down at his daughter. Her eyes were round in fright, and she clutched her doll to her chest.

"Sweetheart, you have to be very brave now. I'm going to drop you out of the window, and the others down there are going to catch you."

"No, I'm afraid," Jenny cried.

Jared pried the doll out of her hand. "Watch, honey." He dropped the doll out the window and it landed in the middle of the outstretched cape. "You see, sweetheart, Bibbie made it down okay. So will you." For a precious second he hugged her, and then kissed her cheek.

"I love you, sweetheart."

The people below were clustered in a group, rain pelting their upturned faces as they waited anxiously.

"Please, God. Please, God," Kitty repeated over and over. Becky stood beside her, crying uncontrollably, unable to watch.

Grasping Jenny by the hands, Jared lowered her feetfirst out the window and held her suspended by his outstretched arms. "It's just like jumping into a swimming pond, honey," he assured her. He looked below. "Ready?"

"Ready," Jake yelled.

They all tightened their grasps on the garment.

"On the count of three," Jared said. He shouted the countdown and released her.

Kitty's breath escaped in a gasp when Jenny landed on the cape. The force of the impact almost knocked Kitty off her feet, but she managed to hold on to the cape.

They quickly wrapped the cloak around Jenny, and Beth took both girls back to the shelter of the carriage.

It was a joyous but very short-lived moment. "How are we getting Jared down?" Kitty asked.

The dense smoke pouring out the window had begun to obliterate the sight of the people on the ground. Jared's eyes were stinging, and he doubled over in a seizure of coughing.

Everything began whirling, and he closed his eyes. Even with the fresh air heavy with rain, breathing had become too difficult, the heat too intense.

He could hear Kitty calling to him. "Jared, we'll get you down."

*No you won't.* He resigned himself to the inevitable. That was the real irony: just when she had convinced him of a real purpose for his life, he was about to die.

Through the smoke and rain, Kitty caught a glimpse of Jared slumped on the windowsill. "Oh, God, he looks like he's passed out," she cried out. "Don't give up, Jared. We'll get you down."

Cynthia had returned, and she slipped an arm around Kitty's shoulders.

"You're the engineer, Dave, what do you suggest?" Jake asked his brother-in-law.

Dave Kincaid looked around in desperation. "You see that tree? What if we climbed it and tossed him a line? Then he could swing over to us."

"But you have no rope," Kitty said.

Dave looked toward the carriage. "But we do have—"

"—harness reins," Jake declared.

When the men ran off, Kitty said worriedly, "But if Jared's passed out, what good will a line do him?"

"Honey, knowing Dave and Jake, one or both of them will swing over themselves if they have to. Trust Dave, Kitty. He's ingenious at moments like this. Did you ever hear about the time he and I were trapped up in a hot air balloon? Dave figured out how to get us down unscathed."

"Thia, I love you dearly, but I don't want to hear it right now."

"I know, darling." Cynthia gave her a squeeze. "I'm just trying to convince you that if there's a way of doing it, Dave will figure out how."

Kitty stared in amazement at Cynthia Kincaid. With time running out, she had the serenity of a general reviewing his troops before a battle. Her trust and confidence that Dave would think of a way to save Jared was absolute—and remarkable to behold.

Kitty drew strength from it.

The men returned with the long reins. Jake got

down on one knee and cupped his hands together; then Dave put a foot in Jake's hands and Jake hoisted Dave up to the lower limb, where Dave tied part of the rein around the tree trunk, then dropped the other end down to Jake, who grabbed it and scaled the tree trunk. The whole thing took less than thirty seconds.

The two men worked their way up the tree until they were level with the window.

"Jared, this is Dave Kincaid. Can you hear me?"

Dave's voice cut through the maze of Jared's dizziness. He raised his head in confusion. "Dave?"

"Over here, Jared. Jake and I are in the tree opposite you. If we toss you a line, do you still have the strength to swing to the tree? Jake will grab you and pull you in."

Jared glanced up. Through the smoke he saw a red glow on the ceiling. Seconds later it crashed down in flames.

"Yeah, and hurry—the ceiling's caving in."

"Dammit!" Dave cursed, when the reins didn't even carry as far as the window. "Jake, take off a boot—fast!"

Jake did so, and Dave wrapped the loose end tightly around the ankle of the boot.

"For God's sake, Jake, hurry! This room's blazing," Jared shouted.

He managed to snag the boot when it was tossed, but he was so weak from smoke inhalation that he couldn't shove off hard enough to reach the tree. He cleared the house but then dangled in the air, swinging back and forth.

Kitty and Cynthia rushed to grasp his legs and hold him steady until Dave and Jake climbed down to assist them.

Jared's arms felt rubbery, and he was too weak to hang on to the reins any longer. They slipped through his fingers and he dropped to the ground, his fall broken by the two men.

Grimacing with pain, Jared clutched his injured leg and lay coughing the smoke out of his lungs. Kitty sat beside him and elevated his head in her lap. "Jared, help's on the way. Try to lie still."

He closed his eyes. The pain in his leg and the rain in his face kept him from passing out—and he relished every moment of it. He was alive!

"Jared." He opened his eyes to find Jake Carrington kneeling over him.

"How are you doing, pal?" Jake asked.

"I owe you and Dave, Jake."

"You're telling me! You just ruined a four-hundred-dollar pair of boots."

The strident clang of a fire bell heralded the arrival of the fire truck, as four horses raced up the driveway, snorting and puffing. A two-horse team pulled the ambulance that followed close behind, and while the firemen swiftly set up their hoses and pumps to draw water from the cistern, Jared and Jenny were whisked off to the hospital. Kitty and the others followed in the carriage.

When the doctors were satisfied that both Jared's and Jenny's respiratory systems were free of the smoke, they announced they were out of danger, but insisted they remain overnight in the hospital. Becky refused to leave her sister's side, so Kitty thanked her family for their help and spent the rest of the night in a chair at Jenny's bedside with Becky curled up asleep on her lap.

The next morning, the glum quartet returned to the house. Fortunately the rain had prevented the fire from doing too much exterior damage. The roof had been cleaned of debris and a tarpaulin covered the damaged part of it. But Kitty hated to think what the inside would look like.

The smell of smoke hung heavily in the air when they entered, but other than some minor smoke and water damage, the first floor had been spared. The walls would need fresh coats of paint, and draperies and the upholstered furniture would have to be aired or recovered, but on the whole the damage was minimal.

On the floor above, the wing directly under the attic had suffered extensive structural damage. Kitty's room was gutted and everything destroyed. And with it came the sorrowful realization that she had no clothes except for the ones on her back.

Although the flames had not reached the twins' room, everything in their suite was drenched from the water that had soaked through from above when the firemen had extinguished the attic fire. And as the twins viewed the damage to all their toys, Bonnie and Bibbie were given a special hug and kiss from their speechless mistresses.

Fortunately, like the floor below, the suites in the other wing suffered no damage other than the need for a thorough airing, cleaning, and painting.

Kitty had seen all she wanted to see. Everything

she'd brought with her from the ranch had been destroyed in the fire, including the picture of Ted and her on their wedding day. The twins followed her downstairs and ran into the kitchen to relate last night's harrowing experience to Charles and Mildred.

After bathing and changing his clothing, Jared found Kitty in the library.

"I'm sorry your room got the worst of it, Kathleen. We'll cover the expense of whatever you've lost."

She shrugged with indifference. "Most of it was only clothes. Those can always be replaced." She ran her fingers along a row of books. "I'm glad the library was spared. I'd hate to think of all these wonderful books destroyed."

Kitty suddenly felt awkward, at a loss for words. She sensed that Jared did, too. The smoke might have cleared, the damage could be repaired, but last night had taken an emotional toll on them that could not be expunged with a mop and pail or by replacing a dress or a pair of shoes.

"Have you notified Jonathan?" she asked, in an effort to make casual conversation.

"Our family's attorney is taking care of it." At her inquiring look, he said, "He came to the hospital this morning."

"I see."

"Kathleen . . ." He floundered and seemed to reach for words. "Kathleen, my family owes you a debt far greater than mere clothing. What you've done for the twins and me can't be measured in dollars and cents."

"Jared, please don't say any more. It's not necessary. You're not to blame for the fire; it was an act of nature."

"You know as well as I, Kathleen, that I'm not referring to the fire." His voice carried a new, gentle softness. "You were right, you know."

"About what?"

"Loving someone more than yourself. When I heard Jenny cry out 'Daddy' in her fright, I never imagined a single word could affect me so deeply. No force could have kept me from reaching her at that moment. And when I found her and held her in my arms, the thought that she might die was so overwhelming that I never thought beyond the moment: that I, too, might die. Nothing crossed my mind except how much I loved her and the need to keep her alive. To think how I haven't allowed myself to love, in fear of being hurt . . . What a fool I've been—the years I've wasted."

Kitty didn't know what to say. She couldn't even look at him. He'd kept so much hidden inside, so much pain. Now he was exposing his soul to her, and she saw how vulnerable he really was. She wanted to hold him, comfort him. The thought of the cruel things she'd said to him wrenched her heart.

"Last night was a frightening and emotional experience for all of us, Jared. But once again, some good came out of a tragedy."

"Your 'door and window' philosophy," he said with a tolerant smile. "The real tragedy, Kathleen, is that it *took* a tragedy for me to recognize what's been before my eyes all the time."

"I'm happy for you, Jared—and for the twins. And perhaps this really would be the right time for me to leave. The three of you no longer need anyone but each other. Furthermore, with all the remodeling to be done, I'd only be in the way."

"You can't leave now, Kathleen. Last night was just a beginning: the first page of a new novel. I know you well enough to believe you'd want to read the final page."

"I know the ending already, Jared. 'They all lived happily ever after.' "

"Will they, Kathleen? Without you? I doubt it. You've become as much a member of this family as any one of us."

"That's very flattering, but really, would you have loved Jenny less in that fire whether I'd been here or not? I didn't create the love in your heart for your children, Jared; it's always been there. Last night merely opened the window for you to let it out."

"Last night was a beginning between the twins and me, but that doesn't lessen their love for or dependence on you. Nor does it change the agreement we made. Have you forgotten that?"

"I'm not attempting to back out. I just thought that under the circumstances, this would be a practical time for me to leave."

"My dear Kathleen, there is no place in the heart for practicality."

Incredulous, Kathleen laughed and shook her head. "*You* are the last person I ever expected to hear that from."

He chuckled and his eyes warmed with mirth.

"You've reformed me. And besides, any military officer will tell you that the best defense is a good offense."

"And if you were to win this skirmish, Captain Fraser, where do you intend to quarter your prisoners?"

He looked somewhat abashed. "Actually, I was hoping you might have a thought."

"Oh, I have an excellent thought, Captain. I can't think of a better time to reconsider going to Washington. I'm sure we can air out your uniform so you look fine and proper when they pin that medal on."

Admiration gleamed in his eyes. "Kathleen Drummond, you make a worthy adversary. The only problem is that I'm never certain if I'm the victor—or the vanquished."

Before she could respond, Charles appeared at the door. "Mrs. Drummond, Mrs. Carrington and Mrs. Kincaid are here to see you. You'll find them in the garden with the twins."

"Thank you, Charles, I'll be right there." She looked at Jared. "Did you ever consider, Captain, that sometimes everyone's the winner?"

# Chapter 12

The twins came running into the library ahead of Beth and Cynthia when they joined them. Cynthia was her usual cheerful self.

"Well, Jared, you look none the worse this morning, considering what you went through last night."

"I feel none the worse, either. It's amazing what a bath and clean clothing can do. I wish we could do the same for poor Kathleen. She's lost everything."

Beth grimaced. "Oh, no."

"Yes, my room and everything I brought with me were totally destroyed. I'll even have to wire home for money to go back to the Triple M and pack up the clothes I left behind. There's so many odds and ends to replace: toothbrush, comb, brush . . . I guess I'll have to sit down and make a list so I don't forget anything."

"I told you I'll replace anything you've lost, Kathleen," Jared said.

"Oh, Kitty, just think of how much fun it will be

shopping for all those new clothes—and at somebody else's expense." Thia grinned.

Beth came over and took Kitty's hand. "You can decide that tomorrow, dear. I'm sure I have anything you need at the moment. Why don't you all come back with me now? We can get you settled in, Kitty and the twins can bathe away any reminder of last night, and then we'll all sit down and have a relaxing dinner."

"Beth, that's very kind of you," Jared said, "but we're not going to burden you with our problems. Jake and Dave already did enough for me to be indebted to them for the rest of my life."

"If you're that beholden to us, then you can hardly refuse my invitation. That would be *so* ungrateful of you, Captain Fraser." She smiled serenely.

"And I'm sure you wouldn't want to do that," Cynthia said with a coquettish smile.

"There's no mistaking you're all related. Is a strong will a characteristic of all MacKenzie women, ladies?"

Kitty folded her arms across her chest. "If you think the women are inflexible, Captain, you should meet the MacKenzie men."

"I can see it would be a fool's errand to try and win this argument, so we'll accept your invitation, Beth. Kathleen and the twins can go back with you now. I have some things to go over with Charles, some wires to send, and arrangements to make for the repair and refurbishing of the house. I'll join you later."

Kitty spoke up at once. "Jared, if anyone should be resting today, it's you. Won't tomorrow be soon enough to make those arrangements?"

"I won't be more than a couple of hours."

"Then let's go, Kitty," Beth said cheerfully. "Why stay here, smelling this unpleasant smoke odor?"

Kitty still felt reluctant to leave. "There's so much I could be doing here. There's clothes, bedding, and rugs to be aired, and the washable clothing laundered. I could even start packing away some of the art pieces in preparation for the repair work."

"Nonsense. I intend to hire a service to do that work," Jared declared.

"I feel as if I'm walking away and leaving the dirty work for someone else."

"Kathleen, your duties are to be a nanny to my children. They need your help more than this house does."

Cynthia linked her arm through Kitty's and led her to the door. "He's absolutely right, darling. Jared, I promised to meet Dave for lunch; if you're driving into town, may I share your carriage?"

"Certainly."

Kitty still had reservations about leaving as she climbed into Beth's carriage.

"Thia, do you and Dave want to join us for dinner tonight?" Beth asked, when they were about to depart.

"No, as much as I'd like to, we have another engagement. Bye, darlings," she said to the twins.

"Good-bye, Mrs. Kincaid," they said in unison.

It had been some time since they'd done that. Kitty glanced back at the house and thought gratefully, *Thank God they are alive to do it.*

* * *

An hour later, after luxuriating in a hot bath and washing the smell of smoke out of her hair, Kitty wondered why she'd ever resisted coming to the Carrington house.

From the moment they returned, Nellie the maid had taken over the twins and saw to their bathing and dressing.

The twins had been given the room next to Kitty, and the former suite of Jake's deceased grandmother had been prepared for Jared's arrival.

Since Kitty hadn't slept more than an hour or two the previous night, Beth had insisted she rest for the afternoon. It hadn't taken much persuasion to convince her. Kitty put on the robe Beth had provided for her, then curled up on the bed. As soon as she put her head on the pillow, she fell asleep.

It was twilight when she awoke. A large stack of boxes had been set in the room while she was sleeping. Kitty felt like a child at Christmas as she opened them. Beth had outdone herself. In addition to an assortment of toiletries, there were lace-trimmed combinations, corset covers with matching slips, blouses, skirts, day gowns, delicate hose, and even shoes.

The underwear she put on was a far cry from the cotton ones she was used to wearing. Made of silk chiffon, the lace-trimmed combination clung to her curves. She couldn't help smiling when she thought of the education she was getting on how wealthy women dressed. Kitty chose a fawn-colored skirt and a white blouse with puffed sleeves and a box-pleated front. She brushed her short curls and added a faint touch of rouge to her cheeks and lips. Finding an atomizer among the toiletries, she sniffed the fragrance and was pleased to discover it was the lavender scent she always wore. Satisfied with her appearance, she went downstairs to join the others.

Jared and Jake had arrived and were enjoying a brandy before dinner. Beth and the twins were at a corner table, involved in a checker game.

When she entered, the two men rose to their feet. "Here's our Sleeping Beauty now," Jake said. "You look rested and lovely, Kitty."

Jared said nothing, but his gaze remained fixed on her.

"I'm so ashamed for sleeping all of this time. I hope I haven't delayed dinner."

"Kitty dear, you look lovely," Beth said, as she came over and joined them.

"Beth, how can I ever thank you for your generosity? These clothes are brand-new."

"I'm not the one to thank, Kitty; Jared's the one who bought them."

Her glance swung to him. "You bought . . . but how . . ." She took a deep breath. "How did you know my size?"

"I prevailed upon Cynthia's advice; she said you appeared to be the same size as she is."

Beth laughed. "Selecting a lady's wardrobe must have been quite an experience. I imagine you had an interesting afternoon, Jared. Challenging, to say the least."

"Actually, a fascinating one. It's amazing, all the

apparel a Western woman wears compared to one in India."

Kitty blushed, thinking of the sheer underclothing she was wearing at the moment. "Obviously you've made a clinical study between East and West, Captain." She had to get her mind on a different subject. Walking away, she went over to the twins.

"Who's winning?"

"I am," Becky said.

"That's because she got to make the first move. But the next game, I get to go first and then I'll win."

Since the twins thought alike, Kitty could see how being first could make the difference in winning or losing between them. It was an uncomplicated theory.

"I'm sure you will, honey," she said.

She watched them for several minutes, but still couldn't get her disturbing thoughts out of her head. Restless, she went to stand by the open door leading to the garden. Lured by the provocative fragrance, she stepped out on the verandah and drew a deep breath, hoping the garden would have its usual calming effect on her. It wasn't long before Jared joined her, and handed her a glass of wine.

"You're angry. Why?"

Kitty didn't look at him. "I'm not angry. Why do you think that?"

"I'm beginning to know your moods, Kathleen."

"I have no reason to be angry. On the contrary, I'm grateful to you for your generosity."

"Then what's bothering you?"

She took a sip of the wine, then looked at him. "I guess I just feel frustrated. I left the Triple M to prove I can be independent and instead I find myself entirely dependent on others, even to the point of having them choose what I wear."

"I'm sorry. It was thoughtless of me; I should have consulted you about the clothing." He grinned, trying to lighten her mood. "You did say women enjoy shopping. I didn't mean to deny you that pleasure."

"That's not it at all, Jared. And I don't mean to sound ungrateful. It was very thoughtful of you."

"I wanted to show my appreciation for what you've done for my family, Kathleen. If you're not satisfied with the selections, we can return them and choose what you want."

She forced a smile. "Your taste is excellent. I love everything."

"Then what is it? You're clearly upset."

"I feel helpless, like I'm losing control of my own life."

"I think the recent chain of events have made us all feel that way."

This time her smile was sincere. "I guess you're right. I am acting rather self-absorbed—forgive me."

What she didn't tell him was that she felt frightened and confused as well. Less than two weeks ago she never knew Jared Fraser existed, and now he was selecting intimate lingerie for her. They had bared their souls to each other, and with every passing day their lives were becoming inexorably intertwined. Whatever her intentions to walk away, circumstances brought her back. It was as if there was a force beyond her control—a juggernaut that once set in motion was beyond stopping. And why? What scheme of fate had placed them in its path?

She stared at him for an endless moment and thought she saw the same bewilderment in his eyes.

Funny, how quickly their roles had reversed. She'd been dwelling so much on her own problems, she'd overlooked that *all* their lives had been shaken up in the past week—even those two little girls in the corner.

Well, as Aunt Maude used to remind her family at times of crises, "Life's often like a boat with a hole in the bottom—either you grab a bucket and start bailing, or you sink."

*Well, Kitty, looks like it's time to grab that bucket again.*

Beth and Jake were relaxing hosts, and dinner was so enjoyable it would have been impossible for Kitty to maintain her dark mood.

Toward the end of the meal, Jake asked, "Is Jonathan aware of the damage to the house?"

"Yes," Jared replied. "I spoke to him on the telephone in my attorney's office today. What an invention that is! Your voice being carried over a wire."

"I agree. I'm having one installed in my office."

Jared nodded. "Technology is moving so fast, I venture to say that by the turn of the century, every city in America will have a telephone and electricity."

"I'll even go one step farther. I'm predicting we'll be talking intercontinentally by then."

Becky frowned. "What does innercontimental mean, Mr. Carrington?"

"Intercontinentally, honey," Kitty corrected.

"It means between continents, Becky," Jake explained. "For instance, I could talk to my office in London by telephone."

"Far be it for me to thwart progress, darling," Beth interjected, "but I would prefer they install indoor plumbing in all the cities before worrying about talking to each other through a wire."

They all lingered so long that when dinner was over, it was time to put the twins to bed. To Kitty's surprise, Jared accompanied her upstairs. When the girls were tucked in bed, he kissed them good night.

Before leaving, Jared asked, "Will you be coming back downstairs, Kathleen?"

"Yes. I'll just be a minute."

"Kitty, are we going to stay here with Mr. and Mrs. Carrington while our house is getting fixed?" Becky asked after her father left.

"No, honey, your father will make other arrangements."

"When are Poppie and Uncle Seth coming back? I miss them," Jenny said.

"I imagine your grandfather and uncle will be back soon."

Jenny giggled. "Boy, is Poppie going to be surprised when he sees the house."

"I'm sure he will be. Good night, sweetheart." Kitty bent down to kiss her and Jenny slipped her arms around her neck.

"I love you, Kitty. Bibbie does, too."

"So do Bonnie and me," Becky said.

"And I love you, too. Even Bonnie and Bibbie."

"Do you love, Daddy, too?" Becky asked.

Kitty was too startled by the question to reply.

"He loves you," Jenny said.

"Girls, your father doesn't love me."

"Uh-huh," Becky insisted. "We can tell."

"You can do no such thing. Now get such foolish thoughts out of your heads and go to sleep, you little dickens." She kissed Becky and hurried out of the room.

*Jared in love with her?* Kitty shook her head in disbelief as she went downstairs. Wherever did the twins get the wild ideas that entered their heads?

After Kitty left, Becky said, "Did you see how Daddy looked at her when he asked if she was going back downstairs?"

"Uh-huh," Jenny said.

Giggling, they looked at each other, then hugged their dolls, and closed their eyes. They fell asleep with the smiles still on their faces.

"So when do you have to report back to duty?" Jake asked as they sat down at a marble table to play bridge.

"I'm being discharged from the service."

"Really? What plans do you have for the future?"

"The government has offered me a position in the diplomatic service, but I'm not interested. The first thing I'll have to do when we return from Washington is decide where we can live until we can move back into the house."

"Don't tell me the army expects you to go to Washington to get discharged?"

Kitty slipped into the chair opposite Jared.

"Didn't Jared tell you? He's being awarded the Congressional Medal of Honor."

"My God, man!" Jake shook Jared's hand. "Congratulations. The Medal of Honor! That's quite a distinction. Beth, did you know we've been entertaining a hero tonight?"

"I had no idea." Beth leaned over and kissed Jared on the cheek. "Congratulations, Jared. Kitty, why didn't you tell us?"

Kitty didn't want to reveal that he'd just agreed to accept the medal today. "I guess in all the confusion, I forgot." She laughed lightly. "Maybe Jake and Dave should be given a medal of their own for preventing Jared's from having to be awarded posthumously."

"Now, that's a morbid thought, Kitty," Beth remarked. "But I have an excellent one. Jake has business in London, and with the children in Colorado for the summer, Jake and I have decided to go together and make a second honeymoon of it. You're welcome to stay here, or at our ranch. Whichever you prefer."

"That's an appealing idea, Beth," Jared said. "My father said he's rented a house in New York and suggested we join him there. Frankly, I prefer remaining close by to keep an eye on the renovation."

"What do you intend to do after you're discharged?" Jake asked.

"I'm seriously considering writing a novel. Literature has always held a particular appeal to me."

"Sounds like our ranch would be ideal, Jared. *La Paloma* is remote and peaceful. The roundup is over and in a week the hands are driving the herd to Fort

Worth, then remaining to attend the rodeo. You'd have the place to yourself for a month."

"The twins would love it, Jared," Kitty said hopefully. *And so would I.* She missed ranch life. "Or if you didn't want to remain close to Dallas, we could go to the Triple M. I have my own house there." She winked at Beth. "Of course, there are no servants to wait on you hand and foot."

Jared looked at her, disgruntled. "That would hardly be an issue, Kathleen. I prefer a closer proximity to Dallas."

Beth interrupted the conversation. "I thought we were going to play bridge."

"You'll have to excuse Beth, folks. From the time we've been married, my wife's been addicted to card games." Kitty sensed there was a story behind the intimate look Beth and Jake exchanged.

Kitty enjoyed the bridge game except when she had to play the hand and Jared was the dummy. He would sit silently staring at her, and his steady gaze made her nervous.

He's doing it on purpose, she seethed in silence. He knows what I have on under this blouse and skirt, and he's using those damn brown eyes of his to let me know he knows.

Nevertheless, she enjoyed the company, and the evening passed swiftly.

Everyone in the household had retired, but Kitty discovered that due to her long afternoon nap she wasn't ready for sleep. She got out of bed, pulled on her robe, then went into the sitting room and sat down at the window.

The sky was star-filled, and a bright moon streaked the treetops and ground with silver. A gentle breeze stirring the leaves carried the garden's fragrance on the night air. In the past two weeks her life had been turned topsy-turvy, yet she felt contentment.

She moved from the window to the connecting door that opened into the twins' room, where a stream of moonlight guided her to their bedside. She gazed down at the sleeping girls. How she'd grown to love them. And she knew they loved her, too. Their trust in her was implicit, and she wondered if it would be shattered when she left them one day.

Adjusting the sheet, she covered each of them, photographing the sight in her memory.

She sensed a presence. Turning her head, she saw a shadowy figure sitting in a corner chair. Kitty wasn't startled or frightened; she knew it was Jared.

He got up and came over to the bed. "They're quite wonderful, aren't they?"

Kitty nodded. "Very wonderful."

"Strange how something so perfect could come from such a catastrophic marriage." His next question caught Kitty completely unprepared. "Do you think she ever loved me?"

Kitty knew he was referring to his wife. "I'm sure she did." Then added intentionally, "As you did her."

"I guess I'd like to believe so. In the past few years I've asked myself that over and over."

"Some loves can be as fleeting as others are eternal."

"Like that you feel for your husband."

"Yes." And she would always love Ted, but the past few weeks had given her the hope that she was capable of building a new life for herself.

Fearing they would wake the girls, Kitty returned to her suite. Jared followed.

"The important thing, Jared, is that you allow yourself to love."

"Or make yourself that vulnerable."

"Is that what frightens you about the idea? Do you believe love weakens rather than strengthens?"

"I'm no longer sure what I believe, Kathleen. It's a new emotion to me. Being unfamiliar makes me leery of it."

"I think we're both experiencing some changes we didn't expect. But from the change I've observed in you recently, I'd say you've made a good start."

"Thank you. You see, even a fool like me can learn."

"I've learned something, too, Captain."

He moved closer, so close she could feel the warmth of him, smell the seductive, musky male scent of him

"What is it, Kathleen?" His voice was thick with huskiness.

With a heady feeling of dizziness, she leaned into him, and his hands grasped her shoulders. "You haven't answered me, Kathleen. You said you've learned something, too."

She couldn't resist the draw of his gaze and looked up into the sensuality of his brown eyes.

"That you're not the fool I thought you to be."

For the faintest of moments they stared in silence

at each other. With each passing second, his nearness became more mesmerizing.

"I enjoyed this evening, Kathleen."

"I did, too, Jared."

"I don't remember the last time I had such an enjoyable time." His voice and eyes had become an erotic stimulant.

"It must have been the company."

"It was definitely the company."

"Beth and Jake are a wonderful couple."

"I'm referring to *all* the company." He lowered his head and kissed her forehead. "Good night, Kathleen."

Then there was only emptiness in the spot that his warmth had once filled. Funny how she once had thought him cold.

# Chapter 13

The following day was spent airing clothing and packing. The twins were excited and couldn't wait until the next day, when they'd board the train for the trip East.

That evening Kitty and Jared played bridge again, and Jared accepted the Carringtons' offer to use their ranch until the repairs on the house were completed.

Bright and early, they climbed on the eastbound train for the long trip to Washington, D.C. They had two sleeping compartments, with Kitty and the twins in one and Jared in the other, but they spent the days in Jared's compartment playing card games or reading.

The twins especially enjoyed eating in the diner car. It was an exciting experience, but by the time they crossed the Mississippi River and reached Chicago, the train had lost its fascination for them. Since they had to change trains in Chicago, Kitty was relieved when Jared suggested they spend the night in the city before continuing with the final leg of the trip.

Everything in this hub of the Midwest was different. They were awed by Lake Michigan, the buildings, and the huge population that not only didn't dress like Texans, but didn't sound like Texans, either.

They watched a trainload of steers being unloaded from Kansas City, and Kitty clapped and burst into tears of excitement when she saw the Triple M brand on a huge number of them.

"Kitty, if you wanted to visit stockyards, we could have gone to Fort Worth," Jared commented in a droll tone.

"Daddy, that's not nice," Jenny said.

"Yeah, Kitty's excited 'cause they're from her ranch," Becky scolded.

"I bet I helped herd some of those cattle," Kitty said, wiping away her tears.

"Think of that when you're eating a steak at dinner tonight," Jared teased.

She gave him a disgruntled look and took the twins by the hand. "Come on, girls, just for that we'll make him window-shop with us."

"Tell you what, as a souvenir of Chicago, each of you can pick out one gift—as long as it will fit into your suitcases," he said.

As they left Chicago's famous stockyards, they saw a poster tacked to a building advertising Buffalo Bill's Wild West Show featuring live Indians and Little Miss Sureshot, Annie Oakley.

Jumping up and down excitedly, the twins asked, "Daddy! Daddy! Can we go?"

"Today's performance has already begun, girls.

That would mean we'd have to stay over another day."

"Please, Daddy, can we?"

Jared looked at Kitty. "What do you think?"

"As long as we can change our train reservations, I don't see why it would be a problem."

"I was afraid you'd say that."

"I'm wise to you, Captain Fraser. If you didn't want to, you would have ruled it out from the start."

He grinned at her. "Is there anything you haven't figured out about me, Mrs. Drummond? Let's check the train schedule."

They took a carriage to Dearborn Station and made new arrangements, then went window-shopping. The twins selected little drawstring purses as their souvenir gifts, and Kitty chose a pair of white gloves. Then they returned to the hotel. Kitty and the twins had connecting rooms, and Jared's was across the hall. After resting and freshening up, they went into the dining room and ordered dinner.

"This has been a good day, don't you think so, Daddy?" Becky asked.

"I enjoyed myself," he said.

"Did you have a good time, Kitty?" Jenny asked.

"A very good time, honey."

As if rehearsed, Becky asked, "Don't you think Kitty looks pretty in that blue dress, Daddy? It matches her eyes."

"I thought it would when I bought it," he said, amused.

"Kitty, don't you think Daddy looks handsome in his uniform?"

"Yes, dear, very handsome." What were the girls

up to now? They acted as if they were on a mission, and the best thing was to end it fast. "If we're all through with dinner, I'd like to go back to my room."

Upon leaving the dining room, the maître d'hotel said, "Good night, Mrs. Fraser, have a pleasant evening."

Rather than correct him, Kitty merely nodded. "Thank you."

Jared trailed behind and she overheard the man say to him, "You have a lovely family, Captain Fraser."

"Thank you, I think so, too," Jared said.

The girls giggled, and Kitty hustled them along before they could say anything embarrassing. "Hush," she whispered. "Some people will say anything to get a tip."

Obviously it worked, because Jared shook the man's hand and slipped him a generous tip.

Kitty's last thought before falling asleep that night was of the truth in the maître d's comment: every day, they were beginning to act more like a family. More importantly, they were beginning to feel like one.

The following morning Jared declined Kitty's invitation to join the twins and her for more sightseeing; he remained at the hotel reading an assortment of newspapers. He joined them for lunch, and then they left to attend the performance of Buffalo Bill's Wild West Show.

The twins sat openmouthed as the mounted men and women rode out with colorful flags and guidons. They clapped and cheered with the other spectators during the staged battle with whooping Indians pursuing a stagecoach, and the cavalry riding to the rescue. It all was exciting, colorful, and entertaining, especially the riding feats of the equestrians.

But the highlight of the show was Annie Oakley. Her marksmanship was extraordinary and even impressed Jared, who had found most of the previous exhibition too theatrical.

"Can you shoot a gun like Annie Oakley, Kitty?" Becky asked.

"No, honey, there's little use for one on a ranch anymore. Still, my father instructed me to never ride out on the range without a rifle."

"I bet you're just as good as she is," a faithful Jenny declared.

"I don't think so, honey, but I *was* taught to hit whatever I aim at. On the range, if you have to use a weapon it usually means you have to shoot quickly. To kill a snake or a charging animal, for instance. That's not the same as taking your time and shooting at a stationary target."

"Did you wear a gunbelt, too, like Annie Oakley does?"

"No, Jenny, I never wore a pistol. But when I was as young as you girls, all the men on the ranch wore gunbelts with Colt revolvers. They don't do that anymore."

"Did you ever have to shoot Indians, like the people in the show?"

"No, Becky. Most of the Indians were on reservations by then."

"I bet your father did, though," Jenny said.

"Oh, yes. When they were growing up, my father and uncles had to fight off Indians and outlaws."

Jared said, "But what you saw here was make-believe, girls. In battle it's not a game. Men die," he said grimly.

After the show, the twins raced over to where Annie Oakley and Buffalo Bill were signing the programs. As they waited for the twins, Kitty said, "I gather you didn't enjoy the Wild West Show."

"Perhaps because the Wild West is no longer *wild*. It's like the South after the Civil War: a way of life ended. Just as we've seen the passing of slavery and Southern gentility, so, too, the gunfights and hangings of the early West. We're growing up as a nation, Kathleen. The past is history and belongs to the scribes and novelists."

"But this is merely meant as entertainment, Jared. Just as vaudeville or any other form of theater is intended to be."

"Buffalo Bill was a Pony Express rider, an army scout, a buffalo hunter, and an Indian fighter. And he was awarded the Congressional Medal of Honor in 1872. Now he's demeaning the importance he and others like him had in building the West, with this kind of theatrics."

Kitty regarded him with a long look of wonderment.

"What?" he asked.

"Why, you're a romantic at heart, Jared Fraser, despite how much you try to appear otherwise."

"I don't know what you're talking about."

Kitty smiled. "I think you do."

Early the next morning, they were bound for Washington. The medal ceremony was scheduled for the Fourth of July, and their train arrived the day before. Jonathan and Seth had already arrived and after a brief reunion with the twins, the three men sat down so his father and brother could apprise Jared of the progress in the case.

The twins were anxious to get out and see the city, but Kitty reined them in and settled them down with a history lesson of the White House, which they were going to tour the next day.

That evening Jonathan recommended that Kitty be given a respite from her nanny duties. He suggested his sons take her out to dinner while he remained with the twins.

Seth embraced the suggestion enthusiastically, but Jared was reluctant to leave the hotel.

"Then stay with Father and the twins," Seth said. "I'll take Kitty to dinner and we'll dance the night away."

Not liking *that* idea, Jared agreed to go with them. As they departed, he couldn't help but notice how lovely Kathleen looked. Her face glowed and her eyes sparkled with excitement. He'd observed in the past that Seth always had that effect on her.

Much to Jared's further disgruntlement, Seth remained attentive to Kitty throughout the meal. When she excused herself for a few minutes, Jared pointed this out to his brother.

"Really, Seth, Kathleen is not like the usual pieces of fluff you're used to entertaining. I'm afraid she might take your attentions seriously."

Seth chortled. "And when did you gain this vast understanding of women, Jared? Considering the choices you've made in the past, I'd say you're the one who needs advice."

"Kathleen isn't anything like those women. That's why I don't want to see her hurt. She's naïve and innocent where men are concerned."

"Really?" Seth said, amused. "I thought you categorized all women as shallow and untrustworthy."

"Kathleen is different. She has a great deal of common sense and the twins adore her."

"And what about you?"

"I've developed a great deal of respect for her," Jared said, uncomfortable with the turn of the conversation.

"Are you sure it's not more than that?"

"I don't know what you mean."

"You know damn well what I mean. Are you in love with her, Jared?"

"As usual, Seth, you're talking like a damn fool. Kathleen and I have reached a comfortable working relationship which is beneficial to my daughters. I don't want to see it jeopardized by your womanizing."

"This, coming from a man who cut his first teeth on Stephanie Lorimer and then married Diane Fleming!" Seth scoffed. " 'Physician, heal thyself.' "

Kitty's return prevented the conversation from getting any more heated, and Seth immediately whisked her off to the dance floor.

Jared's gaze followed the couple as they waltzed. Lord knew Seth was right about his past choices, but Kathleen was nothing like Diane or Stephanie. Like her remark yesterday: only Kathleen would accuse him of being a romantic at heart. No one else would ever entertain such a thought about him, would ever guess how much he yearned for a loving relationship. Those incredible eyes of hers seemed to read his soul effortlessly. And the more she did so, the more he became aware of his own vulnerability.

When the waltz ended they returned to the table, but Jared was gone. Kitty looked around and saw him talking to another uniformed officer near the doorway.

"Seth, we're being very rude leaving Jared alone so much."

"Jared always preferred his own company to that of others. We both know he's an intellectual snob, Kitty."

"That's a very unkind remark to make about your own brother, Seth." She was shocked by Seth's harsh criticism of Jared. "I see a big change in Jared."

"Through no credit of his own."

She felt a rise of anger. "Sometimes the circumstances in people's lives can trigger a need to change, but it's still up to the individuals themselves to do so. Jared had to adjust to a whole new life when he returned home. He's adopted a new attitude with the twins, and they now adore their father. He's a very private person, you know; it must have been difficult to come back to take over the responsibility of raising two daughters."

"It appears to me, Kitty, that you're the one raising them."

"You're being very unfair to Jared," she said angrily. "Why don't you give your brother some credit where credit is due for—" She stopped at the sight of his grin, and was hit by the truth. "Seth Fraser, you said those nasty things just to rile me, didn't you?"

He reached across the table and squeezed her hand. "You're in love with him, aren't you?"

"I certainly am *not*. I simply have a much better understanding of him than I once did."

"You wouldn't lie to a friend, would you, Nanny Kitty?" He clasped her hand between his own. "You're a great gal, Kathleen Drummond. You're good for him, and the best thing that's happened to him other than the twins. No matter what you may think to the contrary, I love Jared. Maybe someday I'll have the opportunity to prove it to him."

Jared returned to the table and his gaze locked on Seth holding her hand. "I'm tired, so I'm going back to the hotel."

"I'm ready to leave now, too," Kitty said, and slipped her hand out of Seth's.

"That's not necessary. Don't let me break up your party." He spun on his heel and walked away.

Seth let out a low whistle at Jared's exit. "Yeah, he sure has changed, all right."

"He's tired, Seth." Kitty got up and hurriedly caught up with him, and Seth joined them as the doorman hailed them a carriage.

The next morning Jared was quiet at breakfast, but Kitty didn't dwell on it. She was as excited as the twins were at the prospect of touring the White House.

By the time they finished the tour it was time for the medal ceremony, which was being held in the garden.

Jared stood tall and handsome in his uniform when he stepped forward to accept the medal. He wore the fixed, inscrutable expression that she had seen often before, as the president read the citation.

"On January 31, 1895 in an act of heroism and disregard for his own survival, Captain Jared J. Fraser, in command of six United States Marines and two civilian employees, defended the United States embassy in Calcutta, India, against a marauding band of rebel insurgents, until a reinforcement force arrived to relieve the defenders.

Although seriously wounded, Captain Fraser, in the finest tradition of the United States Army, single-handedly defended the quarters of the American ambassador and his family when several invaders penetrated the embassy.

With great pride, on this fourth day of July 1895, the United States Congress and a grateful nation award Captain Jared J. Fraser his country's highest distinction, the Congressional Medal of Honor."

Kitty felt the rise of tears as the president hung the medal around Jared's neck and shook his hand. As soon as the six Marines and two civilians were awarded decorations, the band struck up the "Semper Fidelis March," ending the ceremony.

The press's attention focused on Jared, and their cameras' flashes exploded when the twins ran up and hugged and kissed him, capturing a shot that would surely make the front pages of newspapers across the country.

The decorated heroes and their families were feted with a luncheon in the White House; then the Frasers returned to their hotel.

As soon as Jonathan and Seth left to return to New York, Kitty and Jared left the hotel to finish their sightseeing before the Fourth of July parade.

The streets of Washington were in holiday mode, with street vendors selling everything from American flags to frankfurters on buns smothered with spicy mustard, Heinz ketchup, pickles, and relish. They visited the Smithsonian Institute and Arlington National Cemetery, watched the parade with marching bands from all the armed services, then finally settled down on a hillside that gave them a magnificent view of the Washington Monument to await the gigantic fireworks display.

Before long the twins fell asleep, exhausted from the eventful day. Jared stretched out with his hands tucked under his head and closed his eyes.

"Are you going to sleep on me, too?" Kitty asked.

He opened one eye and peered at her. "You want to rephrase that, Mrs. Drummond, before I answer?"

Kitty blushed. "I meant the same as the twins did, and you know it."

He chuckled and closed both his eyes again. "I'm seriously considering it."

"It has been a tiring day, but a very exciting one."

"Uh-huh," he agreed.

"Thank you, Jared."

"For what?" he asked, on the verge of drifting into slumber.

"For bringing me along on this trip. I've really enjoyed it."

"If I hadn't, I would have had to leave the twins behind, and I know their nanny would have disapproved of me denying them the opportunity to see their father get a medal."

"They'll remember this day as long as they live. And so will I."

Jared opened his eyes and sat up. "Why, Kathleen? Why will *you* remember it?" he asked in a low voice made deeper with huskiness.

Her fingers itched to reach out and touch him, to trace her fingertips along the scar on his cheek—or his mouth. He had an incredible mouth; his lips were firm and sensual. They drew her gaze like a magnet.

Lowering his head, he repeated in a whisper. "Why, Kathleen?"

She felt the overpowering need to feel that mouth on hers. Parting her lips, she raised her head.

The whistle of a dozen roman candles shattered the quietness and lit up the sky with a blaze of color, and the twins were jolted to wakefulness with startled cries. Jared drew away and reached for Jenny, and Kitty picked up Becky.

For the next thirty minutes they watched the extraordinary aerial display. But the brilliant bursts of color paled in comparison to the excited beating within Kitty's breast from the awareness of the man who sat so near.

# Chapter 14

The twins were restless on the return trip to Dallas. Kitty tried everything she could think of to keep them entertained, but a train compartment did not provide too many options.

She had bought the sheet music to "The Band Played On" and was teaching the twins how to waltz as they sang the words to the popular song.

Jared was trying to read about four-cylinder automobiles, which were becoming more popular every day and, according to the magazine article, were predicted to replace the horse and buggy completely. But as much as he tried to concentrate, he continued to peer over the top of the magazine to watch Kitty and the twins. The three of them had joined hands and were dancing in the small area.

His gaze was on Kitty. She was so vibrant and seemed to have a contagious enthusiasm for whatever she did.

As they whirled she sang, "Casey would waltz with the strawberry blond . . ."

The twins joined in, "And the band played on."

"He'd glide 'cross the floor with the girl he adored . . ."

"And the band played on," the twins responded.

He couldn't help grinning. They enjoyed one another's company so much, and always had a good time together whether they were reading, singing, or just playing.

As much as he tried to keep the thought out of his mind, he couldn't help thinking about the night he and Kitty had gone to dinner with Seth. Had Kitty fallen for his brother? She acted as if she had, and he couldn't believe Seth wouldn't take advantage of that. At one time he'd thought Seth might have done so already, but since Jared had come to know and understand Kitty, his common sense told him he was mistaken.

And while on the subject of common sense, he sure as hell didn't show any when he came close to kissing her at those fireworks. That would have been a grievous mistake. Yet every day they were together, his desire to kiss and hold her—make love to her—was growing. And when it did happen, as it surely would, he was afraid she'd bolt like a rabbit and they'd never see her again. Why in hell couldn't he keep his mind off her! Disgusted, he raised the magazine.

But within minutes, he lowered it again.

By the time they finally transferred to the Rocky Mountain Central for the short ride to Dallas, they were all wishing for a long walk along the creek at home. The trouble was, once they reached Dallas, they'd still have a twenty-mile buggy ride to the Carringtons' ranch.

It was hot on the train, and the open windows offered only a warm, dust-filled breeze. Kitty sat gazing out the window, her thoughts on the cool water of her favorite swimming hole on the Triple M. Jared was reading in the seat next to her, as usual, and the twins were in the opposite seat drawing pictures on pads of paper.

"What now?" Jared grumbled, when the train slowed to a grinding stop.

When he stood up to check, the man in the seat across the aisle stood up and leveled a drawn Colt at him. "Sit down, soldier boy."

Kitty had noticed the unsavory-looking character when he boarded at the previous stop.

"This is a holdup, folks, so don't nobody try nothin' foolish," he ordered. "That goes for you, too, soldier boy."

Several of the women started to panic, and he snarled, "Shut up, ladies, and stay in your seats. I want your money and jewelry." He grabbed Becky's arm and pulled her out of her seat. "Take your daddy's hat and help me collect this stuff. You can start with your ma and pa there."

"I don't want to," Becky said. "I don't like you. You're dirty and you need a bath."

"And you need a smack across your mouth," he snarled.

"Don't you dare touch her," Jared warned.

"Then tell the brat to do what I say," the outlaw declared, "and nobody'll get hurt."

"Here, Becky," Jared said, handing her his hat.

"While you're at it, throw your wallet in it. And that ring on your finger, lady."

"That's my wedding ring," Kitty said.

"I'm sure soldier boy here will be glad to get ya another one. Now quit stallin'."

Jared put a hand on her arm. "Give him the ring, Kathleen."

Tears glistened in Kitty's eyes as she pulled off the band Ted had slipped on her finger the day they were married. She dropped it in the hat.

The outlaw followed Becky up and down the aisle, making sure the other passengers deposited whatever valuables they had.

A rider rode up to the train leading three saddled horses, and Kitty saw an armed man climb off the other passenger car, and another out of the engine cab.

Snatching the purse from one of the women, the outlaw dumped the collected loot into it, then tossed Jared's hat back to him.

"Here's your hat, soldier boy." He grinned broadly, exposing a row of yellowed teeth. "Thanks, folks, for your generosity. You kin sit down now, brat," he said to Becky.

"You're not nice. I don't like you." She kicked him in the shin.

"Why you little . . . Hold it, soldier boy," he snarled when Jared lunged out of his seat. "I'd hate to hafta mess up that pretty uniform you're wearing."

Grabbing Becky, he used her as a shield as he backed to the door.

Jared followed him. *"Take your hands off her."*

At the last moment, the outlaw shoved Becky at Jared and jumped off the train. The four men galloped away before anyone could get to the pistols in their luggage.

Jared picked up Becky and carried her back to the seat.

"Are you okay, honey?" Kitty asked, hugging and kissing her.

"He was a mean man," Becky said, not the least bit fazed by the incident.

"Weren't you scared?" Jenny asked.

"No, I didn't like him. And he sure was ugly."

Kitty hugged Becky again. "You were very brave, sweetheart."

"And you girls listen to me," Jared declared solemnly. "If an outlaw ever has a gun pointed at you, do exactly what he orders, do you understand? You could have been shot, Becky."

"Or you," Kitty murmured beside him.

The holdup took the boredom out of the rest of the trip, and before they knew it, they were climbing off the train in Dallas.

They were delayed at the station while the sheriff took information about the outlaws. Jared gave him a description of the man who robbed their car, and the engineer and passengers in the other cars filled in the descriptions of the others.

Kitty told him the kind of horses they rode, and the sheriff thanked them and was about to leave.

"One other thing, Sheriff," Kitty said. "He wore spurs."

"Nothing unusual about that, ma'am."

"Cowhands only do so when they're on horseback. I remember thinking how strange it was he had spurs on when he was riding on a train, and that's why I noticed the rowel was missing from the left one."

"Thank you, ma'am. That'll be most helpful when we catch up with them."

Jared hailed a carriage so they could return to the house. Once they were moving, Becky asked, "What's a rowel, Kitty?"

"That's the little wheel with the sharp points on the end of the spurs, honey."

"Why do they wear them?"

"Some men wear them to goad the horse to move faster."

"I bet that hurts," Jenny said.

"It does. My father won't let anybody spur a horse on the Triple M."

Jenny grinned broadly. "I bet I'd like your father."

"I bet he'd like you, too, honey." She gave the girl a quick hug. "I bet he'd ride you around on his saddle just like he used to do with me, when I was little."

Charles and Mildred greeted them warmly when they arrived at the house. The odor from the fire was barely perceptible. The rugs and furniture downstairs had all been cleaned or polished, and the walls freshly painted.

On the floor above, all the charred wood and debris had been removed, the floors and walls of the attic and Kitty's room were already roughed in, and the halls and other suites had been repainted. It was hard to believe it was the same place they'd left less than two weeks before.

"There's no reason why we couldn't stay here tonight, Jared," Kitty suggested. "The twins and I could sleep in either your father's room or Seth's."

"I'd like that, too. This will give us a chance to relax before leaving for the Carrington ranch."

The twins chose their grandfather's room, so Kitty moved into Seth's for the night. After bedding them down, the first thing she did was go out to the garden. The site had become a haven to her, a place where no matter how chaotic the day, she could find solace in its peacefulness.

"Do you have a garden on your ranch?" The question had come from Jared, who was sitting on a bench in the shadows.

Kitty walked over and sat down beside him. "No, I wish I could. I love flowers."

"Pity, seeing how much pleasure you get out of a garden."

"I guess that's what makes one so precious to me. Don't you like a garden, Jared?"

"I guess I've never thought about it. It's just something I take for granted. My mother planted this garden when I was a child. She made Seth and me help plant it, telling us how much satisfaction there would be in watching something grow." His smile was sardonic. "I think the only pleasure we really got out of the garden was bringing girls out here and—"

"Say no more, I get the picture. I can see you boys were in dire need of a sister."

"I never thought about what it would have been like to have a sister. But seeing the twins, I realize how enjoyable it might have been to have a young girl's presence in my childhood."

"Well they say, 'What you don't have—' "

" '—you don't miss,' " he finished. "Nevertheless, I'm sure I would have liked to have known the young Kathleen Drummond."

"It was Kathleen MacKenzie then," she corrected.

"And you and your brother are very close."

"Yes, and Josh was always very protective of me. Of course, that never stopped him or my cousins from teasing me, though. Were you and Seth close when you were young?"

"I don't think we've ever been as close as brothers should be. Seth was always getting into some kind of trouble. He hasn't changed, but at least I no longer have to take the blame for it. I'm afraid his latest escapade will hurt the family name."

"I know it's none of my business, but how is Seth's case doing?"

"Father says it looks very encouraging right now. The man responsible for the fraud has sworn that Seth was unaware it was crooked. He brought Seth into it to capitalize on the Fraser name, because of my father's honest reputation."

"It's unfortunate Seth didn't look into it more."

"To say the least," Jared said, disgusted.

"You two are so different."

His face hardened in a grimace. "So I've been told. The whole time we were growing up. Good night." He started to walk away.

"Jared." He stopped and turned his head. "You don't understand. When I first met you, you appeared to put your own welfare ahead of the twins' to the point of neglect. I've since come to realize you're not that person I believed you to be."

He looked at her intently, then moved back to the bench. "And what kind of person am I?"

"You're the brother with all the strength. Oh, Seth's charming and lovable, but he lacks any direction. He really hasn't grown up, has he? Whereas you've already lived a lifetime and had to deal with its turmoil."

"I had the impression you were very fond of Seth."

"Of course I am. I can't help but feel a fondness for him—as I would for any child. But knowing both of you, I think I understand what shaped this difference between you brothers: you probably were forgotten in the glow of Seth's personality."

"You think I don't love my brother, and that isn't true, Kathleen."

"You're wrong, Jared, I don't think that at all. I'm saying that when you were growing up, Seth probably got all the attention, and you were the forgotten child. So you became the serious and dependable son, and Seth the charismatic, easygoing one. Perhaps one day he'll meet the right woman, change, and settle down. But I think it's a long time off yet."

"I think he might have met her already."

"Really," Kitty said, pleased. "Who is she?"

"I figure it's you."

Her eyes rounded in disbelief. "Me! Whatever gave you that idea?"

"You seem to glow when you're with him. I thought that perhaps you—"

"Jared, I adore Seth the way I do the twins and your father, but I have no romantic attachment to him. Granted, I want children, but I don't want the child to be my husband."

Jared burst into laughter. "You have such a delicate way of expressing yourself, Kathleen."

Kitty was glad his mood had lightened considerably. "Well, I guess I should think about getting to bed. I'm looking forward to tomorrow."

"I have to say, so am I, Kathleen. So am I."

In companionable silence, they walked back to the house.

# Chapter 15

The next morning, while Jared discussed a remodeling problem with the carpenter, Kitty took the twins shopping to get suitable ranch clothing. She also bought whatever supplies she could think of that would be needed for a month's stay.

"We aren't going into the wilds, you know, Kitty," Jared complained, as he loaded cartons of food and supplies into the buggy. "Jake told me there's a town called River Bend nearby where we can purchase anything you need."

"Thank you for your advice, Jared, but I should tell you Ted and I did all the purchasing and kept up the inventory for the store on the Triple M."

"You had an actual *store*!"

"Well, not exactly a store. No one had to pay for what they took; it was funded by the ranch. When you ran out of something, you didn't have to ride to town to get it. There are a number of families on the ranch, so it was very convenient for everyone."

"I'm sure it was, Kathleen. But from the number of crates, you must think you're still buying for a clan. There're only four of us."

She watched with satisfaction as he squeezed in the last crate. "Despite your grumbling, Jared, I see you managed to get it all in the buggy."

While Jared went to give Charles some last-minute instructions, Kitty rounded up the twins, and they were waiting in their seats when he returned.

He climbed in the buggy, took the reins, and they were on their way. Once out of the city, Kitty and the girls sang as they rode along, and even Jared joined in on one or two of the songs.

The Carrington ranch was twenty miles north of Dallas on the west side of the Trinity River. Jared turned onto a road identified as La Paloma and followed a stream that led to a ranch house surrounded by towering oaks and pines.

Slim and Martha Slocum, who had been informed they'd be arriving, came out to greet them. The aged couple lived in their own house on the ranch and had been with the Carringtons from the time Jake had been an infant. Slim immediately informed them that he and his wife would be leaving the following day for Fort Worth, where Martha intended to help out her ailing sister for a couple of weeks.

The original ranch house had a large kitchen, a parlor, and two bedrooms. When their children were born, Jake had added two more bedrooms and another bathroom. The house did not have the luxury or elegance of the Carrington's Dallas home, but the comfortable and homey ambiance of the sprawling ranch house was a delight to Kitty, and even though it was not her home, it would be *her* kitchen for the next month.

The twins immediately claimed a bedroom and Kitty took the one next to them, connected by a bathroom. Jared took the bedroom that obviously was Jake and Beth's, and within the hour the luggage and supplies were unloaded and they were settled in. From the moment they arrived, the twins began pestering to be taught how to ride a horse. Jared insisted they get their bearings first, so Slim and Martha took them on the tour of the outbuildings.

The original bunkhouse was now used for storage, replaced by a larger house with a sitting room and indoor plumbing. There was a smokehouse, a blacksmith shed, and a huge barn with horse stalls and a hayloft that delighted the twins. They immediately proceeded to climb up into it and jump down into the mounds of hay below. A pregnant mare in one of the stalls eyed the goings-on with an impervious stare, then went back to munching hay. Jared put their team into two of the empty stalls.

While he studied the array of bridles and harness hung on wall pegs, Kitty was just pleased to look around at the familiar items she'd known since childhood.

Martha Slocum had already prepared them an evening meal, and Kitty spent the rest of the evening familiarizing herself with the kitchen.

Before retiring, she went outside and glanced around with pleasure at the scattered outbuildings and fenced corral. It felt good to be back on a ranch again, even if it wasn't the Triple M.

The next morning, as the Slocums prepared to leave, Slim explained to Jared the need to keep the stock watered and fed, and the twins away from the south pasture where the bull was penned.

"You best keep the young'uns away from him. Normally Ole Samson—named in honor of Sam Houston—don't give folks a never no mind, but with most of the heifers gone, he's liable to get a mite restless."

"I understand."

"And Bluebonnet ain't due to foal for a couple of weeks. We'll be back by then. Wish there was time to teach you the names of all the horses, but most of them will answer to a whistle." He proceeded to demonstrate, and the piercing sound set the horses in the corral galloping over to the fence.

"Are those two ponies gentle enough for children to ride?" Jared asked.

"You bet. Young Jacob and Rachel rode them all the time. One's named Straw, and the other with the blaze answers to Berry. You'll find saddles and other gear in the barn."

While Slim filled Jared in with instructions, Martha showed the twins how to feed the chickens and collect the eggs. "It's important you do it every morning," she told them.

"We promise," the twins said, thrilled by the responsibility given to them.

"I feel bad about runnin' off like this and leavin' you to your own makings," Martha said, climbing onto the buggy.

"Martha, it's no problem," Kitty assured her. "I was raised on a ranch."

"You sure you don't mind?"

"I'm looking forward to it. I miss ranch life."

And as they watched the couple ride away, Becky asked, "Kitty, what's a blaze?"

"It's a white streak on a horse's face or mane."

"I bet you know everything about ranching," Jenny said with awe.

Kitty looked around her and felt empowered. "You're right, honey. There's not too much I don't know about it."

Her gaze shifted to the corral where a pair of strawberry ponies grazed among the other horses. "You girls get your riding clothes on." She winked at them and they ran into the house. She headed for the barn, and Jared followed her.

"What are you doing?"

She picked up a bridle and grabbed one of the saddles that was slung across a wooden frame. "I'm going to saddle a horse."

"Do you want me to try it out first?"

She turned her head and looked at him. "I beg your pardon?"

"Let me ride it to make sure it's tame."

"Jared, I've ridden horses from the time I've been nine years old, ponies when I was six. In fact, I was going to make the same suggestion to you if you intended to ride."

"I may not have been in the cavalry, Kathleen, but I've done a lot of riding in the service."

"I was thinking about your leg wound. I thought you might prefer a buggy until it's totally healed."

"I'm sure I can mount a horse. Have you one in mind for yourself?"

"I haven't decided yet." She disappeared through the barn door.

Jared snatched a bridle off a peg, picked up a blanket, and grabbed a saddle. "For heaven's sake, woman, slow down," he called, hurrying after her. "We'll be here a month. Five minutes won't make that much difference."

"Maybe not to you, but I've been waiting to do this since I left the Triple M."

Kitty slung the saddle over the top bar of the corral, then climbed up and sat down, hooking her heels on the bar below. Jared came up and stood behind her.

"Well, do you see one you want?"

"I like the looks of that roan mare."

He climbed up beside her. "So is this the real Kathleen Drummond?"

"What do you mean?"

"The split skirt, the boots, that Stetson."

Kitty laughed. "Actually, no."

He cocked a brow. "Really?"

She threw him a sassy grin. "On the Triple M I always wore the jeans my brother had outgrown."

The strawberry ponies trotted over to them, and Kitty reached into her pocket and pulled out a sugar cube for each of them.

"Are you resorting to bribery to win their affection?" Jared asked as the ponies plucked the cubes out of her hand.

"If the twins are going to ride these ponies, I want them to know my scent."

"Did I just hear an old, home-on-the-range custom?"

She gave him a disgruntled look. "Could be, and I know I just heard an old, typically pretentious Jared Fraser question."

"Or Jared Fraser trying to be humorous. I guess I shouldn't try."

"Forgive me, Jared; never give up trying to be humorous." Her eyes twinkled as she added, "No matter how pathetic the attempt may be." Bridle in hand, she hopped down into the corral.

Jared's gaze followed her confident stride as she moved among the horses. When she reached the roan mare, she patted the horse several times on the neck, then took another sugar cube out of her pocket and fed it to the animal. After a couple more pats, she slipped the bridle over its head and put the bit in the mare's mouth. Watching the smooth, effortless action, he decided that there wasn't anything the woman didn't do well.

Grabbing the bridle, Jared climbed down, his eye on a black stallion. Unfortunately he didn't have any sugar cubes to entice it, and the horse shied away from him. After a couple more attempts, though, the stallion let him put the bridle on him. Kitty had saddled the mare by the time he led the stallion back to the fence.

"Need any help?" she asked, adjusting her stirrups.

"I'm quite capable of saddling a horse, Miss Home-on-the-Range."

"I thought maybe some lackey did it for you in the army, Captain Fraser." Grinning, she swung up smoothly into the saddle, trotted over to the gate, leaned over, and released the latch.

"What, you aren't going to jump the fence?" he asked, climbing stiffly into the saddle.

"At the Triple M, we don't jump fences for pleasure or ride to the hounds, Captain Fraser."

Jared galloped several hundred feet to get the feel of the reins and the strength of his horse. Satisfied, he wheeled the stallion and at a full gallop headed for the fence. The horse soared over it without breaking stride.

When Jared reined in, Kitty glared, disgusted. "So you can handle a horse—it still was a fool thing to do. What if that horse couldn't have cleared the fence?"

"Mrs. Drummond, I may not have been raised on a ranch, or ridden ponies at six, but I can judge the strength of a horse when I'm on one."

"Captain Fraser, I don't have the equipment to turn this into a pissing contest, but I think my equestrian experience outranks yours."

He broke into laughter. "Pissing contest, Mrs. Drummond? I'm shocked."

She grinned sheepishly. "With a brother and a slew of outrageous cousins, a girl overhears a lot of things that maybe she shouldn't. Let's just teach the twins how to ride, shall we?" With that, she galloped to the house.

As Jared rode up to the hitching post, she dismounted. "I'll go and get the twins."

After a long moment she came out and with a theatrical flourish announced, "Ladies and gentlemen, now it's time for the main attraction that you've all been waiting for. With great pleasure I present the stars of the show, those two elec . . .

tri . . . fying, fas . . . cin . . . a . . . ting, bo-o-o . . . dacious beauties from Dallas, Texas—Rebecca and Jennifer Fraser!" She dipped in a bow and pointed to the door. "Ta-da!"

Dressed in fringed skirts and vests, cowboy boots and hats, the twins came out of the door and delighted them with a performance of "Home on the Range."

They looked adorable. Jared was so pleased, he almost toppled off his horse as they sang and strutted through the song. When they finished he whistled and applauded vigorously.

"Did you really like it, Daddy?" Jenny asked excitedly.

"I loved it, angel."

"Do we look like the girls in Buffalo Bill's Wild West Show?" Becky asked.

"You're much cuter than they were."

Becky's excitement was evident as she looked toward the corral. "Can we ride the ponies now?"

"It'd be better for you to get to know how it feels to be on horseback first," Kitty said. "When I was very small, my daddy used to let me ride in front of him on his saddle. So your daddy will take one of you, and I'll take the other, and we'll go for a little ride."

"Can Bonnie and Bibbie go, too?" Jenny asked.

"Of course. They're family, too, aren't they?" her father replied.

*Boy, have you changed, Jared Fraser!*

Bubbling over with excitement, the twins ran into the house and came back carrying their dolls.

Jenny ran over to Jared and he lifted her up and

set her down in front of him. She giggled with delight when he put his arms around her and grasped the reins.

Kitty lifted Becky up onto the saddle, and then swung up behind her, gave her a hug, and reached for the reins.

Side by side, they rode off to explore the ranch. With a grin at Jared, Kitty began to whistle "Home on the Range." Soon they were all singing it at the tops of their voices.

# Chapter 16

Jared had never felt as contented as he'd been in the past week. He didn't know if it was the peacefulness of the ranch or Kathleen's presence. Funny, how she had aggravated him when they'd first met; now she was like a soothing balm to a wound.

Their talk in the garden the night before they left Dallas had been a revelation to him. He had to admit he'd been relieved to find out her true feelings for Seth. And he'd been wrong about a lot more where Kathleen Drummond was concerned.

He opened the book he'd been trying to read but couldn't concentrate on the words. What was keeping Kathleen? It had been a good hour since she left to put the twins to bed. Had she retired, as well?

Putting aside the book, Jared followed the low murmur of voices to the twins' room. The door was open and he saw them sitting in the center of the bed, filing their nails and talking.

He grinned as they chatted away about the need for a lady to always keep her finger- and toenails filed. Kitty patiently endured Becky filing at her fingers and Jenny at her toes. He couldn't pull himself away from the sight as they switched around until all six sets of nails had been filed to their satisfaction.

When they were finished, Kitty tucked them in bed, then sat down and began to read to them in a low voice, soothing in its gentle softness.

Returning to the parlor, he sat down and picked up the book.

Life felt good.

Since their arrival, the twins had mastered handling and riding a pony. Apparently Bonnie and Bibbie had done so, also: the twins were waiting to take their beloved dolls with them on the picnic planned for that day. Kitty watched with pleasure as Jared saddled their ponies and teased his daughters about their impatience to get under way.

This stay on the ranch had done wonders for him. He was totally contented and appeared to have taken to ranch life easily. The exercise had helped to work out some of the stiffness in his leg, and the scar on his cheek was barely perceptible under the tan he'd acquired. He'd even begun to jot down notes for his novel.

His adoration for his daughters was evident in the way he now teased or showed patience with them. And they had grown to adore him and felt free to shower the affection they had held within them for so long. Kitty wiped away the tears that had suddenly welled in her eyes, and thought of Jenny's poignant words a few weeks before.

*Yes, sweetheart, your father has become the daddy you always yearned for.*

Kitty finished packing the picnic basket and went out and joined them.

Jared had kept their destination a secret; his only clue was that she would enjoy it. Since she had yet to see anything on the ranch she hadn't enjoyed, her expectations were high. He didn't disappoint her when he led them to a pine-shrouded hilltop and dismounted.

"I discovered this site while out riding one day. Knowing your love of flowers, I thought you'd enjoy it."

Kitty gaped with pleasure. Below them, the valley stretched out in a floral carpet. She took a hand of each twin and they raced down the hillside.

Grinning at their exuberance, Jared followed slowly behind, favoring his leg; but he tired on the steep descent and sat down in the shade of a tree. Kitty had halted and was gazing around in wonderment. Laughing gaily, the twins raced back and sat down beside him.

"You were right, Daddy, Kitty sure loves this place," Jenny said.

Jared's gaze followed Kitty's returning climb. "It's not this particular place, as much as it is the way of life. She's not a city girl, Jenny, and she doesn't need fancy houses or Paris gowns to be happy. A field of wildflowers can do just as well."

"Do you like ranch life, Daddy?"

"I've never lived on a ranch, Becky. All I know about cattle is that I like my steaks rare."

"You can ride a horse real good," Jenny instantly spoke up in his defense.

"I bet you could learn about cattle, too, if you wanted to."

"Yeah, I bet you could, Daddy. You're about the smartest man I know. 'Cept maybe Poppie," Jenny said.

Jared laughed and tossed her short curls. The twins joined in the laughter, and the sound reflected off the surrounding hills.

Becky's head perked up. "Listen, Daddy, the hills are laughing with us."

Jenny grasped his hand, and he liked the feeling. "I would like to live on a ranch *forever.*"

"Wouldn't you get bored? You have no friends here."

"Do, too. Becky's my best friend."

"And Jenny's mine," Becky declared.

"So you're convinced you girls would be content to live on a ranch."

"Oh, yes, Daddy," they said in unison.

"And what of those tastes you've acquired that I'm told women like so much: shopping, going to lunch in fancy restaurants?"

The hopeful gleam in Jenny's eyes was like a glowing beacon. "We like them, too, but then we'd like them even better when we'd get to do them."

"And we could get a ranch close to Dallas, just like this one is," Becky answsered.

Jared chuckled. "You little minxes put up a very good argument."

Continuing their persuasion, Becky said, "And just think, Daddy, how quiet it would be—"

"For you to write your novel," Jenny finished.

"Did Kitty put this idea in your heads?"

The girls exchanged one of their meaningful smiles, which Jared was convinced Eve must have worn when she handed Adam the apple.

They shook their heads. "We thought of it ourselves," Becky said proudly. "But I bet she'd like it, too."

He was putty in their very skillful little hands, but he enjoyed it. "I'll think about it, but I'm not making any promises."

"Hooray!" they shouted, and Jared was pushed to the ground under a fusillade of hugs and kisses.

At the sound of the infectious laughter, Kitty turned her head and saw Jared and the twins in a playful heap on the ground. She smiled in pleasure. How she wished she had children of her own. She had begun to think of the twins as hers—and, more dangerous, she had begun to feel Jared was hers, too. What had put such an idiotic thought in her mind? How long had it been since she'd thought of Ted?

It seemed like the twins and Jared had pushed any thoughts of others to the back of her mind. She hadn't even felt homesick for the Triple M, much less let her mind dwell on the guilt of her marriage. Had the healing begun, as people said it would?

Another outburst of laughter from the twins, followed by the sound of Jared's warm chuckle, brought another smile to her lips.

Yes, the healing had begun.

With the twins' help, Kitty spread out a blanket under a tree and they ate the picnic lunch she'd packed. Not a crumb remained of the apple pie she'd gotten up early to bake that morning, and when they finished eating, Jared stretched out and closed his eyes.

As soon as Kitty walked away to tie the picnic basket on her horse, Jenny leaned over him. "Boy, that apple pie sure was good, wasn't it, Daddy?"

"Uh-huh," Jared murmured.

"Kitty sure is a good cook, isn't she, Daddy?" Becky said.

"Uh-huh."

"I bet Kitty's about the best cook in the world," Jenny said.

"I bet," he murmured, waiting for Becky's turn. It came immediately.

"I bet if Mildred got sick, Kitty could do the cooking at home for us."

"I bet she could," Jared murmured. He was wise to the little schemers, and he couldn't help grinning. "She brews a good cup of coffee, too."

He heard Kitty return, and the twins immediately dashed away.

"You asleep?" she asked.

"No."

"Why did the twins run off so quickly?"

"I think they've got some more betting to do."

"Betting? As in gambling?"

"No, just some wangling, the little connivers."

"What are they up to now?"

"You don't want to know." He continued to lay with his eyes closed and a grin on his face.

Why had he feared for so long to open his heart to these precious girls? Every day spent with them made it easier for him to share the love he'd held in. He knew now that they'd never reject it. Kitty had opened his heart to trust. For the first time in his life, he understood that simple four-letter word was the most powerful motivating force in mankind.

Kitty opened the book she'd brought to read and sat enjoying the peace and tranquillity. Occasionally she'd look up from the page and glance at the twins picking wildflowers below—occasionally Jared would open his eyes enough to watch her do it.

That evening, the infectious laughter coming from the twins' room drew him to their door. "What's going on in here? Sounds like you're raising the rafters."

The twins and Kitty came out of the bathroom, their hair entirely saturated in white, foamy shampoo. Kitty had molded the twins' hair into horns jutting up from each side of their heads. They looked like Puck from *A Midsummer Night's Dream*. They, in turn, had swirled Kitty's hair into a single horn sticking up stiffly from the center of her head.

He laughed in amusement. "I don't believe it."

"Come on, Daddy, we'll shampoo your hair, too." They pulled him over to the sink.

He leaned over the sink, and once they wet his hair the two of them worked the shampoo into a foamy lather; then they made him sit down in a chair. There wasn't much they could make with his short hair and sideburns, so they pressed it tightly to his skull, and added a foamy white beard to his chin.

Stepping back to admire their handiwork, Jenny reflected, "Daddy, that white hair makes you look like Poppie."

The twins' smiles turned to sadness. Bending over, they kissed his cheeks. "We miss you, Poppie."

The task of rinsing out the shampoo fell to Kitty. When it came time to do Jared's, she had him sit on the chair and bend his head back over the sink to get the soap out of it.

"That feels good," he said. "Much better than when the barber does it."

She took a towel and rubbed his head to dry it. "That should do it, but I'm afraid you're going to smell very sweet for a while."

He stood up and his brown-eyed gaze looked into her eyes. "You do already."

Becky and Jenny exchanged smiles.

Later, as she tucked them in bed, Becky said, "Doesn't our daddy have nice hair?"

"Very nice, honey," Kitty said. She moved over to Jenny's side of the bed to tuck her in.

"It's so soft and wavy, don't you think, Kitty?" the girl asked.

"Yes, dear, it's very soft and wavy."

"Do you think Daddy's handsome, Kitty?" Becky asked.

"I would say so."

"Do you like Daddy?" the other twin probed.

"Of course I do. Your father and I get along very well. Now go to sleep, and sweet dreams, darlings."

When she left the room, Jenny murmured, "Dreams of you and Daddy, Kitty." Smiling, she hugged Bibbie to her side and closed her eyes.

Bright sunshine streamed through the open window, snaked across the room, and teased Kitty's eyelids. She opened her eyes, stretched her arms above her head, and enjoyed the glow of the sunny rays.

The Slocums were due back within the week. The days were passing swiftly, and before she knew, it would be time to leave. She hated the thought of leaving the ranch. They'd all been so contented here. It was like a fairy tale—but unfortunately, it would have to end.

Kitty got out of bed and went to the window. At this hour most of the ranch was still asleep, but it looked like the start of a perfect day to do the laundry.

Kitty finally pulled herself away from the window and put on a pair of jeans and plaid shirt to enable her to wash her gowns. Then she went to the kitchen, made coffee and a pan of oatmeal, collected all the soiled clothing and towels, and carried them outside. Filling the washtub with hot water and suds, she proceeded to wash the towels and squeeze out the water with the hand wringer clamped to the rim of the tub. She had them hung up to dry by the time Jared and the twins came out of the house.

"There's oatmeal warming on the stove, so help yourself. I want to continue with the laundry."

"Let's go, girls," Jared said, and went back into the kitchen.

Becky and Jenny lingered outside, eyeing the hand wringer. "Can we help, Kitty?"

"As soon as you eat." She plopped the twins' muddy jeans into the water. "What were you girls doing, rolling in the mud? I'll need a washboard to get these clean. Go ahead inside and eat while I look for a washboard."

Kitty raised the bar that fastened the door of the tiny shed, and was met by a blast of hot air when she swung it open. The corners and shelves were piled with old garden tools, branding irons, and other discarded paraphernalia.

She began to rummage through the scrap.

Jared was enjoying a cup of coffee when the twins came into the kitchen.

"Sit down, girls, and I'll get you your oatmeal."

They exchanged glances, then Becky said, "We can do that. Kitty told us to tell you she needs your help. She's looking for a washboard in that old shed.

He gulped down his coffee and got up. "Eat your breakfast." He went outside and walked into the shed. "What are you looking for in this hot, dusty place?"

"A washboard. I need one to scrub the mud off the twins' jeans."

Suddenly the door slammed shut, plunging the

shed into darkness except for the dim light filtering through a small, dusty vent window up high.

"Be careful, Kitty, you might trip over something. Don't move until I get the door open."

As she waited, Kitty could hear him groping his way to the door.

"Dammit!" he suddenly cursed.

"What happened?"

"The door's stuck. It won't open."

As soon as her eyes adjusted to the darkness, she went over to the door where he'd begun throwing his shoulder against the solid wood to force it open. She added her weight to the effort, but to no avail.

After several minutes, Jared stepped back and swiped away the perspiration that had begun to dot his brow. "It won't budge. If I didn't know better, I'd swear it's been barred shut."

"Who would do a thing like—" Struck by the obvious, she stopped in mid-sentence. "Oh, no, they wouldn't."

"Of course they would." He sounded resigned.

She leaned back against the door in defeat. "Why would they do this?"

"Can't you guess?" He moved nearer.

The huskiness in his query made her acutely aware not only of his nearness, but also of the intimacy of their confinement. Her mind began to whirl in a recollection of a similar situation in the library: the huskiness in his voice, and the heady excitement his nearness provoked. For two years she had not desired any man's touch. Why did Jared Fraser have this effect on her?

He braced his palms against the door on either side of her and leaned into her.

"I can't believe my daughters' smart nanny hasn't figured out what they're up to."

How did he expect her to think when he was so close? She dared not look at him or she'd be lost for certain, so she lowered her eyes. "I don't understand."

"I think you do, Kathleen Drummond. They've made us the hero and heroine of one of those Brontë novels you read to them. The trouble is, they're too impatient to wait for the ending and appear to be writing it themselves. So the least we can do is encourage them."

Curving a hand around the nape of her neck, he slowly lowered his head.

Kitty closed her eyes and parted her lips in anticipation.

His mouth closed over hers. His lips were warm and firm, the kiss intoxicating, drugging. Her feeble attempt to resist its draw only resulted in his deepening it more. Long-suppressed desire surged into an overpowering demand that washed through her in a swelling tide of passion.

When they broke apart, she was trembling. He appeared to be as affected by the kiss as she. With the sensuous taste of one another still on their lips, their bodies demanded more. His mouth covered hers with an urgency that should have been a warning to resist; instead, it fired her with a desire for what lay beyond the kiss.

His mouth devoured hers hungrily, possessively,

inflaming her passion with heated probes of his tongue. He nibbled and tugged at her lips, traced their outline with his tongue, then reclaimed them with his own.

When he caressed her neck and cupped her breast, the barrier of her clothing was like armor between them and she wanted more—she needed more, and wanted to cry out deliriously when he succeeded in unbuttoning her blouse and slipped his warm palm inside. His mouth trailed down her neck and across her breast.

Shoving the blouse off her shoulders, he made quick work of the buttons of her chemise, baring her breasts. He brushed the sensitive tips with his tongue and took one of the nipples into his mouth. Her hands slid to his neck and held his head there as he suckled and laved until her ragged gasps turned to whimpering moans of ecstasy.

Suddenly, Jared jerked up his head and his hands paused at the button of her skirt. He quickly pulled her blouse back up over her shoulders.

No! Not when her body was crying for satisfaction.

Then she heard what had caused his sudden reaction.

"Kitty, Daddy."

Jared was struggling to close the tiny pearl buttons on her chemise. She shoved aside his hands. "I'll do it."

"Are you okay, Kathleen?" There was such a tenderness in his eyes that he had to be just as shaken as she by the untimely interruption—he most certainly had been just as aroused. If she was adult enough to indulge in what had just happened between them, she shouldn't try to fool herself by blaming it on her abstinence for the past two years. It was Jared's kiss and touch, and no other's, that aroused the passion that had lain dormant within her.

Which troubled the hell out of her.

"Kathleen, are you okay?" he repeated.

"Yes . . . Yes, I'm fine."

"You sure?" He sounded contrite—and so vulnerable.

She managed a smile. "I'm sure."

"I'm sorry, Kitty."

"We're both to blame, Jared. It won't happen again."

"Are you so sure? The chapter hasn't ended yet."

"I think it must."

"It can't end until we reach the part where they live happily ever after."

For an infinite moment their gazes locked, then he pressed a light kiss to her lips.

"Girls, unlock this door. And after you do, you'd better run for your lives."

# Chapter 17

The door creaked open and the twins stood with downcast eyes when Kitty and Jared stepped out into the bright sunlight. For a long moment Jared loomed above them, adjusting to the light, then he folded his arms across his chest and glared down at them.

"Well, let's hear it. Why did you bar that door when you knew Kitty and I were inside?" They remained silent. "I'm waiting."

"We're sorry," Becky said.

"You should be. You both need a good spanking."

"It's not Jenny's fault; I thought of it. She didn't think it was a good idea."

"She was right. It was dark in there, it was hot in there, and there were some sharp tools in there that could have injured us. So I'd like to know why you would want to do that to two people who love you very much. Jenny, since you didn't like the idea, why don't you tell us the reason?"

Tears glistened in her eyes as she looked at her father. "Because . . . because we love both of you."

He threw up his hands in a hopeless gesture. "Well then, that explains it. And since we love you, too, I guess we'll have to lock you in the shed to prove it to you."

Tears rolled down Jenny's cheeks. "But I'm afraid of the dark."

"It was my fault, Daddy," Becky cried. "Lock me up, but not my sister."

Kitty put a hand on his arm. "Jared, may I ask a question?"

"Go ahead."

"Jenny, you said you locked us in there because you love us. Why do you think that would prove your love?" The girls exchanged tearful glances, but did not answer. "Becky, honey, will you tell me, since it was your idea?" She was curious to find out if Jared's theory was correct.

Becky's lips were quivering. "We know you love us, and we know Daddy loves us, so I thought if we locked you up together maybe Daddy would kiss you, and then maybe you'd start loving him."

Jared was fighting a grin as he looked at her. "Wherever do these children get such ridiculous notions, Mrs. Drummond? Could it be from those novels you read them?"

Kitty failed to share his amusement. "May I speak to you privately, Jared?"

"Would you like to step into the shed?"

She grabbed his arm and yanked him aside. "Okay, you were right, but I'm not going to let you lock them up in that shed."

"I never had any intentions of doing so. I have the perfect punishment in mind."

He walked back to the girls. "I hope you've learned I will no longer tolerate any more of your pranks on me, on Kitty, or on any other nanny unfortunate enough to come in contact with you. Do you understand?"

"Yes," they said.

"Yes, sir!" he reprimanded.

"Yes, sir."

"And now you can go and muck out the horse stall."

"Oh, Daddy," they groaned.

"Didn't you understand what I said?"

"Yes." They looked horrified.

He frowned. "Yes, what?"

"Yes, sir," they said, and headed for the barn with slow steps.

Jared grinned as he watched them disappear through the doors of the barn, and then watched Kitty stride off with washboard in hand. His gaze followed the sway of her hips in those damn pants.

"We've got some unfinished business, Kathleen Drummond."

By the afternoon things had settled back to normal, and Kitty promised to take the girls riding as soon as she finished taking down the dried laundry. She was hoping to stall long enough for Jared to get back from town and go riding with them, but the girls were eager to be under way. They had climbed into the corral and were playing with their ponies on the far side of the pasture.

Kitty had almost finished her task when the horses began to whinny. She cast an uneasy glance in the direction of the corral; the horses sounded frightened.

Something was spooking the horses, and it wasn't the girls. Either a snake was in the pasture or the horses had picked up the scent of a bear or cougar. Since she hadn't seen a sign of any wild animal since they'd been there, she suspected it was a snake.

"Becky, Jenny, get out of there," she yelled. They were too far away to hear her. Setting aside the clothes basket, she ran to the corral. That's when she saw what had frightened the horses.

Lumbering across the pasture was Samson, the Carrington's huge black bull. In search of heifers, he had obviously broken through the barbed wire in the adjoining pasture and was now heading toward the horses—and the girls.

Bulls were dangerously unpredictable. They were mean by nature, and though often would ignore you completely, other times they would snort and threaten to charge.

The girls were unaware of the bull's approach, and in a few short minutes the huge animal would reach them.

She cupped her hands to her mouth and shouted, "Becky! Jenny! Get over here, and hurry!" This time they heard her and started to run back.

Kitty climbed into the corral and managed to calm the mare who was hugging the fence. There was no time to saddle it, so Kitty grasped a handful of its mane and swung up on the mare's back. The whole process had taken mere seconds, but in her desperation it seemed like hours.

By now the girls had seen the bull and, screaming, were running toward the gate as fast as they could. But Samson had seen them, also, and his lumbering trot had become a thundering gallop. She had to create a diversion.

Kitty galloped across the pasture. She could see the bull was closing fast. Suddenly, to her horror, Jenny tripped and fell to the ground. Becky stopped and ran back to help Jenny to her feet as the animal charged toward the helpless girls.

Kitty cut across Samson's path, narrowly missing the lethal horns that could disembowel a man or horse. As she hoped, the bull swerved and followed. When she was far enough away from the girls, who were again racing toward the fence, she wheeled her horse and reined up.

Kicking up a cloud of dust, the bull lumbered to a halt and surveyed his new target like a boxer in a ring sizing up his adversary.

"Ya! Ya!" she shouted, taunting Samson to keep his attention.

Amazingly agile for the ton of flesh and muscle he carried, the bull pawed the earth, then lowered his head and shoulders, preparing to charge. A quick glance showed her the girls had at least another twenty or thirty yards to go.

When the bull charged, Kitty forced herself to wait until the last moment, then maneuvered the horse to the side. Pounding past her, the bull wheeled his bulk, then once again studied his target.

His snorting nostrils raised dust as he lowered his head to charge again.

Once again, Kitty deftly sidestepped the charge, and looked over to see the twins scamper through the fence. Relieved, she quickly wheeled the mare to leave. In her haste, though, she lost her grasp on the mare's mane, and slipped off the horse. For several seconds she lay flat on her back, too astonished to move—she'd ridden bareback scores of times and had never been unseated. She got to her feet just as the mare galloped away.

Kitty feared she was doomed; she could never outrun the bull—but she sure as hell wasn't going to stand there and wait for him to kill her. She took off in a run, with Samson in pursuit.

Jared had just ridden up to the hitching post in front of the house when the twins rushed up to him. Pointing to the pasture, they cried, "Help, Daddy! Kitty needs help! There's a big bull out there!"

"Get in the house and stay there," he shouted, then goaded the stallion to a gallop. The horse leaped the fence without breaking stride, and Jared raced across the pasture. By the time he reached Kitty, the bull was within a dozen yards of her. Jared leaned over the saddle and reached out his hand. Kitty grabbed it, and he swung her up behind him. She grabbed him around the waist and held on for dear life as they outdistanced the charging bull and reached the gate.

With no stationary target, Samson appeared to lose interest. He turned and trotted away.

Kitty was still trembling when Jared helped her inside, and she sank bonelessly down in a chair.

"That was close. Someone want to tell me what in hell happened?" Jared asked.

As usual, both twins began chattering at once, and Kitty sat in silence, waiting for her trembling to cease.

After hearing the full story, Jared gathered the twins in his arms, kissed the tops of their curly heads, then told them to go to their room while he had a quiet talk with Kitty.

"We love you, Kitty," they said, and kissed her on the cheek. Then they ran off to their room.

Jared knelt down and grasped her hand. "You okay, Kitty?"

"I will be as soon as I stop trembling."

"That was a very brave thing you did. You saved my daughters' lives. I'll never be able to thank you enough."

"It's not over yet, Jared."

"What do you mean?"

She looked at him desolately. "How do we get that damn bull out of that corral?"

For the rest of the day they kept the twins near the house. Kitty made dinner and Jared and the twins did the dishes. While she put away the clothes she had laundered, Kitty's thoughts were on the events of that day.

It had been one of extreme emotions: the incident in the shed that morning, the horror when the bull charged her . . . *the divine warmth of Jared's hands on her breasts*, the laughter of the twins wringing out the wet clothes . . . *the excitement of Jared's kiss,* how they would get that bull out of the corral . . . *the seductive huskiness of Jared's voice.*

"Stop it!"

She slammed the drawer shut and looked at herself in the mirror. *This type of thing happens all the time between men and women.* After all, they'd been together daily for weeks. They'd wondered about that kiss from the time they met; now it was over and they could put it behind them. Tomorrow they'd probably be laughing about it.

She nodded toward the image in the mirror. "Right."

*I don't think so,* an inner voice replied.

By rote, she went through the rest of the evening until the the twins fell asleep. Thoughts of sinking into a hot bath and soaking away the day's turmoil were foremost in her mind. She went into the living room and said good night to Jared.

"Kitty, will you sit down for a moment? I think we should discuss what happened today."

"It was just an accident, Jared. The bull got loose but those things happen sometimes. Mercifully, no one was harmed."

"I'm not referring to the damn bull. I'm talking about what happened between us in the shed."

"Mercifully, no one was hurt there, either." She smiled weakly.

"It's going to happen again, Kathleen."

"Not if I can help it," she said.

"You can't stop it, any more than I can."

"We're both adults, Jared. We have control over our desires."

"And I want you more than ever, Kitty. I'll marry you, if that's what you want."

She raised an eyebrow. "You're willing to make that sacrifice just to have sex with me? How romantic."

"I didn't mean to imply it would be a sacrifice. I meant, I know you wouldn't accept any other arrangement."

"We already have an arrangement, which I thought was working out fine: I'm your daughters' nanny."

"And how long do you think we can continue such an arrangement, when I can no longer look at you without wanting you? Even now I'd like to . . ." He threw up his hands in frustration. "Lord, how I hate trying to reason with a woman! I should just carry you to my bed and make love to you."

"Fornication is not *making love,* Jared. Love is what elevates us above the level of that bull out there in that pasture."

"Desire between a man and woman *is* a form of love, Kathleen."

"Hardly! Love satisfies the heart and the soul—desire merely satisfies the body."

"Are you saying that *every* time a man and woman are intimate, it must be for some soul-searching gratification rather than just physical pleasure?" He looked at her with astonishment. "My God, you've never really experienced real passion, have you?"

*Damn him! How dare he trespass on her most hidden uncertainties!* "How ridiculous! Of course I have; I was married for three years." The whole conversation was becoming more uncomfortable by the minute.

"I'm not referring to a pristine, lights-out, it's-Saturday-night-and-time-for-sex kind of passion. I'm talking about a ripping-the-clothes-off, no-holds-barred kind, where physical gratification is the only thought in your head, and whether your partner's in love with you is the farthest."

Kitty stood up. "I've listened to all I intend to, because if you're right, I'm thankful I don't possess that kind of passion. Good night, Jared."

She started to leave and he grabbed her arm and spun her around, crushing her to him.

"I believe you do, Kathleen. I believe that volatile nature of yours is meant for passion. I got a glimpse of it today in that shed." His lips bore down on hers in a hard, bruising kiss.

She tried to pull away, but he only pulled her more tightly against him.

Kitty whimpered under the pressure of his mouth. She parted her lips to gasp a much-needed breath, and he drove his tongue into the chamber of her mouth, plundering it with sweeping licks. She continued to struggle, but her efforts were useless against his overpowering strength as he bore her down to the floor.

"If you do this, it will be rape," she gasped, when he finally freed her lips.

"I would never do that, Kitty. I just want you to face your physical feelings for me."

Her eyes blazed in contempt. "I have no physical feelings for you."

"We'll see."

He ran his tongue across the swell of her cleavage, and she sucked in her breath. "I know what you're trying to do, and you're wasting your time. You're not going to prove anything with this senseless attempt."

Slipping a hand under her bodice, he cupped the swelling fullness of her breast. She jerked in response.

"Feels good, doesn't it, Kathleen?" His thumb toyed with the nipple as he continued the caress.

"What makes you think your uninvited groping could possibly feel good to me?"

"Ah, but you know it does. Just as it feels so good to me. You fill my hand, Kitty. Tell me you aren't beginning to feel that tingling in the pit of your stomach, that slow coiling in your loins that keeps winding and winding until it implodes into spirals of mindless ecstasy."

She couldn't defeat him physically, but if she wounded his pride she could win the battle of wills. "I think you overestimate your ability to arouse a woman, Jared, so please release me. I'd like to go to bed."

"My thought exactly—but once I prove my point, I don't think you'll make it as far as the bed." He released her breast to move his hand to the buttons of her bodice, and released them. The cool air on her breasts created a startling awareness of how much the heat of her body had intensified.

"Don't you have any pride?" she panted.

"Neither of us will, shortly."

His hungry gaze swept her breasts. "I've thought of your breasts often, Kitty: what they'd look like, what they'd feel like—and what they'd taste like." He dipped his head and ran his tongue across the peaked nipples. "I envisioned these pink tips, hard and pointed as they are now, surrounded by these dusky areolas, Kitty." He laved the areolas, then took a nipple into his mouth.

Her breath had begun coming in gasps, and she shifted beneath him. The movement became a tantalizing friction against his hardened arousal. She stopped the effort at once and lay still.

"Jared, stop and think of what you're doing."

"I've thought of nothing else. I thought of the fullness of these milky mounds," he whispered, cupping one in his hand. "How they can nurture a child, how they can nurture me. And I thought of what I would do to them." He lowered his head and suckled, licked, and caressed them until, despite her resolve, she began to whimper as she felt an agonizing excitement building within her. In panic, she tried to shove him off her.

Jared pinned her arms above her head and gazed down at her. "You should see those sapphire eyes of yours; they're black with arousal. That latent passion you've kept concealed for so long has surfaced, hasn't it? Let it out, Kitty. Show me the real woman who's concealed herself behind her widow weeds."

"I'll never forgive you for this." She turned her head to the side and refused to look at him.

He began an even greater assault on her senses. In a husky, tantalizing murmur, he described her body and what he would do to each part with his hands, his lips, and tongue when she asked him to. He whispered of the delights he had learned in India to increase a woman's ecstasy, and what he wanted her, in turn, to do to him. The more erotic his whispers, the more greatly aroused she became. Each spoken word drew a response from the core of her womanhood until she felt on fire, her body ablaze with a heat that kept swirling through her, blanketing her mind and body with no thought except to feel his kiss, his touch, his manhood driving into her.

She finally began to whimper and squirm beneath him.

"Are you still going to tell me you aren't feeling passion even though you don't love me? You want it now, don't you? You want me to rip off your clothes and you want to rip off mine. Isn't *that* the real truth, Kitty?"

"No! It's not true! It's not true." The cry was meant to convince herself, not him.

"How long are you going to keep lying to yourself?"

The passion that had possessed her with such enormity dissipated with his taunt—or was it because he was right?

He kissed her lightly, then pulled her to her feet. "How long are you going to pretend your body didn't respond? Don't be ashamed of what you thought, what you felt. Rejoice in it. Liberate the woman that's in you, Kitty. Give her what she wants. Free her, for God's sake."

Kitty felt more desolate than ashamed. She was numb and couldn't even feel anger toward him. He'd been right. She'd never suspected she could respond so wantonly to a man's touch—or words. There was a sense of decadence to it.

"Why did you do this to me, Jared? Is proving your point worth destroying our friendship?"

"I want you, Kathleen. But I want that woman I felt in my arms for a few seconds—the woman I could have had. But if I'd taken you then, you'd have hated me. So I'll wait. The day will come when you'll come to me as that woman. Until then, Kathleen Drummond, it will be business as usual."

"How can it be after this? It will be too awkward."

"It will be hard." He stopped and grinned. "A little humor, there. But I believe I can do it. And you're a remarkable woman, Kathleen; I know *you* can. We never need to mention it again."

Strangely enough, she knew he was right. She had learned something about herself tonight, and it was as shocking as it was revealing. For that brief, incredible time, she'd felt the most uninhibited, exquisite sensations she'd ever experienced. Certainly Ted had never raised this degree of passion in her. But Jared could—and did.

What he had tried to show her went far beyond sex. He saw her as an unfulfilled woman—and he was right. She had never brought the passion she harbored into any facet of her marriage—much less the marriage bed. That was the real guilt she suffered when she lost Ted. She had blamed herself, the Triple M, even the virility of the men in her own family, but she now realized it had nothing to do with what was—but more with what wasn't. She had let Ted go to his grave without knowing the real woman he married. And just as tragically, he had been satisfied with that woman. The reality was, they both were at fault—the guilt was no longer hers alone to bear.

Tonight had shown her that the two women within her were as opposite as the two men: Ted had been content with what she chose to be; Jared wouldn't settle for anything less than what she *could* be.

Fulfillment as a woman could come only from the latter.

Kitty looked at Jared and could feel no animosity, only gratitude. He had helped her to face some truths—in more ways than he even suspected. It would take some getting used to. And she knew he understood.

"Good night, Jared."

"Good night, Kathleen."

As soon as he heard her bedroom door close, Jared left the house, shed his clothing, and waded into the cold stream.

When Jared returned to the house, it was dark except for a single lamp burning in the living room. He turned it off and went to bed. For a long time, he lay hoping against hope that she'd come walking through his door. Finally, he drifted into sleep.

*The door opened and Kitty slipped through, then closed it and leaned back against it. She stood there in the shaft of moonlight that revealed the outline of her curves. The satin nightgown he'd bought her clung to the lush fullness of her breasts and hugged her slim hips as she moved toward the bed. He was so hard he ached.*

*His throat dried up and he couldn't speak or even swallow when she stopped at the bedside and lowered the gown's straps off her alabaster shoulders. With a deft shake of her hips that set the blood to pounding in his groin, the gown dropped down to her ankles and she stood naked before him—a moon-kissed goddess.*

*"I've thought of nothing else except the delights you promised me. Here I am, Jared. What are you waiting for?"*

*"Oh, Kitty! Kitty!" Reaching out for her, he rolled over*—and hit the floor! Dazed, Jared sat up and stared around at the darkened room.

"Dammit!"

# Chapter 18

*"Kitty, I want to make love to you," Jared whispered, the velvet strokes of his heated palm caressing her naked flesh.*

*"I don't want your love; I want your lust," she declared.*

*"Oh, Kitty! Kitty . . ."* The bed began vibrating beneath her.

"Kitty. Kitty!"

Her eyes popped open. Becky and Jenny were leaning over her, shaking her awake. They both looked wide-eyed with alarm.

"Kitty, get up. Something's wrong with Bluebonnet."

She jolted to a sitting position. "What do you mean?"

"We went out to feed her like we always do in the morning, and she was lying on her side."

Jenny's blue eyes reflected her sadness. "She looks real sick, Kitty."

"While I get dressed, go tell your father."

"We did. He went out to the barn."

Kitty wasted no time pulling on her jeans and grabbing a shirt. The mare must be foaling, and though she'd often seen it happen on the Triple M, she'd never assisted in one. She quickly pulled on socks and boots, and ran to the barn with the twins chasing after her.

Jared was kneeling beside the downed mare. "Is she foaling?"

He nodded. "She's not having an easy time of it."

"Is she having her baby now?" Jenny asked.

"I think so." Kitty pointed to some nearby bales of hay. "You girls go over there, sit down, and stay out of the way."

Jenny's lips began trembling. "Bluebonnet's not going to die, is she, Kitty?"

"No, sweetheart. She'll be fine once she foals. Now, go over and sit down like I told you to."

Clutching Bonnie and Bibbie, the twins climbed up on a bale of hay and waited with wide-eyed expectation.

Grim-faced, Jared said, "Looks like she's going to need some help."

"Poor thing." The horse began to thrash and Kitty patted the mare's neck to try and calm her. "There, there, Bluebonnet," she cooed. "It'll be over soon, girl." She took some hay and began to wipe the sweat off the mare's coat.

It appeared the mare had been in labor for some time: her lungs were heaving from exhaustion and her protruding eyes were glazed with pain and fright. Seized by a contraction, the mare tried to get to her feet.

"Hold her down," Kitty cried. "Don't let her stand." They struggled to keep the agonized animal from rising. The mare's eyes rolled upward under the pain of another contraction.

Another hour passed as they remained bent over the poor agonized animal.

"Dear God, I've only seen this bad a delivery one time. That's when the foal was turned wrong."

"You think that's the problem now?" Jared asked.

"It has to be." Kitty glanced up at him. He hadn't taken the time to put on a shirt, and the sweat-slickened muscles of his shoulders and arms were taut from the effort of holding down the mare. Even the dark hair on his chest and arms was plastered to his skin.

"What did you do then?" he asked.

"My father tied the foal's legs together and shoved them back into the birth canal."

As if in response to her words, the mare's body contracted in another spasm. Horrified, Kitty saw thin, flailing legs begin to emerge.

"We're going to have to tie them, Jared."

His gaze swept the barn for something to use. "Over there. Those reins on that peg."

Kitty dashed over and yanked them off.

"Hurry, Kitty. All four legs are out."

Precious seconds were lost as she looked around for something with which to cut the reins. Spying an axe, she lopped off a strip of the rein and raced back to the stall.

Drawing from her memory of her father's actions, Kitty carefully folded the foal's legs and bound them together, then pushed them back up into the birth canal.

"Hurry," Jared said, straining to keep the mare down as she struggled to rise.

"Now, this is the worst part. You've got to keep her from moving." She took a deep breath, then cautiously inserted a hand until she felt the foal. As gently as she could, Kitty began to slowly rotate it.

The mare heaved against the intrusion, and Jared flung his body across the panicked animal to hold her down. When Kitty succeeded in turning the foal, she began to ease it out. The mare stiffened in another spasm, and the foal's head and then shoulders slipped out the birth canal, its wedged body enveloped in a protective grayish membrane.

Jared stared in awe at the tiny figure. "Oh, my God!"

Kitty wanted to shed tears of joy, but she had to remain calm. "I need a knife to cut off that rein."

Jared jumped up to find one and she quickly pulled up the end of her shirt and wiped her tears. He returned with a knife and they disposed of the rein. The foal stretched out its thin, scrawny legs.

"Isn't it beautiful, Jared?"

"Looks all legs." He looked at her with admiration. "You did a superb job, Kathleen."

"Thank God we could help. Well, we've done our part, and now we should get out of here and let Bluebonnet do hers." She got up and left the stall.

Jared paused at the door for another look. He shook his head in wonderment, then closed and locked the stall.

Throughout the birth, the twins had sat quietly, mesmerized by the miracle unfolding before their eyes. Jenny was the first to find her voice.

"Is it a boy or girl, Kitty?"

"It's a little colt, honey. He's just beautiful. If you go up in the loft, you'll probably have a good view of the stall." She had avoided suggesting that sooner in case the birth ended tragically, but from what she could tell, mother and son were both doing fine.

Jared followed the twins into the loft and they stretched out on their stomachs. He put an arm across each of their shoulders, and drew them to his sides. Kitty came up and sat down beside them, hugging her knees to her chin.

The twins eyes glowed with rapt attention as they watched the scene below.

"What's Bluebonnet doing, Kitty?" Becky asked, when the mare began to lick the colt.

"I bet she's kissing her baby," Jenny said.

"No, honey, she's giving it a bath."

"I'd do that for her," Jenny said, "if she wanted me to."

"She's not only cleaning her foal, Jenny; she's familiarizing herself with its scent and it's learning hers."

The twins watched with fascination as the mare cleaned the colt's entire body. When she finished, the mare began to gently nuzzle the foal.

"Is Bluebonnet kissing it now?" Becky asked.

"No. Just watch; you'll see. It's time for the colt to stand up and test its legs."

"Babies can't stand up," she declared.

"Human babies can't, Becky," Jared said. "But animals can."

"Look," Jenny cried, "the baby's getting up."

The twins held their breath as the little colt raised itself up on its frail, wobbling legs. For several seconds it threatened to collapse, before it finally managed to straighten out its legs and stand firmly, under the protective head of its mother.

They all applauded and Jenny immediately asked, "Can we feed it now, Kitty?"

"No, for now, we all must stay away and let Bluebonnet care for her foal. She won't want anyone touching her little one yet."

"Who's going to muck out the stall?"

"We'll let your daddy do that." She grinned at Jared.

"I think we should let Kitty do it, don't you think so, girls? She's the horse expert."

Both of the traitorous little imps nodded in agreement. "Yeah, Daddy. She's sure the horse expert."

"And we don't want Bluebonnet to get mad at us."

"Thank you, Jared," Kitty replied in a singsong voice. "But we're not through yet; we still have Ole Samson to deal with out in the corral, don't we?" She smiled sweetly at Jared. "Fortunately for us, *bull* is your daddy's expertise."

She climbed down from the loft.

Once back at the house, both Kitty and Jared had to bathe. Cleansed and properly dressed, they lingered over coffee at the breakfast table, while the twins occupied themselves in their bedroom.

"That bull is still out there, Kitty. Do you have any suggestions?"

"We haven't ridden the the northern section of this ranch. I can't believe there aren't some heifers still around. The Carringtons never ran much cattle but they wouldn't have sold off their whole herd."

"What do you have in mind? Driving the bull to them?"

"It's a darn sight easier to drive a few heifers to a bull than to try to rope a bull and pull him to the heifers."

"What if we don't find any heifers?"

"We could get the horses out of the corral, but Samson could break through that fence, too, if he took a notion to. I'd feel more comfortable for the twins' safety if we got him back where he belongs. A couple of heifers will do it."

"Okay, madam, I'm game if you are. Let's go and find Delilah to keep Ole Samson happy. Will Bluebonnet be okay in our absence?"

"She'll be fine; all she needs is some fresh hay and water. We'll need to hitch up a buckboard, though."

"Why a buckboard?"

"To haul the barbed wire we'll need to mend the fence in that south pasture. That's probably how Samson got out. I'll get the horses; you'll find the wire in that shed."

"Maybe you should let me get the horses, Kitty. You never know what that bull will do."

"Not on your life, Captain. I'm not going near that shed again. I'll take my chances with the bull."

In a short time, they had hitched a team to the

buckboard, then loaded wire and the supplies they needed, including saddles and lariats to drive the cattle. The twins found it all very exciting.

When they reached the pasture, they discovered several dozen heifers and their calves grazing on the grama grass.

"You don't intend to drive all those cows, do you?" Jared asked.

"No, just about a half dozen of them."

"Half dozen! What's wrong with just one?"

Kitty looked at him with a pained expression. "Now, what do you think Samson was looking for when he broke out? Have a little pity on the poor heifer, will you? Let's get that team unhitched and saddled."

"What about the twins?"

"We'll ride double."

Cattle could be as stubborn as mules, and it was a slow process to round up six heifers without experienced help. When Kitty finally succeeded, they started for the south pasture, the calves trailing along with their mothers.

It was several miles, and when they reached their destination they found where Samson had broken through. While Jared straightened the fenceposts, Kitty cut out two of the heifers and drove them into the corral. Downwind from them, it didn't take Samson long to pick up their scent. He came thundering across the pasture.

As soon as she saw him coming, Kitty drove the heifers back behind the wire, and they trotted back to the rest of the herd.

When Samson thundered past without a glance

in their direction, Jared remarked, amused, "Now there's a man on a mission."

She didn't dignify it with a retort. "Let's just close up this fence as fast as we can."

"Kathleen, I've never strung barbed wire in my life."

"Then you're about to learn." She handed him a pair of wire cutters. "Stringing and mending fence is the first thing we teach greenhorns on a ranch."

They completed the task without any further threat from Samson—who was well occupied elsewhere.

The day had been long and strenuous, but one they probably would recall throughout the rest of their lives.

With dinner and dishes out of the way, Kitty and the twins were sitting on the floor stringing beads.

This time Jared wasn't trying to hide behind a book or newspaper. He watched them openly, unaware of the grin on his face as he listened to their conversation.

The twins were still awestruck by the birth they had witnessed that morning. When they had returned to the house earlier, they rushed to the barn and spent the next hour in the hayloft staring in wonderment at Bluebonnet and her colt.

"Can we give the baby a name?" Jenny asked as they continued to string the bright crystal beads.

"It's not ours to name, honey. Bluebonnet and her foal belong to the Carringtons."

"I sure wish we had a ranch," Becky said. "Then

we'd have baby horses, too, and could give them the names we want."

Jenny leaned over and whispered, "Daddy said he'd buy a ranch."

"Really?" Kitty glanced at him in surprise.

He shrugged. "I said I'd think about it."

"And just where would this ranch be located?"

"He wants it near Dallas, like this one is," Becky volunteered.

Kitty laughed. "I think he'll have trouble finding one. These are gentlemen ranches—not working ranches."

"What does that mean, Kitty?"

"Well, the people who own these ranches really don't have to make their living from the ranch. These small ranches are more like summer homes for those who want to escape the city's heat. My Aunt Garnet's from Georgia, and she told me that was quite popular among the wealthy in the South before the Civil War. The Carringtons' ranch is larger than most of the surrounding spreads, but Jake Carrington is a very wealthy man like the rest of them."

"That may be true, Kitty," Jared said, "but I've known Jake Carrington since we were young. He has a genuine love for ranching, but a keener mind for business. Railroads, banking, and technology have always challenged him. He told me recently that he believes black gold will be the next bonanza in Texas."

"Black gold? What's that, Daddy?"

"Oil, Becky. It'll be as valuable as gold one day.

Matter of fact, he's invested heavily in a stretch of land called Spindletop near Beaumont, down on the east coast. He persuaded me to do so, too. But if Jake Carrington wasn't such a visionary when it comes to business matters, he'd probably have built La Paloma to the size of the Triple M."

"Is your daddy a gentleman rancher, too, Kitty?"

"No, Jenny; the Triple M is a working ranch. It's his livelihood, as well as my uncles' and their families. Everyone depends on the ranch. We run forty or fifty thousand cattle a year, and we grow, make, or raise practically everything used on the ranch."

Becky's eyes rounded. "Wow! That sure is a lot of cows."

"Bet you've got a lot of horses, too," Jenny said.

"That's right, honey. And a lot of people to ride them. Now, let's see that charm of yours."

Becky removed the bracelet she wore. She'd never taken it off from the time Jenny had given it to her. The cheap chain had turned green, but the charm was fine. Kitty slipped the soldier charm on the middle of the half-beaded string.

"There, that looks good. After you finish stringing the beads, you'll be able to wear it around your neck just like Jenny does the locket you gave her."

"This is a good idea, Kitty," Jenny said, delighted by the result of their efforts.

"You always have good ideas, Kitty," Becky agreed.

*Yes you do, Kitty,* Jared thought. In the past weeks he had come to marvel at the workings of her mind. She never shrank from any challenge, and met the mundane with fresh and interesting approaches.

He couldn't say the same of his ideas, and none was more stupid than the one he'd had last night. How in hell did he ever think he could come that close to having sex with her and then pretend it hadn't happened? Lord, how he wanted her! If he didn't get it off his mind, he'd end up in that damn cold stream again tonight.

He got up to walk it off.

Kitty watched Jared's broad shoulders disappear through the door. Had he become bored with ranch life? The last couple of days had been anything but boring, but maybe that wasn't the excitement he yearned for.

Maybe his mind was on last night, and those unbelievable moments of passion they'd shared. Though they'd vowed never to discuss it again, how could she *not* think about it?

They had opened Pandora's Box, and there was no closing it now. No matter what they tried to tell themselves.

# Chapter 19

The following morning, Jared hitched up the buckboard and they rode to nearby River Bend. The small hole-in-the-wall town got its name because it was located on the bank of the Trinity where the river curved toward Dallas.

Nearer to Fort Worth than Dallas, the town had sprung up around a Spanish mission built at the time of the conquistadors. Shortly after the turn of the century, abandoned by the church, the mission had become a whorehouse frequented mainly by Mexican army officers until Texas won its independence. During the Civil War, a Comanche attack wiped out most of the town's residents. Those who survived moved to more populated areas such as Dallas and Fort Worth, which had become hubs for the famous Texas cattle drives in the decade that followed.

River Bend was typical of the hundreds of small towns in the West that were becoming extinct due to the advent of the railroad. Since it was not on a railroad line—or map—the town was only accessible by horse, the river, and a small freight line in Fort Worth that serviced it on a monthly basis. The merchants depended on local ranchers and drifters passing through for survival.

The advantage to living in the town was that it held little attraction for the lawless. It had neither a saloon, a prostitute, nor even a bank to rob, thus negating the need for a sheriff. It offered neither a local newspaper nor the latest Paris fashion, but could boast of a telegraph office and a small Catholic church—a carryover from its early religious roots. The Protestants congregated on Sunday mornings in the back of Ben Wilks's general store.

Kitty loved the town on sight. Although it was smaller and less advanced than Calico, the town nearest the Triple M, River Bend captured some of the flavor of her hometown.

While Kitty went into the store with a shopping list, Jared went to the telegraph office—which also served as the post office—to check for any mail. The twins stayed outside to look at an armadillo penned in a small area.

"Boy, armadillos sure are ugly," Becky said after studying it for several minutes.

Jenny nodded. "With all those hard shells on it, you couldn't even pick it up and hold it on your lap. It doesn't make sense why anybody would even want one."

"Probably just because it's so different."

"I'd rather have a colt. Least it's pretty to look at, even if you can't hold it on your lap."

Sitting down on the ground, they bent their knees in front of them, propped up their elbows, cradled their heads in their hands, and proceeded to stare more at the armadillo.

After several more minutes of intense concentration, Becky said, "It doesn't even move."

"It doesn't say anything, either," Jenny added.

"Sure seems dumb to keep an animal that doesn't move or say anything. 'Least dogs bark, and cats go meow."

"And horses neigh and cows moo."

"Yeah, even a donkey goes hee-haw, but this dumb animal doesn't do anything," Becky declared.

Whenever anyone in passing paused and looked at it before moving on, the two girls shook their heads.

"Sure doesn't make sense."

"Sure doesn't." Finally Jenny said, "Let's go back. It's hot in the sun, and I'm getting tired of waiting for it to move."

They got up and moved to the shade of a building and sat down again.

"We'll wait just a little longer. Maybe it's getting ready to move, and then we'd miss it."

Two pairs of jean-clad legs and dusty boots came into view and paused at the pen. Suddenly Becky sat up straight when she saw that the spur on the left boot of one of them was missing a rowel. She looked up and recognized the outlaw who had robbed the train.

Poking Jenny, she whispered, "Look, that's the man who robbed us on the train."

"What should we do?"

"Let's go and get Daddy."

"But Daddy doesn't have a gun," Jenny said. "What if they shoot him?"

"Yeah, we better not do that. You go and tell Kitty. She'll know what to do. I'll stay here and watch them." The two men started to move on. "Hurry, Jenny, before they get away."

Jenny raced back to the general store, and Becky got up and followed the two outlaws.

The men went into the livery stable. One of the doors was ajar so she approached it cautiously, then glanced back, but there was still no sign of Kitty or anyone else on the street.

Becky sneaked up to see what they were up to, and peeked inside. Suddenly a hand reached out and yanked her into the stable.

"What the hell are you sneaking around here for?" The man was much younger than the one from the train.

"I'm looking for my cat."

"We ain't got it." He released her. "Get the hell out of here."

Just then the other outlaw came out of one of the stalls. He recognized her immediately. "Eddie, that's the kid from the train we held up."

Becky turned and dashed away. Eddie caught up with her at the door and grabbed her by the scruff of her neck, breaking the string of her beads. The necklace fell to the ground and the crystal beads rolled in the dirt. He yanked her back into the stable.

"Now look what you've done—you broke my beads!" She was so angry she kicked him in the shins. Cursing, he grabbed his leg.

Becky tried to run again, but the other one grabbed her.

"Let me go!" She kicked and squirmed to get away, but he managed to hold on to her. When she started to cry for help, he clamped a hand over her mouth and she bit him.

"Muzzle this brat," he shouted, slamming the door shut. "And bar the damn door before someone walks in."

Eddie gagged her with a bandana and the other man cut up a rope and bound her wrists together, and then her feet.

"What in hell are we going to do with her?" Eddie asked.

"We'll have to take her with us and get rid of her somewhere else."

"I ain't gonna be no part of killin' a kid, Gus. Let's just leave her here and ride away."

"And have a posse of vigilantes on our ass? They're worse than a sheriff's posse; they'll hang us on the spot. No, we'll take her with us. Nobody'll know she's gone till we're long out of here. Now get saddled up and let's ride."

Kitty had just paid for the supplies when Jenny burst through the door. "Kitty, we saw him! He's here!"

"Who, Jenny?"

"That man who robbed us on the train. He's here with another man."

"Oh, no! Where's Becky?"

"She's watching what they're doing."

"Oh, dear Lord."

"What should we do, Kitty?"

Kitty looked at the storekeeper. "Is there a sheriff here?"

"No, ma'am. We've got a vigilante committee, but we ain't had much call to use it."

"Now's a good time—there are some train robbers in town."

"Well, ma'am, I reckon they're just passing through. We get all kinds here, but they don't stir up any trouble when they're in town."

Kitty couldn't waste another minute talking to this bumpkin while Becky's life could be in danger. She bolted out of the store into the arms of Jared, who was on the verge of entering.

"Hey, what's the hurry?" One look at her and his tone changed. "What's wrong, Kitty?"

"The twins recognized the outlaw who robbed the train we were on. Jenny came to tell us, and Becky's following him."

"She's *what*?"

"You heard me."

They ran out to the street, but could see no sign of her. Kitty started shouting for her. "Where can she be?"

"We'll find her. Jenny, you get back into that store and stay there."

"I want to help find my sister."

"I said *stay* there."

Jenny turned back to the store, but when Kitty and Jared hurried away, she followed.

Kitty and Jared searched each street. There was

no sign of Becky, and they had no way of knowing if she might have followed the men inside one of the buildings.

They reached the livery and found both doors locked from the inside. "Becky," Kitty shouted. When there was no answer, Jared tried calling for her.

He shook his head. "It's locked up. We're going to have to start checking—" He knelt down and picked up a handful of dirt.

"What is it, Jared?"

Several crystals sparkled among the dirt granules. "Aren't these the—"

"Yes. She's in there. And they must have discovered her. Oh, God, Jared, what if they've harmed her?"

He glanced up at the loft window. "I'm going in."

"How?"

"With those." He pointed to several bales of hay stacked up to be taken inside.

They shifted the bales under the window and Jared climbed up and entered. He heard voices and crawled across the loft. Two men were in the stall below, and he recognized one from the train.

"You heard those people calling, Gus. We should have forgotten the girl and ridden out of here, like I said."

"Shut up, Eddie, and let me think. They ain't calling no more, so they must have moved on. We best get out of here now."

Jared glanced behind him and saw that Kitty had followed him into the loft. His eyes swept the stable in search of Becky and finally spotted her squirming, trussed-up body in one of the empty stalls. He felt a rise of blind anger.

"Eddie, go up in the loft and take a look to see if there's anyone out there."

Jared and Kitty dived into a pile of hay in the shadowed corner. When Eddie came up and went to the window, Jared stole up behind him, tapped the man on the shoulder, and when Eddie turned around, Jared socked him in the jaw. Eddie hit the floor with a loud thud, sending loose straw raining down from the loft.

"What in hell are you doing up there?" Gus shouted.

Jared put a finger to his mouth to warn Kitty to be quiet. He slipped the pistol out of Eddie's holster and handed it to her.

"Eddie, what's going on?" Gus shouted.

"I fell," Jared mumbled, in the best imitation of Eddie he could muster.

He knew he couldn't climb down without Gus seeing him, so he'd have to leap down.

"Eddie, is it clear out there?"

"Yeah."

Gus opened the stable doors and went over to pick up Becky. "Time to go, brat."

Jared knew he would never have a better chance. Leaping from the loft, he landed on Gus, driving them both to the floor. A shock of pain shot to his leg and for several seconds he fought the blackness that threatened to overpower him. Gus used those precious seconds to roll away and reach for the gun at his hip.

"Don't try it," Kitty ordered. She stood on the top

rung of the loft ladder with Eddie's gun pointed at Gus. "If you like living, you'll slip that Colt out very slowly and lay it on the floor." There was a telltale click when she cocked her pistol. "Hear that, Gus? That's the only cock of a pistol I want to hear. Understand?"

"Okay, lady." He did as she told him to do, and then raised his hands in the air.

"Where're your other two friends, Gus?"

"How do I know? We broke up weeks ago."

"And what did you do with the ring you took from me when you robbed the train?"

"You think I remember what I did with some cheap ring? I probably gave it to some whore in the last town I was in."

"The ring may have been cheap to you, Gus, but it had value to me. I ought to put a bullet through you just for pleasure."

"Leave him to me, Kitty," Jared growled. "Gus and I have some unfinished business."

"Are you sure you're okay, Jared?"

"I'm fine. Take care of Becky." Impervious to the pain in his leg, he advanced on Gus with clenched fists.

As Kitty untied Becky, the sound of blows and groans filled her ears as Jared and Gus fought. As much as she feared for Jared's welfare, she dared not interfere.

"Did they hurt you, honey?" she asked, hugging the child in her arms.

"No, they just tied me up, and Gus said they would get rid of me." Becky frowned. "That doesn't make any more sense than that dumb armadillo. If he wanted to get *rid* of me, why was he taking me with him?"

"Oh, honey." Kitty hugged her again at the thought of what might have happened if they'd gotten there too late.

Jared delivered a knockout punch and Gus dropped to the floor. Jared came over and gathered Becky in his arms.

"Are you okay, baby?"

Becky slipped her arms around his neck. "I'm okay now that you're here, Daddy." Then she crawled around on her hands and knees until she recovered her precious locket.

"I'll get you a chain for it, honey," Jared assured her.

Kitty caught a glimpse of a shadow crossing the door and realized Eddie must have regained consciousness and climbed out of the loft. She grabbed a lariat off a nearby peg and ran outside. She didn't have to go far.

Eddie was frozen in his tracks, staring with mouth agape at Jenny standing in his path.

"How did you get out here? I just saw you inside."

When he saw Kitty, Eddie started running. Twirling the lariat above her head, she chased after him. When the fleeing outlaw looked behind to see if she was gaining on him, he failed to notice an obstacle: the armadillo had burrowed beneath its pen and now lay in his path. He tripped on the hard-shelled animal, breaking his stride. Kitty released the lasso. The rope looped over his head and shoulders, and she gave it a hard tug that jerked him off his feet. With a deft motion, she twisted the rope around his hands and feet, hog-tying him.

Jenny ran up to her, and smiling with satisfaction, Kitty said to the wide-eyed child, "That may not have been championship speed, but I wouldn't be a MacKenzie if I couldn't rope a critter."

When Becky came up and joined them, the two girls clasped hands and stared at the armadillo, which had begun to burrow itself into the ground again.

"Guess that dumb armadillo finally moved," Becky said.

Jenny nodded. "Yeah. Maybe it's not so dumb."

Jared dragged Gus up to the several residents who were gathered around the trussed-up criminal. "Do you have a jail in this town?" he asked.

"Yes, but we don't have much call to use it," the storekeeper said.

"You do now. These two men are train robbers, and there may be a couple more of them around. Wire the Ranger office or the sheriff in Dallas. Either will be glad to take them off your hands." He looked at Kitty. "Are you ready to go, Annie Oakley?"

"Any time you are."

Jared took Becky's hand, Becky clasped one of Jenny's, Jenny slipped her hand into Kitty's, and four abreast they walked back to the buggy and drove away.

Slim and Martha returned a short time after they got back to the ranch. Jared and Slim walked to the barn, and Jared told him of the events that had taken place in their absence.

After dinner, he sat down and read the wire he'd received from Charles, informing him that all of the remodeling had been completed and the rooms were ready to be occupied. It looked as if they could return to Dallas in the morning.

After tearful good-byes to Bluebonnet and her colt, Straw, and Berry, the twins climbed sadly into the buggy early the following morning.

Jared reined up when they topped a rise, and they all glanced back for a final look at the ranch house set snugly in the trees.

Horses grazed peacefully in the corral, and two strawberry ponies trotted over to the fence and cocked their heads in their direction.

The twins raised their hands and waved. Tears rolled down their cheeks as they murmured plaintively, "Bye, Straw. Bye, Berry."

"You, too?" Jared said, when he saw tears welling in Kitty's eyes. "Women!" He flicked the reins. "All I can say, ladies, is between charging bulls, foaling colts, and chasing outlaws, if one is looking for peace and quiet, a ranch is hardly the right choice."

Kitty glanced askance at him, and then sang out, "And the skies are not cloudy all day."

As the buggy rolled along, they all raised their voices in harmony.

"Home, home on the range . . ."

# Chapter 20

As soon as they got home, the twins raced upstairs. Their sadness was put aside at the sight of their newly decorated rooms. It would be an extensive job to replace the toys that had been destroyed, but the girls could hardly wait to get started.

Kitty's room was so elegant she was thrilled. Mildred told her that Jared had insisted the decorator use a floral pattern in the wallpaper.

As she started up the stairway to thank him, the bell tingled. Seeing no sign of Charles she opened the front door. Waiting on the porch was a small man dressed in gray from his top hat to the spats on his polished shoes. A pencil-thin mustache formed a caret under an unusually long nose, and his lips were almost as narrow as the mustache.

"*Bonjour,* madame. Are you the lady of the house?"

"No, I'm not. Actually, there is no lady of the

house; this is a bachelors' household, and I'm the children's nanny."

He raised a monocle to his right eye and studied her intently. "I see." Then he arched his brow and the monocle dropped from his eye.

Kitty grabbed for it instinctively, and discovered that a gold chain attached the eyeglass to the lapel of the man's suit coat. She let go of it, and the monocle dropped to his chest and dangled from the end of the chain.

"I'm sorry, I thought your eyeglass was falling."

His nose began to twitch like a rabbit's. "Will you inform Capitaine Fraser that Monsieur Francois Poinget is here to see him, madame."

"Captain Fraser rarely sees guests, Monsieur . . ."

"Poinget. Monsieur Francois Poinget." His lips narrowed to a thinner line than the mustache. "Capitaine Fraser is expecting me, madame."

"Oh, I beg your pardon. Please come in." Kitty stepped aside and the little man entered.

"May I be of service, Mrs. Drummond?"

Kitty turned around and smiled in relief to discover Charles had arrived on the scene. He could take over. "Charles, this gentleman—"

"Monsieur Francois Poinget." The Frenchman pronounced each syllable slowly and distinctly.

"Monsieur Poinget is here to see Captain Fraser, Charles."

"I'm sorry, sir, but Captain Fraser doesn't see anyone. He is recuperating from an injury."

Poinget sucked in his lips and now only a slit remained for a mouth. "I have an appointment," he hissed through his clenched lips.

"Very well, sir. If you'll be seated, I'll inform Captain Fraser you are here."

Poinget sat down on a chair and crossed his gloved hands over the top of his walking stick.

"I'll tell him, Charles." Kitty started up the stairway, passing the twins descending them. "I'll be right back, girls. Wait for me on the front porch."

Becky and Jenny went over and stood staring at the stranger.

Poinget doffed his hat. "*Bonjour, mademoiselles.*"

"Who are you, mister?" Becky asked.

"I am Monsieur Francois Poinget." He raised the monocle to his eye and peered at them.

"Does it hurt much when it grows, mister?" Jenny asked.

"I beg your pardon?"

"Your nose," Becky explained. "It looks like Pinocchio's. My sister wants to know if it hurts when it grows."

"And who is this Pinocchio, mademoiselle?"

"A little boy whose nose grew every time he told a lie."

Jenny rolled her eyes in wonderment. "Boy, mister, you *really* must have told some whoppers."

Hand in hand, they skipped outside to wait for Kitty.

Jared called out for her to enter when Kitty rapped on his door. She stuck her head in. "Jared, there's a Monsieur Francois Poinget waiting in the foyer."

Jared glanced up from the letter he'd been reading. "A what?"

"It's a who, not a what. Monsieur Poinget says he has an appointment with you."

"An appointment? Oh, yes, I forgot. He must be the caterer."

"A caterer?" Kitty stepped into the room. "Are you planning a party, Jared?" She couldn't believe Jared Fraser would even attend a party, much less give one.

"Yes. I've decided that since my return from India, I've been rather reclusive."

"To put it mildly."

"And my daughters' nanny suggested I make an effort to socialize more for their sake. I believe her exact words were, 'to stop closeting yourself behind a closed door.' "

"Then I advise you not to keep the monsieur waiting." She started to leave, then pivoted. "Oh, by the way, I'm taking the twins for a walk."

"I was hoping you'd attend this meeting with me. I'd like to get your opinion."

"I promised the twins. They're waiting for me right now. Besides, Jared, I know nothing about planning a fancy party. Back home all we had were square dances and shivarees."

"Will you listen, at least? I trust your judgment, Kitty. Tell the girls to be patient and I'll take them to lunch." He looked up with a sly glance. "Their nanny once told me females enjoy going out to lunch."

"I can hardly refuse such a complimentary request; but I didn't think you trusted my judgment about anything."

This time his look held astonishment. "Are you serious? I trust you with my children, don't I?" He came over to the door. "I think we've kept Monsieur Poinget waiting long enough."

Once downstairs, Kitty told the twins of the change of plans. They were delighted to hear they were going out for lunch and immediately dashed upstairs to dress for the occasion.

After a short conversation establishing time and date, Monsieur Poinget toured the lower level. When they reached the dining room, he announced with an all-consuming sweep of his arm, "This rug and furniture will have to go, Capitaine, and the chairs and table in the foyer, of course."

"And where do you plan for them to go, Monsieur Poinget?" Jared asked in a patronizing tone.

"Have you not an attic, Capitaine?"

"Yes, we do. But my intention is to have a garden party."

The caterer's eyes bulged in indignation. "Francois Poinget does not prepare fine cuisine to have it consumed by flies and beetles."

Hoping to cool the rising tension, Kitty felt impelled to join the conversation. "So it's your intention to serve the food indoors."

"But of course, madame. Shall we move on."

When they entered the kitchen, Poinget raised his monocle and looked around. "The size appears to be adequate." He removed his gray gloves, pulled a white pair out of his pocket, and put them on.

With arms akimbo, Mildred watched Poinget's inspection of the kitchen. Each time the Frenchman ran a gloved finger over the top of a cabinet or the carvings on the doors, he checked the finger for any sign of dust.

"Hmmm." Bending down, he opened the oven door and stuck his head inside for a closer look.

Charles quickly put a hand on his wife's arm to restrain her when Mildred made a threatening move in that direction.

Finally, Poinget removed the white gloves and replaced them with gray ones. "It will do, Capitaine."

"My relief is boundless, Poinget."

Kitty knew Jared's temperament well enough to know he was on the verge of picking up the little man and tossing him out the door. From the fire in Mildred's eyes, she feared that if Jared didn't do it, Mildred would.

"Shall we discuss the menu, Capitaine?"

"Why don't we do that in the library?" Kitty hurriedly grabbed Poinget's arm and literally tugged him out of the kitchen.

Jared and Poinget spent the next quarter hour deciding between foreign or domestic wine, caviar or liver paté, sandwich kabobs stuffed with salmon or miniature bouchees stuffed with chicken; and, of course, the necessity of serving Parmesan cheese with the profiteroles was of major importance to Monsieur Poinget. They finally got down to deciding what the main entrée should be.

"May I recommend lamb baked in a soubise sauce, Capitaine?"

"No. Many of my guests are cattlemen, not sheepherders."

"Then perhaps pork fillets wrapped in puff pastry."

"Make that beef fillets and a rib roast. You can throw a ham on the grate, too," Jared said.

Poinget threw up his hands in despair. "Capitaine, Francois Poinget does not prepare barbecues. He prepares fine cuisine."

"Poinget, Jared Fraser doesn't serve his guests anything he wouldn't want to swallow himself. It's more important to my palate for the cuisine to be prepared finely than to be merely prepared fine cuisine, Poinget. So be sure that rib roast is served rare."

Poinget blanched. "As you wish, Capitaine. And what is your preference for a vegetable?"

"Potatoes."

"Prepared in what fashion, Capitaine?"

"I'll leave that up to you, Poinget. I like potatoes any way they're cooked."

"And for a dessert?"

"A variety; just make sure one of them is chocolate. My daughters like chocolate." He glanced at Kitty. "And flowers. Flowers everywhere. Mrs. Drummond is very fond of flowers."

Becky and Jenny were sitting on the stairway with bonnets in place and purses in hand when Kitty and Jared showed Poinget to the door.

"Congratulations. You won," Kitty said as soon as the door closed behind the Frenchman.

"Won what?" Jared asked.

"The contest to see which of you could sound the most pretentious."

His chuckle brought a smile to her face. "I knew I

could count on your vote, *madame*," Jared said. "Shall we go to lunch?"

Kitty soon found out how well known Jared was in the community. He took them to the same restaurant where she and the girls had dined before. The maître d'hotel greeted Jared like a long-lost friend and set the waiters into a flurry with instructions to make sure Jared got nothing but the finest service. On the way to their table, Jared stopped half a dozen times to shake hands or exchange a greeting.

People glanced at her with a speculative gleam of interest, but other than introducing her, he made no attempt to explain she was the twins' nanny.

Once they were seated, a stunning blond woman approached the table. "Jared, what a surprise!"

He got to his feet and kissed her hand. "Hello, Stephanie."

"This is the last place I'd expect to see you, darling," Stephanie said.

"I promised to take my daughters to lunch. Girls, this is Mrs. Lorimer. Stephanie, these are my daughters, Rebecca and Jennifer."

"How do you do, Mrs. Lorimer," the girls said simultaneously.

"Oh, Jared!" Stephanie's hand fluttered delicately to her breast. "These precious girls are your daughters!"

"And I'd like you to meet Mrs. Kathleen Drummond."

The woman's blue-eyed gaze narrowed on Kitty. "How do you do."

"Fine, thank you," Kitty replied.

"Have we met before, Mrs. Drummond?"

"Not that I remember, Mrs. Lorimer."

"Mrs. Drummond is a cousin of Elizabeth Carrington and Cynthia Kincaid."

"Really! I know both of them quite well. Have you been in Dallas long, Mrs. Drummond?"

"A few weeks."

"Well, dear, we must meet for lunch someday."

"Yes, of course." Thank goodness she didn't plan on remaining in Dallas permanently, Kitty thought in relief.

Stephanie turned back to Jared. "Now, you naughty boy, when will I see you again?"

The twins broke into giggles.

"Father's not a *boy*, Mrs. Lorimer," Becky said.

"You're right, darling." She smiled seductively at Jared. "Your father is all man."

Kitty lowered her gaze and stared at the shiny porcelain plate in front of her. She could feel the hot blush consuming her. Why she was blushing was a mystery to her; Stephanie Lorimer should be the one embarrassed. Her open flirtation with Jared was disgusting.

She raised her eyes enough to peer at Jared through her lowered lashes. He looked impatient and she was glad. Then she told herself it didn't matter to her one way or the other.

"Well, I must be off. I'm keeping my friends waiting. It was a pleasure meeting all of you. And, Jared darling, do come calling. You're always welcome."

Kitty raised her gaze in time to see Becky roll her eyes at Jenny.

"Mrs. Lorimer sure is pretty, Daddy."

"Yes she is, Jenny. Quite lovely."

"I don't think she's as pretty as Kitty. Do you think so, Daddy?" Becky asked.

"Beauty is in the eye of the beholder, Becky." His eyes searched Kitty's face. "Mrs. Drummond is *very* beautiful."

To disguise another rising blush, Kitty picked up the bill of fare and hid behind it.

Throughout lunch, Jared entertained his daughters with stories of elephants and Bengal tigers. As Kitty listened with the same fascination as the twins, she realized this was the first time Jared had spoken of his experience in India. Little by little, he was revealing more of himself to his daughters—and to her.

Later that night, after the twins were in bed, Kitty tapped on Jared's door. As usual, he was at his desk when she entered.

"Do you have a minute, Jared?"

"Of course. What is it, Kathleen?"

"It's regarding your party."

"That's a coincidence. I just finished preparing the guest list to take to the calligrapher tomorrow."

"I know how to do calligraphy, Jared. I'll be glad to write them for you."

"I don't want to impose on you, Kathleen."

"It's no imposition. I enjoy doing it, and there are few occasions to do so. Come to think of it, perhaps a job with a printing firm might be a good option to pursue in New York."

He handed her several sheets of paper. "Here's

the invitation, and there are about fifty names on the list."

Kitty read through the text of the invitation. It would not be difficult to complete; as with anything Jared said, the message was succinct.

Her eyes lit up with a sudden thought. "If you take over the children, I could devote my whole day to it and finish them tomorrow."

Jared chuckled. "Beware of Greeks bearing gifts. I shall be delighted to spend tomorrow entertaining my daughters."

"And, of course, you won't fail to inform me when you find out what a delightful experience that actually is."

"I've already discovered that for myself. Before I interrupted you, you said you have a question regarding the party?" he said.

"Yes. I wonder if you'd object to purchasing new party dresses for the twins. I think they'd be thrilled."

"Didn't you just buy them new dresses a few weeks ago? I don't want to spoil them."

"Actually, they didn't select new dresses earlier, because they couldn't buy the same dress."

"Since I no longer have the problem of telling them apart, the girls can dress as they wish."

"Thank you. I know they'll be happy to hear that."

"Thus far, in the past few minutes, you've convinced me to agree to two of your wishes. You're a remarkable woman, Kathleen Drummond. If you'd been at Napoleon's side at Waterloo, the French flag would be flying over the British Empire today."

She did feel quite pleased with herself. As Jared had pointed out, she'd succeeded in accomplishing two goals today on the twins' behalf. He'd proven not to be the ogre she once thought him to be.

On the other hand, she mustn't forget that Jared Fraser was a military man, not the type to lose a battle without putting up a fight. Was there a strategy that lay behind that brown-eyed gaze? The situation called for a quick withdrawal—a change of subject.

"Do you think only two weeks is an adequate amount of time to notify your guests, Jared?"

"They'll come no matter how short the invitation. They're curious to get a look at me."

"Jared, you're too cynical."

"I know Dallas society, Kathleen. I should have made this a masked ball and disappointed them."

"If you expect me to be sympathetic, you're mistaken. The wound on your cheek has healed and is merely a narrow scar that will ultimately become less noticeable. Furthermore, when you act like this, I find the scar to be less unsightly than your disposition."

He gave her an irritated glance. "You can be a real harridan, Kathleen. I've asked myself a dozen times why I tolerate it."

"Then why do you, if it troubles you that much?"

"Because I'm left with only two options: one is to discharge you, which I have no intention of doing; the other is to marry you, which *you* have no intention of doing."

His sudden statement caught her off guard. She decided he was attempting to be humorous, so she laughed.

"I'm glad you found it amusing, Kathleen." His voice had sharpened with rancor. Walking over to the window, he stood gazing out of it, his hands crossed behind his back. She could tell by the set of his shoulders that he was mad.

The old Jared would have ordered her out of the room; the new Kitty fought the urge to go over and comfort him.

"I'm sorry, Jared. I thought you were joking. Why are you so angry?"

He whirled and glared at her with eyes darkened with fury. "Because you drive me to it, Kathleen."

She was just as capable of losing her temper as he. The difference between them was that she didn't take it out on everyone within shouting distance. "If that's true, then perhaps you should discharge me."

As quickly as his anger had materialized, it dissipated, and his tone became speculative. "You know I won't do that. In truth, I enjoy our relationship. You understand me. Not too many people do."

"I enjoy our relationship, too, Jared, but from the beginning, it was meant to be only temporary. Remember?"

"What if I told you I want the relationship to be more than temporary, Kathleen? The time we spent on the ranch led me to believe that we could have a pleasant life together."

She couldn't believe her ears. "Are you seriously suggesting marriage again?"

"What if I am?"

"Jared, you don't want to marry me; you just want a mother for your children."

"I *know* what I want, Kathleen. Furthermore,

many successful marriages are those of convenience. A good match can be often more enduring than love."

"And you think if we marry it would be a good match."

"I think it would be an extraordinary match."

"Extraordinary or not, Jared, I have no desire to marry at this time. Since I desire children of my own, I most likely will wed again one day, but if and when I do, I'd never marry a man if I didn't love him, or he didn't love me."

"Then why not consider a different arrangement for now?"

It took her several seconds to grasp his meaning. Appalled, she asked, "Are you suggesting I become your mistress?"

"Why not? Physically, we aren't repulsed by one another. The incidents on the Carrington ranch proved that."

"This conversation has become ludicrous. If you'll excuse me, I'm going to bed," she said coldly.

She got no farther than the door before he grasped her by the shoulders and spun her around to face him. There was a dangerous gleam in his eyes, and she recognized the raw hunger that lurked in their depths.

"Ludicrous, Kathleen? Is it so ludicrous to think that one day you'd come to desire me as much as you did your deceased husband?" She turned her head away and he forced her to look at him. Cupping her face in his hands, he gazed down at her. "Or is it so ludicrous, Kathleen, to hope that one day you could bestow on me one of those soft smiles you give so freely to my daughters, my brother, my father? We were happy on the ranch, weren't we?"

"Yes, we were happy, but you were a different man there. Is it this city that changes you? Your friends? Here you turn into a pretentious, cynical snob. That's not the man your daughters have grown to love. You talk of marriage, but which Jared Fraser would I wed? You told me to release the real woman inside me, to let her out. Well, which is the real Jared Fraser: the Jekyll or the Hyde?"

She couldn't continue to look into his compelling eyes, so she turned her head away again. "Please, Jared."

Her breath caught in her throat when his fingers on her chin forced her face back to his again. Lowering his head, he murmured, "Please what, Kathleen? Is that a plea to hold you or release you?"

From the instant his mouth covered hers, the kiss was masterfully forceful—so sensually provocative that every nerve within her seemed to leap to its demand. She struggled to resist the temptation of it, but as the kiss deepened her body began to throb in response.

His mouth freed hers just long enough to draw some much-needed breath, then reclaimed hers again. His tongue and lips began the same tantalizing torture her body remembered so well. She closed her eyes and savored the moment.

When she opened her eyes, he was gazing down at her with the same bemused expression she recalled from their first kiss.

"If you can tell me now that you don't desire me as much as I do you, I swear I won't try to touch you again. Tell me that tonight you won't be thinking of me when you're lying in bed tossing and turning, as I will be."

"I can't tell you, because it would be a lie. But a marriage built on sexual desire? I don't think I ever could. I need time, Jared. This is all too sudden . . . too confusing. I must have time to think."

"How much time do you need?"

"I'll give you my answer the night of the party."

For a long moment he held her gaze in one of his soul-searching probes that could set her legs to trembling, then he released her. His hands were an erotic slide along her arms as he stepped away.

"Good night, Kathleen."

"Good night." She slipped out the door.

Troubled, Kitty returned to her room. Life had suddenly taken another very complicated turn. Thoughts of Jared flooded her head as she undressed for bed. Ever since those two incidents on the ranch, she had wondered how it would have ended in the shed or on the floor of the ranch house. Wondered! She had fixated on it, fantasized about its outcome.

Jared appeared convinced they could sustain a marriage on sexual desire. She had once believed she could never desire any man unless she loved him. He had proven what a false belief that had been; she desired him as much as he did her. But it *wasn't* enough to sustain a marriage. The devil's advocate in her argued that, on the other hand, it wouldn't have to be. They had other things in common: a mutual love of the twins and a love of literature, just to name two. And their enjoyment of mentally challenging each other would certainly prevent a marriage from ever being dull.

But she needed to feel loved, too. Her marriage to Ted might not have been the passionate, erotic one a marriage to Jared would be, but at least it was a loving one. And she couldn't imagine a marriage without that basic ingredient. Could the twins' love fill that void? Her mouth curved in a soft smile. How she loved those girls. Could the thought of knowing she'd never have to leave them deceive her into believing she could be happy in a loveless marriage? No! Impossible! Her body might be satisfied, but her heart could never be.

You couldn't build a marriage—have children—without love. She smiled tenderly. Without being a mommy and daddy.

If Jared merely wanted a mother for the twins, it was clear the blond, man-eating shark in the restaurant today would be amenable to such an offer. And it was clear they'd been intimate. She hated the woman—she envied her.

Kitty sat down at the dressing table to brush out her hair. Leaning forward, she studied her image in the mirror. Her lips were still swollen from his kisses, and she brought her hand to her mouth. Her fingertips tingled from the contact, as if they were touching his. Oh, dear Lord, how she desired him!

Jerking her hand away, she yanked the pins out of her hair and brushed it vigorously until her scalp stung, but that failed to shake the feel of his lips on hers. Disgusted, she put aside the brush and looked sorrowfully into the mirror.

"You're pathetic. It's bad enough you have to

fight him, without having to fight your own treacherous body, too."

Kitty pulled a robe on over her nightgown and headed for the library to select a book to read.

It was going to be a long night.

# Chapter 21

After Kathleen left, Jared stood deep in thought, staring into his snifter of brandy. Drat the woman! She was an enchantress. He took a deep swallow. Stubborn? Yes! Irritating? Lord, yes! Unreasonable? Beyond a doubt! But an enchantress, nevertheless. The most fascinating and desirable woman he'd ever known.

His daughters adored her and so did he. She was no vain, self-absorbed shell of a woman like Diane, or a man-preying piranha like Stephanie. Kathleen Drummond was the perfect woman of his dreams. She had the intelligence to challenge his intellect and the sensuousness to fire his passion. She had love and compassion in her heart to be a mother to his children and a mate to him. And by all that was holy, he wasn't going to lose her—he was going to marry her even if she still loved her husband!

For the next hour he tried unsuccessfully to read, then put the book aside and got out of bed. The pain in his groin was becoming unbearable. Those sapphire eyes, the tilt of that determined little chin, those luscious curves . . . She fired his blood. From the first time he saw her, thoughts of her plagued both his mind and body. And the incidents in the shed and the ranch house had proved to him she wanted him, too. She was just too damn stubborn to admit it. But he'd seen the admission in her eyes that night, and thank God she'd recognized he was right.

But that didn't help him now. His body couldn't take even another kiss until he knew the outcome would be physically fulfilling.

Maybe he should force the issue and compromise her? Then she'd have to marry him to preserve her reputation. But she'd hate him if he did. He couldn't bear her hatred—he needed her love.

The more he thought of her, the more aroused he felt. Lord, how he wanted that woman! He tottered between the thought of a cold bath or a drink, and settled for the drink.

Moving to his desk, Jared discovered the decanter was empty. Since he couldn't sleep anyway, he decided to go down to the library. There was a brandy decanter there.

The room glowed invitingly from the fire burning on the hearth. He paused in the doorway and sucked in his breath. Deep in thought, Kathleen sat on a rug in front of the fireplace

His gaze caressed her. In the fire's glow, streaks of carmine shimmered in the glossy silkiness of her dark curls.

And at that moment he realized that his feeling

for her went far beyond a physical need for satisfaction—he was in love with her. He'd vowed that he'd never again utter those words about any woman, but Kathleen had proven him wrong again. She was twined around his heart. She had rejuvenated his life, had brought laughter into it again, and above all had brought love into it again, and he was a better man for it.

They both had wounds to heal in mind and body—peace to make with their own consciences, but for now, there was tonight—and the need to feel her in his arms.

He stepped into the room, closed the door, and turned the key in the lock.

Oblivious of his presence, Kitty stared into the fire, mesmerized by the dance of the flames. She had no idea how long he'd stood watching her before she sensed his nearness. Slowly, she turned her head and their gazes locked, desire blatant in his eyes. Her feminine instincts sensed that this time there'd be no turning back—no last-minute reprieve.

She made no effort to rise, but watched wordlessly as he came over and stood towering above her. His eyes were warm with reverence, gentleness, desire, and love—everything she had yearned for from him.

He lowered himself beside her, and his touch was exquisitely tender as his fingers caressed the delicate line of her jaw.

"We've let so many precious moments pass, Kathleen. Are we to waste this one, too?"

Firelight glimmered on the firm line of his jaw, the sensual draw of his lips, his compelling, soul-probing brown eyes. The quickening of her breath matched the rhythm of his, and for that interminable minute their hearts beat as one.

Gently, lovingly, she traced the scar on his cheek. "No, Jared, we won't waste this one." With a sigh of surrender, she closed her eyes and parted her lips.

His weight bore her back to the floor as his mouth covered hers, warmly, persuasively, and possessively. It tantalized and electrified, devouring the breath from her.

When breathlessness forced them apart, he covered her face with tender kisses, then reclaimed her lips. Despite the heat of their bodies, she shivered when he pulled her against him and slid his tongue past her lips, exploring the chamber of her mouth with warm, sweeping probes. Slipping her arms around his neck, she returned the kiss with the fervor of her own passion.

"Kitty. Kitty," he murmured in a reverent litany and pressed a kiss into the softness of her hair.

Lowering his head, he trailed a line of tantalizing kisses along the column of her neck as he inched the robe off her shoulders. Immediately, his gaze was drawn to the hardened tips of her breasts poking at the thin cambric of her nightgown, and it fueled his passion to lust. He lifted the gown, his mouth laving the aroused nipples as he pulled the garment over her head.

Kitty lay naked before him, her body shimmering

like translucent satin in the light from the flames. His warm touch stroked her shoulders and slid the length of her arms; then he filled his hands with her breasts.

For an infinitesimal moment, she wondered how her body appeared to him. Was he comparing it to Diane's, or any other woman he'd known? Those troubling uncertainties were instantly sent adrift by a floodtide of sensation when he lowered his head and closed his mouth around a breast, toying at one and then the other until her gasps turned to moans.

He raised his head, and she opened her eyes. "You're so beautiful, Kitty. So beautiful."

She reveled under his hungry gaze. It thrilled her, drove her passion to a greater urgency. Her fingers trembled as she unbuttoned his shirt. Then they were body to body, their flesh as naked as their desire for each other.

And as he had done to her, she slowly trailed her fingers along the slope of his shoulder, across the muscular pectorals, and into the dark patch on his chest. The soft hair tickled her fingertips, and she dipped her head and licked one of his nipples.

With a ragged gasp, he buried his hands in her hair and drew her head away, his need for her overpowering. He gathered her into his arms so that she rested on his arms beneath her, and reclaimed her mouth with breath-devouring kisses.

The pressure of his firm thigh anchored between her legs caused the heated core of her being to throb with such intensity she began to feel mindless. She curled her arms around his neck and wrapped her legs around his long muscular one, amazed to discover how the softer curves and hollows of her body conformed to the hard, muscled length of his.

His hands, his mouth, his tongue acquainted themselves with the most intimate parts of her body, returning always to the temptation of her parted lips. She in turn familiarized herself with whatever parts of his body fell under her reach.

Her exploring fingers lightly stroked his erection, and she swallowed his groan as he rolled over onto his back. Slipping his hands under her arms, he suspended her slightly above his head with her hips and legs resting on his. The bulge of his arousal pressed against her in a heated pulsation that electrified every nerve in her body. He closed his mouth around her breast and began to suckle. Crying out his name in rapturous sobs, she grasped his shoulders and threw back her head, reveling in the ecstasy.

With a feral growl, he rolled over and entered her. As the tempo of his movements escalated, her passion neared explosion. Her pulses pounded, and she wrenched breath into her heaving lungs.

His jaw was clenched tight, the muscles in his neck tautly corded. He was so male—so masculine.

When the final moment came, and their bodies and minds were flooded with waves of sensation, he kissed her and murmured his love.

As his breathing slowly returned to normal, he stretched out on his side, propped up an elbow, and cradled his head in his hand to gaze at her.

"What are you thinking about?" she asked.

"I have a confession to make."

"I believe there's a church several blocks from here. I'm sure you'll find a clergyman," she teased.

"I thought if we made love, you might marry me to protect your reputation."

She sat up and pulled on her nightgown. "So, I am to believe this was a cold, calculated act on your part?"

He lay back. "Curses, foiled again! You're on to me, Mrs. Drummond."

She didn't believe him for a moment. Her face curved in a smile. "You must think I'm a fool."

"I didn't, until now."

Kitty leaned over him and began to trace the outline of his lips with her finger. "Well, I'm not. You made love to me because you've wanted to do so—"

"Forever," he said. He nipped at her finger and sucked it into his mouth.

"It would be rather vain of me to think that you've wanted to do so all of your life, when you haven't known me the better part of it."

"You're wrong. The better part *began* when you climbed on the same train that I was on, my love."

"Darn you, Jared. You're going to make me start crying."

He kissed her lightly. "Then I should warn you that as soon as I get my strength back, I intend to try again to convince you to marry me. I won't let you go, Kitty. Not now."

He hugged her closer and she sighed and laid her head on his chest. "I'm glad, Jared."

"About what?"

"That you didn't let this moment pass."

"Only one thing could have prevented me from making love to you, Kitty."

She raised her head and saw that his eyes were now somber. "What?"

"If you'd said no."

Fascinated by his mouth, she let her fingers toy with his lips. "I wanted you to make love to me, Jared. I've wanted you to for a long time."

"I would have, but I knew you were still in love with your husband."

"Oh, Jared—I'll always love Ted, but until I met you I never realized what had been missing from my marriage. I see now I was more of a friend to him than a wife. More a nursemaid than a lover.

"From the time we were children, I loved Ted and worried about his health. Our marriage just was a continuation of that friendship. We enjoyed each other's company and were comfortable with each other. We never quarreled or questioned each other's motives. You challenge me, Jared; you force me to confront my motives—and my beliefs."

"As you do to me, my love. I think that's why I fell in love with you."

"Ted and I never had anything new to discover about each other. Even our lovemaking fell into the same comfortable pattern as the rest of our relationship."

"You mean no raw passion, no ripping off the clothes."

"Never."

"No arguments. No kiss and make up."

"None."

"So he never saw how exciting your eyes can be

when you're angry. Or felt the need to cut off that anger and kiss you until you beg for more than just a kiss."

"Have you?"

"Practically every day from the time I met you."

Her hand traced one of his dark brows. "And I never knew the quickening of my heart when he entered the room, no roman candles when he kissed me, no wanting to kiss away the pain of his heartache."

"Have you now?"

"Practically every day from the time I met you."

"Oh, God, Kitty." He kissed her with an intensity that went beyond the body and claimed her soul. Whatever occurred from this moment on, she belonged to him.

She sighed and drew a deep breath. "Ted was the dearest, kindest man I've ever known. His loss has left a void in my life that no one can ever fill. I loved him dearly, and I'll never regret marrying him. But I believe he'd regret our marriage—even our friendship—if I spent the rest of my life mourning him. My parents tried to convince me of that, but I couldn't accept their argument at the time."

Jared kissed her forehead and gave her a quick squeeze. "Then maybe I wasn't being too hasty in asking you to marry me."

Kitty remained silent.

As much as she wanted to, she couldn't make that commitment tonight: she wasn't certain Jared really loved her. Her brother and cousins had often laughed over how they thought they were in love every time they had sex. Was Jared making that mistake with her?

His voice had turned guarded. "It's not a complicated question, Kitty: a simple yes or no will do."

"I'll give you my answer in two weeks, Jared, just as I said before. And now I think it's time to go to bed."

"Stay here, Kitty. This can be our bed for tonight."

"If the twins find us here, how would we explain what we were doing all night?"

"You know those little minxes have been hoping we'd get together as much as we have."

"I don't think their young minds are quite ready for *this*, Jared Fraser." She tried to duck out of his reach, but he was too fast for her and managed to grab her ankle. She tripped and ended up sprawled across him. Eye to eye, their gazes met, and devilment danced in his.

"Jared, behave yourself. Think what would happen if they came down here this very minute."

"They'd find the door locked."

"Ha—then you *did* plan this all the time. I thought it was spontaneous! A precious, never-to-be-forgotten moment."

"I don't know about you, but I'll never forget it." The laughter left his eyes and they filled with tenderness. "It was beautiful, Kitty."

Her eyes were wide and luminous as she looked at him. "I think so, too."

Brushing aside some errant strands of hair clinging to her cheek, he grinned like a mischievous child. She eyed him suspiciously.

"What are you thinking now?"

"How ugly you are."

She broke into laughter. "Oh, you're an impossible man! Why do I tolerate you?"

She tried to get up, but he pulled her back. Laughing like children, they rolled over, and this time he ended up on top. He suddenly winced and rolled off her.

She could see he was in pain. "What's wrong? Is it your leg?"

He lay back and stretched out his leg. "Yes. It cramps up every now and then."

She glanced down at the gash that ran from his knee to his groin. Her heart ached for him, and she lowered her head and trailed kisses along the scar.

"Oh, God, Kitty," he said in a husky murmur. "You're so sweet. So incredibly sweet." He pulled her back into his arms. Her body tingled wherever their flesh touched, and once again the smoldering passion between them sparked to life. "Lord, how I love you, Kathleen Drummond," he whispered, and covered her lips with his own.

Throughout the night they touched and kissed, made love, or lay contented in each other's arms. Toward dawn she fell asleep, curled against him with her head on his chest.

The ashes had long cooled on the hearth when Jared pulled on his trousers, gathered up their scattered clothing, and picked her up in his arms to carry her up to her bed.

He paused in the doorway to look back at the rug in front of the fireplace.

As long as he lived, he would revere that spot.

# Chapter 22

"Wake up, Kitty. Wake up."

Kitty was shaken awake and opened her eyes to find the twins leaning over her.

"Good morning." She sat up and yawned.

"Did you forget that today's the party?" Becky asked.

"We get to wear our new dresses," Jenny added, excitement shining in her eyes.

The party was the farthest thing from Kitty's mind at the moment; just the memory of Jared's touch lit a burning excitement in her body. Every whispered word and moment of their fervent love-making was vivid in her mind.

For the past two weeks, since that first glorious night in the library, he had come to her each night. He had raised her body to heights she never suspected existed. And in those rapturous moments they had come to know each other's bodies as well as they knew their own.

"Wait till you see it, Kitty," Becky said. "There's some men in the yard and they're stringing lanterns between the trees!"

"And putting up tables," Jenny added. "Oh, it's going to be so lovely!"

"It certainly sounds like it. You girls go back to your room and I'll join you as soon as I get dressed."

They scrambled off the bed and ran back to their room, from which they had a bird's-eye view of the activity below.

Kitty drew a bath, the memory of last night's love-making etched on her mind, body, and soul forever.

The shocking realization that she had fallen in love with him came unexpectedly that day as she'd watched him pushing the twins on the makeshift swings he'd hung from a limb of the very tree that had helped to save his life the night of the fire. It had triggered the beginning of a long list of memories they had shared since that night, and she'd realized that somewhere tucked among those memories was the truth of her feeling for him. It had not been during the heat of his passionate lovemaking or the delight that brought to her, but rather recalling how he now embraced his daughters with loving arms. No longer did he disguise the real Jared—the caring and tender man who had finally found what he'd yearned for throughout his life.

This was the Jared she'd come to love.

In her heart, she hoped their lovemaking might lead to her becoming pregnant. How she would love to carry Jared's child! But she doubted that these past few nights could produce what three years of marriage to Ted had failed to do.

Her heart now was committed to Jared—as well as to the twins—but her mind still asked if his heart was as committed to her.

Right now, the only thing she knew for certain was that the memory of Ted would not keep her from loving and committing herself to Jared. That was the one belief she had once thought would be impossible to overcome, but she had made her peace with her conscience and the guilt she had struggled with for the past two years.

She plopped the sponge into the water. Why was she doing this to herself, dredging up doubts? She'd had enough of this pondering the rights and wrongs of her feelings and his. There were no certainties in life. Enough was enough! She was old enough—intelligent enough—to *know* what was in her heart: the time had come to seize the moment.

Tonight, she would tell Jared she'd marry him.

Kitty hummed exuberantly as she dressed. It was a glorious day, and it would be even a more glorious night: when Jared made love to her, she'd tell him she would marry him.

On the verge of going downstairs, Kitty paused at the top of the stairway and glanced at the balustrade. The satin finish of the hard-carved Chippendale banister had been polished until it shone—and she'd been fighting a particular child-like urge from the time she stepped into the house. Glancing around to make sure she wasn't being observed, she swung her leg over the railing and rode it down.

The railing was as slick as ice, and she flew off the bottom right into Monsieur Francois Poinget, who had just rounded the stairway. The impact knocked him off his feet, and she ended up sprawled across the startled Frenchman.

*"Mon Dieu, madame!"*

She jumped to her feet. "Oh, I'm so sorry, Monsieur Poinget. Are you all right?"

When he stood up, she began to brush him off. He pushed her hands away. "That is not necessary, madame." He squared his narrow shoulders, and muttering something in French, he walked away.

Giggling, Kitty headed for the kitchen.

The twins were seated at the kitchen table awaiting breakfast. After pouring herself a cup of coffee, Kitty slid into a chair and joined them.

"I'm told there's going to be a party here tonight."

The girls giggled with pleasure.

"Wait till you see outside, Kitty," Becky said.

Jenny nodded. "It's like a fairyland."

"And outside is where it better stay," Mildred declared. "Morning, dear." She put down a platter of eggs and toast. "Eat up, darlings. It's probably the last decent food you'll have today."

"Aren't you excited, Mildred?"

"It'll get more exciting if that Mon-ster Poin-gut don't stay out of my kitchen."

"It is monsieur, madame, Francois Poin-shay," the Frenchman articulated, entering the room.

Mildred shook the frying pan at him. "Well, this is *my* kitchen, you little gallnipper, and I don't want you stepping foot in it."

Poinget's eyes pinched into narrow slits and his mouth puckered in disdain. Once again, Kitty was amazed to see his nose actually twitching.

"I shall speak to Capitaine Fraser about this."

"You do that, Mon-ster Poin-gut."

The little man threw his hands up in the air and stormed off in a huff muttering, "Poin-shay. Poin-shay."

"Mildred, weren't you a little hard on him? You know he and his assistants must have access to the kitchen."

"I know, Miz Kitty, but he makes my skin crawl. Ain't we got enough varmints in Texas without letting a little weasel like him cross our borders?"

For the next few hours Kitty struggled to keep the twins from being underfoot. But much to the annoyance of Monsieur Poinget, the girls wanted to watch everything that was happening. Flinging his arms in the air in a gesture of hopelessness, the Frenchman erupted in a huff of temperament.

"Francois Poinget cannot create with this distraction, madame! He insists the mademoiselles leave the house or remain in their rooms."

Confused, Becky asked, "We thought *you* were Francois Poinget, mister."

"Maybe he's a twin, just like us," Jenny offered in explanation.

"Hey, mister, do you have a twin brother?"

"Francois Poinget has no twin brother." Poinget clasped his hands together in a prayerful position and looked heavenward. "Help me, *mon Dieu*."

Kitty hustled the children away. Since getting them to concentrate on lessons was an impossibility, she took them for a long walk along the creek to work off some of their energy.

However, by the time they returned, Kitty was

exhausted and the twins seemed to have been energized.

In late afternoon Kitty convinced them to lie down and rest since they would be up beyond their usual bedtime. She doubted they'd sleep, but it gave her the opportunity to kick off her shoes, take off her clothes, and stretch out on the bed prior to bathing and dressing for the party.

A light tap sounded on the door and she sat up. "Come in."

Jared entered and closed the door behind him. He came over and sat down on the edge of the bed. "Did I wake you?"

"No." She lay back with her head on the pillow. "I was just relaxing. The twins are so excited; they've worn me out. Did you know this is their first party? They've never had a birthday party or attended one."

"I never knew that. I've got so much to atone for on their behalf."

"Well, if I have anything to say about it, there'll be a big change on their next birthday."

He reached out and stroked her cheek. "It's my hope you'll have *everything* to say about it." Leaning over, he kissed her.

His kiss caressed her lips as gently as his hand had just done to her cheek. She parted her lips, and his mouth moved over hers with slow, drugging kisses that sent shivers of desire coursing through her.

Raising his head, he asked, "You haven't forgotten what today is, have you?"

She slipped her arms around his neck. "How could I?"

"Have you made up your mind, Kathleen?"

She wanted to cry out her answer, to shout it from the rooftop—but it would be more romantic to wait until later that night, when all the tension and excitement of the party would be behind them. They could make love until the sun rose.

"Later, Jared. I'll tell you later . . . tonight."

The last word came out in a gasp when he pressed a moist trail of kisses down her neck. The musky scent of him was an aphrodisiac, and a shiver raced along her spine. She arched against him. His body was warm and hard—and felt so good. He reclaimed her lips in deep, demanding kisses that she returned with all the hunger of her own passion.

When he parted her robe, though, she protested, "Jared, we mustn't. Not now."

His gaze swept her nakedness. "*Now* is when we must," he whispered in a husky murmur.

Lowering his head, he tantalized her nipples with his tongue and then drew the hardened peaks into his mouth. For several exquisite seconds he toyed and suckled until she had to press her lips into his hair to muffle the sound of her moans. His tongue traced a trail to her navel, and her heart began to hammer when she guessed his intent. The heat of his hands skimmed along her hips and parted her legs as he continued his mouth's descent.

Her gasps grew to groans when his mouth found the throbbing core of her femininity. Her head whirled dizzily her senses throbbed, and her body rocked with exquisite tremors of fulfillment.

She lay in the afterglow of the ecstasy, then opened her eyes.

Jared was divesting himself of his clothing. The hunger glowing in his eyes rekindled her appetite, and she blushed at her insatiable hunger for him.

He lowered himself to her and the hard angles and muscles of his body found the soft curves and valleys of hers. His gaze devoured her with such tenderness, she felt her heart would burst.

"You're blushing, Kathleen. It's so beautiful."

Then he kissed her, and once again swept her up to that glorious summit of ecstasy.

As soon as Jared left, Kitty quickly bathed, then checked on the twins. To her amazement, they'd fallen asleep. She woke them up, got them properly groomed and in their new dresses, then returned to her room to finish her own toilette as the guests began to arrive.

The twins had followed her and sat on the edge of the bed, watching her every move. Kitty forced herself not to rush her preparation. When she was satisfied with her grooming, she finally put on the dress Jared had bought her.

She had never owned such an exquisite gown. The cream-colored dress flowed to the tips of her cream slippers, where a pink underskirt peeked out from under the scalloped hem. The enormous puffed sleeves, so fashionable at the time, had pink, lavender, and cream layers. Elegantly simple, it had a fitted bodice with a low, square neckline in front and back. Two pink streamers, attached to the snug lavender band around the waist, dropped in swags to below the knees.

"You look so pretty, Kitty."

"Why, thank you, Jenny. So do you and Becky."

"I bet you'll look prettier than that Mrs. Lorimer," Becky said.

Kitty gave her a quick squeeze. "And I bet you're just a little bit biased, *Mademoiselle* Fraser."

She hugged the girls to her sides and studied their images in the cheval glass mirror.

"We do look pretty good, don't we?"

"We look beau—ti—ful!" Becky said.

"Stu—pen—dous!" Jenny exclaimed, adding her approval.

Kitty nodded. "I think you're right. Shall we join the party?"

Laughing, hand in hand, they hurried from the room.

Engrossed in conversation, Jared glanced up and sucked in his breath. Kitty was descending the stairway holding Becky's hand on her right and Jenny's on her left. The sight of them took his breath away.

They were so beautiful, his chest swelled with pride. They were his family. *His family.* It was still difficult for him to think in those terms. When he was a young man he'd harbored such a hope, but the fantasy had been broken by the disillusionment of his marriage.

Now the fantasy was within his grasp. He wouldn't let it slip through his fingers again.

Seeing their grandfather, the twins raced over to Jonathan, and Jared reached out a hand to Kitty. "You look very lovely, Kathleen."

Kitty blushed. "Thank you."

He loved the way she blushed after a compliment. It added an appealing quality to her already beautiful face.

He had to excuse himself to greet some newcomers, so Kitty joined Jonathan and the twins.

"You're the loveliest woman here, my dear," he told her.

"Thank you, Jonathan."

Kitty looked around in curiosity. With the exception of Stephanie Lorimer, the rest of the guests were strangers to her, and she smiled in relief when she saw Dave and Cynthia arrive.

As the evening lengthened, the party continued to go well. Despite how irritating Monsieur Poinget was personally, he proved to be an exceptional caterer. The food tasted as appetizing as it looked, and everyone appeared to be enjoying it.

A small orchestra had encouraged most of the guests to move indoors to dance, and although Jared's injured leg kept him from taking to the floor, Kitty enjoyed a final waltz with Dave Kincaid before she had to take the twins upstairs to bed.

# Chapter 23

"She's so unaware of how beautiful she is," Jared said, when Kitty and Dave waltzed past.

"What did you say?" Cynthia asked.

He hadn't realized he'd spoken the thought out loud. "Nothing important."

"Jared Fraser, look at me." When he glanced up hesitantly, a soft gasp escaped her. "You're in love with her."

Jared felt a rise of resentment. "Does that surprise you?"

"I guess I shouldn't be; Kitty is very lovable."

"And I'm *un*-lovable, is that it?"

"Frankly speaking, Jared, I've never had the impression you're the warmest person I've ever met."

"I guess I had that coming. But Kitty's changed me."

"Obviously. The Jared Fraser I knew would never

make such an admission. Does Kitty feel the same way about you?"

"Are you asking does she feel the same as I do about her, or as you do about me?"

Cynthia laughed in delight. "Now, that's the old Jared I'm familiar with. You were always such an irritating precisionist."

"You MacKenzie women are remarkable. Candid to a fault, but remarkable."

"It's in our blood, Jared. I don't think any of our husbands married us intending to keep us barefoot and pregnant."

"And I've observed from your choices of husbands, none of the women married men they expected to dominate."

"Nothing would be more boring. Tell me, Jared, have you met Kitty's parents?"

"No, why do you ask?"

"If you think the women are remarkable, you should meet the MacKenzie men. I'll never forget my first glimpse of Luke, who is Kitty's father, and his brothers, Flint and Cleve. Their father was my father's only brother, but Uncle Andrew died before my sisters and I were even born, so we never met him. We didn't even know we had cousins. My father lost contact with his brother after Uncle Andrew left home; then Dad went to California during the gold rush, and finally settled in Colorado. He heard later that Uncle Andrew died at the Alamo."

"Yes, Kitty mentioned that her grandfather had died fighting for Texas independence. She's very proud of her Texas legacy. So how did you finally meet your cousins?"

"It was an extraordinary coincidence. Cleve MacKenzie and I happened to meet on a ship returning from England and discovered we were cousins. He was the handsomest man I've ever met, and still is, I should add." She smiled coquettishly. "That's not to take anything away from Dave.

"But getting back to the story, our cousins and their wives came up to Colorado for Angie and Giff's marriage. You've met the Giffords, haven't you?"

When Jared nodded, Cynthia continued, "The sight of all three of them took our breath away. They're tall Texans, incredibly handsome men, and formidable. An army unto themselves. And they all married women who are just as strong and impressive."

"Cynthia, did you ever meet Kathleen's husband?"

"Oh, yes, on several occasions. Ted Drummond was likable enough and he certainly loved Kitty; but between you and me, Jared, I think he took advantage of her."

"Good God, Cynthia, he obviously was ill. The man died young."

"I know, and that's very tragic. But from what I understand, he had Kitty waiting on him even when they were youngsters."

"Kathleen puts herself into that role, Cynthia. I've noticed she does the same with the twins, too. She dotes on them."

"The irony of it is that she left the Triple M because she felt her parents were being overly protective."

Jared was struck with a sudden thought. "Would

she deceive herself into believing she loved a man just because he needed someone to take care of him?"

"Of course not. She *would* love him."

"Hmmm. So the weaker one appeared, the more she'd love him."

Cynthia eyed him suspiciously. "Jared, what are you thinking? I'm not going to stand by and let you manipulate Kitty into marrying you."

"I'd only stoop to that as a last resort. But if necessary, my dear Cynthia, I shall use whatever means I must to get Kathleen to do so." He bowed slightly. "And thank you; you've been very helpful." He winked at her and walked away.

When the waltz ended, Kitty went to get the twins, and Dave joined Cynthia.

He gave her a wary look as soon as he saw her. "Oh, oh! I've seen that look before. What are you up to, Miz Sin?"

"Oh, nothing much," she said casually. "You know how you're always telling me to stop trying to play cupid with people's lives?"

Dave groaned. "You didn't! I hope it's not whom I think it is."

"Whom do you have in mind?" Cynthia asked with an innocent smile.

"You were talking to Jared Fraser while Kitty and I were dancing. It's him, isn't it?"

"Lucky guess."

"And who's the woman?"

Cynthia shook her head. "It's so obvious—but men are so blind."

"Come on, Thia, who is it?"

"Kitty, of course."

"Kitty!"

"They make a perfect couple, and she already adores his children. It's a match made in heaven. Just like ours, lover." Cynthia kissed him on the cheek.

"Isn't there an old-fashioned custom about marrying for love?"

"Sweetheart, they're already in love. I merely planted a thought in Jared's head. A subtle suggestion in case all else fails."

"Knowing you, it was probably about as subtle as a sledge on a rail spike." He grabbed her hand. "Come on, Miz Sin, let's dance."

Kitty beamed with parental pride as, poised and politely, the twins passed among the guests saying good night. They looked like little ladies.

Jared stopped Kitty at the foot of the stairway. "You're coming back down, aren't you?"

"Yes, at least until the Kincaids leave."

"Good. Would you like me to come upstairs with you?"

"You're the host; it wouldn't be proper to leave your guests. I'll be back soon."

Jared stood at the foot of the stairway and watched the three most important people in his life climb the stairs. When they reached the top, he turned back to mingle with his guests.

It took Kitty a while to get the excited twins settled in bed.

"We sure had a good time at the party," Becky said as Kitty tucked her in and kissed her good night.

"Uncle Seth told us we were the belles of the ball," Jenny said. "Can we have another party soon?"

"You'll have to ask your father about that."

Becky's face scrunched into a frown. "I don't think Daddy had a good time at the party."

"What makes you say that, honey?"

"Poor Daddy." Jenny sighed. "He didn't get to dance one single dance."

"I suspect that soon his leg will be better, and there'll be other dances."

"I hope so," Becky said. "That Mrs. Lorimer asked Daddy to dance, and he told her he couldn't because his leg was too sore."

Jenny rolled her eyes. "Then that Mrs. Lorimer said that they should go out in the garden and sit the dance out together."

"Really?" Kitty could see she should have paid closer attention to Jared, instead of accepting dance invitations from other men. "Did he go into the garden with her?"

Becky shook her head. "No. Daddy told her he had to keep an eye on his guests."

The twins squelched their laughter and Jenny said, "We could tell he didn't want to go with her, 'cause the only one he was watching was you."

"And you weren't even one of the guests," Becky said.

"So, he was watching me, was he?" Kitty was pleased.

"Kitty, why would somebody hold a candle to you? You could get burned," the girl said earnestly.

"Was that why Daddy kept watching you? In case somebody did that?" Jenny asked.

"What are you talking about, dears?"

"We heard Daddy tell Poppie that you're so lovely—"

"That no one there could hold a candle to you," Jenny finished. "I bet that's why he kept watching you—in case somebody tried to do it."

Kitty tried not to show her pleasure. "Enough talk. It's time you get to sleep."

When Kitty bent down and kissed Jenny, the youngster slipped her arms around her neck. "Will you do us a favor, Kitty?"

"If I can, sweetheart."

"Well, we kissed you, and Poppie, and Uncle Seth good night, but we forgot to kiss Daddy."

"Will you kiss him for us, Kitty?" Becky asked.

"Well . . . ah—"

"Please, Kitty?" Jenny pleaded. "Nobody ever kisses poor Daddy."

"Grown ups usually don't kiss each other good night, girls."

"Uh-huh," Jenny said firmly. "Mommies and daddies do."

"Well, I'll see. Good night, girls."

"Good night, Kitty," they said in unison.

"Do you think she will?" Jenny whispered as soon as Kitty left.

"If she doesn't, we'll just have to think of something else."

Many of the guests had already departed by the time Kitty went downstairs. Jared was in the foyer saying good night to Dave and Cynthia. Kitty couldn't help smiling when Dave slipped an arm around Cynthia as they walked to their carriage.

"You look very pleased," Jared said.

"I was watching Dave and Cynthia. They're so in love."

"I don't doubt it, but how can you be so certain? Many people put on a show for the benefit of others."

"My mother always told me that the little gestures tell how people really feel about each other."

Amused, he said, "I'm new to the game. What kind of gestures?"

"Oh, the romantic little ways he touches her in passing, or maybe the way they look at each other when they make eye contact. And just now, the way Dave slipped his arm around Thia. It wasn't a protective gesture; he was saying, 'I love you.' "

Jared scoffed. "I wouldn't think a public display of affection is vital to your sense of security, Kathleen."

"It's not. It's the casualness of the gesture—the spontaneity of it—that makes it so appealing."

"Kathleen, when a man pats his wife on her derriere, he's not saying I love you. His mind's on the bedroom."

"You're wrong. And, furthermore, you're wrong about being in love, too. It's not the game you claim it to be."

"Then what is it? You either win or lose, and you ante your heart and soul. Stakes don't come any higher."

"You're making it sound too much like a gamble, Jared."

"Sounds like one to me."

"That's because you're a cynic. I'll admit you're right about giving your heart and soul; but you give them as a gift—not offer them up as an ante. And being in love includes words like commitment, devotion, compromise, and a dozen more. But love goes far beyond mere words. It's the way your heart flutters and your breath quickens when he enters a room, or the smile you can't restrain when you think of the last thing he whispered in your ear when he left that morning."

Kitty continued on in a whimsical voice. "It's your sense of security when you hear his voice and know he's near—and feeling him beside you even when he isn't." She smiled indulgently. "I can see you have much to learn about being in love, Jared."

His tender gaze caressed her face as he raised her hand to his lips. "Fortunately, I have an excellent instructor, Kathleen Drummond."

Then, to her surprise, he led her to the edge of the dance floor. "May I have this waltz, Kathleen?"

"But your leg, Jared. Do you think you should?"

"All evening, I have purposely avoided the dance floor so I could have this waltz with you. I don't care if they have to carry me off when it's over."

"It's not necessary, Jared." Drawing on what the twins had told her, Kitty's eyes danced with devilment. "We could go out to the garden and sit out this dance."

He grinned, and it was so boyish and appealing the breath caught in her throat. "I intend to do that with the next waltz."

He swept her onto the dance floor into the rhythm of the music. Kitty closed her eyes and felt as if she was floating.

"What are you thinking about, Kathleen?"

She opened her eyes and smiled up at him. "What a perfect night this is. The music. Waltzing in the arms of the man I love. It's the romantic fantasy of every woman."

"Is that an admission that love is really just a fantasy?"

"Surely men have romantic fantasies, too."

"Oh, yes, we do! Only they're usually played out in the bedroom, not a dance floor."

"Despite what you believe, Jared, love goes far beyond the bedroom."

"Honey, if it's spontaneous pats and hugs you're looking for, we'd never get out of the bed."

"I swear you haven't a drop of romantic blood in you. Why have I let you invade my fantasy?"

He laughed. "You have enough for both of us. Won't that do?"

"I guess it will have to. Now hush up and let me go back to enjoying that fantasy." She closed her eyes.

Had she opened them again, she would have seen the adoration on his face as they finished the dance.

It did not go unobserved by the few remaining guests in the room—one of whom was Stephanie Lorimer.

Afterward, Jared took Kitty's hand and led her outside. Monsieur Poinget and his crew had cleaned up, removed the tables and chairs, and left for the night.

Aware that they were alone, Jared pulled her into his arms. His mouth covered hers hungrily. Kitty savored every second of the long, lingering kiss.

"I'll tell you now that there's nothing spontaneous about this. I've been thinking about it all evening." He pulled her closer and kissed her again.

When breathlessness forced them to break the kiss, she leaned her head against his chest.

"I love you, Kathleen." The tender words were a provocative whisper at her ear.

"I love you, too, Jared."

"Will you marry me?"

"I'd say it's about time you make an honest woman of me."

He stepped back and looked at her warily. "Is that a yes?" She looked up at him and nodded. His face broke into a wide smile. "Oh, baby." He pulled her closer again and kissed her. "Let's go upstairs."

"What about your guests?"

"To hell with my guests. I need you now, Kathleen."

He kissed her again passionately, his hands sweeping her back and spine. She felt her passion rise, and leaned into him.

"Am I interrupting, darling?"

Surprised, they pulled apart. The question had come from a woman standing in the doorway. She was exquisite-looking, with a tall, slim figure and blond hair.

Kitty didn't remember meeting her earlier. Confused, she looked at Jared. He looked pale and shocked, as if he'd just seen a ghost.

"Aren't you going to introduce me to your playmate, Jared?"

"What in hell are you doing here, Diane?" His voice was taut with anger. Kitty gasped aloud at the mention of the name. "Kathleen, this is my ex-wife, Diane . . . Ah, what is your name these days, Diane?"

"Why Fraser, of course, darling. You see, I'm still your wife."

# Chapter 24

Kitty felt like a spectator in a dream. The people around her seemed to be speaking and moving in slow motion.

"What are you talking about? I signed the papers," Jared said.

"But I never filed them, darling," Diane said. "And when I saw the picture of you and our beautiful daughters in the newspaper, my heart broke into pieces. I had to come back. I made a terrible mistake, Jared. I never should have left the twins. They need me; I'm their mother."

"It's a little late for your motherly instincts to surface. The girls needed you four years ago, when you deserted them," he said coldly.

"I was young, Jared. Irresponsible. Restless. Bored. I've learned my lesson."

"It's too late for regrets. You aren't getting near the twins."

"The court might take a different view, Jared."

"I doubt that. You deserted them, remember? Ran off with your lover. The court will have reservations about turning the girls over to an adulterous mother."

"Or let them remain with an adulterous father. At least my actions weren't in the very house the children live in. I think the court will think twice before they let you keep custody of the girls, since you board your mistress in the same house as your children."

"You'd rather see them made wards of the state than remain with me?"

"What do you expect me to do, Jared? You and your whore are setting a bad example for them. As their mother, I have a responsibility to correct this."

"I'll see you in court, Diane. Get the hell out of here."

"I have thought of a compromise. Rather than embarrassing ourselves in a public trial, perhaps we should consider splitting up the twins and each take one."

"You have a sick mind, Diane. I won't be a party to splitting up those two girls. They worship each other. I'll fight you in every court in the country if I have to."

"Always the warrior, Jared, rushing uncompromising into battle. You haven't changed in eight years."

"Not quite. I'm no longer that naïve cadet who once believed you loved me."

"Love you?" Her laugh was as cold as her green eyes. "You *are* naïve, Jared, but as long as we're still married, I'm willing to continue the farce for the twins' sake. I can't help wondering what our daughters' reaction would be if they found out their mother came back to be with them, but their father wouldn't allow her in the house."

Kitty was too shaken to listen to another word. "Excuse me." She hurried away.

"Kathleen, wait," Jared called.

She didn't. She raced up to her room and locked the door, then slumped down on the edge of the bed. Her body was trembling and she took several deep breaths to try and calm herself. It didn't help; she couldn't stop shaking. And she felt cold. So cold.

Lying back, she curled up with her knees drawn up to her chest and sobbed into the pillow.

A short time later Jared tapped on the door. "Kathleen, may I come in? I must talk to you."

"Go away, Jared. We'll talk in the morning."

"No. We must talk now. Please, Kathleen?"

Kitty got up and walked wearily to the door. She felt drained. Her eyes were red and puffy from crying, and she just wanted to be left alone. But she knew he wouldn't go away. Resigned to the worst, she unlocked the door and opened it.

"I'm very tired, Jared. Can't this wait until tomorrow?" He reached for her, but she avoided him. "Please don't touch me."

She might just as well have slapped him in the face. "My God, Kathleen, surely you don't believe her."

"I don't know what to believe. What would she gain by lying?"

"Who knows what her motive is? But the truth will come out."

"She told you what her motive is: she wants the twins, Jared, or at least one of them."

"Well, she's not going to get them."

"Diane's your wife, their mother. She has legal ground to stand on."

"She is *not* my wife. We're divorced."

"Do you have evidence of that?"

"There's a problem, but as soon as I can contact my attorney it'll be resolved."

"What problem?"

"My father just told me he'd thought I received the final divorce papers; I thought *he* had received them. Dad remembers a large packet of legal papers arrived from my attorney, while I was in India, but he didn't open them because they were marked personal. I'd sold off some property at the time, and he thought the papers related to that."

Kitty's hopes rose. "Then you have proof of the divorce!"

"There's a complication. Dad had put them in a file cabinet in the attic and—"

"They were destroyed in the fire." She felt dizzy and sank down in the nearest chair.

"For God's sake, Kitty, I'm sure my lawyer will have a copy in his file. The trouble is, he's in England right now. He's Jake Carrington's lawyer, too, and is handling that business transaction. In the morning, I'll wire him and we'll get this damn mess straightened out."

"I see." She had a premonition that it wasn't going to be as easy as he thought. "I'm tired, Jared. If you don't mind, I'd like to go to bed."

"All right, Kathleen."

Jared came over to her, but she didn't rise. "I understand this has been a shock to you. To me, too. Get some rest, darling. It will be resolved. Trust me." He tipped her chin up; his eyes were steadfast with purpose. "I love you, Kathleen. And there's not a force in the world that will keep us apart or take my daughters away from me."

Kitty sat in stunned silence as he left the room. She knew she was faced with the hardest decision she'd ever have to make.

Did she have the fortitude to do it?

After a night of trying uselessly to sleep, Kitty got up at dawn and packed her clothes. The best thing she could do for Jared and the twins was to leave. They couldn't even speak of marriage if he was still married to Diane; and as long as she remained in the house, it gave more credibility to Diane's accusation of adultery. That could influence the court's decision about custody of the twins.

The thought of Becky and Jenny being split up was horrifying. Even if Jared had divorced Diane as he claimed, it would be more humane for him to let Diane have them both than let them be separated.

She felt certain if she left, Jared wouldn't go through with a divorce. He would probably go back to closeting himself in his room, but at least the twins would have a mother and father . . . her eyes welled with tears . . . if not the mommy and daddy Jenny yearned for so badly.

And perhaps Diane had changed. Perhaps she *had* seen the wrong of her ways. Or maybe Jared and Diane could put the mistakes of the past behind them and start afresh for the welfare of their children.

One fact was certain: they'd never do it as long as she remained in the picture.

She finished her packing, then sat down and wrote a letter to the twins and one to Jonathan, but she knew she'd have to face Jared.

Kitty stopped at the doorway of the twins' room for a final look at them. As she gazed at the sleeping girls, her heart ached so badly she thought it would burst. She yearned to kiss them and hug them just one more time, but she dared not in fear of waking them—and then she would never be strong enough to leave.

Jared had been right. People were fools to allow themselves to love. If people were wise, they wouldn't make themselves vulnerable to the pain of good-byes.

She turned away and continued down the hall.

A light glowed from under Jared's door. She doubted he had slept any more than she did.

Kitty tapped on the door and opened it. Jared was at the window and turned when she entered. She didn't have to say it.

"So you're leaving."

"I think it's best for everyone, Jared. My continued presence here would do more harm than good."

"You don't believe anything I said, do you?"

"I believe you're sincere in what you said; I just think you're wrong. Diane wouldn't threaten to take you to court if she couldn't prove what she claimed."

"Kitty, you don't know her. She's devious. It's all just an empty threat."

"Jared, you have nothing to prove she divorced

you. How can you possibly think you have a chance at winning in court?"

"Because it won't end up in court. She's bluffing."

"For what purpose?"

"Who in hell knows? That's Diane."

"And that's my point: you *don't* know. There's a bigger issue here than just you and me. Are you willing to risk the twins' future by calling her bluff? And what if, by the time you're able to prove anything, the court has given her guardianship of the twins—or at least one of them? If we let that happen, we'd end up hating each other."

"If you believed in me, Kathleen, you wouldn't be so ready to run. Is this an example of the MacKenzie intrepidness that you boasted about?"

"Please, Jared, this is hard enough for me as it is. Let's not reduce this to name-calling. Nothing you say will convince me to stay. Once I'm gone, you can try and rebuild your marriage; if not for your sake, for the sake of the twins."

"Since you've arranged my life for me, what do you intend to do with your own?" he asked sarcastically.

"I don't know. I suppose I'll go back to the Triple M. I wish now I never left it."

"Yes, run back home to your mother and father, Kathleen. Why not even marry the son of the nearest rancher? Then you can live happily ever after in your home on the range. God forbid if he doesn't know how to fire a Colt or strum a guitar."

Kitty felt the heated flush of anger. "Maybe I'll do just that. He's always had a crush on me."

"Do you really believe you'll find what we have in

another man's arms? You settled for something less once before. Are you willing to do it again?"

He had pushed her too far. "How dare you bring Ted into this argument! He's no part of it."

"He's very much a part of it, Kitty. You chose a marriage of complacency before, and now, when you're faced with the possibility of discord, you cry havoc as if you're the spirit of the betrayed Caesar crying out from the grave. You're the betrayer, not the betrayed, Kitty. Why not just stick a knife into me, as Brutus did to the man who trusted him?"

"Oh, please, Jared, spare me the dramatics. I tried to make this as easy for both of us as I could, but there's no reasoning with you; you're too obsessed with your own needs to see beyond the moment. This is the time to face realities. How have I betrayed you?"

"By running away. You're guilty of the same thing you once accused me of—you're afraid of love, Kitty. You run from it when it threatens your tranquillity."

"That's not true. I admit I had no wish to marry again, but that was before I fell in love with you."

"I was a fool to ever believe you were different," he said coldly. "For a few moments of fantasy, I let you convince me there could be an intimacy between us that went beyond making love. Damn you, Kitty. Why did you ever come back?"

"I thought it was for the good of the twins," she said, forcing an iron control she held tenuously. "Later I realized it was for a different reason."

"And what was that?"

She answered with simple honesty. "So you wouldn't be left alone."

For the first time in the conversation, she saw a glimmer of hope in his eyes. "Then don't do this to us, Kitty. Somehow we can work this out. I can't let you go."

His desperate plea was so agonizing that her heart shattered, knowing how much his misery matched her own. She choked back her tears. "I'm afraid you'll have to, Jared. I love you, and I love your daughters. But I have no right to any part of your lives. You have a wife; they have a mother."

"Then go—get out. Take your talk of lasting love with you. I don't need you. And I never want to see you again."

His bitter tirade gave her the strength to walk to the door.

"I once asked you not to leave; now I'm begging you not to. But if you walk out of that door, Kitty, don't think I'll ever ask you again."

Tears misted her eyes as she paused with her hand on the doorknob. Without turning, she said, "Good-bye, Jared."

Kitty went directly to the train station and learned there was no train passing through Calico until the following day. With Beth and Jake still out of the country, she went to Cynthia and Dave's.

One look at her and Cynthia opened her arms. Kitty couldn't hold back her tears, and ran into Cynthia's embrace. Her cousin held her and let her vent her tears.

"Are you ready to talk about it?" Cynthia asked when Kitty finally stopped crying. Kitty nodded and Cynthia led her into the parlor. "How about a cup of tea?"

"I'd like that."

"Did you and Jared have a falling out?"

"It's much more serious than that, Thia."

Kitty told Cynthia about Diane's arrival, her accusation, and the threat to take the twins.

"Diane wouldn't dare take Jared to court, Kitty. She was cheating on Jared for years even before she divorced him."

"She now claims she hasn't divorced him."

"That could be, unless Jared has proof she did. Diane was not known for her diligence. Her forte was sniffing out rich men. She's like a bloodhound treeing a coon."

"Is Jared that wealthy?"

"His mother was a Pennsylvania Scott. Big steel money, honey. When she died, she left Jared and Seth a fortune. And Jonathan, of course, has made a fortune in banking."

"If Jared is that wealthy and Diane is that materialistic, why would she leave him?"

"She likes men, honey, and Jared wasn't around. That's why it could very well be that Diane didn't follow through with a divorce. I doubt that Italian count she ran off with ever intended to marry her. He might have gotten tired of her and booted her out. That may be why she's come back."

"Does she have personal wealth?"

"I have no idea. I doubt it."

The maid came in with a tea tray and a plate of freshly baked croissants. Kitty was too upset to eat, but she welcomed the hot tea. She sat back and felt its warmth seep through her.

"Kitty, did Jared ask you to marry him? He implied to me he intended to."

"Yes, and I had just agreed to do so when Diane showed up."

Cynthia arched a brow. "Well, if Diane is telling the truth, it's a good thing she did. Bigamy wouldn't sit too well with the court, either."

Kitty forced a smile she didn't feel. "I don't know which would be worse: being married to a bigamist, or the mistress of an adulterer."

"Well, honey, since Jared Fraser is the man in question, most women wouldn't complain."

"Except there's a major issue here, Thia: the twins. Have you forgotten about them?"

Cynthia patted her knee. "Of course not, honey. I'm just trying to lift your spirits."

"I know you are, Thia." Kitty got up and walked to the window. "I'm in love with Jared. I didn't think I was ready to love again, but I do. And now I've lost him, too."

"You've done the right thing for now. Besides, if I know Jared, once this situation is resolved he'll come looking for you. He told me there's no force on earth to keep him from marrying you. I believe him."

Kitty couldn't help recalling Jared's last words to her. "I wish I had your optimism, Thia."

Cynthia came over and linked her arm through

Kitty's. "Well, as long as you're planning on leaving Dallas tomorrow, let's go out and look in shop windows, then have lunch."

"Thia, I really don't feel like it."

"All the more reason for going. I'm not going to let you sit around and mope. Let's get going."

# Chapter 25

No matter how much her cousin tried to bolster her spirits, Kitty just couldn't raise any enthusiasm for looking in shop windows.

They'd pause at a window and Cynthia would ooh and ah over a purse or a hat, or comment on how lovely a particular dress would look on Kitty or Beth, and even confided once in a whisper how much Dave enjoyed seeing her in the flimsy lingerie displayed. But Kitty's heart just wasn't in the excursion.

Throughout lunch, despite Cynthia's valiant effort at conversation, Kitty paid little attention to what was said. Cynthia finally declared, "All right, Kitty, this is enough. I understand exactly how you feel. I ran away from Dave before we were married, and the decision to leave him was the most difficult one I ever made."

"At least it wasn't lasting. The two of you obviously reconciled your differences."

"Yes, we did. And I'm convinced that if it's meant to be, the same will be true with you and Jared."

"And if it's not meant to be?"

"Then you go on with your life. You felt despair when Ted died, didn't you? And then Jared came into your life. There's a reason for everything that happens. The Lord never closes a door without opening a window."

Shocked, Kitty murmured, "Oh, my God!"

Alarmed, Cynthia asked, "What is it, Kitty?"

"Those are exactly the same words I always said to Jared. He calls it my 'door and window' sermon. At the time, I didn't expect that door to be slammed in my face again. I'd like to kick the damn thing in."

Cynthia chuckled. "Now you sound like a MacKenzie. That had a spunkier tone than I've heard from you all morning."

For the first time in the past twelve hours, Kitty smiled with sincerity. She reached across the table and squeezed Cynthia's hand.

"Thank you, Thia, for reminding me of something I lost sight of."

Cynthia glanced up and paled. "Oh, good Lord!"

"What's wrong?" Kitty turned her head and saw the reason for Cynthia's reaction: Diane Fraser and Stephanie Lorimer had just entered the room, and were being seated at a table near the door.

"We must be in store for a full moon tonight—they've released the hounds."

"Are they close friends?"

"Oh, yes, indeed! Stephanie's bragged that when her husband was alive, the three of them would often indulge in a *ménage à trois*. It's no wonder Brian

Lorimer died of a heart attack; those two vampires are enough to suck the life out of any man. She's even admitted that she and Diane have experimented sexually with each other."

The thought of the twins being raised by such a woman made the hair stand up on Kitty's neck. She started to tremble again, and felt on the verge of screaming.

"Thia, I have to get out of here now. And we'll have to walk right past them."

"Just leave it to me, honey. Don't you even look at them and don't stop."

As they passed the table, Diane exclaimed, "Cynthia, darling. What a surprise."

When Cynthia paused at the table to return the greeting, Kitty kept walking as Cynthia had told her to do until she was out of the door. Still within earshot, she could hear as well as watch the conversation.

"Diane!" Cynthia exclaimed. "So you've returned from Europe. You look exhausted, my dear. It must have been a long swim back."

Diane's green eyes glittered like ice. "Stephanie tells me the whore who's having an affair with my husband is your cousin."

"Really, what cousin would that be, Diane?"

"Kathleen Drummond, the woman you just had lunch with."

"Kathleen's my cousin, but she's certainly not a whore. Isn't that more your expertise, darling? Now, don't you girls stay up too late tonight baying at the moon. Ta ta." Cynthia flicked her wrist in a wave and left them looking confused.

If Kitty had any hope of the whole nightmare being resolved quickly, the evening newspaper convinced her to the contrary. It carried a paragraph that made reference to the forthcoming court battle. Kitty had never felt so frustrated in her life. She wondered how the twins had spent the day, and what Jared told them about her leaving. Did they know about their mother's return? Consumed with anguish, she was helpless to do anything for them—they were now at the mercy of the court.

Her lack of sleep the previous night made it possible for Kitty finally to sleep, but bright and early the next morning, she was packed and ready to return to the train station. Unfortunately, the train wasn't departing until noon.

Anxious to be under way, she wandered restlessly from room to room. Gazing out the window, she noticed a man in a derby hat and suit who appeared to be watching the house. She remembered catching a glimpse of him the previous night.

"Thia, who is that man?"

"I've never seen him before," Cynthia said, after joining her at the window.

"I'm sure he's the same man I saw last night, too."

"He's sure not dressed like any Texan I know. He looks like an Easterner."

"The neighbor next door has his house up for sale; maybe the man's a prospective buyer."

Four hours later, as they were preparing to leave for the railroad station, the man approached them.

Cynthia took the initiative. "Sir, may I ask why you've been loitering outside my home?"

"I'm looking for Kathleen Drummond."

"What do you want with me?"

"Are you Mrs. Kathleen Drummond?"

"Yes, I am."

"Why didn't you just come up here sooner?" Cynthia asked.

"I had to wait for this to arrive." He handed Kitty a document, then doffed his hat. "Good day, ladies."

"What is it?" Cynthia asked, as Kitty read the document.

Befuddled, Kitty looked at her. "It's a summons."

"A summons! Whatever for?"

"I've been subpoenaed to appear in court next week to testify in the suit of Fraser versus Fraser for the custody of Rebecca and Jennifer Fraser."

Cynthia picked up Kitty's suitcase. "You might as well unpack, honey. I don't think you're going *anywhere* for a while."

In the week that followed, the newspapers carried daily reports of the ongoing trial, complete with pictures of Jared and Diane. The whole story made exciting copy in a week where there was little noteworthy national or international news.

Much was made of Jared's wealth and the fact that he'd recently been awarded the Congressional Medal of Honor.

One of the newspapers known for printing sensationalism actually carried pictures of the twins at play in their yard, along with an interview with Harriet Whipple, who depicted them as spoiled, undisciplined rich girls.

Stories of how Jonathan Fraser had accumulated his wealth in banking hinted of irregularities, with nothing to substantiate the claims. Seth's recent involvement with fraudulent bond investments was referred to time and time again, without one word that he had been exonerated of the charge.

And Diane Fraser was characterized as a loving mother who'd been deprived of her children and driven out of the house because of her humble beginnings.

The paper referred to Kitty as Jared Fraser's mistress posing as a nanny in his household, even though she was the daughter of one of the largest ranch owners in Texas, and referred to it as "The Naughty Nanny Trial." Even her cousins were brought into it when the paper mentioned her relationship to two of Dallas's most notable families: the Michael Carringtons and David Kincaids.

The night before Kitty was due to testify, anticipation for her appearance in court had swelled to a fever pitch. Beth and Jake had returned that day from Europe, and Cynthia brought them up to date on what was happening.

Jake was furious after reading the evening edition. "My God, Kitty and Jared are being tried in this rag newspaper, not the court. The whole Fraser family has been put on trial."

"Most likely Diane has bestowed her 'favors' on this stupid reporter who's doing the interviews," Cynthia said.

"I can't imagine how Jared can abide this," Beth commented. "He values privacy, and his family's being crucified. Even the twins are being made targets of this abuse."

"It's called freedom of the press, Beth," Dave said. "They try people in the court of public opinion before they listen to what the accused has to say under oath. Did you notice this newspaper never printed quotes from people who had positive things to say about the Frasers? Sensationalism sells newspapers—not unbiased reporting."

"I want to thank all of you for being so supportive," Kitty said quietly. "I've been nothing but trouble for you from the time I came to Dallas. I know you'll be glad when I go back where I belong."

"Let's not hear any more of that kind of talk, Kitty Drummond," Beth said. "We're family, remember?"

Kitty felt too emotional to try and keep up an intelligent conversation. She excused herself by saying she needed to get some rest before her big day tomorrow, then sat up most of the night wondering what the next day would bring. Jared was sure to be present in court and she didn't know if she could face him. And what questions would she be asked? She prayed she'd make it through the day without causing the Frasers any additional scandal—but she doubted she'd be that lucky.

The following morning, the Kincaids and Carringtons accompanied her to the courthouse. A hundred butterflies fluttered in her stomach when she saw the crowd gathered on the street and steps.

Shouts of "There she is now," and "There's the Naughty Nanny," sounded from the crowd gathered on the street and steps. Cameras flashed in her face when she stepped out of the carriage, and the mob surged forward.

If it weren't for Jake and Dave, Kitty would have been crushed. The two men managed to push through the mob of reporters, photographers, and spectators. Many had come out of curiosity, but the majority shouted jeers and taunts at her.

Strangely enough, rather than demoralize her, the people's actions angered her. They had no right to judge her so harshly without hearing her side of the story. By the time the men got her into the security of the courthouse, Kitty felt righteousness was on her side.

Jared's attorney waited for her in the lobby. Milton Hamilton was one of the most famous lawyers in Texas, and Kitty had met him previously when he came to the Kincaids to speak to her. Satisfied with her responses to his questions, he had not contacted her again, preferring to keep her testimony fresh and uncoached.

Greeting her now, he told her to collect her thoughts, and keep her answers honest and succinct, and above all not to volunteer any information not asked for.

"I understand you have become very attached to the twins."

"I love them very much, Mr. Hamilton."

"Then for their sake you must remain calm, Kathleen. The plaintiff's attorney will undoubtedly ask you many personal and disturbing questions in an attempt to provoke you. It is vital you do not lose your temper and say something that could be harmful to our case. Do you understand?"

"Yes."

He patted her arm. "Good, I'm sure you'll do just fine."

The courtroom was packed to capacity when Kitty was called in to testify. Despite her resolve, the butterflies started fluttering again when she was sworn in and sat down in the witness chair.

Kitty had vowed she wouldn't look at Jared, but she couldn't resist. Her heart sank to her stomach at the sight of him. Clearly the trial had already taken a toll on him; he looked drawn and tired, and stared ahead of him with an inscrutable expression. Her heart ached to think of how much he hated her for what he believed was her betrayal of him.

All the love she felt for him swept through her in a tidal wave. She wanted to shout out how much she loved him, and it was all she could do not to rush across the room and throw herself into his arms, just to feel them around her again.

Fearing that her eyes would reveal her yearning, she dropped her gaze to her lap as Milton Hamilton approached the witness stand.

He asked her a few perfunctory questions about her age and background, and established the fact that she'd been widowed for two years before coming to Dallas.

Then he asked her how long she'd been employed as a nanny in the Fraser household, and established the fact that she'd accepted it as a temporary position until a new one could be hired, that her intention was then to go on to New York.

"Who employed you as the nanny for the Fraser twins, Mrs. Drummond?"

"Mr. Jonathan Fraser, the twins' grandfather."

"And in that capacity, please tell the court what you witnessed between Jared and Diane Fraser the night of August the twelfth."

"The Frasers were having a party to celebrate the

remodeling of their home, which had been damaged in a fire. Most of the guests had already left by the time Mrs. Fraser arrived. Jared—Mr. Fraser appeared very shocked when she informed him they were still married."

"Why was that, Mrs. Drummond?"

"He said he'd signed the divorce papers several years before, while he was serving in India."

"Did Mrs. Fraser deny this?"

"No. She said she never filed them, so they were still married."

Ezra Pike, Diane's attorney, stood up. "Objection, Your Honor. This testimony is hearsay."

"It's a statement made by the other party that goes toward the offering of the truth, Your Honor," Hamilton said.

"I'll allow it. Objection overruled," the judge declared.

"Please continue, Mrs. Drummond," Hamilton said.

"Well, she went on to say that after seeing the picture of him and the twins in the newspaper, she realized how much she missed her family, and suggested they resume their marriage."

"What was Mr. Fraser's response to her?"

"He told her to get out, and that's when she threatened if he wouldn't take her back, she'd take him to court to gain custody of one of the twins."

Hamilton's voice rang with outrage. "Do I understand you to say that Mrs. Fraser threatened to *separate* these eight-year-old twin girls, just to get even with their father?"

A low murmur of shock circled the courtroom; the judge pounded his gavel and demanded silence.

Pike bolted to his feet. "Objection, Your Honor: the witness has no way of determining what Mrs. Fraser was thinking as far as motive is concerned."

"I withdraw the question, Your Honor." Milton Hamilton looked as pleased as a cat that had just lapped up a bowl of cream—he had made his point.

"What was Mr. Fraser's response to the threat of taking the matter to court?" Hamilton asked.

"He said she'd deserted the twins four years before, and the court would never turn custody of either of them over to her. I didn't wish to listen to any more of the argument, so I returned to my room."

"Are you still employed by the Frasers?"

"No, I left the household the following morning."

"Thank you, Mrs. Drummond. No more questions, Your Honor." Hamilton returned to the table and sat down in his chair next to Jared.

"I think this is a good time to adjourn for lunch," Judge Howard said. "Court will resume in ninety minutes."

Kitty rejoined the two couples outside the courtroom, and they went to a nearby restaurant. By this time, the crowd outside had been reduced to a few curious stragglers.

"How are you feeling, dear?" Cynthia asked when they were seated at a table.

"I just wish it was over."

"You did fine, Kitty, and you sounded very convincing," Beth assured her.

"The worst is still ahead of you, though," Jake

warned. "Pike's got a reputation for being slick and unscrupulous, so don't let your guard down."

"I can assure you, I'm not looking forward to his cross-examination," Kitty said.

She saw Jared, Jonathan, and Seth seated at a nearby table in deep discussion with Milton Hamilton. Kitty tried to avoid looking at them, but she invariably glanced in that direction throughout lunch.

Much to her displeasure, after the four men finished their meal, they approached her table.

Jonathan and Seth greeted her warmly, while Jared introduced the Carringtons and Kincaids to Milton Hamilton. Then Jared looked at her.

"Hello, Kathleen. How are you?"

"Fine, thank you. How are the twins?"

"They miss you."

"Will you give them my love?"

"Of course."

"Kathleen, I'd like to talk to you for a few minutes before court resumes," Hamilton said.

"I'm finished eating now."

"Fine. Why don't we go where we can talk quietly?" He said good-bye to the others, and she left with him.

As she walked away she heard Jake ask, "How does it look, Jared?"

He replied, "A lot is riding on the cross-examination today."

Jared's remark didn't help to bolster her confidence, but Milton Hamilton did. They sat down on a bench. "You're a very credible witness, Kathleen. You're coming across as honest and sincere."

"Mr. Hamilton, I believe I met Judge Howard at a

dinner my cousin gave when I came to Dallas. That's the same night I met Jonathan Fraser."

"That's no reason for the judge to recuse himself. Judge Howard has a reputation for integrity, Kathleen. A friend couldn't affect his decision any more than the newspapers can. He's a superb officer of the court. That's why it's very important you do not misrepresent any facts. Pike is going to try every trick he can think of to confuse you. You must stay focused and think carefully before you answer. A mistaken yes or no at the wrong question can lose us the case."

"I understand."

A short time later, Kitty was back in court facing one of the meanest little men she'd ever seen. If her Uncle Flint ever saw him, he'd probably describe Pike as looking like he was "rode hard and put away wet."

She recalled Mr. Hamilton's reminder to stay focused and Jake's warning that the worst was still ahead of her, and gazed steadily at the man.

# Chapter 26

"How do you do, Mrs. Drummond," Pike said pleasantly. "I know this is unpleasant for you, and this shouldn't take too long. I just have a few questions to ask you."

"Thank you," Kitty replied. The little toad didn't fool her for a moment.

"Now, you testified previously that Jonathan Fraser employed you as a nanny in the Fraser household. Is that correct?"

"Yes, sir."

"What prior experience did you have to qualify you to seek such a position?"

"I didn't seek the position, sir. Mr. Fraser was without a nanny for his granddaughters and I accepted his offer on a temporary basis, until he could find a replacement for the one he lost."

"So you never knew Jonathan Fraser prior to meeting him the night before, at a relative's house."

"That is correct."

"Did you know Jared Fraser previously?"

"No, sir."

"Isn't it true, Mrs. Drummond, that you and Jared Fraser arrived in Dallas on the same train together?"

Kitty had forgotten about the incident on the train. "We may have *arrived* on the same train, sir, but we weren't acquainted."

"You claim not to know him, yet you were seen sharing the same seat. We can produce a witness who can swear she even saw you sitting on his lap at one time. Isn't that true, Mrs. Drummond?"

"That was an accident. The train lurched—"

"Just answer yes or no, Mrs. Drummond. Were you and Jared Fraser together on that train?"

"Yes, but that was coincidental."

"Coincidental!" Pike smirked. "Just as *coincidental* as your being hired that same evening to work in the Fraser household."

Hamilton jumped to his feet. "Objection, Your Honor. Mr. Pike is speculating. What is the question?"

"Sustained," the judge said. "Parse your statements in the form of a question, counselor."

"Yes, Your Honor."

Kitty had begun to loathe the smug attorney; the little toad was as slick as Jake had said.

"Isn't it true, Mrs. Drummond, that despite having no previous experience as a nanny, the day after you arrived in Dallas on the same train as Jared Fraser, you moved into the Fraser household?"

"Objection, Your Honor," Hamilton said. "Asked and answered already."

"Sustained," Howard said, frowning at Pike.

"And isn't it true, Mrs. Drummond, that while you were in his *employment* Jared Fraser personally selected and purchased items of clothing for you, among which were a considerable number of intimate pieces of lingerie?"

"My clothes were destroyed in—"

"Yes or no, Mrs. Drummond?" Pike demanded.

"You're not giving me a chance to explain," Kitty said.

Pike turned to the judge. "Your Honor, will you direct the witness to answer the question?"

"Mrs. Drummond, please answer the questions as requested," the judge said.

"Yes, it's true." She felt as if the weasel were tightening a noose around her neck.

"And isn't it true you traveled to Washington, D.C., with Jared Fraser? And admit it, Mrs. Drummond," Pike fired quickly, "didn't you then spend a month together on the ranch of a family member, as you and this married man continued your illicit relationship?"

Hamilton was on his feet. "Objection, your Honor. He's badgering the witness and not giving her a chance to respond."

"Sustained. The court recognizes the defense counselor's objection as a continuing objection, Mr. Pike, so I warn you, counselor, you are nearing crossing the line."

"Yes, Your Honor. Isn't it true, Mrs. Drummond, you knew Jared Fraser was married when you entered his household under the pretense of being his children's nanny?"

"No, I did not," she cried out.

Pike's voice rose accusingly. "In fact, madam, you and Jared Fraser were carrying on an adulterous relationship the whole time you lived in that household, weren't you?"

"No, that's not true."

"Are you denying that you and Jared Fraser were intimate while you were living in the Fraser household?"

The answer froze in Kitty's throat. She opened her mouth to speak, but couldn't get the words out.

"Yes or no, Mrs. Drummond?"

Kitty glanced in desperation at Jared. He was leaning forward with an intense look.

Pike pounded the table and shouted, "Must I remind you that you're under oath, Mrs. Drummond!"

His shouts thudded in her ears like a drum, driving out all reasoning except the need to get away from his twisted accusations. Driven by her pent-up despair of the past week and the abusive interrogation, Kitty's control snapped.

"Yes," she cried out, and broke into sobs. "Yes, we were intimate."

Hamilton bolted to his feet. "Your Honor!"

"Sit down, Mr. Hamilton," the judge declared. His eyes gleamed with anger when he turned to Pike. "Counselor, you have previously been admonished by the court for this line of questioning. If you continue, I shall find you in contempt of court."

"Just one more question, Your Honor," Pike said.

"Would you like the court to take a brief recess, Mrs. Drummond?" Judge Howard asked.

Kitty just wanted it over. She wiped away her tears, then shook her head.

"Very well, Mr. Pike," the judge said. "You may continue, but choose your words very carefully, counselor."

Pike strutted forward like a bantam rooster to deliver his coup de grâce. "The truth is, Mrs. Drummond, you're in love with Jared Fraser, aren't you?"

Kitty raised her head. She looked at Jared, then she looked back into the smirking face of Ezra Pike. With all the dignity she could muster, she replied, "Yes, I love Jared Fraser. I'll always love him."

"And love him enough to continue this illicit affair, even though he's a married man. Isn't that right, Mrs. Drummond," Pike said contemptuously.

"I warned you, Mr. Pike," Judge Howard declared. "I now find you in contempt of court."

Pointing a finger at Kitty, Pike announced, "It's a small price to pay to expose that woman as the adulterous harlot that she is."

"You sonofabitch!" Jared snarled. He lunged for Pike and grabbed his shirtfront, slamming him down on the table. Milton Hamilton and a bailiff finally succeeded in pulling Jared off him.

Pandemonium broke loose in the courthouse. Shoving and stumbling over one another, reporters tried to rush out in their haste to get their stories to press, and photographers attempted to set up their cameras. The sound of the judge's pounding gavel rang above the melee.

When the chaos quieted, the judge ordered the bailiffs to clear the courtroom. Disgruntled, everyone filed out until only the principals and their attorneys remained.

Throughout the fracas, Kitty had sat stone-faced in a state of shock.

"Mrs. Drummond, you are dismissed," Judge Howard said. When Kitty looked at him in confusion, he explained, "You are dismissed as a witness; you're free to leave and not return."

His forceful gaze swung briefly to Jared. Then he said, "Mr. Hamilton, if you cannot control your client in my courtroom, I shall order him put in restraints."

"Yes, Your Honor," Hamilton replied.

"I apologize, Your Honor," Jared said.

"You have not been given permission to address the court, Mr. Fraser," Howard snapped. He turned a wrathful gaze on Ezra Pike. "As for you, Mr. Pike, I found your actions to be the most deplorable I've ever witnessed in my court. Mrs. Drummond is neither a defendant nor codefendant in this matter. Her character is not more questionable than that of some of the witnesses you have brought before the court, or that the plaintiff's attorney has failed to bring before the court—such as the individual with whom your client consorted when she abandoned her children."

"We tried, Your Honor," Milton Hamilton said, "but the gentleman in question has diplomatic immunity."

"Not another word, counselor," Howard warned, with a scathing glare at Hamilton.

He swung his attention back to Pike. "This is a serious issue, Mr. Pike, involving the future of two eight-year-old girls, and the intent of your questioning is clearly to exacerbate the sensationalism that some of the press has already generated, rather than determine a solution for these girls' future. I find you in contempt of court and fine you one hundred dollars. If the fine isn't satisfied within the next thirty minutes, I shall have you incarcerated and brought before a disciplinary committee."

"You can't do that, Your Honor," Pike protested.

"Your fine has just been raised an additional fifty dollars, counselor, and you have twenty-nine minutes remaining to pay it.

"Court's adjourned until nine o'clock tomorrow morning," Howard declared, gave a quick rap of his gavel to make it official, and departed.

From the time they arrived back from court, Kitty had been in and out of bouts of crying. As she listlessly packed her clothing to leave the next day, she felt tomorrow couldn't come fast enough. She couldn't wait to get out of Dallas and back on the Triple M. She couldn't understand why Ezra Pike hated her so much, when he'd never met her until that day. And how could he call her those horrible names? Was she any worse than the client he was representing? Certainly Milton Hamilton wasn't calling Diane Fraser such names.

A tap on the door interupted her ruminating. "Kitty, may I come in?"

"Of course, Thia."

Cynthia stepped in hesitantly. "Honey, Jared Fraser is downstairs asking to speak to you."

Even though her heartbeat quickened, Kitty didn't want to face him after the embarrassing scene in court. Her testimony must have totally ruined his hope of winning the case.

"Tell him I'm in bed."

"Are you sure that's what you really want to do? You don't solve a problem by running away, Kitty."

"That's not true, Thia." Kitty's quick laugh was cynical. "I ran away from the Triple M and solved my trouble with Ted's death. I've discovered the whole trick to solving a problem is to create a different one."

"All right, Kitty, I'll tell Jared you're not available." There was an unusual shortness in her tone.

"You disapprove."

"It's not my life, honey. It's yours."

"What would you have done in my place?"

"I'm the wrong person to ask, Kitty."

"Why do you say that?"

"Because the moment I saw Dave, I wanted him. He was the chief engineer on the railroad my father was building from Colorado to Dallas. I had no pride; I actually chased after him—followed him to where they were laying track. I was nothing more than a wild playgirl whose only thought was how to have fun. Dave was just the opposite: serious and hardworking. He loathed me and my lifestyle. Kitty, for the next couple years, I watched this man lay track through rugged mountains and arid desert, build bridges to span rivers, fight Mother Nature, and a few outlaws along the way to fulfill that dream of my father's. To me he was brilliant, invincible, loyal, and dedicated—any admirable adjective you can think of. And this fabulous human being fell in love with me. As brilliant, powerful, and successful as he was, he loved *me*. I was his woman. The woman he bared his soul to, told his most intimate secrets. The woman he sought to soothe his weariness or calm his turmoil. The one with whom he shared the joy of his accomplishments or the anguish of his failures. And I'm the woman he lay beside and reached for in the night. I didn't care what people thought, or what they said about me. *I was his woman*. Nothing and no one could have separated us." With an apologetic smile she squeezed Kitty's hand. "You see, honey, I told you I was the wrong woman to ask."

"But what if the welfare of his twin daughters was at stake?"

"Thank God I didn't have to face that consideration."

"But if you had, what would you have done, Thia? I've got to know. Have I been wrong? Is Jared right to accuse me of betraying his love?"

"If Dave and I had been faced with the same problem you and Jared are, I'm ashamed to say that Dave would have had to make the decision for us; I would have been too weak. I don't have his strength or yours, Kitty. You're a very courageous woman. And Jared's wrong: you haven't betrayed his love, Kitty, you've betrayed your own heart." She walked to the door. "I'll send him away."

"No, I'll come down. I suppose it would be childish not to. Just give me a few minutes."

"Good for you, Kitty. I'll have him wait in the library. You'll have more privacy there."

Kitty glanced in the mirror. Seeing her eyes were

red and puffy from crying, she dabbed some powder on her face.

Jared was standing with his back to the door, paging through a book. He turned when she entered and closed the door. His expression was as inscrutable as ever, but his probing gaze searched her face.

"I'm sorry to disturb you, Kathleen."

"That's quite all right. I was just finishing my packing. It seems packing and unpacking is all I've been doing since I came to Dallas."

"So you're leaving."

"That's always been my intention."

"You'll find New York is quite different from Dallas."

She saw no reason for telling him she had made up her mind to return to the Triple M. "Why did you come here tonight, Jared?"

"I wanted to tell you I'm sorry for the ordeal you went through today. I wish there was something I could have done to prevent it."

"It all could have been prevented if you had accepted Diane as your wife. Why couldn't you have done that, Jared? Now the twins are at a greater risk than ever."

"I will not have that woman in my house, Kathleen."

"If today's court session is any indication, I imagine you won't have your daughters there much longer, either."

"Diane will not get custody of my daughters."

"Oh, for heaven's sake, Jared, face the realities.

Diane is their mother. Your wife. Even if you intend to divorce her, by then the damage will be done. If you don't lose both of the twins, you'll surely lose one of them."

"The case isn't over yet, Kathleen. If we can prove she's lying—"

"Do you have proof that she divorced you?"

"Not yet, but Hamilton's legal team is tracing records to establish that we are. And we can produce witnesses who will substantiate Diane's an unfit mother. Do you think for a moment she actually wants the twins? She never would have left them if that were so. She has no visible means to support them, and she lives off men, flitting from one affair to another. Her life has no room for children. She needed a place to live, so she came back here until she could latch on to another man. And she knows that before I'd let her take one of the girls, I'd pay her off."

"Then why didn't you do it before it got this far?"

"Because it's the same as blackmail, Kathleen. After using up that money, she'd show up again for more. I called her bluff. This way she can never pose a threat to the twins again."

"I hope for their sake it succeeds."

"I have confidence it will. I only wish you felt the same."

"Is that what you came here for, Jared? A final accusation of my betrayal?"

"No. There've been enough accusations today."

"Thank you for that much."

"I didn't come here to argue, Kitty. I came to tell you that Pike's conduct came as a surprise to us. He had promised Hamilton if we took it easy on Diane, he would do the same with you. He double-crossed us. Otherwise, I'd never have let this go to court. I would have given Diane what she wanted."

"Well, it's done. I'd say there's no sense in crying over spilled milk, but I know how much you hate clichés."

"On the contrary; they're one of the things that I grew to love about you." For the length of several heartbeats, his gaze swept her face. "One of many."

She floundered in a misery so acute she could barely breathe. *Don't do this to me, Jared. Not again. I can't bear any more.*

"I'll always love you, Kathleen. A day will never dawn that I won't think of you and what we once shared—and lost."

"As I told you, the important lesson is learning how to give love, no matter how short-lived it may be."

"And I had such a good instructor."

The words were a tender echo of the love and joy they shared before the world came crashing down on them.

"Well, I'm keeping you from your packing. If there's anything I can do—or anything you ever need, please—"

"I will," she said, cutting him off. "And give my love to the twins."

He put down the book he'd been holding. "I don't think I'll ever be able to pick up a novel again without thinking of you. Good-bye, Kathleen."

"Jared," she called as he was about to open the door. He turned his head and looked back at her.

She hungered with the remembrance of his touch. "Despite everything, I don't regret it ever happened. I'd do it again."

"I would, too. For a short time we almost had it all, didn't we, Kitty?" His smile caressed her face. "We came so close."

She closed her eyes to hold the image of that smile in her memory.

The next morning, Kitty stood on the observation platform of the train and waved good-bye to Beth and Thia. As much as she loved both of them dearly, she never intended to return to Dallas again.

# Chapter 27

"Oh, look Becky. She looks so sad."

Becky peeked around the corner and saw Kitty on the platform of the train depot, saying good-bye to Mrs. Kincaid and Mrs. Carrington.

"Now, the first thing we have to do is get on the train without being seen together. People always notice twins."

"Then why did we dress alike and you shove your bangs under your bonnet?" Jenny asked.

"So that everyone will think there's only one of us. And we'll have to take turns hiding in the ladies' room."

"What if Kitty sees us? She'll know."

"So it's better if she doesn't know before the train gets moving, or she might make us go back," Becky said.

"What if she won't let us stay after we get to Calico?"

"Jenny, you heard what Daddy told Poppie: our mother wants to separate us."

Jenny looked forlorn. "I'd die if that happened."

"That's why we can't let Kitty see us now. Okay, get on the train and go and hide in the ladies' room. I'll wait a few minutes, and then get on."

"What if the conductor sees me?" Jenny fretted.

"Tell him Kitty's your mother, just like we planned it last night. Don't be afraid, Jenny."

"I hope this plan works better than some of our other ones."

"If it doesn't, we'll just have to think of something else."

"All right. Good-bye, sister." Jenny kissed Becky on the cheek.

"It's not *good-bye*. We'll just be apart for a few minutes. Try not to let anyone see you."

Clutching Bibbie in one hand and her small satchel in the other, Jenny got on the train.

As soon as Becky saw Kitty board, she climbed on at the other end of the car and showed her ticket to the conductor.

"You traveling alone, little girl?"

Becky gave him her sweetest smile. "No, sir. My mother's that beautiful lady sitting up in the first seat."

"Why aren't you sitting with her?"

"Because I want to sit with my grandmother." She quickly sat down in the last seat next to an old lady. "Hello, Grannie."

The old lady smiled at her. "Why hello, my dear. Would you like to sit next to the window?"

"No, thank you, Grannie."

"Have a pleasant trip, ladies," the conductor said and moved on.

Becky hoped her nose wasn't growing.

She heaved a sigh of relief when the train started moving, then got up and went to the ladies' room.

Jenny was waiting for her. "How long do I have to stay in here?"

"You can go out now, and I'll stay for a while. I'm sitting next to an old lady in the last seat. Her name is Mrs. Marshall and she's going to Albuquerque to visit her daughter and six grandchildren. Kitty's sitting in the front seat alone. She looks very sad; all she does is stare out the window. Come back in fifteen minutes and we'll change places again. This is one of the best ideas we've ever had!"

For the next hour, the twins switched back and forth every quarter hour.

"My goodness, my dear, you must have drunk a lot of water before you left," Mrs. Marshall said when Jenny excused herself again. "Would you like me to hold your doll for you while you're gone?"

"No thank you, Mrs. Marshall. Bibbie doesn't take to strangers too well."

"Bibbie? I thought you said her name was Bonnie?"

"She answers to either name, ma'am." Jenny hurried away.

Becky had just returned to the seat when the conductor announced that they would be serving lunch in the dining room for the next two hours. To Becky's relief Kitty remained in her seat, so she went in with Mrs. Marshall. As soon as they finished eating, she and Mrs. Marshall returned to their seats and Becky excused herself and joined Jenny.

"Go into the dining car and have lunch now. The chicken salad is very good."

Jenny entered the dining car just as the conductor was leaving. "Didn't you just eat lunch, miss?"

"I didn't eat it all, so my mother said I should come back and finish my meal."

"Why doesn't your mother eat with you?" he asked.

Jenny cocked her finger and motioned to him to come closer. He lowered his head. "She's going to have a baby and said if she eats she'll puke."

He blanched. "Oh, my! We don't want that, do we?"

She widened her eyes. "Noooo."

Becky was back in the seat when Kitty got up to go into the dining car. She quickly buried her head on Mrs. Marshall's shoulder and pretended she was sleeping when Kitty passed by.

Kitty was listlessly pushing the food around on her plate with a fork when the conductor came by and stopped at her table. "Madam, you're eating!"

"Yes, thank you."

"I certainly hope you don't get ill."

Perplexed, Kitty glanced at her plate. "Is there something wrong with the food?"

"Not at all, madam. I only thought that in your delicate condition, perhaps just a cup of tea would have been more advisable." He walked away shaking his head. *What a strange family.*

*What a strange man.* Shoving her plate aside, Kitty returned to her seat.

Jenny was also having an unpleasant time. The chicken salad was not sitting too well on her stomach, so she wanted some fresh air. Peeking out the door, she saw the coast was clear and headed for the observation platform.

The air felt so good, she decided to stay there for a while instead of in the stuffy ladies' room. She felt so glum she wanted to go and talk to Kitty, but Becky had told her not to do so until they got off the train.

When it drew near the time to change places with Becky, she was about to go inside when the conductor opened the door and came out on the deck.

He did a double look when he saw her. "Didn't I see you inside, little girl?"

"Sure, lots of times."

"I mean just now."

"Mister, how could you see me inside when I'm outside?"

"You're right." He shook his head. "Just be careful out here." He went back inside. "I must be coming down with a fever," he mumbled, and brought his hand to his forehead to see if he was hot.

Kitty felt so desolate by the time she climbed off the train at Calico that she was on the verge of tears. In response to her wire, her father was at the depot to meet her. He opened his arms and she rushed into them. As soon as she felt them close around her, her tears opened up in a floodtide.

He let her shed her tears, the warmth of his embrace more comforting than any words could ever be. And when her tears began to wane, he picked up her luggage and led her to the buggy.

"Kitty! Wait!"

She turned around, and had the shock of her life.

Throughout the whole day in court, Jared had thought of nothing except how Kitty looked when they said good-bye last night. He went straight home after leaving court. He had a lot to decide and wanted to be alone to be able to work it all out in his mind before taking any action. When he entered the house, Mildred was swiping tears out of her eyes and anxiety was written all over Charles's face. Wordlessly, the butler handed him an envelope with the word "Daddy" written in a childish scrawl. He ripped it open and read the letter within.

"Oh, my God!" Stunned, he slumped down in a chair.

"I tried to get it to you as soon as we discovered the twins were missing and found the letter, Captain Fraser. They wouldn't allow me in the courtroom."

"I understand, Charles."

Just then Jonathan and Seth arrived, and Jared gave them the letter to read. Both men's reactions were the same as Jared's.

"What if they didn't make it to Calico? Or what if they were hurt, or fell into the hands of the wrong person?"

Jonathan squeezed his shoulder. "I'm sure they're with Kitty, Jared."

"Who knows if they are? The letter says she didn't even know they were going to follow her."

"We can wire the MacKenzies," Seth suggested.

"Wires take too long. I could be there in the time it takes to get an answer. If only there were a train . . ." He bolted to his feet. "Maybe . . ."

He ran out of the house, climbed into a carriage, then thundered down the driveway like a chariot driver in the novel *Ben Hur*. Jared rode to the Carrington house and there explained the situation to Beth and Jake.

"They're so young!" Beth lamented. "I can't believe they'd try this on their own. And Thia and I were at the station this morning when Kitty left. We didn't see a sign of the twins."

"I've got to get to the Triple M to find out if they made it there. Can you help me?"

Jake glanced at the clock, then hurried to his desk and pulled a schedule out of the drawer.

"The Rocky Mountain's got a Denver-bound freight train that leaves in about forty-five minutes. You can hop a ride on that, Jared."

"Thank you. I'll go back to the house and let Dad know."

"Okay, I'll pick you up in fifteen minutes," Jake said.

Once back at the house, Jared was hurriedly throwing some items into a suitcase when his brother came into his room.

"I came to say good-bye. I'll be leaving Dallas as soon as we hear the twins are okay," Seth said.

"Where are you going?"

"I figure I owe you and Dad a big favor, and I thought of a way I can do it. I spoke to Diane after the judge's decision, and I'm taking her to Paris."

"What? Damn it, Seth, I don't have time for this nonsense. What in hell are you talking about?"

"I figure as long as Diane hangs around Dallas, she'll continue to be a problem for you and the twins. Diane's just looking for a bankroll and a good time; so why not?"

Jared stopped and really looked at his brother. "Seth, you don't have to do this."

"I know. Who knows; I might enjoy it."

"I don't know what to say."

"One more favor, big brother. Marry Kitty. Don't let that damn pride of yours foul it up."

"I'll have to convince her first."

"And give those little minxes a kiss from me."

"I will."

As the two men shook hands, Jared pulled Seth to him in a hug. He couldn't remember the last time he had hugged his younger brother.

Thirty minutes later, Jared was in the caboose of a Denver-bound freight train—with an unscheduled stop to be made at Calico, Texas.

The sun was a bright ball peeking over the horizon when Jared got off the train and waved good-bye to the engineer and brakeman.

A sign on the ticket window read "Closed." Jared ignored it and rang the bell continually until a light popped on in the rear of the station. A sleepy-eyed, grizzled man, still in his nightshirt, came to the window.

"We don't open for another two hours, mister."

"I just need some information. Are you acquainted with Kathleen Drummond?"

"Sure. Knowed her all her life."

"Do you know if she returned to Calico today?"

The man eyed him warily. "What's it to you, stranger?"

"I have to know if my daughters were with her. Twin eight-year-olds with short dark hair. Did you see them?"

"Ain't sayin'. You figurin' on causin' Kitty some trouble, stranger? You'll be bitin' off more than you kin chew, if you try. Them MacKenzies are mighty protective of their womenfolk."

"Certainly not. I just want to know if my daughters arrived here safely."

"I reckon they're the two who were with her."

"Thank God! Thank God!" Jared cried, torn between joy and gratitude to the Almighty. "Do you have any idea where I can find them now?"

"Triple M, I reckon. Luke MacKenzie came into town with a buggy and they drove out with him."

Jared's mood had exhilarated almost to the point of giddiness. "May I prevail upon your good nature, sir, for directions to the Triple M?"

"Take the road straight through town; the main entrance to the ranch is about ten miles down the road."

"Thanks again. Where can I rent a horse and send a wire?"

"The livery stable and Western Union office, most likely. But they don't open for two more hours, either. Now I'm goin' back to bed, stranger."

"Thank you. Thank you for everything."

The local restaurant was closed as well, so he couldn't even get a cup of coffee. For the next two hours Jared sat on a wooden bench in front of the telegraph office, nervously tapping his foot as he waited for it to open. He finally was able to send a wire with the good news to his father, rented a horse, and rode out of Calico headed for the Triple M Ranch—the bastion of the MacKenzies.

# Chapter 28

Inside the compound, Jared rode up to two men who were standing in front of one of the several houses.

"What can we do for you, stranger?" the taller of the two inquired.

"I'm looking for Kathleen Drummond."

The other man straightened up to his full height, which was quite appreciable, also. "What do you want her for?"

"That, sir, is between Mrs. Drummond and myself."

Jared's words had an immediate effect on the two men. Both looked quite formidable as they regarded him intently: one with hostility, the taller one with curiosity.

"Is that so?" The hostile one folded his arms across his chest—which, too, was quite appreciable. "Reckon, then, there's something that's between you and me. Wheel around that horse you're sitting on and get your ass off the Triple M, or I will personally boot it off."

Jared was taken aback by the man's antagonistic outburst. "I beg your pardon?"

" 'Pears like your hearing's ailing." He clenched his hands into fists. "You get out of here, or I'll have to beat the hell out of you."

"It would be ill advised of you to try, sir. I will warn you that I was the pugilistic champion of my class at West Point."

The taller of the two men stepped forward. "Now, gentlemen, let's try to remain calm and resolve this. I'm Cleve MacKenzie, young man. How about you answering my brother's question before tempers get any shorter?"

"Are you Mrs. Drummond's father?"

"No, he ain't but I am. Luke MacKenzie's the name. And I'm sick and tired of you yellow-rag reporters nosing around the Triple M."

Jared dismounted and walked over and extended his hand. Cleve MacKenzie shook hands with him, but Luke ignored the proffered handshake. "How do you do. I'm Jared Fraser. It's a pleasure to finally meet you, Mr. MacKenzie."

"Fraser! You're the last man I expected to see around here. What do you want?"

"I intend to marry your daughter, sir."

"Last I heard, you have a wife, Fraser."

"I do not have a wife, Mr. MacKenzie. That was a mistake."

"Hers or yours, Fraser?"

"Mr. MacKenzie, I do not wish to be rude, but this is between Kathleen and myself. Will you please tell me where I can find her? I'm not leaving without her. And I'd appreciate it, sir, if you'd stay out of this."

Flint MacKenzie, accompanied by his wife and sisters-in-law, came up and joined them. "What's all the shouting about?"

Seeing Luke glaring at the young man, Honey MacKenzie walked over to her husband. "What is it, Luke? What's wrong?"

"This is that Fraser fellow from Dallas. Kitty doesn't want any part of him."

"What do you want, Mr. Fraser?"

"Are you Kathleen's mother, ma'am?"

"Yes, I am." She offered her hand. "How do you do, Mr. Fraser. I'm Honey MacKenzie. You must be Becky and Jenny's father."

"Guilty," he said in a lighter tone.

"We adore them, Mr. Fraser. Now, what's this about you and Kitty?"

Thank God he was dealing with someone other than that unreasonable father of Kitty's. "Please call me Jared, Mrs. MacKenzie."

"Very well. Now let's get back to the issue. Kitty doesn't want to see you, Jared. Why don't you just ride away and leave her alone."

"Good luck in getting a straight answer to that one," Luke warned. "The fellow's an expert at dodging them." The remark was accompanied by another scathing glare at Jared.

Undaunted, Jared weathered it. "Mr. and Mrs. MacKenzie, I'm in love with your daughter."

"That's understandable, but aren't you a married man?"

"No, I am not. That's what I came here to explain."

At that moment, Kitty rode up in a wagon with the twins. Seeing Jared, the girls jumped out.

"Daddy!"

Jared knelt down and they huddled together, hugging and kissing. He felt on the verge of crying, he was so glad to see them.

"Someone's got some explaining to do," he declared, with a stern frown meant for his daughters.

Kitty had stood in silence until then. "I figure I'd be the one you blamed." She walked past him and into one of the houses.

"Kitty, we have to talk," he called after her.

"It wasn't Kitty's fault, Daddy," Becky said.

"She didn't even know we were on the train," Jenny added.

"You girls did a terrible thing. Do you have any idea how worried I've been about you? How much you've upset your grandfather and uncle?"

"But we wrote you a letter and told you not to worry."

"Not to worry! How could I *not* worry?" He hugged them again.

"We were afraid our mother was going to separate us; that's why we ran away."

"You don't have to ever worry about that again. The judge awarded me complete custody." He stood up.

"Jared, I'm happy to hear about your custody," Honey MacKenzie said. "But since you're a married man it still would be wiser if you'd leave."

"Trust me, Mrs. MacKenzie, I am *not* married."

Lord, did anyone around here ever listen? It was time for action. Jared tipped his hat. "Excuse me, ma'am." He strode toward the door.

When Jared entered the house, Luke started to follow, but Honey put a hand on his arm. "Stay out of it, Luke."

"He might harm her."

Honey shook her head. "He's not going to harm her, Luke."

Kitty's raised voice could be heard through the open window. "Don't you touch me, Jared Fraser."

"Listen to that? She needs my help."

"Luke, she doesn't need your help," Flint's wife, Garnet, assured him.

Adee MacKenzie agreed. "Men can be so dumb when it comes to women."

Cleve slipped an arm around her shoulders. "I wouldn't say that. I think I was pretty smart to pick you for a wife."

Kitty knew she was in trouble when Jared came in. She'd seen that look in his eyes enough times to know he was determined to have his way. He strode toward her purposefully, and she backed away.

"Don't you touch me, Jared Fraser."

Those sapphire eyes smoldered with glaring reproach.

"Good Lord, Kitty, calm down and listen to me. I'm not leaving without you and the twins."

"I don't understand this. You made yourself very clear how you felt about my *betrayal* of you, Jared. Now you come here declaring that I must leave with you. Maybe I didn't make myself as clear to *you*. I am not becoming your mistress, Jared. And even if I were inclined to do so, *nothing* on God's green earth would ever entice me to return to that wretched city! So get out of here, or I shall start shouting at the top of my lungs!"

"You're already shouting loud enough to be heard in Dallas," he said, shoving aside the chair that separated them. He followed when she moved to the table, and stalked her around it.

"If I cry for help, my father and uncles will come in here and make mincemeat of you, Jared."

"Kitty, I am not intimidated by your father and uncles." He lurched across the table, but she managed to avoid his grasp.

Kitty stopped in surprise and looked at him with suspicion. "Of course you are; everyone is."

He sighed deeply, a combination of impatience and frustration. "Kitty, you're the only one who can intimidate me."

She stood stock-still. "What!"

Jared approached her cautiously, fearing she would bolt again. She backed away slowly.

"Dammit, Kitty, will you stand still?" He bumped into the corner of the table and a shock of pain shot through his leg. Clutching his thigh, he staggered against the table.

"Oh, Jared, your leg!" Hurrying over to him, she slipped an arm around his waist. "Let me help you." She eased him onto a nearby stuffed chair. "You know the doctor said you have to be careful. I'll—"

He pulled her down on his lap, and his kiss smothered her cry of surprise. Instantly the passion of their anger became the passion of hungry need.

One kiss led to another, and then another, until they were both breathless.

"Jared, you know as well as I that nothing can be gained by this, no matter how much I love you," she finally said breathlessly.

He gently cupped her cheek in his hand and gazed into her eyes. "Kitty, Diane lied; we were legally divorced. She backed herself into a corner with that lie and it backfired."

"And the custody of the twins?"

"She didn't really want them. That was a ploy to get money out of me. When the judge heard the whole story, he gave me complete legal custody."

"I can't believe it!" Kitty's heart was beating so joyously, she feared it would burst.

He grinned. "Sweetheart, there's so much I want to say. I didn't mean what I said to you the day you left. I was a damn fool striking back because I felt so betrayed. I love you, Kitty. You've rejuvenated my life. You've taught me how to love again, my darling, and you've taught me so much more: to trust again, to laugh again. Kitty, you've opened my heart and driven out the bitterness and self-pity I've wallowed in for years. I had blamed Diane for everything as an excuse to indulge my own self-pity. But you were right about that, too: despite her infidelity, it wasn't Diane's fault that I shut the twins out of my life. I was afraid to show I loved them for fear of being hurt some more. I was a stupid fool, Kitty, whose only redeeming quality is my love for you."

"You were indeed," she agreed.

The penitent Jared offered no argument. "How can I convince you now how much you mean to me?

You've shown me a whole new life I never thought I'd ever know. Don't snatch it from me, Kitty. My fate's in your hands. It has been from the moment I first saw you. Blame me for being the arrogant, overbearing boor that I am, but, sweetheart, don't ever doubt how madly that overbearing boor loves you."

Harboring grudges was never one of Kitty's faults, especially toward a man she loved beyond reason. Her heart full of gratitude, she smiled at him tenderly. "You can start by kissing me again."

So for the next few minutes, Jared devoted his attention to doing just that.

Kitty's voice was throaty with breathlessness when she raised her hand and lightly brushed her fingers down his cheek. "I do love you, Jared. I couldn't have stayed away from you much longer—married or not." She sighed in contentment and laid her cheek against his chest. "And what you said to me that day was true. I *was* running from love. When Ted died, I vowed to never fall in love again. I closed my heart to the very thing I needed the most. Then, when I heard you and Diane were still married, I believed it was retribution for betraying that vow. But I learned by loving and losing you that no one can decide their own destiny. The ability to love is the one thing we can't relinquish. My father tried to tell me that after Ted's death."

Kitty's mouth curved in a soft smile. "If you knew my father—"

"I have had the pleasure of meeting him," Jared said, tongue-in-cheek.

Kitty glanced at him, amused. "You really aren't intimidated by my father or the other MacKenzies, are you?"

Jared couldn't help grinning. "No. Why should I be intimidated by them?"

"Don't you find them rather . . . ah . . . formidable?"

He nodded. "I'd say so."

"Well . . . don't you find that intimidating?"

"My darling Kitty, I've already told you that you're the only person who can intimidate me." He kissed her again.

Kitty leaned back in his arms and gave herself up to the sheer pleasure of his kiss. Several more kisses followed.

"Well, maybe your mother is a little intimidating," Jared said.

"My mother!" The idea was ludicrous to Kitty.

"I suspect she rules with a fist in a velvet glove on occasion. Matter of fact, I'd have to say that the MacKenzie females are far more intimidating than the men."

"Obviously you are unaware that the MacKenzie men have faced down some of the worst outlaws in Texas."

"Having recently faced down both male and female MacKenzie factions, I hold to my opinion."

"I'm one of those MacKenzie females, Jared Fraser."

"I rest my case."

She slipped her arms around his neck and pulled his head closer so that their lips almost touched. "I think we should take this discussion to the bedroom, where I can show you just how intimidating a MacKenzie woman can really be."

Swooping her up in his arms, he stood. "I accept the challenge—and I warn you I don't intend to give in without a struggle."

Nipping at his ear, she murmured, "That's what I'm hoping for, Captain."

She giggled, so deliciously appealing that he doubted they'd even make it as far as the bedroom.

Outside, Luke raised his hand. "Be quiet, everyone. Listen. It's quieted down in there. What if he's hurt her, and we stood by and let it happen?"

Garnet arched a brow. "I'm sure he hasn't hurt her, Luke." The three women exchanged meaningful glances.

"It's just too damn quiet in there. What do you suppose is happening?"

Honey shook her head in disbelief. "Luke MacKenzie, I know you too well to believe you're *that* naïve. Figure it out for yourself."

"Are all fathers this dense?" Garnet asked. The three women started giggling.

Luke shoved his hat to the top of his forehead. "Figure what out? Dammit, will you women stop looking like three cats licking their whiskers?"

"I think what our wives are trying to say, Big Brother, is that Kitty and this Fraser are in love," Cleve said.

"In love?" the normally reticent Flint questioned. "They were doing a mighty lot of shouting for two people in love."

His remark sparked an immediate response from

Garnet. "You've got a short memory, Flint MacKenzie. All *we* did was holler at each other before you finally broke down and admitted you loved me."

Cleve chuckled in amusement. "I've got to agree with her, Brother Flint. You and Garnet did more than your share of shouting at each other. I thought on that cattle drive we made, all your noise would stampede the herd."

"You know, Little Brother, you can be plumb irritating at times," Flint warned.

Cleve shrugged his broad shoulders. "I can't help that I understand women better than my older brothers."

It was too good an opportunity for his wife to ignore. "Maybe that's because you spent half your life making a study of women?" Adee teased.

"Only until I met you, Angel." He flashed the appealing smile that always melted her heart.

Still hesitant, Luke looked askance at Honey. "I hope you're right about our daughter, Jaybird."

Whenever he called her by the pet nickname, Honey knew the fight was out of him. She tucked her arm through his. "Let's go back to our house, everyone. I think we have a wedding to plan."

At that moment, Josh and Emily came riding up. After greeting everyone, Josh said to the twins, "Let's go, girls—we promised to take you for a ride and show you Amigo's Marida."

"Kitty told us how it got its name," Becky said.

"It's such a beautiful story," Jenny added.

"It makes us cry—"

"—every time we hear it."

Flint scratched his head and glanced at Cleve.

"Hey, Little Brother, do you reckon those two little gals figure out in advance what words they're gonna divvy up before they say 'em?"

Cleve chuckled and walked on, holding Adee's hand.

Luke shook his head. "You know, Jaybird, if what you gals say is true, we're going to have eight-year-old twin granddaughters. Sleeping with a grandma is gonna take some getting used to."

Josh slapped his father on the shoulder. "Well then, Grandpa, I suggest you start getting used to it, because Em and I have an announcement to make. We're going to have a baby."

"Well, it's about time!" Honey looked about to burst with pleasure. "Just think, these two darling girls, a new baby, and a new son-in-law to boot." Tears of joy glistened in her eyes as she smiled up at her husband. "Our cup runneth over, Luke."

"Wow!" Becky declared.

"Does that mean we're going to be aunts?" Jenny asked.

"No, sweetheart," Em replied. "Cousins."

"Cousins? Hmmm." Becky's adorable face puckered up in reflection. "That's good, too."

Her statement produced a burst of laughter, which attracted the attention of Zach and Rose. Flint's son and wife came hurrying up to join them.

"Hey, what's all the excitement about?"

"We're very sorry, Zach, but we can't be your cousins anymore," Becky informed him in apology.

"Josh and Em are having a baby and we're going to be its cousin," Jenny clarified.

Zach grinned at Josh. "Sounds like congratulations are in order all around."

Rose nodded. "We've been saving our news for the right occasion, and I guess this is as good a time as any. I'm going to have a baby, too."

"Well, I'll be dam . . . darned!" Flint declared, beaming with pride as if he were the father, instead of the future grandfather. "With all these babies coming, I reckon we best start cleaning up our language around here." He gave his daughter-in-law a big hug. "Thank you, gal. Garnet's been yearning to rock a little one in her arms for a long time. He cast a loving glance at his wife. "Ain't you, Redhead?"

Amid kisses, squeals of happiness, and tears of joy from the women, the group began to move on.

Frowning, Becky and Jenny hung back. As they were so often, their thoughts were as identical as their faces.

Becky frowned. "Being cousins to little babies is going to be great fun, but—"

Jenny finished the thought. "It would be more fun to be sisters to a little brother."

Becky nodded decisively. "Looks like we're going to have to do something about that."

Jenny pondered intently. Finally, she looked at her sister. "Becky, maybe we should let Daddy do something about it."

The twins looked at each other and broke out in similar grins. "I'm sure *he'll* think of something," they said in unison.

Hand in hand, they skipped after the others.

* * *

Long after the sun had set, Kitty and Jared lay entwined in bed.

"We've missed dinner. How am I ever going to face the family? I know what they'll be thinking."

"That we've been in bed all day making love."

"Exactly! Josh and Zach will never let me live it down."

"I half expect your father to come through that door with a shotgun."

"He wouldn't do that; in truth, he's the most softhearted one of the lot. But being the patriarch of the family is a big responsibility."

Jared hugged her. "I know. And I promised the twins we'd live on a ranch, remember?"

"So they said."

"I never said it had to be *my* ranch."

Kitty looked at him with a hopeful gleam in her eyes. "Are you suggesting you'd be willing to live on the Triple M?"

"You think these MacKenzies could tolerate a writer in their midst?"

"I think they'd love a writer in their midst."

"Could be that hero of my novel might have to be a cowboy."

She cuddled against him. "I love you, Jared Fraser. I know my family will, too."

He kissed the curls on the head pressed against his chest. "And I know I'm going to like these MacKenzies."

"I hope so. Marry one, and you get all of us, you know."

"That's not so bad. I can handle them."

Blissfully happy, Kitty raised her head and

looked down with adoration at the man she loved. "I think you will. I think you'll get along with them just fine."

Jared curved his hand around the nape of her neck, then slowly drew her head down to meet his own. Just before kissing her, he whispered,

"And we'll all live happily ever after, my love."